COUNTERFEIT NATION

Book Two of The Remains Saga

COUNTERFEIT NATION

Book Two of The Remains Saga

By Mark T. Sneed

Table of Content

DEDICATION

To my mother, family and friends that continue to inspire, encourage, and challenge me to be a better person, even when no one is around.

THANK YOU

To the various minds that continue to thrive despite the lack of resources, equipment, and education.

We carry our future on our backs.

COUNTERFEIT NATION

Book Two of The Remains Saga

COUNTERFEIT NATION

Book Two of The Remains Saga

By Mark T. Sneed

Chapter One.

Return to the Remains

The helicopter crossed the outer wall and then the inner wall of the Remains before the first signs of the houses of the thousands living in the walled compound below. The bruised and battered teen smiled at the idea of being in a helicopter for the hundredth time and watched as the heavily armored whirlybird headed toward the hills of what had once been the Oakland and Berkeley hills and now were known as the Remains. The helicopter banked to the left and slowed as it gently landed on the roof of a multi-storied dark brick building overlooking a disused highway heading toward a dark pair of tunnels bored into a mountain.

Inside the chopper were eight enforcers armed and prepared when the helicopter arrived. The first two enforcers, inside the helicopter with Ralphie and the others, stepped off the helicopter and assisted Ella Buchanan from the transport. Ralphie, a Miller, tired and in pain, tried to watch all the activities once the helicopter landed. The enforcer closest to Ralphie stuck out his arm to restrain the injured teenager.

"We got some minutes before we get off," the enforcer smiled. "So, relax."

Ralphie listened and cataloged the enforcer's number. 7734? 7734, the enforcer with the blunt chin and three long scars across his cheek, leaned back and took a breath, relaxing. After a few breaths, the enforcer looked at Ralphie.

"Take it easy, kid. Good luck," the scarred enforcer said.

The son of Benjamin Reynolds blinked holding his left arm and looked at the enforcer and back to Bailey who was being moved carefully from the airship and to an awaiting gurney. The enforcers secured Bailey to the gurney and moving her away from the helicopter as the rotor blades slowed their rotation.

"What's your name?" Ralphie asked curiously, bandaged, and connected to an IV. The teen looked as if he had fallen into a tiger trap with a tiger and barely made it out alive.

7734 turned and looked at Ralphie with a small grin on his face. He seemed genuinely surprised and a little shocked by the question.

"Me? They call me: Monday," 7734 said.

The survivor of the Pandemonium Challenge nodded.

Ralphie still injured and woozy just smiled and watched as the enforcers went into action. He would have been the first to climb out of the helicopter, but his body felt like it had run over by a steamroller. So, all the teenager could do was watch as the enforcers moved Bailey toward a doorway and disappeared from the roof of the unknown building.

Ralphie looked up and toward the cloudless sky. The sun was setting and there were just a few fingers of light as the enforcers, who had been waiting on the rooftop, entered the copter and examined Ralphie.

Simultaneously enforcers with assault rifles slung across their backs climbed out of the quieting transport with essential equipment. Monday, the enforcer, and another enforcer had an exchange and the named enforcer scribbled something on a notebook computer the smiling bearded enforcer showed him.

"All right, kid," 7734, now Monday, said. "This is where I hand you off to this jamoke. He is responsible for getting you to the Buchanan complex," Monday said with a small smile. "Take care. Be safe. Don't do anything stupid."

The battered teen smiled at the enforcer's advice. With those words Monday, the enforcer climbed off the helicopter and disappeared.

He was instantly replaced by a diamond-faced man with a close-shaven beard and mustache, beady eyes that sat under a protruding brow and an extremely small mouth. Ralphie, instinctively looked at the enforcer's ID and logged it in his head; 9990.

"Hi, you are under my supervision for now," the enforcer said showing his small teeth. "I'm supposed to get you from here to the estate, safely," 9990 said, reading the machines and a report on his notebook computer. "I think you'll be fine. You just look pretty beat up, like you went ten rounds with a badger," the new enforcer said with a puzzling small tooth smile. He, like all the enforcers had his assault rifle, a service weapon on his hip, along with a notebook computer and a visible earbud. "Do you have any acute pain at this moment?"

The curious teenager looked to the left and saw that the pilot of the helicopter and another person were still in the cockpit. There was only Ralphie and two other enforcers aboard. The helicopter seemed suddenly hollow and quiet. Ralphie tried to stand and felt the clawing of pain in his right side radiate from his hip up to his arm pit. He winced and bent to the discomfort.

Ralphie leaned forward and before he could climb to his feet he was encompassed by darkness. He felt the tilt. He reached out. Ralphie did not recall anything else.

*   *   *   *   *

When Ralphie opened his eyes, he was immediately uncertain of his surroundings. Nothing seemed familiar. He was firmly but comfortably supported by the bedding beneath him. In the darkened room there were two lights softly glowing, like candles, but not candles. The curious teenager tried to press himself up and onto his elbows and noted that his left arm was immobilized somehow. Ralphie, in the darkness felt with his right hand and found that his left arm had been taped or secured so that his left elbow rested locked against his side.

Ralphie twisted onto his left side and pushed up a little in the luxurious bed to see better. The bed he lay in was expansive, the fifteen-year-old thought. The bed could sleep four or five easily.

Was it all a dream? It was dim in the room. He did not move immediately. Instead, he tried to recall the last thing that he remembered. There was darkness. Then he had heard distant voices. In his memory he had recalled continual movement.

The teen attempted to sit up and the first thing he noticed was that he was cushioned, held in the most comfortable bedding he ever experienced. He lay in a four-poster bed that looked as if it was an antique and manufactured by hand and not machine. The teen studied the artisanship of the fluted posts and marveled at the workmanship. It was a real treat to see handmade work in the room he was in.

The inquisitive Miller looked down and found his right arm in an air cast. His right hand was bandaged. His body felt as if he had fallen down McDonald's hill carrying an armful of knives.

Ralphie smiled and felt his jaw was sore as well. He took a deep breath and there was a constant sting in just breathing, but not like when he had been on the island. He looked left and right and for as far he could see to the left there was white Egyptian linen. To the right, there was an ornate door on the far wall. Between the door and the bed there was a bedside table and on it a silver bell, and a lamp with a paneled crystal lampshade. Also, on the table sat an analog clock that had eight faces.

The healing teen stopped sightseeing to focus on the manufacture and genius of the analog clock. He marveled at the clock and the moon phase face of the timepiece. The clock was an old-fashioned creation. It sat on the wooden table a piece of art.

Ralphie attempted to sit up and though there was a stinging hurt everywhere at once he pushed through the veil of eye closing and stabbing spasm.

"Pain was temporary," Ralphie thought. Someone had told Ralphie and all the Millers that when he was yet to be a teenager. "Pain only lasts a minute, an hour, or a day, but eventually it fades, and life goes on. We endure pain," some instructor told him.

To be a Miller was to know suffering. The teenager was used to sacrifice. The hurt was not as bad as he imagined. Ralphie winced. He looked toward the two paned windows and in between those panes stood a great mirror. In the mirror Ralphie saw a glimmer of himself. He tried not to get distracted. He saw his reflection and knew that he looked like he had fallen in a woodchipper.

The fifteen-year-old sat up with effort and felt a dull, throbbing bite in his right side. The twinge felt like a punch in the gut, but it did not stop him. Instead, the ache and the ache slowed him. He gritted his teeth and moved gingerly to a seated position.

In his quiet grand room, that was twice the size of his bedroom was a pair of wooden chests beneath the two windows framed panes. The night sky let stars and clouds frame the window. From Ralphie's vantage point there was no moon visible that night.

The curious bruised boy looked around the room and decided to climb out of the bed and find something to wear. He was dressed only in a white T-shirt and boxers. He padded across the wooden flooring to the door closest to the bed and tried the doorknob. The knob gave under his hand and inside the dark closet Ralphie found heavy coats and boots. He searched inside the closet for anything that he could wear but finding nothing he redirected his attention to the wooden chests beneath the four paned windows.

He moved gingerly to the first wooden chest and opened it to find sweat tops and jeans. He bypassed the sweatshirts as they seemed all declarations of the love of the Innovator line. So, Ralphie grabbed a pair of blue jeans and hesitated. What was he going to do? He did not know where he was. He was injured. Well, he was in pain from seven days on Pandemonium Island. He replaced the jeans in the chest and gingerly headed back toward the luxurious bed. Ralphie sat on the edge of the bed and tried to think what his next move was.

There was a sound outside of his room. The noise startled Ralphie. He braced himself for whoever appeared. Ralphie watched as the door to his room opened. In walked the slightly fox-faced daughter of Gordon Buchanan dressed in royal blue high collared evening dress, that had a white accent that lined the front of the dress. Ella Buchanan had dark eyes and her hair was swept up and away from her neck into gravity defying hairdo that looked a bit like a black curled waterfall.

Dangling from her earlobes were two strings of diamonds. The dress was sleeveless and showed off Ella's tone arms. On her shoulder was a small sequined blue purse. Ralphie smiled seeing that the Innovator firebrand was wearing a pair of matching royal blue Doc Marten combat boots.

"Hey, Miller, you awake?" Ella asked. Her question seemed more song than words as she walked into the room by herself. "Hope I didn't catch you indecent," she continued.

Ralphie smiled from the side of the bed.

"You aren't supposed to be out of bed," Ella pointed out to Ralphie.

Before Ralphie could respond Ella continued.

"I came in to check up on you. I usually do a few hours before I go to bed," Ella confessed. "You are my responsibility."

"How?" Ralphie asked, confused.

"I did liberate you and Bailey from the challenge," Ella said with a smile.

The curious Miller blinked and recalled the challenge and Bailey and Campbell and the imploding building that had nearly killed him and left Bailey buried. Ralphie could not remember how he had hurt his shoulder.

"What happened to my shoulder?" Ralphie asked curiously.

"I'm not too certain, we were in flight at the time," Ella stated. "From what I get from the Revolutionaries, my people," she said, placing her hand near her mouth. "They say you tried to shoulder an I-beam for some reason when you were fighting the First Gen, Emmett Carson, who you didn't like," Ella replied.

Ralphie nodded. What she said sounded correct.

"How long I been here?"

"Just a few days," Ella said.

"A few days?"

"Yeah. Three days, I think. How are you feeling?" Ella Buchanan asked with a big smile displaying her perfect smile.

The bruised teen smiled from the edge of the bed.

"I'm... I'm fine," Ralphie said.

"No pain?" Ella asked.

"No, pain," Ralphie smiled. His breathing was a little painful. He pressed his elbow to his right side and found that there was still a sharp ache there.

"What did the doctor say? I mean, are your injuries serious?" Ella Buchanan asked.

Ralphie did not respond.

Ella looked at the quiet Miller confused.

"You did talk to the doctor?"

The stoic Miller lowered his eyes.

"Ralphie? Did you see the doctor?"

Ralphie shook his head.

"Why?"

Ralphie shrugged his shoulders and felt his fingers, forearm, and upper arm tingle with a light wave of pain as an answer to his movement.

Ella frowned.

"What doctor?" Ralphie asked carefully.

"You didn't meet him?" Ella asked, frowning.

The cautious Miller felt that he stepped into a trap and poked out his lower lip. "No," Ralphie admitted.

Ella Buchanan frowned. She pouted. She crossed her arms in front of herself suddenly angry. Ella looked left and right, frustrated.

"It's not a--" Ralphie began.

Ella Buchanan raised her pointer finger. She was an attractive girl when she was lighthearted. Ralphie noticed that when Ella Buchanan frowned, she looked like an angry bullfrog in her high collared evening gown that looked like it should have been on some cartoon hero instead of Ella. Ralphie shook the image from his mind. He was a guest in Ella Buchanan's home. He knew that having rude thoughts of his host was wrong. He was raised better than that.

The quiet Miller watched as Ella marched across the room to a dark corner further in the room and stopped in front of yet another table. On the table was a phone that looked more decorative than functional. The Shaker lifted the receiver of the phone and tapped the phone once. Ella looked back at Ralphie, briefly and smiled mirthlessly.

Ralphie listened unsure what to do at that moment.

"Doctor Sherman, this is Ella Buchanan," Ella Buchanan said through gritted teeth. "I need you to come to the second floor on the west wing and our guest's room and check-in with your patient." She paused, listening. "He says you have not introduced yourself." She paused again. "I don't care. Make yourself available," Ella demanded and replaced the phone.

Ella turned around and her smile that was there earlier slowly, painfully made its way back on her triangular face. The frown was gone. She looked at Ralphie and noticed that he seemed uncomfortable.

The Maker closed the distance and with each step she seemed to brighten. By the time she had reached Ralphie the pinched look on her face was completely gone.

"I'm sorry, Ralphie, you are a guest in my home, and you should be comfortable here. I apologize," Ella said.

Ralphie nodded, silently.

"Are you going to a party?" Ralphie asked the girl standing in front of him. Ella was lost in thought.

"Yeah, my parents throw them pretty regularly," Ella declared. "This one is for some re-election campaign of one of the administrators or something."

Ralphie nodded not knowing what Ella was talking about.

The bright-eyed daughter of Gordon Buchanan shook her head and refocused.

"I can't believe that you haven't seen the doctor," Ella said with a shake of her head.

The healing Ralphie squirmed a bit, uncomfortable.

"Maybe I should fire him? Maybe I should tell daddy to fire him and his staff if he isn't doing his job," Ella said more to herself than to Ralphie.

Ralphie listened not sure if Ella was talking to herself. Ralphie remained quiet. He simply watched Ella ping pong back and forth over whether she should have Ralphie's doctor fired.

A few minutes later there was a knock at the door.

"Come in," Ella sang.

In walked a tall and thin chestnut brown man dressed in a white lab coat accompanied by a nut-brown man wearing glasses, and a big eyed intelligent looking, dark-haired woman. The doctor walked directly to Ella Buchanan and stopped in front of her.

"Miss Buchanan is there a problem?" Asked the man wearing glasses.

"Yes, there is a problem," Ella Buchannan said with tension in her voice. "My father pays you well, to be our on-call doctor. We expect quality service. I was informed by Ralphie that he has not seen any of the medical staff since he has woken up," Ella pointed out.

Gone was the gentle smile replaced with that intense pinched look that Ralphie saw before she had made a phone call.

"But we patched him up and monitored his progress," the doctor said, looking at the girl dressed in an evening gown.

Ella Buchanan raised a finger and the doctor stopped. She was annoyed. She looked at Ralphie and then back to the doctor.

"Introduce yourself to our guest." Ella said. She crossed her arms in front of her and looked sternly at the doctor and his two assistants.

"I'm doctor George Washington Carver Sherman, I attended to you when you first arrived," the doctor smiled. "As I said, we patched you up. You had a few bruises and lacerations from your time... on the island. But nothing seems permanent. The worse was your dislocated shoulder. We reset it. You should be right as rain in ten to fourteen days."

The cautious Miller nodded. The doctor reached out his hand and shook Ralphie's left hand awkwardly, looking at Ella all the time.

"I'm Ernest Gaines Floyd," the spectacled round-faced man with short, cropped hair said, with a flashy smile. He was dressed in a light blue polo shirt, khakis, and blue and gold basketball sneakers. Floyd was the only one not wearing a lab coat. He was also carrying a notebook computer in hand.

"I'm Josephine," the nurse smiled. "I'm Josephine Baker Howard and I'm your nurse." Josephine Howard, the nurse, looked a little like an old-fashioned long-legged model with loose curly black hair that fell just below her ears and framed her jewel-shaped face. She was dressed in a dark blue dress and matching high heels. Over her dress, Josephine wore a matching white lab coat.

Ella Buchanan had her arms crossed in front of her chest. She seemed impatient.

"All right, all right," Ella said, annoyingly. "So, I am a bit confused as to you not being here or talking to or checking in on our house guest," Ella said with a pout.

Doctor Sherman opened his mouth only to close it silently. He smiled.

"Miss Buchanan, we have monitored young Mister Reynolds since his arrival," Ernest Floyd said, nervously checking his notebook computer. "He was resting, and we also have been checking on Miss Bailey as well."

"This is *my* house guest," Ella pointed out again. "I think that to find that he has just woken up and to have no one here to make sure that he is not frightened or confused or to answer any questions about his injuries or whatever is the least you could do," Ella Buchanan trailed off, losing energy.

"Well, Miss Buchanan, the patient was unconscious for nearly 72 hours. That was most of our initial examination. As I said he had a dislocated shoulder. He had numerous lacerations. None of them were life threatening. So, after the first twelve hours of observation I instructed Josephine to check in on him every... few hours." Sherman seemed to be reading from a script. "Josephine has checked on Mister Reynolds periodically. He might have woken but it was never for extended periods of time without supervision." Sherman stopped, thinking. "His body is healing. He suffered a lot of physical trauma."

"He has been checked on every four hours," Ernest Floyd said, looking at his computer screen.

"Are you trying to mansplain something to me?" Ella asked, narrowing her eyes at the pair.

"No, Miss Buchanan," Doctor Sherman smiled.

"That is the most chauvinistic and antiquated and not to mention condescending thing to do to a woman," Ella hissed.

"I just wasn't sure if you understood the extent of young Mister Reynolds condition," Sherman backpedaled.

Ella Fitzgerald Buchanan crossed her arms again in front of her evening gown. She studied the three and seemed to be making a silent decision. Ralphie was not sure what he was supposed to do or say. Ella Buchanan nodded, satisfied but still annoyed.

"My father pays you well for your services. We have two guests in the house and they both need attendance. You promised my father that they would receive the highest quality of care. Are you saying that you cannot offer that to Ralphie?"

"No, I'm not saying that," Doctor Sherman said, stammering. "We are monitoring both patients. We continue to give them both the highest quality of medical service. It is my goal to reassure you and your family that you and your guests are in the best hands in the medical field."

Ella brushed off the explanation, suddenly bored with the conversation. She pouted. She looked at Sherman calculating.

"Can he walk?" Ella asked.

"Right now?" Sherman asked.

"No, not right now," Ella rolled her eyes. "I need him up and mobile tomorrow. Mummy and daddy want to introduce him, as soon as possible, to a few people."

The cautious Miller listened and realized that Ella was talking to the doctor as if he wasn't there.

"Based on my overall examination, he might have a few cracked ribs." He turned to Ralphie. "Your breathing may be a little painful but that's to be expected. You have been put through the wringer. You have been sleeping a lot. That is a good sign. That means that your body is healing."

Sherman looked at Ralphie who had a question he needed answered. The doctor nodded and added, "You have slept on and off for three days."

"Will he be able to walk?" Ella stepped forward and regained Sherman's attention.

"Wait," Ralphie said, suddenly unconcerned about Ella or the doctor's power play. "Do my parents know that I'm alive? Do the Millers know where I am? What is the Pandemonium Committee doing right now?"

Ella smiled. "Our wallflower is suddenly involved and questioning?"

"Ella," Ralphie rasped. His voice cracking. "Can you answer my questions. I'm all turned around here. I've been here for three days?"

"I said that," Ella said.

"So?"

Ella nodded and smiled, standing near the foot of the bed. Sherman was to her right. Next to Sherman was Ernest Floyd. On the left was the round-faced nurse.

"Do my parents know that I'm here?" Ralphie asked, concerned.

Ella giggled. She smiled impishly. Reluctantly, she nodded.

"Well, yes and no," Ella said.

The cautious Miller exhaled realizing that he had held his breath for Ella's response. He smiled because Ella smiled. Then he looked at the Innovator skeptically.

"Okay, I have to kind of explain that answer," Ella said.

"What do you mean?"

"I mean, my father had someone go to your compound and tell your parents that you were safe, I think," Ella explained.

"What?"

"It's a little delicate," Ella Buchanan grinned. "The Pandemonium Committee is none too happy with me and my father for the interruption of the challenge."

"They," Ralphie began only to stop. He shook his head, confused. "I don't care about that."

"The problem is that you need to care. We all need to care," Ella noted. "We are under the protection of the Innovators Collective. They have guaranteed that the Pandemonium Committee will not do anything until you and Bailey are able to return to your compounds."

"What do you mean?" Ralphie asked, confused.

Ella shook her head. "My Daddy will tell you more. I am supposed to take you to breakfast tomorrow and then things will be explained."

"But I don't understand," Ralphie said.

"My dad will tell you more in the morning." With that Ella stopped answering Ralphie's questions. She instead turned her attention back to Doctor Sherman.

"Before my guest and I got sidetracked I had asked you a simple question and you had not answered me," Ella Buchanan reported. "Do I need to repeat myself?"

Doctor George Sherman looked at Ernest Floyd and back at Ella Buchannan and nodded.

"He may have a little pain," Sherman said.

"Manageable?" Ella asked.

"A little pain," Ernest Floyd said with a shrug of his shoulders.

"A little pain," Ella said and frowned. She pouted. Ella looked at Ralphie and smiled. "You are a tough guy. Right? Miller, aren't you?" She asked looking at Ralphie.

The bruised teen looked at Ella confused. Ralphie looked to the doctor.

"It's unavoidable this early in your recovery," the doctor said with a shrug. He looked to Ella. "I have wrapped him up and in a few days he will be fine. It just takes time," Sherman explained. "He should be able to manage the pain by tomorrow."

"Based on our estimates the patient should be fully recovered in fourteen days," Ernest Floyd, the doctor's assistant smiled.

Ella Buchanan turned and stared the assistant to silence. She returned her attention to Doctor Sherman.

"Based on our estimates, Miss Buchanan, our patient should be fully recovered in the next ten days," the doctor repeated and smiled at the daughter of Gordon Buchanan. He smiled again and added, "I think that based on a number of factors, and the extent of his injuries, Mister Reynolds should be feeling nearly one hundred percent in a week."

"Mister Reynolds should rest," Josephine Howard smiled. "It is the best thing for him."

Ella Buchanan stared at Josephine Howard. The nurse fell silent.

"Mummy and daddy want to meet you, as soon as possible, and since you are up now and talking, I will plan on a brunch meeting tomorrow. It makes the most sense."

Ella Buchanan fished out her cellphone from her tiny purse. She quickly punched in a message.

"So, I want him ready for tomorrow morning by.... nine," Ella Buchanan said.

"Based on his alertness he should be more than capable, with enough preparation," Sherman said.

Ella Buchanan looked at her cellphone and smiled. "I just got a text from mummy, and they are happy to hear that Ralphie is awake. Mummy said she will make plans for tomorrow morning. She will arrange all the details," Ella was saying to anyone who would listen. "It should be fun. We haven't had a brunch get together in a while." Ella looked to the doctor and froze him with her dark stare. "So, I need some answers. What is his eating schedule?" Ella said with the slightest old-world British accent that came out a little more pronounced the more she used old-world sayings, Ralphie mused.

Doctor Sherman looked to his nurse and assistant. Howard smiled uncomfortably to Ella Buchanan. Floyd flicked through screen after screen on his notebook tablet.

"He has no eating restrictions. We have taken care of all his injuries. His right shoulder is in restraining cast against his side," Ernest Floyd over shared.

Ella Buchanan looked at Ernest Floyd annoyingly.

"Very well," Ella Buchanan accepted.

The three stood waiting to be dismissed.

"You can all leave," Ella said.

Sherman nodded. Ernest Floyd looked to his boss. Josephine Howard looked from Ella to Ralphie and back to Sherman. George Sherman was the first to move. Then, Ernest Floyd and Josephine Howard stepped to the bedside of Ralphie and shook his hand.

"If you need anything, just ring the bell," Josephine Howard smiled with her bobbed haircut. She pointed to the silver bell on the bedside table that Ralphie had noticed when he climbed out of bed earlier. He nodded.

"I'm going to let you sleep," Ella Buchanan smiled. "In the morning we can go do a tour," the daughter of one of the most powerful Innovators said with a grin.

After everyone left Ralphie's room the fifteen-year-old was unsure what his next steps were. He laid back in bed and watched the dark sky out of the four paned windows and tried to think what his family must be doing and thinking about him at that moment in the Remains.

Chapter Two.

Culinary delight

Raphie thought about his father, Benjamin O. Davis Reynolds. He might be in his study pouring over his paperwork from the days before. He was one of the bigger construction companies in the Remains. As a result, he was always busy. He was always taking phone calls and having meetings with important people from all over the Remains. His father had taken Ralphie, when he was young, with him on his meetings. Now, he was sure that his father, had called in favors to figure out what was going on with Ralphie, his only son. At least, that was what Ralphie believed.

His mother, Ralphie thought, would try to keep busy to keep her mind off Ralphie not being home. She would check on his father. He would shoo her away, busy himself. She would have made dinner, or they would have eaten, and she and Macy would have cleaned up the kitchen. Macy, his younger sister, would have run to her room after helping clean the kitchen. Her mother would straighten up. She might listen to music or check the Interweb before checking in on Macy and appreciating her daughter's need to check in, Ralphie thought. His mother and sister would comfort each other while he was out of the house.

Ralphie's mother, at this time of day, was trying to get Macy to bed. It was late and Macy, without Ralphie in the house, might be a little jumpy. She liked visiting Ralphie before she went to bed. Ralphie not being home would be hard for his little sister to deal with.

Instantly, Ralphie felt a heaviness wash over him. He felt the emptiness swirling around a hole that only seemed shaped for his family. He dreaded and longed for his father's steely glance. Ralphie hated to admit it, but he felt the inexplicable desire to see his mother's worry and concern about him.

Of his family, it was the mere idea of his younger sister Macy that made Ralphie smile effortlessly. Only nine years old Macy was a curious and gentle warrior. She incredibly bright and rarely backed down when she believed she was correct. Macy liked being nine. She liked being a Miller. She liked everything about the Remains.

The recovering teen recalled how Macy had brought him a crossbow after he had been selected for the Pandemonium Challenge.

"First things first," Ralphie had said spinning around in his desk chair, in his bedroom, when the little girl, dressed in T-shirt, overalls and sneakers, who looked so innocent with Afro puffs, walked into his room with a loaded crossbow. "Where did you get that?"

"Ralphie, you have to concentrate," Macy had said. "You don't have time to play. You must prepare for the challenge."

"What are you doing with a crossbow?" Ralphie asked, ignoring Macy's logic.

"This kid at school told me he had one and I told him that you might need it to practice with for the challenge."

"Macy I am not going to use a crossbow," Ralphie had told his apple cheeked sister. Macy had her unruly hair combed and brushed neatly into two Afro puffs on either side of her diamond face.

Ralphie fell asleep recalling Macy bringing him a combat knife the next day with the same intention.

"You can never be too prepared," Macy warned.

Ralphie slept for a few hours only to wake to to the heady smell of his dinner sitting next to his bed. On a dinner tray sat Ralphie's dinner on three small plates. There was a typed menu folded above each plate. On one plate sat warm Mediterranean mixed olives. Next to the olives was lavender baked goat cheese, White fig alidade, chicories, crostini, crudité and Provencal brandade. Ralphie spooned the whipped salt cod. He smelled the Yukon potatoes. There was Norwegian smoked salmon, fingerling potatoes with curried crème fraiche, pickled onions, which Ralphie avoided. There was a small glistening pile of black pearls shaped into a pyramid, next to Levian crisps. On the third plate sat Monterey calamari, covered in Romasco sauce with chickpeas, aioli, and a side of tortilla chips.

The knicked up teen picked at each plate. He had to eat using his left hand. Ralphie enjoyed spearing the olives with his fork. It was entertaining to spear the black and green olives. He ate all of them. He ate a couple of bites of the goat cheese and decided he didn't like the taste. He spooned the whipped salt cod but did not eat it. Instead, he picked at the Yukon potatoes. He ate three of the potatoes and focused on the Norwegian smoked salmon. He ate most of the salmon. Ralphie sampled the black pearls but found them too salty for his taste. The teenager ate the calamari awkwardly with his left hand. He could not do anything but spear the calamari and chew. Ralphie washed his meal down with a tall glass of water.

After his dinner, Ralphie found himself falling asleep. He napped. He woke up a few hours later to the sound of piano music. Ralphie with a full stomach listened to the sound of the piano and the lightest of laughter below his feet somewhere in the place he was resting. He listened absently to the piano being played and fell back to sleep under the blinking stars in the sky just on the other side of the four paned windows.

The next morning a copper toned round faced girl with braids was sitting in a chair beside Ralphie's bed when he woke up. The girl was dressed in a white nurse's outfit with a peaked cap, white jacket, and white skirt. The girl was reading a comic book Ralphie had seen in his own library.

The beaten-up teen moved his elbows, just a little, and sat up painfully.

The motion drew the nurse's attention.

"Good morning, Mister Reynolds," the new nurse smiled.

"Good morning," Ralphie smiled, with a slight grimace. He tried to sit up and clumsily edged to an almost sitting position. "Who are you?"

"Me? I'm Patricia," the nurse with the headful of braids braided to one side of her head said. "Patricia Bath Moore."

"How long you been there?" Ralphie asked.

"Not long," Patricia Moore smiled. She looked casually out the window at the sunlight starting to stream into the room and back to Ralphie.

"What time is it?" Ralphie asked.

"Nearly seven o'clock," Patricia responded. "You slept a long time. That's good. Your body needs rest to recover." Patricia had a notebook computer on her lap and a small bag by her chair. Ralphie could see that the computer was monitoring his vitals like the four or five machines by his bed. He also noticed in Patricia's bag there were other comics inside.

"Are you hungry?" Patricia asked.

The recently awakened teen smiled and then looked around curiously.

"The food isn't scheduled to arrive just yet. I will text the kitchen and tell them you are awake. The food should arrive in a few minutes." Patricia smiled, closing her comic, and tapping on her notebook computer before climbing to her feet. She was tall and long limbed, curvy but not voluptuous. She looked more like a runner.

Patricia walked to stand beneath one of the four paned windows in the bedroom. She crossed the space in three steps. "We have a variety of food choices to offer but today you only get a small snack," Patricia continued. She tapped a few things on the table where she stood. There were monitors there as well.

Ralphie raised his left hand. He waved at Patricia who had walked toward the window instead of toward Ralphie for some reason. She was clearing off a table near the window.

"I'm sorry," Ralphie apologized. "I need to go to the bathroom. I also need to brush my teeth and clean up before I eat anything," Ralphie admitted.

Patricia turned on her heels like a ballet dancer. She smiled and nodded. Patricia was boyish in her shape, Ralphie noticed. She was wide hipped and small chested but stunningly attractive. She had this grace that suggested a dancer.

"Sorry, I don't know what I was thinking," Patricia said, grinning looking at her notebook computer. "You haven't gone to the bathroom since last night," Patricia said with a small grin. "This room's bathroom is having some plumbing issues. So, we must use the other bathroom." She moved quickly to the bedside and as she stepped toward the bed, she grabbed a small toiletry kit and bath robe that were lying at the foot of the bed. She silently helped Ralphie out of the bed. Ralphie slipped on the robe a little slower than he preferred, still tender from his injuries.

"It's just a short walk to the end of the hallway," Patricia said with a narrow smile. She was grinning as she slowly walked Ralphie across the space between the bed and the single dark door.

"This is a bedroom?" Ralphie asked.

"Why yes," Patricia said. "What did you think it was?"

"I don't know," Ralphie said. "I have a bedroom, but it is not even close to this size."

"Well, you are in the Buchanans primary home," Patricia said. "It is not like any other house," the nurse said.

Patricia smiled. Ralphie moved gingerly toward the door. They paused at the ornately designed door and Patricia opened it.

The recuperating teen was surprised to find a tall man dressed in a matte black uniform of the enforcers just on the other side of the door. Instinctively, he looked for the enforcer's ID number. The guard was positioned on the left of the doorway looking at his computer attached to the forearm of his uniform. He snapped to attention and stood rigidly watching Patricia and Ralphie.

The still healing Ralphie moved out and into the hallway and found that he had not seen the enforcer's number. It was not easily visible from his vantage point. Ralphie found it interesting that Ella and her family had enforcers in their private home.

Enforcers, in the Miller compound, where Ralphie lived, were government agents and seen exclusively on streets, at the Gathering Center, in public areas and near government buildings. They were the ones that defused potentially dangerous situations. The enforcers were trained in hand-to-hand combat. They were fearless and one enforcer was equal to three or more untrained residents.

Ralphie knew that enforcers armed or unarmed were dangerous. The Miller teen had seen one enforcer subdue five teens by themselves. Enforcers were serious and brutal street protectors.

The idea of a private enforcer in someone's home was unbelievable and unimaginable. Ralphie was stymied by the sight of an enforcer so close, protecting the hallway. He looked from the enforcer and back to Patricia, his nurse, formulating a question.

"How? Why is there an enforcer here?"

"It's a precaution," Patricia said and walked away from the bedroom.

The injured teen did not push the issue. He had to think about why Patricia didn't see the problem.

Ralphie, had he been healthy and not injured, would have craned his neck to find the enforcer's ID number but then and there he was too sore and trying to fight through the aching in his side to look. Besides, Ralphie needed to make it to the bathroom. His priorities were focused on getting to the bathroom.

What Ralphie did note was on his hip was a gun belt, pistol, and holster. The enforcer snapped to attention seeing Patricia and Ralphie. The enforcer watched Ralphie and Patricia as they walked down the hallway toward the closest bathroom. The dark hallway did not end but bowed to the right and into darkness.

"This way, Ralphie," Patricia smiled directing Ralphie toward the right and away from the enforcer. They walked one hundred feet, to the edge of the dark hall, and Patricia stopped at a hidden door on the left side of the hall. "We are in the main building. I want to apologize for the inconvenience. Luckily, we aren't in the far western wing of the house. On this floor there are sometimes plumbing issues for some reason. It's a bit of an inconvenience for the guests but.... I hope this isn't too big of an issue for you," the tall nurse said handing Ralphie his toiletry kit.

"I'll be fine," Ralphie said.

The nurse, smiled awkwardly, looking to the left and then the right.

The still bandaged Ralphie smiled and nodded and entered the hall bathroom. The bathroom had a claw-footed bathtub on the far wall. The commode sat just a few feet from the tub. There was a vanity that was made of black stone. On the opposite side of the vanity were three open shelves that held towels and a few vases. The closest thing to the door was a small wash basin that was mostly just a white porcelain bowl held by the brass works that resembled fluted petals of a flower. The flower image was continued to the floor with the stem being the one-foot radius three-foot-high stem that housed the waterworks and ended in a circular fluted foot that was bolted to the tiled floor. Hanging over the wash basin was a three-foot-high mirror. Ralphie examined the efficient room and realized that this was really a bathroom.

He opened the toiletry kit with his left hand and after a little effort did his morning ablutions. He was in the small bathroom fifteen minutes at most. When he opened the door, he found Patricia smiling down at him.

"Have you been waiting for me all this time?"

Patricia smiled.

"I'm sorry, I didn't know," Ralphie said.

"It's not a problem," Patricia said. "We'll head back now to your room," she added.

Patricia and Ralphie walked back to the room that were the only room in the hall. The nameless enforcer watched as Ralphie returned to his room.

"Are there enforcers guarding every room?"

Patricia smiled but did not answer. Instead, the round-faced beauty helped Ralphie back into bed and went to retrieve the breakfast that sat on the table under the four-pane window.

"You need to put a little something in you before your brunch." Patricia advised. "You can't meet the benefactors and have your tummy all growling," she said with a little grin.

The unemotional teen looked at the plate and tray and back to Patricia.

Patricia smiled. "You are supposed to be eating with the Buchanans this morning," the nurse said. "That is a very big deal."

Patricia smiled nervously.

Ralphie nodded. He examined the food and decided that it couldn't be poisoned. He was to meet with Ella's parents that morning. Ralphie ate his breakfast snack and wondered what would come of the day.

For the second time in as many days Ralphie found himself with a delight for his palette that he did not know how to describe. Now, he had orange juice and apple juice when he was in the compound but for some reason the orange juice and apple juice tasted fresher, sweeter and he did not want to think it, but he could not shake the idea that the orange juice was fresh squeezed. There again was a typed menu folded above the plate. On one plate was a single wedge of bacon and leek quiche. Beside the wedge was a neatly formed pyramid of blackberries. The berries were gently sprinkled with confectionery powder.

After Ralphie was done eating Patricia started to take the tray away.

"What can you tell me about Ella's parents?" Ralphie asked.

Patricia smiled but did not answer.

"Come on," Ralphie said. "Are they nice? Mean? Crazy?"

"They are nice people," Patricia said.

"Oh yeah," Ralphie said. "What makes them nice?"

"I don't know," Patricia said. "I think they treat everyone fairly."

She took the tray away and sat it near the door. Patricia returned from the door with a rolling rack that was filled with some clothes for Ralphie to wear, when meeting the Buchanans.

He had several options. There were several pairs of jeans. There were four pair of sneakers and several blue and various shades of blue combat boots. There were seven T-shirts to choose from. At the end of the fashion rack were four hooded sweatshirts.

"How did you know?" Ralphie asked.

Patricia smiled. "We saw you on the challenge and know that you prefer these over other choices."

The still battered teen dressed himself. He was clumsy and slow, but he slipped into the jeans and basketball sneakers and pulled on a short sleeve blue T-shirt. He chose not to wear the hooded sweatshirt offered. The selection was all Innovator gear and Ralphie would not be caught dead in a hoody that was not a Miller hoody.

A few minutes after Ralphie was dressed Ella Buchanan walked into Ralphie's room without knocking. She was dressed in a red blouse, gold zip front hooded sweat top, dark blue loose-fitting jeans, and spiked Doc Marten boots.

"Let me take you on a tour of our home," Ella said smiling to Ralphie as they left Patricia behind.

Ralphie blinked and tried to take in the hallway he was in. There was this muted red print carpet on the floors with a golden threading in it that Ralphie wondered about. On the walls were easily a dozen framed paintings that Ralphie was sure he had seen on museum websites. As he walked toward the stained-glass end of the hallway Ralphie noted that there was even a suit of armor in the hallway.

"You okay to walk?"

The impassive Miller nodded.

"Okay, we'll go to the patio and have breakfast with my parents," Ella said. "Now, be prepared to be asked a million questions. They have invited a few people over for brunch as well."

Ralphie stayed silent. He did not know what to say even if Ella would have seemed interested in what Ralphie thought. So, he followed the heir to the Buchanan riches.

For the next few minutes Ella Buchanan walked at a slow pace and talked non-stop about her home. "Okay, here's the whole Buchanan estate history, as best I know. Let's see," Ella said, with a pause. "This was a private country club at one time. My dad knows all the dates and particulars. All I know is it was once a country club. I forget the original name. It doesn't matter. It is now and forever the Buchanan estates. We own everything that we can see for as far as the eye can see. I think it was built in 1900, but I could be wrong. I know that it was owned by one of the Livermores. I'm just not certain if it was the important Livermore or not. There are three buildings that make up the main estate. The main building, what daddy likes to call: the mansion, has fourteen bedrooms. It is four stories tall. Your room, unfortunately, has a plumbing problem and the bathroom in your room is not working, as you know."

Ralphie nodded.

"The estate has an 18-hole golf course which my daddy loves," Ella said. "There are seven tennis courts, two outdoor swimming pools and above us the quietest neighbors ever," Ella said with a toothy grin.

"What do you mean?"

"Well, above us, on the other side of the hill, is a cemetery," Ella said, with a sly smile.

Ralphie seemed a little shocked by the news but chuckled despite the information.

"It's okay, they didn't rise from the dead when things went bad and I don't think they are planning on doing that now," Ella said.

The injured teen shook his head. Ella seemed to be all laced up and proper and then she would drop these dark, twisted jokes. Ralphie and Ella walked around the second floor of the mansion.

"My father told me that not his father, but my grandfather's father purchased this property nearly half a century ago, after the flash and the majority climbed aboard their secretly built spaceships and left this place," Ella said. "The rich here, back then, climbed on the Arc and the Wanderer and headed into the stars."

Ralphie had heard stories of the world pre-flash, pre-Remains, pre-walls, and challenge but in the back of his head never really given them credence. Yet, Ella was talking about the Arc and the Wanderer that had been launched and carried 52,000 of the richest and most powerful people in the nation into the stars to search for another earth.

"Wait, that stuff about the Arc is true?"

Ella sneered. "Of course," the Innovator chuckled. "The oppressors escaped to the stars and left us with the fallout of the flash."

"I thought that was all just fairytales and stories they told to scare us," Ralphie said, unbelieving.

"No, the truth is sometimes scarier than the fiction that we want to believe," Ella said with a smirk.

"What do you mean?"

"I mean, that the oppressors, the one percent, who had amassed all this wealth, had years to create an escape plan," Ella said. "They were planning an exit just for them in case things went bad. They were so focused on themselves that they didn't try to do anything for anybody else. All the while everyone else believed that the world leaders would correct the problem brewing between two penis measurers with their hands on world killing technology. Few knew that those two chest beating idiots wouldn't walk back the war talk like they had many times before."

"Yeah, so," Ralphie said. "I know all that."

"Did you know that the oppressors plotted and planned and sent into space all these parts of what most did not know were essential for the Arc and the Wanderer?"

Ralphie shook his head.

"The other nations, rich and wealthy and focused on saving their elite, did the same things." Ella shook her head. "So, when they blasted off with the flash and the world killer virus and its effects already making its unstoppable march across earth, they left knowing there was no way to stop the flash or the virus. They left our ancestors for dead. They expected the earth to die." Ella said with a tinge of distress in her voice. "When those not dead learned of the one percent's plan it seemed a fool's run."

"It was a dead-end run," Ralphie said. "I mean, they can't live in space forever."

"The one percent aren't risk takers," Ella said. "Little did anyone know, except those aboard, their supplies and rockets and experimental propulsion systems floated above our heads ready for the oppressors to assemble and take off toward the planets to restart their idea of humanity."

The dispassionate Miller did not say anything. Again, he and countless others had heard of the oppressors escaping the earth in rockets, but most believed that they had run away only to die in space. They *had* to die in space.

"Hey, can I ask a question?" Ralphie asked beneath a Kehinde Wiley painting that spanned the length and width of a doorway.

Ella smiled.

"Do you think that any of them survived?" Ralphie asked, looking up toward the ceiling of the mansion.

Ella smiled. "I'm not sure. I don't think anyone here really knows," Ella said. "The rich always have a way of avoiding punishment like smoke or rats through cracks." The Innovator cut her brown eyes at Ralphie. "Is that what you really want to know?"

"Well, I also wanted to know," he paused. Ralphie looked at one of the paintings on the wall that he knew he had seen on a museum website. "Can we see Bailey before meeting your parents?" Ralphie asked.

Ella Buchanan smiled.

"Don't smile at me," Ralphie said with a slim smile, suddenly embarrassed.

"I was expecting you to ask. I figured I would just wait you out," Ella said.

Ralphie smiled awkwardly, suddenly feeling Ella's eyes on him. He squirmed in the hallway.

"Yeah, sure," Ella said as they got to the head of the hallway. She turned to the left and walked Ralphie down another hallway. "Don't forget that we all saw you and Bailey promising not to gut each other." Ella smiled romantically. She clasped her hands together and tilted her head to the right. "It was just so cute."

Ralphie turned away embarrassed. In the heat of the challenge, he sometimes forgot that sometimes seventy to eighty percent of the Remains were watching everything that was happening on Pandemonium Island.

"Do you think that you love her?" Ella asked with a wry smile.

Ralphie did not respond to the question.

Ella looked back at Ralphie and smiled knowingly. "Sometimes saying nothing speaks volumes," the Innovator said smugly.

At the second hallway the pair walked down the hallway that was bathed in natural light. The hallway was distinct in that the windows looked out toward a courtyard compared to the darker hallway that held Ralphie's room. The second hallway seemed brighter. The sun was streaming in from the half dozen four paned windows.

Standing in the middle of the hallway was another enforcer, Ralphie noted. The enforcer in this hallway was just a little shorter than the enforcer guarding his room in the other hallway. Seeing the second enforcer jarred Ralphie. He slowed not sure what to think.

Ella did not slow or stop. She simply pushed past the enforcer. 8129 scowled at Ralphie as he followed slowly behind the Innovator. Ralphie could not stop looking at the enforcer with his blockish features staring at him.

"How many enforcers does your family have?"

Ella shook her head at the question and kept walking, ignoring the question, and pushing past two women in white lab coats. Ralphie stopped short seeing the pair of women dressed in white. He smiled. The two women were not unattractive but not as stunning as Josephine or Patricia.

They both smiled at Ralphie as if he was a chocolate treat. The woman on the right was wearing rectangular glasses. Her hair was a finely braided hairdo that resembled twisted chunky cornrow braids that fell to her rounded shoulders. The other woman, big eyed, caramel colored and heavy chested was slightly doughy with wide hips. She had short curly red dyed hair on her round head.

"Ralphie, come along," Ella said, demandingly.

The overwhelmed Miller smiled awkwardly at the two women and moved gingerly past them. He lowered his eyes and moved painfully behind the Innovator. Ella Buchanan waved her hand toward the three people standing around a giant four-poster bed with a canopy. Ralphie drew closer to the bedside.

Ella stood and studied Bailey Beaumont lying on the bed unmoving and hooked up to several machines. Ralphie looked and was mildly shocked to see that Bailey was attached by a dozen tubes to four machines. There was one machine that was monitoring her heartbeat and some other function. There were three pouches of liquid hanging from separate racks near Bailey. One of the pouches was clear. Another was a lightly tinted blue pouch that dripped into a tube attached to Bailey. The last was a golden liquid hanging from a rack that was slowly being pumped into one of Bailey's intravenous.

"How is she?" The still mending teen asked.

The doctor turned and Ralphie was surprised to find that the doctor was not doctor Sherman but a chubby woman in her forties with a short black Pixie haircut wearing a lab coat. She had hazel eyes and a thoughtful look on her balsa wood tinted face. The doctor smiled, seeing Ralphie.

"You are Ralphie Reynolds," the doctor nodded. "I saw you on the Interweb." She smiled widely and for an instant Ralphie thought the doctor might hug him. He smiled awkwardly. "I'm Doctor Sarah Farro Willis," she extended a hand to Ralphie. Ralphie shook the doctor's hand awkwardly with his left hand.

"Doctor Willis, how is Bailey doing?" Ella asked, rolling her eyes at the two.

"She is doing better," Doctor Willis said. "For the first 36 hours (about 1 and a half days) she was touch and go. We could only hope that she would survive her various injuries. Thankfully, we have had a few days to stabilize her." Doctor Willis looked at Ella and then Ralphie. "Based on the videos we saw a building fall on her. It's a miracle that she's not dead or paralyzed."

Ralphie nodded, hesitantly moving to the bedside, and paused. He looked at the beaten and bruised Bailey laying on the sumptuous bed that could have easily fit eight people on its luxuriousness. She looked like a toffee-colored baby doll pretending to be asleep in the milk white of the bedding and pillows. The only thing that broke the image were the intravenous lines that ran from the crooks of both her arms to fluid bags that dripped from the IV poles and the various wires that monitored her breathing, heartrate, pulse, and various other needs.

Ralphie reached out and placed his left hand on Bailey's hand and stood there for a moment. He studied her cut, bandaged face, and saw that Bailey had a huge bandage around her head. Ralphie turned and looked at the doctor who was watching Ralphie holding Bailey's hand.

"What happened to her head?" Ralphie asked, turning to Doctor Willis.

Doctor Willis pouted before answering. "When she arrived, she had bleeding on her brain," the doctor said. She raised her index finger and looked seriously at Ella and Ralphie. "Like I said, it was touch and go. Thankfully, she had the best medical care available." The doctor nodded. "Now, all she needs is time to recover."

Ralphie let what the doctor said sink in. He shook his head at the idea that Bailey could have died on Pandemonium Island if she had not been brought to the Innovator's compound. It, the idea, seemed unimaginable.

The injured boy looked up and noticed that there were at least seven people in the room with Bailey. One of Doctor Willis's aides was at Bailey's bedside but looking at Ralphie with a silly lovesick puppy look on her brown face. Ralphie looked at the other three and they were all watching Ralphie next to Bailey.

Doctor Willis smiled seeing Ralphie looking at her assistants.

"You two are a bit of celebrities here," Doctor Willis gushed. "We all watched your heroics and self-sacrifice."

The still mending teen smiled and looked at Ella. Ella seemed genuinely amused.

"I don't watch the challenges too often but when Mister Buchanan told us that little Ella was going to be in it, well, I had to," Doctor Willis said with a pencil-thin smile. "We all watched. We were so worried for our little Ella."

Ralphie smiled at the concern the doctor had for Ella. He cut his eyes toward Ella who was already shaking her head, annoyed and embarrassed. Ralphie smiled at little Ella. The usually overconfident and confident Ella shook her head.

"So, I watched and heard Mister Buchanan had gotten Ella out safely and I sort of lost interest," the doctor said. "Then I heard that there was an underdog, a Miller, who was surprising everyone. I tuned back in to see you, a Miller, outwitting all the other lines with your pluck and persistence. It was incredible."

Ralphie felt awkward and anxious. He smiled and nodded.

"It was quite impressive," Doctor Willis said, with a wispy smile.

"How long until she fully recovers?" Ella asked.

"I cannot say for sure," Doctor Willis said to Ella. She had a tablet in her hand and referred to it. She scanned some data before speaking again. "I don't want to say a week if it will take longer. She broke a few bones. Her left arm is broken. That will be at least, at least eight weeks recovery. She also broke her right leg. She is pretty scraped up. But I don't think there is any long-lasting damage." Doctor Willis concluded. "We expect her recovery to be quick." The doctor paused. "Maybe, six to eight weeks."

Ella looked at her smart watch and nodded.

"We have a brunch date, Ralphie," Ella said, changing the topic.

Ralphie nodded approvingly. Ella nodded to the doctor and assistants. Ralphie patted Bailey's hand and turned to leave.

Doctor Willis blocked Ralphie's exit by stepping into his path. She smiled from ear to ear.

"Thank you for proving them wrong about you, Ralphie," the doctor said, smiling broadly.

Ralphie edged around the doctor and felt one of the assistants clap him on the back and say: "Good job." Another assistant whispered, "I was pulling for you."

Ralphie looked back to Bailey only to find the smiling and adoring faces of the women in Bailey's room blocking his view of the girl in bed. Ralphie turned back toward Ella as she reached the door and exited, never looking back.

Chapter Three.

Once outside of Bailey's room, and just a few feet from 8129, the enforcer, at the door, Ralphie reached out and stopped Ella. Out of the corner of his eye Ralphie watched 8129 pretending not to watch. Ralphie knew he was a raised voice or look away from being beaten to a pulp if Ella so deemed. The Influential daughter turned and looked first at the hand and then up to the concerned squarish face of Ralphie. She smiled. Her smile perfect, even, and white.

"What is going on?" Ralphie asked.

"What do you mean?" Ella asked with her perfect smile framed between her perfect, full lips.

"I mean," Ralphie said, confused. "Why is everyone all... I don't know?" He gestured with his left hand back toward Bailey's room. He seemed frustrated. Ralphie rubbed at his forehead.

"Well, Ralphie, as far as I can figure," Ella said, now beside him and starting to walk. Ralphie moved slowly forward. Ella was walking at his pace.

"You are a big deal," Ella said. "You survived. You didn't die," the girl in the hoody said. "You were thrown to the lions, as it were, and came out alive." She paused and looked at Ralphie. She shrugged and started to walk away.

Ralphie stopped her again. He looked at Ella Buchanan who he had not known before the Pandemonium Challenge. The girl in front of him, dressed in a golden sweat top, who had risked everything to save him, smiled and tilted her head to the right, curiously.

"But--," Ralphie said, unsure.

"This challenge is bigger than people understand, Ralphie. It's barbaric, Ralphie," Ella said. "I hate it. I hate that we give into it. Yet, this year, after a lot of convincing, you and Bailey and I made a difference," Ella said, defiantly.

"How?"

"We threw a monkey wrench in the system," Ella said, with a thin smile.

"I don't get it," Ralphie said, confused.

"It'll all make more sense when you meet my father," Ella said. "For now, I'm supposed to be taking you on a tour of the house... and a tour you will get." Ella shook her head and seemed to morph from the firebrand into the effusive tour guide instantly.

The switch was a little jarring. Ralphie frowned, confused. He shook his head and took a deep breath, resigned to follow Ella. He held his thoughts to himself, hoping for a better explanation from her father.

From the hallway Ella took the next five minutes to talk about the mansion. The Buchanan mansion sat on what had once been a golf course before the flash. The house and course sat unseen just off what had been Broadway Avenue. The mansion was hidden behind ten brick apartment buildings on Broadway Terrace in ruin and disuse. The family had purchased all the land surrounding the mansion including the now empty apartment buildings. It had taken a decade to refurbish and empty any and everyone in the surrounding buildings for three blocks in all directions, Ella explained as a matter of fact. According to the wealthiest person Ralphie had ever met, that purchase, and ownership made their home the only inhabited home for a mile just off the broken highway to the west.

"This place we are in is over five hundred years old," Ella smiled as she described the mansion, her family took it over. Ralphie listened but suddenly had about a hundred questions he needed answered.

The main building was four stories and had been built in 1900 by some famous architect. Ralphie half listened, and half worried suddenly not sure how he should feel. As Ella led Ralphie down to the main floor The injured teenager found that he did not seem to care too much about the history of the Innovator's 45+ room Tudor home.

"Ella, this is crazy," Ralphie said, trying to understand all the things that had happened to him. "We're in a mansion. There are enforcers here. You have private doctors?"

Ella smiled at the foot of the stairs to the main floor. Ella turned and watched as Ralphie slowly descended the last few steps. At the bottom of the stairs there were two other hallways that led, Ralphie did not know. Directly behind the pair was a stained-glass window which was an intricate work of art above the landing that created kaleidoscope-colored hallway that morning.

At the end of that brightened hallway was the main door, again delicately stained glass colored the carpeted floor from the door all the way to the foot of the stairs. Early that morning there was little to no sound in the house.

Ella smiled. Ella pointed toward a woman standing or leaning in the shadows near the front door. Ralphie was a little surprised to see the woman enforcer dressed in matte black and blending in completely with the shadows of the entryway.

"Why are there enforcers everywhere?" Ralphie asked, uneasily.

"They are our personal team," Ella said. The Maker turned to Ralphie and smiled. "Ralphie, you are suddenly important. More important than me or my family," Ella said.

"How?"

"How? Well, each year they try and make us all believe that their distraction keeps us unharmed and not at each other's throats," Ella said. "They have made up their own rules and only allowed one champion to survive," Ella said. She seemed suddenly angry. She seemed hurt by the words she said.

Ella stopped herself. She exhaled. She regained her composure.

"Sorry about that," Ella said with a weak smile. "The challenge is a horrible thing. We are pitted against one another like animals. For the pleasure of others." Ella shook her head. She smiled again and continued into the dark hallways.

Ralphie liked the passion of Ella. It was at times intense. Yet, she was sincere. None of her words seemed hollow or for performance.

Ralphie paused at the entry to yet another hallway in the mansion. Ella looked back, curious.

"Where is everyone?"

Ella smiled at a short, carpeted stairway.

"This is an incredibly big place," Ralphie said. "I can't imagine how many people are here on the regular." He stopped and looked at the art on one of the walls. "You have brothers and sisters?"

Ella smiled as an answer.

Ralphie followed feeling a slight scratching in his side as he walked.

"I thought we were going to be having brunch with some of your family's friends?" Ralphie paused. They had just come down from the lighter and brighter second floor and into the darker, because of the dark wood, and seemingly closer interior of the main floor.

Ralphie thought Ella had said something about her home being on twenty acres of land on the brief tour. There was the main building and its east and west wing, the guest house and two swimming pools and seven tennis courts on the property.

Ella gestured and walked to the right and into a dark wood hall on the right. Ralphie followed slowly, feeling a little better the more he moved. In the dark hall he saw gigantic paintings and pictures on the wall.

"So, what's with all these old pictures," Ralphie said after entering the dark wooden hallway and seeing two long dark wood tables separating the hallway from the hall, changing the subject.

Ella shrugged her round shoulders. "All these pictures are valuable. According to my mom they are priceless for some reason," Ella said.

Deeper into the space, away from the windows was a large room that looked like it could easily hold sixty people with ease. The pair walked through the hallway and under the eye of half a dozen statues. Ella noticed Ralphie staring at one of the statues. "The statues are priceless as well," the Maker said pointing to the two Art Deco statues that sat on either side of the staircase guarding the stairs.

"Why do you have so much art?"

"My daddy said that there are three things that continue to increase in value: land, art and gold." Ella Buchanan paused. "There's tons of land now. There's excess resources thanks to the fact that the population has decreased by eighty percent. So, the only thing that has increased in value nowadays, consistently, is gold and art."

"Gold," Ralphie said curious.

"Yeah, gold," Ella said. "We love gold. It is just one of those limited resources that rarely loses its value."

Ralphie nodded. He looked at Ella and asked a simple question. "All art?"

"Most art," Ella stated.

"How do you decide?"

"Well, I don't, really," Ella smiled. "My dad and the people that work for him spend hours researching valuable art pieces that might still be around."

Ralphie smiled, thinking that Macy would love to have a Banksy piece if Ella had one.

"Wait a minute," Ralphie said, confused. "You mean your dad, or his people, are going out and finding the art?"

"Well, not him," Ella said with a faint smile. "He has people he pays to go out and dig it up."

Ralphie listened. The injured juvenile thought about what Ella had said. He thought absently that Ella and her father were treasure hunters, except with tons of money. The thought tickled him. The Innovators were not that different than the others in the Remains. They were trying to unearth history in their own way. He shrugged the thought off, thinking of his baby sister as he walked past an oil painting that he knew had been in a museum.

"You ever hear of Banksy?"

Ella Buchannan reflected on the question for a moment before answering.

"You mean the ancient colonist graffiti artist?"

"Yeah, my little sister likes him," Ralphie smiled.

"I think my mom doesn't support that kind of art for some reason."

"What does that mean?" Ralphie asked.

Ella shrugged her shoulders in answer.

"Well, Macy, my little sister, likes him. He might have been a colonist, but I don't think he was a colonist with bad intentions."

Ella laughed at Ralphie's words.

"What?" Ralphie asked as they walked.

"Nothing," Ella Buchanan said, smiling her perfect white and even smile. "The more you look at something," Ella said with a tilt of her head. "The more you can see what's wrong with that something."

Ralphie made a face.

"I don't know too many colonists that didn't have bad intentions," Ella said. "Their title alone told on them."

Ralphie smiled at Ella's lesson.

"I shouldn't have said anything," Ella said apologetically. "I don't know anything about that. You can ask mum. We may have some of his art somewhere, but I'm not sure. We mostly display Black artists." Ella paused, pivoting. "I am more into the Renaissance artists like Aaron Douglas, Jacob Lawrence, Romare Bearden and Laura Wheeler Waring. Classic artists. You know, black artists that were saying something with their art."

The pair were walking through the hall that was filled with oaken furniture which had to be hundreds of years old and had stood the test of time. There were two tables made of carved wood that ran the length of the room. At the front of the room was another wooden table where the most important guests sat, Ralphie imagined.

"What is this place?" He asked with a tip of his chin.

"It is one of the four dining halls in our house," Ella said. "This one is named the Oak Hall."

Ralphie nodded.

Ella turned abruptly right again and walked down a stairway to another level with Ralphie gingerly following, nursing his ribs as he made his way down the short flight of steps. Ella turned at the bottom of the stairs and Ralphie followed.

The entire left side of the room they entered was eight six-foot-high and six-foot-long panes of glass that looked out onto the rear of the Buchannan property. Ralphie saw four tables just on the other side of the glass. The round tables held yellow and blue umbrellas on a deck made of wood that extended out fifty feet. The wooden deck stretched out from the back of the house and ended on the manicured greens of the sculpted golf course.

"Whoa," Ralphie uttered.

Ella Buchanan smiled.

At the door that led to the decking stood another enforcer man dressed in matte black like the other enforcers. The distinct difference to the enforcers in the mansion was that they did not wear helmets like the enforcers in the Miller compound.

The man, seeing Ella, opened the door and held it for her as she exited. As Ella walked Ralphie out and onto the decking and backyard of her home Ralphie studied the enforcer. Ralphie noted that the enforcer at the doorway was 2163. The enforcer nodded as Ralphie stepped out of the mansion.

Once out of doors Ralphie took in the grove of trees which sat three hundred yards from the mansion's decking and that divided the course in two. On the far side of the course, just visible through the grove was a gentle slope that led back up and away from the house. On the side, closest to the house, was another gentle slope that bowed out and led down toward the western end of the property.

"Come on," Ella said, reaching out and gently guiding Ralphie. Ella Buchanan continued to the right and Ralphie stopped, stunned to see that the deck continued down toward the rear of the course. Straight ahead of him on the far side of the course was a canyon wall covered in greenery and above it sat a dozen homes. He looked at the manicured lawn and right to the decking and people as well as two smaller buildings. Smaller was relative, Ralphie thought. The two smaller buildings were the size of two normal houses in the Miller compound.

"Ralphie, come along," Ella said with a faint smile.

Ralphie turned to follow Ella and found himself looking at a putting green at the end of the wooden deck. One hundred feet from the putting green Ralphie saw people dressed like they were either going to play tennis or heading to a cocktail party.

Not one hundred feet from Ella and Ralphie sat a couple under one of the umbrellas covered tables. Ralphie noted a thin man standing by the table wearing a dark blue baseball cap on his rectangular head. He was a small-faced, broad nosed, tall, and thin shouldered man with bony knees and thin legs that ended in white socks and white tennis shoes. He wore a pink and blue striped polo shirt.

The smiling woman who was rocking in her chair to get enough momentum to get out of it. The yellow and white striped blouse rippled as the woman extricated herself from the chair and pirouetted expertly to take in Ella and Ralphie. She stood a foot shorter than the man beside her. She was a pumpkin headed woman with no visible neck, round shoulders, heavy chested and wearing a green and blue tennis skirt that showed off her thick, stumpy legs. She too wore white tennis socks and shoes. She wore pricey sunglasses and tipped her chin in the direction of Ella and Ralphie once Ella as the pair approached..

Ella waved and Ralphie waved weakly with his left hand because Ella had waved. The couple waved back.

"Ella? Is this the famous Ralphie?" the pumpkin headed woman asked after grabbing and hugging Gordon Buchanan's daughter.

"It is Missus Pippin," Ella said, smiling and stepping back. Ella grinned and shook her head, waiting for Ralphie to catch up.

As Ralphie finally reached the couple the man extended a thin hand toward Ralphie.

"Ralphie, I am George Crum Pippin," the man said with a firm handshake and a smile. Ralphie grimaced as Mister Pippin gripped his left hand and pumped it vigorously. Ella seeing Ralphie's wincing stepped in quickly and stopped the handshake.

"Sorry, Mister Pippin," Ella said. "You know Ralphie is still recovering."

"Oh, sorry about that Ralphie, I didn't mean to hurt you," George Pippin said.

"I'm okay," Ralphie said. He moved his shoulder slowly to make sure he was unharmed.

"What are you doing all the way over here?" Ella asked looking back toward all the activity at the other end of the decking.

"You know that after the "Hello" and "How are you" some of the crew can be a bit of a bore," Mister Pippin said to Ella with a wink. "I chose to give my Marie and myself a little space to avoid the required bullshit."

Ralphie smiled at Mister Pippin's characterization of the people he was about to meet.

"Well, Ella, Gordon told us you have been misbehaving," the curvy woman said with a soft smile.

"I can't help it, Missus Pee," Ella said, with a pert smile. "Suppose mummy and daddy raised a rabble rouser." Ella turned and looked back in the direction of the far end of the decking.

The woman laughed and shook her head. Mister Pippin, now beside his wife, laughed as well. They seemed nice enough, Ralphie thought.

"Suppose we'll see you over there in a bit?" Ella nodded to the Pippins and guided Ralphie forward and away from the couple. Ella moved Ralphie toward the far end of the decking and the group of people standing in front of the two smaller buildings.

Just a few feet away from the Pippins Ralphie laughed. Ella looked at Ralphie out of the corner of her eye. She smiled.

"What?"

"Your family's friends are pretty funny," Ralphie said with a scant smile.

"Don't pay them any mind, Ralphie," Ella said. "They are some of daddy's oldest friends. They come here most weekends and enjoy the view and the quiet of the place."

Ralphie looked back as the couple sat under the umbrella talking and sipping drinks.

"My daddy is really looking forward to talking to you," Ella said. She smiled broadly and pointed in the direction of activity. There were groups of people at the far end of the decking where there was the first small building. In front of the smaller building were a dozen tables and patio umbrellas where some people were sitting and some talking. In between Ella and Ralphie were a small group of to people talking, all dressed alike.

"Now, be warned. We are going to have brunch with my parents, but there are a few people here to meet you," Ella said as she continued moving toward a half a dozen men and women dressed in white shirts and black trousers. Ralphie studied the people and immediately knew they were the wait staff, there to wait on the gathered influentials.

Moving down the wooden decking Ella slowed and made sure Ralphie was beside her as she parted the wait staff. The wait staff nodded or bowed as Ella and Ralphie passed. Ralphie did not speak feeling uncomfortable amongst so many people that he did not know.

On the other side of the wait staff Ralphie saw there were a dozen tables with white linen cloths draped over them. Just a few feet from the wait staff were a sprinkling of women talking amongst themselves. Behind them were a knot of men dressed in outlandish and garish colored pants that ran the spectrum from plaid, check, yellow, green, and pink. The men were sipping on drinks and talking to or being talked to by a sole stout man with jowls. The jowly man was standing on the grass that was climbing back toward the end of the deck. The turkey necked man was wearing a blue polo shirt, white golf pants and golf shoes and had a putter in his hand.

People waved and mouthed hellos to Ella, but the daughter of one of the most influential Innovators ignored them. Ralphie noted the disregard and felt uneasy with Ella's slights.

Ella charged ahead through the dozen people on the other side of the wait staff and toward a smiling woman with loose black curls and a bright yellow and blue blouse seated beneath a patio umbrella at the large round table at the head of the triangular setting of tables.

"Prepare yourself for all the glitter and grandness that are my mummy and daddy," Ella advised over her shoulder.

As soon as Ella stepped to the woman with loose black curls, the woman stood up and smiled broadly and extended both her arms to Ella. Ella picked up her pace and walked into her mother's arms. After a brief embrace, Ella separated and held her mother's hand. Spinning to see Ralphie, Ella smiled broadly.

"Mummy, I want you to meet Ralphie Reynolds," Ella smiled.

Missus Buchanan was an attractive woman with a symmetrical face and big brown eyes, dressed to attract bees, Ralphie imagined silently. Ralphie smiled and nodded respectfully toward Ella's mother. Ralphie noted that Ella must take more after her father.

"None of that Ralph Ellison Reynolds," Ella's mother said with one of those perfect toothpaste smiles. "My baby risked life and limb to get you out of that God-awful challenge," she said stepping toward Ralphie her arms open wide. She had a gigantic smile on her pie face. "Come and give me a hug."

Ralphie took a few steps and closed the distance between him and Ella and then Ella's mother. Ella smiled broadly. Ella's mother embraced Ralphie. He expected her hug to awaken the sleeping pain, but the embrace was gentle and delicate. The hug was loving and perfumed, as if he had been hugged by lilac and honey scented softness.

Others seeing Ella's mother hugging the newly crowned celebrity stranger, gathered around.

"Now, Ralphie, I hope you don't mind me calling you that," Missus Buchanan beamed, looking at the guests suddenly converging on her and her daughter and guest. "I must introduce you to the people that have wanted to meet you for the last couple of days."

Ralphie smiled, awkwardly. Missus Buchannan turned Ralphie toward the small group and announced clearly, "This is Ralphie Reynolds, everyone."

With that everyone gathered, including the wait staff, smiled, and clapped.

Ralphie looked at Ella. Ella smiled in her foxy way.

"You are sort of a big deal," Ella said at Ralphie's elbow.

Ralphie did not respond.

Missus Buchanan and Ella walked Ralphie around and introduced him to people that he would never remember. People smiled and shook Ralphie's left hand. By the time he had done the initial rounds and returned to the Buchanan's table Ralphie knew had met twenty people whose names he could not recall for the life of him.

Well, that is not true. When Ella's mother brought him back to the point on the deck where she had introduced him, Ella stepped forward. Ralphie thought they would sit down and maybe he would finally meet Ella's father. Instead, Ella placed a hand on her mother's arm to get her attention. She cut her eyes in the direction to the left of Ralphie.

To the left of Ralphie was a man that stood out.

"Mister Nelson is here to meet you," Ella said. "It is sort of a big deal."

Ralphie looked at Ella, confused. Before she could ask anything, Ella's mother was beside him smiling.

The stout and jowly man was dressed in a blue polo shirt and white golf pants and moved slowly toward Ralphie and Ella and her mother. He was clean shaven and as Ralphie was introduced to the turkey necked man the jowly man smiled and studied Ralphie with his goldish brown eyes. He had no eyebrows and a pinched look about him. Ralphie noted that the man had a wedding ring on his finger and no other jewelry.

"I am Michael Jackson Nelson," the man said in a bit of a rasp. "I am one of the men behind the online financial systems instituted in the Remains."

Ralphie nodded. Nelson was just one of many that he met that day, but Ella did not let Ralphie forget Nelson. Ralphie tried to decipher what Mister Nelson did.

"We need to watch out for him, Ralphie," Ella said.

"Long as you're around, little Ella, I won't have to watch out for him alone," Ralphie said with a smile.

"Seriously," Ella said.

"Okay," Ralphie said, not understanding Ella's tone. What was important about the turkey necked fat man? Online financial systems, in Ralphie's mind meant computer money of some sort. Then it hit him. Nelson had something to do with the computer betting and accounting of money for the Pandemonium Challenge.

As the trio returned to their table Ella leaned in and spoke close to Ralphie's ear.

"He might be trouble," Ella said.

Ralphie suddenly understood the possibility of trouble. He looked back at the short, fat man that looked more like a bowling ball than a threat. He was talking to some others that Ralphie had recently met and looking back at Ralphie. Was Nelson someone to worry about?

Missus Buchanan broke Ralphie's concentration, placing her hand on Ralphie's forearm, to get his attention.

"Are you hungry, Ralphie," Missus Buchanan asked. "I'm sure you are."

They were standing at a table that afforded at least eight people to sit comfortably. At that moment, up walked Gordon Buchanan who was a fox-faced, average-sized man with short-cropped hair and a trimmed moustache. He was not very tall, compared to Ralphie and could not be five-foot-six-inches-tall. He was dressed in a diagonally stitched blue and gold polo shirt and wearing Coke white golf trousers and white golf shoes. On his wrist was an oversized diamond and gold wristwatch. On his finger was a single band of gold.

"Daddy, I want to introduce you to Ralphie," Ella said. Ella stood and waited for her father to recognize her. Once he turned from his wife to his daughter Ella ran to give her father a hug. Ralphie saw the immediate family resemblance. Ella had inherited her father's small brown eyes, straight nose, and wide mouth.

"Good morning, Ralphie," Gordon Buchanan said, extending his hand toward Ralphie. Ralphie extended his left hand. Mister Buchanan smiled at the awkward handshake.

"Heard you are a little banged up," Gordon Buchanan said. "To be honest, I thought that the challenge was all fake." He paused, smiling at Ralphie and Ella. "I suppose it isn't *all* fake."

Ralphie did not respond.

The blue and gold dressed man leaned in, curious. He studied the still healing teen effortlessly.

"Ralphie I've heard so much about you," Mister Buchanan smiled. "You started a fire under this one. Once she got back to the Remains, she would not let go of returning to the challenge and saving you."

"Me?" Ralphie asked.

"He means whoever was left," Ella corrected.

"I knew that it might cause a stir, but Ella made a good argument for our involvement. I mean, she was right. The challenge is barbaric. It is our shame. It is our modern-day gladiator games," Gordon Buchanan said as an explanation. "We, here, attempted to distance ourselves from all the toxic classism and racial self-hate that had weaved its way into our culture long ago but there are still some, even here, that profit from the sweat and blood of others."

"Daddy don't lecture Ralphie," Ella scolded.

"Sorry angel," Mister Buchanan said to his daughter.

"Ralphie, we're going to eat and then talk, if you don't mind," Mister Buchanan said, turning and looking to one of the guests Ralphie had been introduced to earlier.

"Come on, let's sit here," Ella said, pointing to a pair of seats.

Ralphie sat down and found everyone sitting and smiling at him.

"Is this normal?" Ralphie asked, tipping his head in the general direction of the people smiling at him.

"They all heard about you, but you being here is unique," Ella said. "I think this is the first time a challenge winner has been in our compound."

"Unique? How?"

"They don't see too many people from the other lines of the Remains," Ella said, with a broadening smile. "Then, again, you are a celebrity now."

"A celebrity?"

"Yeah, you survived the challenge," Ella said. "That is a big deal, even for us."

Ralphie shook his head at Ella's comments. He looked at the people sitting at the tables looking at him. The teenager suddenly felt awkward, well more awkward than before.

"You know everyone here?" Ralphie asked, looking at Ella.

"Yeah, I grew up with most of their sons and daughters," Ella said.

"Where are they?"

"They did not invite them here today," Ella said poking out her lower lip.

"Why?"

"This is a business meeting, of sorts," Ella said.

"A business meeting?"

"Yeah, they have to make some business decisions about how to deal with the Central Government and the Pandemonium Committee that wants to blame someone for their money loss because of my little stunt," Ella said.

"Wait, you're in trouble, little Ella?"

"I'm not in trouble Ralphie Reynolds," Ella said with a laugh. "I'm the daughter of one of the most important persons in the Remains." Ella paused. She snickered. "I know how it sounds, but with power comes the ability to weather storms that might destroy others."

"What's that mean?"

"It means that the Remains will never punish me for doing right as long as my father's last name remains Buchanan," Ella said.

Ralphie shook his head, confused.

At that moment up walked a rugged looking dark eyed man wearing a light blue button front short sleeved shirt, matching light blue trousers and white golf shoes. Beside the dark eyed man was a striking woman with a curly natural Mohawk and a nose ring.

"Ralphie," Missus Buchanan said, once her husband and the other couple drew close. "Let me introduce you to Vincent LaFleur and his wife Justine. He is the man in charge of our compound."

"Pleased to meet you," Ralphie managed to say and awkwardly stood and extended his left hand to shake hands with Vincent LaFleur and then with his Mohawk wearing wife.

"Pleased to meet you," LaFleur smiled as if Ralphie was the catbird. His dark eyes seemed cold and calculating. "You don't know what getting you and your First Gen beau cost us, but that is unimportant. As Gordon pointed out there is no point in power if you don't use it."

Ralphie sat back down and looked at Ella. She rolled her eyes and played with her water glass while her father and Vincent LaFleur talked with Ralphie.

"So, would you have really gutted your girlfriend?" LaFleur asked pointedly. He was a man used to getting answers, Ralphie could tell. Dressed in a light blue button front short sleeved shirt, LaFleur looked a little like a bully to Ralphie.

Ralphie tried to figure out what to say. Thankfully, Mister Buchanan spoke and gave Ralphie a reprieve.

"I'm more interested in what made you decide to sign-up for the challenge," Mister Buchanan said.

"I'm interested in that as well," said LeFleur to Mister Buchanan with a nod. "Yet, I think everyone in the Remains wants to know if young Ralphie would have let Bailey gut him or would he have greased her," Le Fleur said with a Cheshire cat smile.

"I'm suddenly interested in the conversation," Ella's mother chirped.

Ralphie did not respond.

"I think that was the most interesting part of the challenge to me," LaFleur said. "Was that staged?" LaFleur asked Ralphie.

"Staged?" Ralphie repeated, confused.

"Did they set that up beforehand?" LaFleur asked.

Ralphie shook his head.

"That wasn't staged?" Justine LaFleur, honey colored, with arched eyebrows, big brown eyes and straight nose above pouty lips asked. "If it wasn't, it was the best thing I've seen on the Interweb in forever. That was better than the best Remains network dramas they wheel out for ratings."

The conversation switched to Remains dramas for a few minutes.

Ralphie listened and in that moment realized that Justine LaFleur had been a video actor long ago. He tried to recall the video series she had been on. It was something popular in the Remains.

Ralphie leaned to Ella and touched her on the arm.

"What?"

"What was the name of the video series she was in?"

"Oh, yeah. She was in that old show, Newbies. You know about some newbies living in the Remains," Ella said.

Ralphie nodded. He recalled the TV show. It was about a bunch of friends living on the borders of the Remains and trying to get by. Justine LaFleur played one of the friends who was friends with two other girls on the show. It was a show Ralphie had watched a dozen times and then got bored with.

"All right everyone we are going to begin service," Missus Buchanan announced. Instantly the guests and wait staff were in motion. As the guests found their seats the wait staff were already bringing out the first course for brunch.

Chapter Four.

Playing checkers

Gordon Buchanan sat down at the table. Missus Buchanan sat next to Ralphie with Ella on his right. To the right of Ella was a man with broad shoulders and average build with dark eyes and a pensive look on his face. On his right was a slender rectangular faced woman with a nose ring and a bold half shaved natural Mohawk but the thing that was eye-catching close-up to Ralphie was the razored sides and triangular sideburns that gave her a playful tomboyish look.

"Ralphie, are you feeling better?" Missus Buchanan asked.

Ralphie looked at Missus Buchanan and then across the table. There was nothing on the white linen draped circular table as they sat and Ralphie looked to Ella curious.

"I imagine you are just happy to be alive," Mister Buchanan said, next to his wife. "That challenge was just so damn brutal."

Ralphie winced at the comment. The injured juvenile had lost all his friends in the challenge. He had nearly died a dozen times. It was by sheer luck that he or Bailey had been found and brought to the Innovator compound. The memory stung and made his eyes tear up. He looked away only to find Ella looking at him, curiously.

"I think that when you return to the Millers you will have a story to tell," LaFleur said. "Do you know what you will do when you return to the Millers?"

At that moment, the wait staff saved Ralphie. They brought the first of five courses for the Innovators luxurious brunch. The first course was a variety of natural fruits and fresh squeezed juices.

"Dig in," Missus Buchanan said, with a silky smile.

Ralphie was amazed at the fruit at first because he had not seen the fruits before. Ralphie lifted an orange teardrop piece of fruit and asked Missus Buchanan: "What is this?"

"That Ralphie," Vincent LaFleur watching him like a hawk smiled. "That is a persimmon. Have you ever had one?"

Ralphie turned and looked at Vincent LaFleur. He smiled nervously. LaFleur was watching Ralphie the way that he imagined a cat watched a mouse.

"No, sir, I have not," Ralphie admitted.

"Not everyone likes them. They are an acquired taste," LeFleur said.

"How do you eat them?" Ralphie asked picking up the persimmon with his left hand.

"Me, I eat them like an apple," LaFleur grinned, and his smile spread across his smooth hairless face. He did not break his stare from Ralphie. LaFleur picked up a persimmon and took a sizeable bite out of the persimmon. Ralphie watched agog.

Ralphie studied the persimmon in LaFleur's hand and for some reason the teen thought the fruit was more like a tomato, but its consistency was more like an orange.

LaFleur took another bite of the persimmon.

Ralphie nodded. He studied the orange skinned fruit. He lifted it to his mouth and took a bite. The skin gave and the sweet pulpy and juicy fruit flooded Ralphie's mouth. Ralphie smiled at the delicacy. Ralphie looked across the table to LaFleur. The Innovator leader smiled. Ralphie nodded.

The table got quiet as the first course arrived. Ralphie sipped a cold glass of water in front of him. He cleansed his pallet.

The staff delivered a choice of scrambled eggs, poached eggs, eggs Benedict and omelets. Every table had a selection of fruits. The drink choices were orange, apple, and grape juice. The alcoholic beverage choices were champagne, wine and cocktails.

Ralphie had scrambled eggs and a small sampling of blueberries, blackberries, strawberries, and grapes on his plate. As Ralphie attempted to figure out how to eat left-handed, Mister LeFleur caught his attention. Ralphie looked at the leader of the Innovators curiously.

"Try a more stabbing motion. It's not going to be pretty, but it will be more efficient," LeFleur said with a fancy smile.

Ralphie nodded and began stabbing at his food. It was not pretty or delicate, but Ralphie got food on his fork and into his mouth. Ralphie smiled at the simple solution. He looked at Ella and then her parents. They seem focused on their food. He looked to Justine LeFleur. The trophy wife was eating scrambled eggs. Ralphie's eyes landed on Mister LeFleur. Mister LeFleur was eating eggs Benedict. He paused and smiled at Ralphie. The teenager smiled, grateful for the advice.

"I had asked you about your intentions at the challenge before the food arrived," LaFleur reminded. "Well? What say you? Were you going to gut your girlfriend or allow her to gut you?"

Ralphie smiled and rubbed the back of his neck nervously, thinking. He knew that his answer was not going to be popular no matter what he said. So, he shrugged.

"I don't know," Ralphie said, looking up from his plate. He looked at Vincent LeFleur. "I mean, I think that I sort of was focused on trying to figure out if I was going to make it to Campbell before passing out."

"Okay, say you had," Justine LaFleur said, her voice nasal and rattly, like there was something in her throat. "What would you have done? I mean, Bailey threatened you."

"She didn't mean it," Ralphie smiled. He reached out and sipped at the fresh squeezed orange juice.

The LaFleurs chuckled at Ralphie's answer.

The second course was organic fruit Pop Tarts made from wild huckleberry or pineapple, Straus yogurt fried almonds and honey. The third course was a grilled broccoli rabe, hummus, favas, shaved fennel, drizzled with an apricot salsa.

"Ralphie, I hear you like art," Missus Buchanan said as the wait staff cleared the plates for the main meal.

"Well, I wouldn't go that far, ma'am," Ralphie said looking at Ella out of the corner of her eye. The Buchanan daughter seemed quite amused. "I like what I like," Ralphie said with a tiny smile.

"Well, Ella says that you were curious if we collected any Banksy works," Missus Buchanan stated. "His work is usually on walls and the few print pieces are rarer than unicorn blood."

"We have discovered a number of artists that had been lost," Mister Buchanan said, sipping his champagne and orange juice concoction. "They are mostly here, in the main house."

"I noticed," Ralphie said with a small smile. "Very impressive. I think I have seen a few of them on museum websites."

"To the victor go the spoils," Mister Buchanan said.

Ralphie smirked at the comment.

The wait staff served the main meal, the fourth course, was some of the tastiest cage free eggs, plant-based meat substitutes and gluten free pancakes Ralphie had ever tasted. If he had not known that the sausages were plant-based, he would have imagined them to be from an animal.

The last treat of the morning was several water crackers and small single shallow bowl of the black salty pearls Ralphie had seen the night before or grilled Acme Lavian toast, whipped butter, and guava jam.

"Excuse me," Ralphie smiled to Vincent LaFleur. "Can you tell me what that is?" He was pointing to the bowl of black pearls.

"Caviar, Ralphie," LaFleur beamed, cutting his eyes at Gordon Buchanan.

Ralphie nodded and ate the toast.

The meal was one of the best Ralphie had ever had.

After brunch everyone wanted to take a picture with Ralphie. He did not mind. If he did, he concentrated on Ella and her antics. She loved attention and when Ralphie was the center the Buchanan daughter did the silliest things to stay relevant. Ella situated herself just in the eyesight of Ralphie and every time he was asked to take pictures did something silly. She hugged a boy on the wait staff and the boy froze not wanting to be inappropriate. She fell into the arms of one of the female wait staff, just to see if they would catch her. Ella did an impromptu dance and on and on.

"You know you are silly?" Ralphie asked.

"Can you hum a few bars I might have played it at a recital," Ella joked.

Two hours later Vincent LeFleur and Justine bid their goodbyes. They were the second to last to leave. The Pippens seeing the LeFleurs leaving reluctantly left.

When all the guests left the decking, the mansion was secured. it was just the Buchanans and Ralphie left on the deck. There were a handful of wait staff cleaning up the plates and deck.

"Now, Ralphie, you have to tell me, about your take on the challenge, if you are up to it," Mister Buchanan smiled. They, Ralphie was seated next to Mister Buchanan, Ella was behind the two, as they were riding in a solar powered golf cart up the backside of the golf course that seemed to stretch for miles.

"Well, sir, I don't know what I can tell you, really, other than it was hard... harder than I expected," Ralphie attempted.

"I know it was hard Ralphie, but the whole life and death scenario," the Innovator said as he navigated the golf cart up a slight incline. "Ralphie, I am more curious why you entered. Why did you enter the challenge?"

Ralphie listened to Mister Buchanan and noted that off to the left was a white flag flying from a thin white pole with the number seven on it.

"Well, sir, I wanted to be legendary," Ralphie said. "I mean everybody I know wants to be legendary. Right?"

Ralphie lowered his head, holding onto the golf cart with his left hand as Gordon Buchanan weaved left and then right around a sand trap.

"Legendary?" Mister Buchanan asked. He was silent for a moment. "Everyone wants to be remembered?" Mister Buchanan asked. He steered the golf cart around the course effortlessly. "Do you think you achieved that? Are you legendary?"

Ralphie did not respond.

"Did you gain in the challenge? Or did you just lose?"

Ralphie bit his tongue and looked at the man in the polo shirt behind the wheel of the golf cart.

"Daddy," Ella said. "He is probably still suffering from post-traumatic stress from the whole ordeal," the daughter of one of the most important Innovators opined.

Gordon Buchanan turned the golf cart to the left and up a gentle rise that paralleled a piece of property that seemed to dip drastically toward a small hut.

"Ralphie, you would tell me if I was pushing too hard? Right?"

"Yes sir," Ralphie smiled.

"You see, baby girl," Mister Buchanan smiled broadly to Ella in the back of the golf cart. "Ralphie and I are just chatting casually. We aren't talking about anything too significant or triggering. I just want to hear his perspective on the matter. I mean, I did spend a sizeable sum to ensure that he and Bailey weren't...cheesed," Gordon Buchanan frowned. He looked back at Ella, curiously. "Is that the correct nomenclature of the day."

Ella leaned forward and into the front of the golf cart. "Yes, daddy, that is the way we say it. But don't you ever say it again."

Ralphie chuckled at the exchange between Ella and her father. Ella rolled her eyes as the three rolled across the course. Ralphie held on tightly to the golf cart as Mister Buchanan drove around the golf course seemingly oblivious to the idea of brakes or the need to slow down.

"Where are we going?" Ralphie asked Ella as he held onto the seat for security.

Ella looked at Ralphie and pointed ahead. Ralphie looked and saw that there was a tunnel ahead. Ella smiled and placed a hand on her father's shoulder. "Daddy loves to show anyone who has never been here the reason our family secured this estate." Ella looked at Ralphie and reveled. "You get to see the priceless view."

The golf cart swung through the tunnel which was just a little wider and taller than the golf cart and out the other side. Mister Buchanan made a hard left and the golf cart slowed briefly only to pick up speed as he turned right and parked on a slight incline.

Before Ralphie could say a word Ella and her father were out of the golf cart and walking toward the top of the small hill. Ralphie climbed out of the golf cart and after a little effort caught up with the two Buchanans. The two held hands and for a moment Ralphie could imagine Ella when she was younger with her father.

At the top of the rise Gordon Buchanan stood silently. Ella looked back and smiled as Ralphie closed. Ralphie just tried not to focus too much on the slight ball of hurt in his side.

"You see this," Mister Buchanan said, looking out and over what had once been miles and miles of land where people lived, but was now just desolate. The homes had been abandoned. The buildings were dark and in disrepair. The population of eight million people had fallen to less than half a million.

"This view is worth all the headache and planning that was done to secure our private shelter for our family and staff," Gordon Buchanan said, and Ella rolled her eyes as her father spoke. She stuck out her tongue, while looking at Ralphie and tilted her head, as if she were dead.

"But this used to be a city and the homes of millions of people," Ralphie stated looking out over what had been the Bay Area, which stretched for miles to the edge of the Acid Bay. The Acid Bay was still, dead, no waves or motion on the mirror like surface. Ralphie knew the liquid in the bay was poisonous. Some said it was caustic. Ralphie was not sure about either claim. All he knew was that the one-time San Francisco Bay had been dammed under the destroyed Bay Bridge and Golden Gate Bridge long ago and that now the Pacific Ocean was protected from the poisoned acidic liquid found in the Acid Bay.

"Yeah, but once the flash was over most of these buildings were virtually empty," Ella pointed out.

"Think my family had a Miller, maybe your dad or his dad, build the gate to our estate," Mister Buchanan said.

"Your family welders?"

"No sir," Ralphie said. "We do construction."

Gordon Buchanan nodded. He looked out and toward the Acid Bay and pointed. "Our compound stops at the elevated rail station," he said with a shrug of his shoulders. "What is going on in the Poppies and First Gen compounds is anyone's guess. Our compound is secured and protected by a barrier wall." He paused. "I think the Poppies are the ones that party and drink and whatever is clever to get their creative juices flowing. The First Gens are more subdued," Mister Buchanan recalled. He reached back and pulled Ralphie up beside him. With Ella on the right and Ralphie on the left, Mister Buchanan seemed pleased with himself. "They are plotters, like all the Gens."

"What do you think they are plotting?" Ralphie asked looking to the south and in the direction of the First Gens compound. He tried to recall what he remembered of going to the First Gens compound with his father. He had only been five or six years old at the time. His memories were jumbled.

"Not sure," Mister Buchanan said, looking at Ralphie with a gentle smile. "They are the tech brains of the Remains. We must watch them closely. They might be building robots in their garages for all we know," Buchanan said with a chuckle.

"Don't listen to him, Ralphie," Ella said. "My daddy doesn't trust them because he feels the Gens don't really dislike each other, but that they are pretending to divide the Remains based on loyalties."

Ralphie did not speak. He understood what Ella had said, but the concept of dividing the Remains to benefit the Gens seemed outlandish. What would be the result of a divided Remains? Who would benefit from that division?

"There are some manipulative people still roaming this broken marble," Mister Buchanan said. "We must be aware that just because they look like us doesn't mean that they have the same interest as us." Gordon Buchanan drew Ella closer. "It is a lesson that my brilliant daughter still does not fully understand."

Ralphie nodded.

"My dad says the same thing," Ralphie said.

"But here we are in the Remains," Ella began. She looked at Ralphie and her father. "Everyone is Black, brown or an outcast. There is no division unless we create it."

"You know in Africa, before all this, there were tribes that fought other tribes over land and food," Mister Buchanan said. "Skin color or everyone being the same doesn't guarantee anything. There were conflicts in Japan against other Japanese. The Swedish fought each other. The Chinese, the most homogenous culture in the world, created divisions to subjugate others." He paused, thinking. "Mandarin is the official, was the official language of China despite there being other languages. Separation and division is as natural as breathing to us. Humans are selfish, jealous and cantankerous and violent."

Ella quieted. Ralphie did not speak.

"What?" Gordon Buchanan asked. "No snappy retort?" He chuckled. "I didn't bring you up here for a history lesson. I just wanted you to know that division is always possible. If you want something or value something, then you have to be willing to fight for it."

Ella nodded. Ralphie did not respond. The three just stood and took in the view.

"New topic. The best part of this place is sunrise or sunset. Hell, anytime you can get here and just stand or sit or get quiet. If there is no fog rolling in," Mister Buchanan said after a long pause. "You can see the skeletons of the three bridges and the tollway that had once been the entrance to the Bay Bridge." He paused and took a deep breath, impressed with the view or himself. He looked at Ella. "Ella, you said you walked on that for the challenge."

Ella nodded. She smiled at Ralphie and shook her head. She looked at Ralphie and slightly lifted her chin toward Ralphie.

"It's a great view, sir," Ralphie said.

"This view is priceless," Mister Buchanan said.

The three walked from the knoll where Gordon Buchanan pontificated to a copse of trees. Ralphie noted that there was a flag and pole there that read: 14. Ralphie smiled at the flags and the craziness of his being on a golf course owned by Gordon Buchanan. In the shade of the trees sat a wrought iron bench and next to it a matching chair. Beside the chair was a golf ball washer. Mister Buchanan sat in the wrought iron chair.

"Ralphie, you never did answer my question earlier," Mister Buchanan said, his dark eyes burned on his triangular face. Gordon Buchanan looked at Ralphie with his bushy eyebrows, thin nose, moustache and pointed chin.

"Sir?" Ralphie smiled, not sure what Ella's father was referring to at the moment.

"Did you gain anything from the challenge? Or was it all loss?"

Ralphie smiled emotionlessly. For a nanosecond, Ralphie thought that Mister Buchanan was joking. The Pandemonium Challenge took so much from him and all who participated in the event. Ralphie had lost all the friends he ever knew in the challenge. The one girl he had thought he might love was crippled, broken, and unconscious in the mansion below.

What had he gained? Could he have gained anything? It seemed as if the challenge took everything and gave back nothing to the challengers. Perhaps, the winner gained something. Everyone Ralphie knew wanted to be legendary. Was Ralphie legendary? He could not say. The teen thought about the question but did not answer.

The narrow-faced man stared back at Ralphie, coolly. He did not blink. Ralphie looked to Mister Buchanan's side and found Ella looking at him expectantly. Ralphie knew Gordon Buchanan wanted an answer. He needed an answer.

"Well, the thing is, sir, I'm not really sure," Ralphie began, haltingly. "I mean, I guess I got to meet Ella," Ralphie said, jokingly. He shook the words out of his head and got serious. "I thought I'd get something out of the challenge, but I didn't think it would be nightmares." Ralphie paused.

Ralphie instantly thought of Jax and Zeke, Tee, Dame, Isaac, Gina and Maddy. Their faces floated in front of his eyes. He remembered Jax sitting and eating one of those taffy like protein bars and making faces. There was Zeke being all serious and important. Tee, Ralphie could not believe that he felt his stomach tighten at the thought of the girl who had pointed out the magical lizard being gone. Dame, Isaac, Gina and Maddy he had only met in the challenge and in the challenge, he grew to like them for the fleeting time they had.

"All I think about are my friends. I lost all my friends." Ralphie paused. "All my friends," Ralphie said, feeling the emotions well up inside. The thoughts overwhelmed Ralphie, and he felt his eyes water.

"Friends are important," Mister Buchanan said solemnly. He paused. He looked to Ralphie. "Are you and my Ella friends?"

Ralphie did not answer.

Mister Buchanan nodded. He placed a hand on his daughter's shoulder and looked again in the direction of the Acid Bay. Ralphie watched Mister Buchanan.

"When my daughter explained to me what she was thinking," Mister Buchanan said. "I had to take that in." He looked at Ella and smiled. "I know we aren't all kumbaya here Ralphie, but Ella made a point about the lines with the least being used by the Pandemonium Committee the most."

Ralphie frowned at Mister Buchanan's words.

"I mean, for all the fanfare the challenge is just a modern-day dog fight," Mister Buchanan said, bluntly. "No one thinks twice about the planet dying or that there might be real danger just on the other side of the walls trying to get in. The Pandemonium Committee have distracted everyone with the Challenge. They don't care that we are beginning to repeat the things that led to the destruction of this planet." Gordon Buchanan looked at Ella and Ralphie. "The populous couldn't care less. They are busy wagering and betting on the shiny bauble before their eyes and not concentrating on the lack of hope, even if we all know we have no hope." Buchanan was playing with his wedding ring. He looked at Ella and then to Ralphie.

Ralphie smiled.

"I made decisions, Ralphie. I found to myself here, standing on the knoll, looking out toward the Acid Bay, and thinking," Mister Buchanan said gesturing back toward the knoll. "My actions and my actions alone saved you and Bailey Beaumont." Mister Buchanan paused. "We have all lost something here. None of us are without scars or regrets."

Ralphie nodded, wiping at his eyes.

"The flash took something from all of us. In return we were given something in return," Buchanan pointed to the walls that bordered the Remains. "The ultra-rich villains escaped and left in their wake the flash ravaged earth, billions of dead and the flash created abominations that threaten to destroy us every day."

"Abominations?"

"Yes," Mister Buchanan said. "The abominations that stalk outside of our walls can be called nothing else. They are ghouls and grotesque creations created for...God only knows," Mister Buchanan said, with a knowing shake of his head. "The problem is that reports from our point people is that their numbers are increasing." Ella's father climbed to his feet and adjusted himself and leaned against one of the trees. "We saw the numbers after the Exodus level out, but for some reason the numbers have begun to increase," Mister Buchanan said, standing in the shade of the trees of his golf course. "The bastards that escaped secretly stockpiled technology for years for their inevitable escape. They abandoned us."

"Daddy," Ella said, bored. "We all know this." She shook her head. "There's videos of the Exodus."

Gordon Buchanan stopped at Ella's words. He looked at her and she quieted.

"The thing about all of this is that the five of the six billion that were on earth are gone," Mister Buchanan said, looking out toward the incline and the eerily quiet Remains. "There are just half a million people still alive here in the Remains. This place used to have eight million living and breathing souls," Buchanan said. He stopped and looked at Ralphie. "The only thing that protects us are the walls. I believe part of the wall was built by your line." Mister

Buchanan looked at Ralphie and smiled. "There was death and destruction everywhere. People panicked. People locked themselves away. They feared leaving their homes. There was no logical, scientific explanation for what was happening."

"Daddy," Ella said, annoyed.

"I know you think you know all this," Gordon Buchanan said. "At least, my little angel believes you should. But the thing that they don't tell you is that this place, the Remains, is held together through our various lines' cooperation. We have a personal stake in each line's part in this collective. Your line builds and maintains all these wonderful things. The Poppies contribute the great art. The Gens deal with technology and so on." Mister Buchanan paused. "This brings me back to the question I asked you earlier. Except, now I will ask it in a different way. Do you still have faith in the leadership of the Remains?"

Ralphie had been listening half-heartedly. He knew Mister Buchanan had stopped talking. So, he looked up and found Ella and her father looking at him.

"I'm not sure, sir," Ralphie said, unsure of what he was answering.

"Well, it is this that we need to know," Mister Buchanan said. "We hold this construct together based on the trust of the lines and their leadership. We know on the other side of the walls there are freakish things trying to get through the gates to kill us," Ella's father said.

Ralphie listened and looked from Mister Buchanan to Ella. Ella looked away. She suddenly found an interest in the flock of birds winging through the quiet buildings near the estate.

"Ralphie, there is no free lunch, here, or anywhere," Mister Buchanan said, looking at him seriously. "A small group of like-minded people are interested in using you and Bailey's celebrity to correct some issues that we have not been able to... correct," Mister Buchanan said.

Ralphie looked at Ella's father confused.

"There is a belief that our dangers are increasing and not decreasing," Mister Buchanan continued. "I want you to understand that there are a few things in place. We have an interest in you and

Bailey," he said. "Just need you to know what is at stake and what we fear."

"What are you talking about, sir?"

"Well, there is a belief that the aberrations outside of the walls are increasing, but not naturally but in a strategic and methodical way," Mister Buchanan said.

"Wait. What?"

Mister Buchanan nodded.

Ella looked at Ralphie and nodded as well.

"We want to offer you and possibly Bailey, based on her recovery, a job," Mister Buchanan said.

"A job?"

Ella smiled. Ralphie looked at Ella. She shrugged her shoulders. Ralphie shook his head at Ella.

"Yes," Mister Buchanan said and paused. "Perhaps, I am a bit premature in saying a job. More a task. Not a job. A mission if you like." He paused. "We need you to find out if what we believe is true or not. Nothing more." Mister Buchanan stopped. He raised a hand to signal he was done with the conversation. "We will talk more and in detail when you feel a little better," Ella's father said. "This is just... the introduction... the groundwork."

Ralphie suddenly felt completely alone despite the golf course with Ella and Gordon Buchanan. He took a deep breath and exhaled, thinking. He was a Miller. He was, in the eyes of Gordon Buchanan, nothing more than a working-class stiff born to work and build for the Remains and nothing more. A worker. Hired labor.

Ralphie felt he had been brought to the Innovator's compound for another reason that he did not understand. He felt as if he was a pawn in a bigger game. He was unaware of what Mister Buchanan was getting at completely. He was not even sure if Mister Buchanan was the person who held the real power and was really offering Ralphie the job.

If nothing else, Ralphie knew that Ella's father or the Innovators were playing in this bigger game he was somehow involved in without his understanding, acknowledgement, or choice. It made Ralphie aggravated.

Ella reached out and touched Ralphie on the forearm, getting his attention. She looked at Ralphie with those big brown eyes and shook her head, ever so slightly. Ralphie pursed his lips, choosing not to ask his burning questions.

"We'll head back now," Gordon Buchanan said, with a brilliant smile. "You need to rest. Tomorrow you will be meeting with some of the Remains elite."

"What?"

"You and Bailey are important Ralphie. They want to meet you," Mister Buchanan said as he walked back toward the golf cart.

"The Remains?"

"We have held them at bay, but as soon as they see pictures of you up and about, they will push to meet with you," Gordon Buchanan said.

The three made their way back to the golf cart silently. Ralphie looked at Gordon Buchanan and then his daughter. Ella kept her head down, avoiding Ralphie's eye contact.

At the golf cart Ralphie climbed in and sat beside Ella's father. Ella sat behind Ralphie. She placed a hand on his shoulder.

Ralphie did not look back. He had some things to think about. Ralphie foolishly thought that he had been saved by Ella out of the goodness of her heart. He thought that Ella had saved him and Bailey out of the goodness of her heart, but after listening to her father Ralphie knew that was not completely the case. There was an ulterior reason that Ralphie did not yet fully understand.

Mister Buchanan engaged the golf cart and it slowly rolled across the manicured grass. Ralphie adjusted his grip on the golf cart as the terrain leveled out just a bit. There was a small river that they skirted. To the right Ralphie noticed the hills that naturally hid the golf course from any that might have searched for it.

The three rolled through the golf course path and into another tunnel to cross under a street overhead. On the other side of the tunnel Ralphie found himself on a stretch of manicured green that had a slight bank to it. Buchanan drove the golf cart easily toward the west and the once non-acidic San Francisco Bay.

Mister Buchanan navigated the golf course expertly. In a few minutes, the golf cart was parked and one of the staff members of the Buchanan estate was driving the cart to wherever the cart went over night.

Ralphie climbed gingerly onto the wooden decking and found the area and everything that had been there cleared. The still hurt and aching Ralphie looked around for the dozen tables. Where they were stacked Ralphie was uncertain. He looked at Ella and her father, but they did not seem to pay him any attention as they walked back to the main building.

"There are a lot of people here," Ralphie said to Ella catching up with her.

"I don't really notice," Ella said, with a shrug of her shoulders. "It's just something that I take for granted."

"There is a working staff of thirteen here at all times, that doesn't include the dedicated group of enforcers devoted to the mansion," Mister Buchanan said. He paused and looked up at the main building. "We sleep soundly here."

Ralphie nodded, taking in all the information.

"You don't have to wait for me," Ralphie said to Ella.

"Nonsense," Ella said with a gentle smile. "I don't mind. It's better than dealing with the watchers."

Ralphie nodded.

The pair moved close to the main building where 2163 waited. 2163 opened the door for Ella and watched silently as the pair entered the mansion. He closed the door behind Ralphie silently.

"Have you always lived here?"

"Yes," Ella said.

Ralphie looked around as he walked to the small stairway that Ella had used to descend to this floor.

"You know this isn't normal?" Ralphie asked as they walked up the stairs and back to the Oak Hall. "I mean, this place could probably house just in this building alone, I don't know, maybe thirty or forty people, easily."

"But there aren't thirty or forty people living around us, Ralphie," Ella said. Ella smiled at Ralphie. "I think our closest neighbor is on the other side of the highway," Ella said pointing in the general northernly direction. Ralphie investigated the space where the two tables sat and nodded.

The pair continued walking. Ralphie shook his head. Ella simply smiled. Ella and Ralphie walked past the eight four pane windows and to the main lobby of the mansion with the stained-glass windows. The mansion was a private museum, Ralphie thought, except Ella and her family lived there.

As Ella and Ralphie stepped out of the Oak Hall, Mister Buchanan was leaning against a doorway. Mister Buchanan pushed off the woodwork and stood in the doorway to another part of the mansion. Seeing her father, Ella stopped and Ralphie stood in the lobby of the entryway to the Buchanan mansion. Ralphie investigated the shadows of the entryway and saw the outline of the enforcer lurking near the door.

"Ralphie," Mister Buchanan said. "I hope you can get some rest before dinner." He paused. "I think we'll have dinner at seven, if you are up to it," Mister Buchanan said. "Hope to see you there. I have enjoyed my time with you."

Ralphie smiled at Ella's father and nodded.

"We will be dining in the Great Room tonight," Buchanan said to Ella. "We have a few guests coming by. So, no jeans or throwbacks to the punk rock era."

Ella smiled at her father and rolled her eyes. With that Mister Buchanan turned and walked down the hallway.

"Punk rock age?" Ralphie asked, looking down and pointing to the spiked Doc Martens.

"My daddy thinks he's funny," Ella said.

"He's kind of funny," Ralphie said.

Ella shook her head. Ralphie smiled.

"Come on," Ella said. She walked to the stairs and looked back as Ralphie slowly followed. Ella stepped on the first step and waited.

Ralphie mounted the stairs and he and Ella moved slowly up to the second floor of the mansion where his temporary bedroom was located.

Chapter Five.

How the Rich and Famous play

Ralphie dressed in a green suit jacket, white collared shirt, dark green trousers, and black leather lace-up shoes met up with Ella and headed to the Great Hall. Ella was dressed in a canary blue off the shoulder evening dress that fell below her knees. Around her waist was a one-inch-thick gold belt with ruby stones. On her delicate wrist was a handful of gold and ruby bracelets. To compliment her blue and red look, Ella was wearing canary blue high heel shoes with red bottoms. Ella's hair was pulled back and away in loose curls from her face.

"You look really nice," Ralphie said with a small awkward smile.

"Thanks," Ella said. "But I am seeing someone."

Ralphie shook his head confused.

"Besides, I thought you were interested in Bailey?" Ella asked.

Ralphie shook his head in answer. "I just said you looked nice. I didn't say let's go out."

"Ralphie, you are interesting and all but not my type. I need someone more my intellectual equal. Nothing personal," Ella said.

Ralphie laughed at Ella. "Ella, I'm glad you told me now so that I could deal with it and still be friends with you," Ralphie said, with a goofy smile, despite the serious tone.

"I like to be honest with people about my intentions," Ella said.

"Thanks again for your honesty," Ralphie said with a small smile.

Ella and Ralphie walked to the main floor of the mansion and turned to the left and into the dark oaken hall that led to the Great Hall. On the walls were artworks Ralphie knew he had seen on museum websites.

The pair arrived at the entrance to the Great Hall. At the entry of the hall there were two fluted wooden columns and leaning against one of the columns was a dark dread headed photographer. He was dressed in a blue denim shirt, baggy jeans, and comfortable boots. Around his neck hung a Judah lion medallion. The dread headed photographer took several pictures of Ella and Ralphie.

Ralphie looked awkward in front of the camera.

"Smile, Ralphie," Ella said. She posed and smiled as the photographer took pictures.

Ella walked into the Great Hall with a narrow smile still on her face.

"What's going on?"

"This is my life," Ella said. "When the big wigs get together there are always photogs around," the Innovator said with a shrug. "Just roll with it."

Ralphie grimaced and looked back only to realize that there were three other photographers with cameras and video cameras. There were four camera people, three men and one woman roaming the Great Hall. The dread head stayed near the entrance to the Great Hall and either caught the guests coming or going. The other two camera operators wore tight fades and were bearded and dressed in collared shirts and trousers. The woman had small eyes, a broad nose, small pouty lips, and a pointy chin. She was boyish in her shape except for her wide hips. She was dressed in a black pants suit and blue collarless blouse.

The Great Hall was enormous. It sat on the farthest point of the western side of the mansion just beneath the main lobby of the mansion. Although Ralphie had not been to the western wing of the Buchanan mansion it seemed as if the Great Hall took up much of the far wing.

The hall was decorated in paintings and pictures that should have been in a gallery, Ralphie thought. The Great Hall was dominated by a deep oak dining table that stretched from one end of the hall to the other. There was a sumptuous centerpiece in the middle of the extended table. The centerpiece was made of a few brilliant flowers, fully bloomed, blooming and in bud form. The centerpiece aroma was heady and fragrant. Ralphie noted that the closer he got to the centerpiece the more pungent the floral fragrance.

The hall was decorated with bright blue cloth banners with gold stitching which bordered the crown molding. Above the blue cloth banners were gold ropes that led to a dazzling chandelier which looked made of thousands of individual crystals that reflected the light ten times more than usual. There were at least eight smaller chandeliers on either side of the grandiose chandelier to illuminate the rectangular space.

At the far end of the hall Ralphie noted a pair of swinging doors that, he presumed, led to the kitchen. Wait staff entered and exited the swinging doors with trays of drinks and finger foods.

Along the back wall was a piece of art that dominated the space. It was an abstract piece that looked initially like a hodge-podge of red, black and white paint that was incredibly textured, detailed, and seemed to be a sea of colors which moved from one side of the canvas to the other and spanned at least fifty feet from end to end.

"You like it?" Ella asked. She was suddenly at Ralphie's elbow. Ella had her hair swept up into a loose bunch of curls on her head. Dangling from her earlobes were golden obsidian heart shaped drop earrings.

Ralphie did not answer.

"It's one of my favorites," Ella said. "Whenever I come here, I always find myself standing in front of it and trying to look away." Ella smiled. "It's hypnotic."

Ralphie nodded.

"This is our main dining room," Ella said.

Ralphie smiled at Ella.

"We don't usually eat in here," Ella said, with a slight smile. "This is definitely done to impress."

"Who are you trying to impress?" Ralphie asked.

Ella cut her dark eyes toward Ralphie. Ralphie smiled awkwardly. Ella smiled.

"Well, first, it's not me trying to impress anyone. It's my parents. I think there's going to be three leaders of the lines here tonight," Ella said. "Security is going to be pretty tight tonight."

Ralphie shook his head, confused. "Why?"

"Come on, Ralphie, what happened on that island was sort of big, even for you," Ella said. She smiled, but the smile was thin and pained. "Even I know that what I did was going to cause some problems." Ella paused. "There's got to be something coming. So, my daddy and his people have been trying to build an alliance." Ella smiled and shook her head.

"An alliance?" Ralphie said.

"Ralphie, you need to stop repeating everything I say," Ella said with a cartoonish smile.

Ralphie opened his mouth and closed it looking at Ella. He looked at Ella and nodded.

"Yeah, the whole saving you and Bailey had a cost," Ella said. "Like he said, 'Everything comes at a cost.' My daddy said that doing what we did comes at a cost. We just don't know exactly what Central Government will try to do to punish us."

"Pun--" Ralphie said only to stop himself. "What do you think they are going to do?"

Ella smiled at Ralphie. She didn't answer immediately. The teenager dressed in her evening gown studied Ralphie before answering.

"I don't know, really," Ella said. "I figure that whatever it is will be minimal for us." Ella walked Ralphie slowly to the windowed wall.

There were people near the window drinking and talking. Several women wore feathered hats. Most of the men were dressed in suits, ties, and shiny shoes. Some had champagne glasses. Some were drinking from cocktail glasses. The wait staff, all dressed in white collared shirts, black trousers, and black shoes, were weaving in and out of the well-dressed gathering offering hors d'oeuvres and retrieving glasses.

"Ralphie, how's your arm?" Someone Ralphie had met at brunch asked.

Ralphie smiled and nodded, not wanting to engage in a conversation with someone he didn't know. Ralphie walked away. He was separated somehow by the crowd from Ella.

The awkward and injured teen found himself in a group of adults he didn't know. They surrounded him and peppered him with questions.

"Ralphie? What was the first thing you ate when you got back to the Remains?" A woman with small eyes and full lips asked dressed in an aquamarine v-neck dress. She had an exotic look about her with heavy mascara on her eyes. "I have a restaurant that would love to have you come by."

Ralphie smirked.

"Ralphie, have you done anything fun since you have been back in the Remains?"

Ella appeared and stood and waited. He was peppered with questions which he tried to answer. Most of the questions were about Bailey and Ralphie.

After a round of questions Ella stepped in and saved Ralphie.

"Thanks," Ralphie said, walking away from the group.

"I thought of letting you squirm a little longer, but it didn't seem hospitable," Ella said with a wry smile.

"You seemed to enjoy me squirming," Ralphie said.

"It wasn't boring," Ella said with a little smile.

Ralphie shook his head at Ella. Ella chuckled. Ralphie took a deep breath and exhaled.

"Let me show you the best part of the Great Hall," Ella said.

Ella navigated the assemblage and moved to the left side of the wall of four paned windows. Ralphie followed. Ella stopped and smiled, framed against the darkened window.

Ralphie looked at Ella and behind her, in the darkness, he saw the dozen or so lights blinking in the dark. The teenager seeing the lights blinking turned his head past Ella and looked down a tunnel of trees. The darkness seemed sliced in two by the dark absorbing trees that made the darkness darker if that was possible. Yet, it was the light, stars, Ralphie imagined but discounted when he realized he was looking toward the Acid Bay.

The thing that drew Ralphie's attention was the wall of windows that looked out and into the woods beyond. Ralphie looked and saw that somehow the trees had been pruned and planted to allow a sliver of the Bay beyond. The idea of the creation of the natural window of trees that created a window to the Acid Bay was an architectural and forestry marvel. Ralphie blinked. The time and energy that had to be invested in the creation of the windows and then the planting to assure the view of these two disparate creations was mind numbing.

"How did they do that?"

Ella shrugged.

Ralphie looked at Ella and twisted his lips, questioning.

Ella rolled her eyes.

"How you not know?" Ralphie asked looking at Ella slightly unsure.

"I'm smart but I don't know everything," Ella said with a faint smile.

"I suppose," Ralphie said with a thin smile.

Ella and Ralphie walked away from the window and found themselves on the far side of the gigantic dark wood table and the eight four-paned windows that looked out into the darkness that was the Buchanan backyard. Ralphie saw a lighted tennis court.

"How long does it take to walk this place?"

"I don't know," Ella said. "I have never timed it, but I assume it would take a long time."

Vincent LeFleur and his wife Justine crossed the great space and said their hellos.

"This is Alex, my assistant," LeFleur said. His assistant was a clean-shaven man with a crown of black curly hair, big ears, dressed in a brown suit, blue tie, and comfortable shoes.

"You need to say hello to Gary Covington, the treasurer," LeFleur said, pointing to a man dressed in a blue suit.

The bearded treasurer for the Innovators compound, Gary Covington was a muscular man with a tight fade dressed in a blue suit. Next to him stood his wife, a tall and thin woman with short blonde hair dressed in a yellow blouse and layered skirt, were there as well.

There were at least thirty men and women gathered in the Great Hall. Beautiful people, Ralphie thought. Rich and powerful people, Innovators, that determined things in the Central Government. These people had the ears of the Central Government.

Ralphie looked around and was shocked to find an incredibly handsome man who was thickly muscled and dressed in leather pants and combat boots and a bright neon blue silk shirt with a thick gold chain around his neck stood between three stunning women.

"Who is that?" Ralphie asked, once away from the adults and with Ella.

"That's James Weldon Lawrence," Ella said, with a knowing smile. "The Interweb artist."

Ralphie nodded and smiled. Ralphie liked music and he had heard of James Weldon Lawrence. He was one of the Remains top ten musical Interweb artists. He had consistently been on the charts for the last three years. He had won countless awards for music and video production.

A few minutes later Ella touched Ralphie's shoulder to get his attention. The gathered turned with the entrance of the host and hostess.

"My parents always make a production of their entrances," Ella said with a casual smile.

Ella's mother was dressed in a red, black, green, and white asymmetrical sexy V-neck cocktail dress. The dress showed off Ella's mother's curves and delicate neck. Her hair was braided and pulled back from her round face.

Gordon Buchanan was dressed in blue and black suit and trousers and white collared shirt without tie. He entered and as soon as he did the wait staff disappeared and the Great Hall table was quickly set for the guests.

"Come on, Ralphie," Ella said, reaching out but not touching him. He looked around and followed behind Ella. Ella fell in step behind her parents.

Mister Buchanan sat at the head of the table. His wife sat on his left. Ella sat on the right-hand side of the table. Ralphie sat next to Ella. Justine LeFleur sat next to Ralphie. Mister Pippin sat next to Justine LeFleur. On the far side of the table next to Missus Buchanan sat Vincent LeFleur, then Missus Pippin, then people Ralphie did not know.

The table was filled, and food was brought out.

Everyone was given an entrée selection before the salad arrived. The choices were Truffle Honey-Chicken or Chicken Parmesan Pizza slices.

The salad was a baked goat cheese with garden lettuce.

The main course was Bucatini all 'Amatriciana which was long, hollow pasta strands with house-cured guanciale and spicy house-made tomato sauce.

When dessert was offered Mister Buchanan and Vincent LeFleur climbed to their feet and Mister Buchanan tapped Ralphie on the shoulder.

"Come with me, Ralphie," Mister Buchanan said. He did not wait for my response. I climbed to my feet and followed the ten people that were up and moving to the rear of the hall.

The ever-present Vincent LeFleur was suddenly beside Ralphie. This time his wife was not with him.

"Mister LeFleur," Ralphie said to the leader of the Innovators. Ralphie reached out and touched Mister LeFleur's arm to get his attention.

"Yes, Ralphie?"

"Mister LeFleur how are you related to the original LeFleur?" Ralphie asked with a wee smile. He looked at the handsome man next to him. "The one that started the Innovators?"

"Well, he was my great grandfather," LeFleur said with a toothy smile. "I was named after him," LeFleur said placing a hand on Ralphie's shoulder. "The LeFleur family has been involved in the plans of the Remains for a very long time."

Ralphie nodded.

The group slowed and in the unseen conference room hidden in the rear of the darkened Great Hall was a glass fronted conference room with a circular table. The doors were guarded by two enforcers.

Ralphie entered the room and cast his eyes on the round table that could seat ten people comfortably. Ralphie looked back and tried to understand how he missed the conference room portion of the Great Hall. He brushed it off to sensory overload. The teen stood against the wall and watched quietly as the conference room filled.

Mister Buchanan walked to the table and shook hands with all those in attendance. Standing with his arms crossed in the rear of the hall was a bearded man who looked like he would be more comfortable in a T-shirt and jeans instead of the blue and green camouflage suit jacket he wore that night. Behind him were two bearded men dressed in dark blue and green jackets.

The familiar face of Maya Higgins, the leader of the Millers, loomed in front of Ralphie. The teen was shocked seeing the leader of the Millers in the same room.

Higgins, big-boned, short and moving with a slight limp, looked distinctly different that night. Her hair was brushed up and away from her pie face. She was wearing Miller inspired dangling earrings. Ralphie smiled seeing, that true to her nature, Higgins was wearing a dark blue pants suit.

"Ralphie, we are so glad to see you alive," Higgins said with a nod. "Of course, I am speaking for all the Millers. You have done us proud."

Ralphie smiled, awkwardly.

"I am glad you are alive as well," the round-faced woman with an Afro and wide mouth said. "More importantly I am glad that you decided to spare our Bailey," the woman next to Maya Higgins said.

Ralphie did not respond, confused.

"Ralphie, this is Sonia Sanchez. She is the leader of the First Gen compound," Higgins said with a thin smile.

Sanchez extended her hand and Ralphie awkwardly shook it. Sanchez was a curly-haired attractive blockish woman dressed in a high collared dark blue dress that fell to the floor in a waterfall design of sequins. She had a high forehead, thick eyebrows, brown eyes, a straight round nose above her wide mouth. Ralphie noted that the leader of the First Gen had big arms and painted nails.

"Sorry," Ralphie said, confused.

"No, need to be sorry, Ralphie. You were willing to sacrifice yourself to save our lone challenger," Sanchez said.

Ralphie did not argue. All around him there were people talking. The lone camera operator was taking pictures from the edges of the room. Ralphie was aware of the camera and never totally comfortable and always aware of where the bearded camera operator was in proximity to himself.

Gordon Buchanan standing at a chair cleared his throat and with that the gathered sat. Ralphie stood awkwardly as the gathered found seats. Vincent LeFleur and Maya Higgins gestured to Ralphie and though a Miller, Ralphie sat between the Innovator leader and the Miller leader.

Vincent LeFleur sat at the round table closest to Buchanan. Sanchez, the leader of the First Gen, sat next to LeFleur on his left. Ralphie found himself seated next to the leader of the Innovators on his right. Beside Ralphie sat Maya Higgins and then the gruff man in the blue and green camo suit. The seat next to the camo suited man was empty. Exactly opposite of Ralphie was an open seat. The last three seats that closed the ten seats were empty.

Ralphie was about to say something when in walked an angular faced man with curly black hair and a tired look on his face dressed in a blue suit with muted green checks. The man had a scruffy beard and mustache and determined look about him. He walked with a limp and the assistance of a silver bird headed cane. Ralphie noticed that with the stranger's appearance the room quieted. Ralphie noticed that the camera operator in the corner of the room focused on the stranger's entrance.

Ralphie leaned close to Vincent LeFleur and asked:

"Who is that?"

"That is Jean-Michel Goodman, the grandson of the founder of the Boomers," LeFleur said.

"It is a great honor to have you here Jean-Michel," Buchanan said interrupting LeFleur. "I appreciate your coming out tonight. Obviously, we have important things to discuss and need your input."

Jean-Michel Goodman sat next to the blue and green camo suit jacket wearing man.

The last person to arrive was a dark woman wearing braids. She was dressed in a dark blue dress that had golden cuffs and shoulders. The woman was big eyed with a round nose and full lips. She was curvy and had a big butt.

"Sorry for being late," the woman said, looking around the table and sitting next to the founder of the Boomers and opposite Vincent LeFleur.

"That is my co-director Twyla Brooks," Vincent LeFleur said to Ralphie.

Ralphie nodded. The injured teen leaned toward Maya Higgins and silently tried to get her attention.

"Yes," Higgins said.

"Where is Mister Fields?" Ralphie asked.

"Well, some of us do not have the ability to leave our compound and plot against the Central Government with impunity like others," Higgins said with a smile. She shook her head and smiled at Ralphie and LeFleur. "Fields is in the compound keeping up appearances. The Central Government is suddenly interested in our compound's activities and investigating all our activities a little more than usual."

Ralphie listened, confused. He looked at the three empty seats at the table and wondered who had decided not to attend this meeting.

"Be careful who you give your allegiance to tonight, Ralphie," LeFleur said under his breath as Gordon Buchanan began the meeting.

"Let me begin by thanking my dear friends for coming here on such short notice," Buchanan said. "As you know there has been a much-needed push for us in the rescue and return of Ralphie and Bailey to the Remains." The influential man paused. "We suddenly have a visible way to address the barbaric nature of the Pandemonium Challenge while, at the same time, trying to do something about the inevitable end that we all are aware is not too far away."

"Gordo, I came all the way here for a plan not a speech," the bearded brute dressed in the blue and green camouflage suit jacket said. "We need a plan. You promised us a plan. The number of attacks on the wall are increasing. No one knows why. There have been rumors that the outer wall may have already been breached," the gruff man said. "The Central Government refuses to give any details."

"Who's that?" Ralphie asked.

"That's Jim Brown, leader of the Boomers," Maya Higgins said to Ralphie.

"JB, I understand your concern. Your line is at the northern end of the compound and your complex would be the first to be destroyed if the wall were to buckle."

"Gordo, this is serious. The Central Government seems to be interested in everything and anything but this. We need answers. I came tonight because I am worried about everything, but I am really worried about the safety of all our lines," Jim Brown said.

"You know I do not speak for the Central Government," Buchanan said. "I simply invited you here to meet Ralphie and to discuss our plans for the biggest issues in the Remains." He smiled. "The wall is one of those problems but as you all know there are bigger problems, we, as a collective, face." Buchanan, seated and commanding the room, paused, and looked at the people gathered. "This world is dying. Our resources are limited, at best, and we find that the flash aftereffects have poisoned our lands while creating deviants that make gathering resources perilous. The worse part of our limited resources is that we cannot store enough food stores to stave off our diminishing food supplies." Buchanan paused. "If our projections are correct, we have about three to five years to fix this before things are untenable."

Ralphie listened and thought about what Mister Buchanan was saying about the food. Was the food not real food? It didn't seem logical.

Mister Buchanan concluded saying this: "We must send out teams, beyond the wall, to... if nothing else, find another supply source. At best our scouts might locate an alternative location." Buchanan scanned the men and women in the room. "We had thought we had more time, but our timetable has moved up significantly based on our best projections and now that we have shown our hand," the Innovator said. Mister Buchanan smiled. "Yet, showing our hand is not a negative. Here, with Ralphie and Bailey, we can direct our concerns for relocation and so many issues we are facing through the artifice of the barbaric nature of the Pandemonium Challenge," Buchanan said.

"So, is this more talk?" Jim Brown asked placing his gigantic hand on the table.

"Absolutely not," LeFleur said. "With Ralphie and Bailey as the faces of our much-needed change and rethinking we can remind those who believe the Remains should not be our final home. For some the Remains might be their final resting place. For those on the fence and uncertain which side to take we can use our saved challenge survivors to remind them that we can save the Remains. We just need to focus our case for exploration beyond the walls during their tour of the lines while there is high interest in Ralphie and Bailey's survival."

"Have we identified potential relocation spots?" Sonia Sanchez asked.

"What are you hearing on the Interweb?" Twyla Brooks asked Sonia Sanchez.

"I heard that most of the East Coast is gone. There are reports that some people are living near the Great Lakes," Sonia Sanchez said.

"Well, the closest location that might be possible would be Nevada or Arizona," Jean-Michel said.

"There's always Utah," Jim Brown said.

Several people rolled their eyes at Brown's suggestion.

"What choices do we have?" Maya Higgins asked.

"The choices are limited, at best," LeFleur said with a nod.

"How would we get there? Wherever we go?" Jim Brown asked.

"We would have to go by wheeled transport," Higgins said.

"The airplanes are no longer flying?" Jean-Michel asked.

"We have plenty of gasoline, but jet fuel is scarce," LeFleur said.

"There's no way to travel that distance by helicopter?" Sanchez asked.

"We don't have enough helicopters to make that a reality," LeFleur said.

"So, what are you thinking?" Higgins asked Buchanan.

"Well, I will let Vince speak. He knows more and is privy to more details than I would ever pretend to know," Buchanan said with a big smile and gesture to Vincent LeFleur.

"Tonight, in this little meeting, we are more than half of the lines and we have a true opportunity to create significant change," LeFleur said with his hands on the table.

"Come on Vince, cut to the chase," Jim Brown said.

"Very well, JB, based on my understanding of what we see ahead the Remains cannot sustain its present situation. At the soonest, we have numbers suggesting three years," Vincent LeFleur said.

"We've heard this Vince," Jean-Michel said, interrupting LeFleur.

"Okay," LeFleur said with a nod. "Three years, 36 months (about 3 years), we have to save the Remains. Simple as that. We know that the Central Government refuses to listen to the predictions, which is problematic. We all know that hubris has destroyed the greatest of human creations. The Remains is no exception," LeFleur said.

"What is the Central Government doing to punish your dalliance into their sacred challenge?" Jean-Michel asked.

"They want to punish the three lines involved in the hiccup that happened the last day of the challenge. To us, that is no biggie. They are going to give us slaps on the wrists. All theater. But the thing that matters is that they will tip their hand. We can push for change in front of the Remains," Vincent LeFleur said. He looked to the imposing Jim Brown. "Now, as for the concerns of the wall and the Remains all that will be addressed with the use of Ralphie and Bailey. We all know of the wall and the threats, JB. To that end, we have enlisted the services of Sonia Sanchez and her IT team to try and figure out what is causing the rise in threats. Attacks on the wall anywhere is an attack on us all."

Sanchez stood at that moment.

"I want to point out that we alerted the Central Government to the increases in attacks during the Twentieth Pandemonium Challenge and... nothing," Sanchez said. "We thought it might be connected to the increase of white noise created to broadcast the signal of the challenge to all the Remains. Of course, we were laughed out of the chamber by the Pandemonium Challenge Committee's scientists."

"Well, is it connected?" Jim Brown asked.

"We don't know," Sanchez said, annoyed. "We know there is a connection, but as of yet we have not been able to connect the challenge's signal with the rise of attacks on the wall," Sanchez said and sat down. "I should point out that there are reports of creatures in between the walls. The wall enforcers have faced and eliminated two types, but there is a troubling third type that they have yet to address."

"What is this third type?"

"Some strange hybrid. Not a lone wolf. Not the typical slow moving pack group either. Something different," Sanchez said.

Jim Brown looked at Jean-Michel twirling his cane. Gordon Buchanan and Maya Higgins frowned. The two did not seem thrilled by the announcement.

"We are getting off track," LeFleur said. "We have plans in place. We have only to wait for the right moment. Things are about to ramp up quickly to the inevitable. Just be prepared. Tonight, we hold the majority in advance of the coming theater that we all face."

"Agreed," the assembled said.

As the brief meeting ended Ralphie found himself looking at Maya Higgins. Ralphie reached out and touched the arm of the Miller leader.

"What is it Ralphie?" Higgins asked.

"I'm going to be some kind of poster boy for some cause, all of a sudden?"

"You have been a poster boy since you were selected for the challenge, Ralphie," Higgins said. "The only difference is now you will be working for the Remains and not for the Pandemonium Challenge Committee."

Ralphie robotically returned to the table and Ella and Missus Buchanan. He listened but did not have words suddenly. The dinner, the business meeting, the Innovators, all the line leaders who had come for the special meeting and their plan, was bigger than Ralphie could understand.

He was gut punched by Higgins comment. All around him the dinner party and partygoers chatted, ate, and socialized. In Ralphie's head he was trying to understand what he had gotten himself into by allowing Ella Buchanan to pull him out of the Pandemonium Challenge.

After the dinner and meeting ended and all the security and staff retreated to wherever they retreated Ralphie found himself once again on the stairs leading back to his temporary bedroom and talked with Ella Buchanan.

"Did you know?" Ralphie asked. He looked at Ella coolly.

Ella chuckled. She shook her head, no.

"I don't like feeling like I am being used," Ralphie said, hurt and confused.

"Well, there isn't any other way to feel when you are around powerful people," Ella said, looking at Ralphie.

"So, were you a part of this?" Ralphie asked, frowning.

Ella laughed.

Ralphie rethought the question.

"Who's on our side?"

Ella smiled. Ralphie looked at Ella, annoyed.

"Sides? It isn't a this side or that side thing, Ralphie," Ella said, with a frown. "No one wants the Remains to fail. This is about power. The problem is that people get comfortable with things and don't want to change." Ella stopped. She studied Ralphie. "There have been protests against the challenge since it began but it took me and my daddy... and his helicopters to do something about it." Ella stopped and pouted. "It is the same way with the limited resources in the Remains. We have been here for four decades waiting for the end. We all know that the planet is on life support." Ella paused. "It seems to be done and then something happens."

Ralphie nodded.

"We all know there has to be something better, but we have refused the idea of finding another place, any place other than here," Ella said.

"Okay," Ralphie said, growing annoyed. "But you understand how crazy this all sounds? Right?"

"Crazy? I don't agree with that," Ella said.

"Well, okay, maybe not crazy, but damn near close," Ralphie said.

Ella didn't respond.

"So, who doesn't support this?"

"Well, there's seven lines. The Trads don't like change too much. There's the Second Gens. I think they just are opposed to anything the First Gens support. They have a bad history." Ella paused. "The ones that surprise me are the Poppies. I would think they would be 100% behind shutting down the challenge. I think they would be with all the possibilities." She stopped. "I mean they're artists. They should be all over change and new frontiers."

"I think the Poppies don't want to leave Cosson Hall," Ralphie said.

"On Pandemonium Island?"

"Yeah," Ralphie said. Ralphie thought momentarily of Pablo, Pablo, and Robert Nesta, who he had found at Cosson Hall. He blinked and shook the memory from his head. "They think it's sacred or something."

Ella nodded.

"So, what now?"

"You get some rest and when you are healed things get weird," Ella said.

Chapter Six.

The Revolutionaries

For the next seven days Ralphie found his recovery progress improving. In fact, when he walked a few days after the dinner with the leaders of the Remains lines there was little sign of the ball of hurt. There was still discomfort, but that discomfort was manageable.

One morning Ralphie woke and still felt the raking of his insides as he tried to sit up in bed. He winced from the unexpected grating and ragged hurt.

"You know you are still healing? I mean, you did have a building fall on your head," nurse Patricia said with a sweet smile.

"I suppose," Ralphie said struggling to sit up despite the dull ache. Somewhere inside his body Ralphie imagined there was a prickly monster with three-inch claws that climbed up and down his right side whenever he moved in the wrong direction. Simultaneously, Ralphie imagined, that if he ignored the prickly monster it would die from lack of attention, and he would heal.

The copper toned nurse put her reading away.

"What are you reading?"

Nurse Patricia smiled and looked away from Ralphie coyly.

"I know its comics," Ralphie said, with a toothy smile as he finally adjusted himself to sit comfortably in the bed. "I was just curious which one? I mean, there used to be this great debate as to which comic group had the greatest heroes and villains." Ralphie paused and smiled. "Don't tell me you are into some independent edgy comics and not interested in the big comic book houses."

Patricia smiled, awkwardly.

"Not saying that there's anything wrong with independent comics at all," Ralphie said, trying to sound nonjudgmental.

"I am in a phase," the big-eyed beauty said. "I always find myself in phases when I read. Right now, I am into the stories of McDuffie, Moore, Gaiman and Graham and just fascinated by what they were able to accomplish and say in 48 pages of Bang! Pow! And Zaps!"

"So, what are you reading right now?" Ralphie asked with a painful laugh.

"Static Shock," Patricia said, reluctantly.

"Why you say it like that?"

"Because you were talking about the great debate and I suppose I fall on the side of Marvel because they hired McDuffie," Patricia said.

Ralphie smiled and laughed, feeling the invisible monster inside his right side claw up his ribs just a few inches and rest under his elbow.

"I was kind of kidding," Ralphie said, with a pained smile. "If we had known that the best way to get recognized was the Interweb, I think we would have all gone that route long ago and with less headaches."

"Agreed," Patricia said with a large smile.

When he woke each morning Ralphie was happy to see Patricia reading her comic books or monitoring the equipment or just scribbling something on a clipboard.

After going to the bathroom and several tests, Doctor Sherman showed up with his assistant Floyd.

"How is Bailey?"

"She is healing," Doctor Sherman said. "She seems to be doing quite well."

Five days into his recovery Doctor Sherman removed the sling and air cast. He checked Ralphie's range of motion on his shoulder daily.

"How does your shoulder feel?"

"Good," Ralphie said, rotating his arm and smiling at the doctor.

"Don't try punching anyone," the doctor said with a grin.

"I'm not planning on it," Ralphie said.

Ralphie had lunch with Ella and her mother in the rear of the estate at one of the two swimming pools. The pool where they ate was empty for some reason.

There were a few round tables set out around the empty pool that day but only Ella and her mother and the attentive wait staff present. Ralphie smiled and sat beside the two Buchanans.

Ella, dressed in bright blue top and acid washed jeans with yellow Doc Martin combat boots on, giggled.

Her mother, dressed in a dark blue short-sleeve top and blue jeans smiled at Ralphie.

"Ralphie, it seems as if you are feeling better," Missus Buchanan said with a wide smile.

"I am," Ralphie said, sitting beside Ella.

A pair of camera people were in the periphery. Ralphie bit at his lower lip, uncomfortable.

"Is Mister Buchanan joining us?"

Missus Buchanan looked at Ralphie, uncertain. She followed Ralphie's line of sight to the camera person shooting video or taking photos. The wife of Gordon Buchanan smiled and nodded at Ralphie's question. She looked back at Ralphie.

"Ralphie, as you know, Mister Buchanan is a busy man. He will not be available today. Hopefully, he will be back for dinner, but no promises. He is dealing with some delicate negotiations," Miss Buchanan said.

"Empire building," Ella said in a whisper.

Ralphie and Ella smiled.

"Today, you are going to be interviewed by three reporters for the lines news services," Ella's mother said.

"What?"

"It's okay, your line leader should be here in a few minutes. We are just laying the groundwork so that the Remains sees you as the hero you are," she said. Missus Buchanan raised a hand and the wait staff brought out lunch for the day.

That day the wait staff were dressed all in white. There were two young women serving the Buchanans and Ralphie that afternoon. Water was brought out. A glass of water was filled for all three.

"What would you like to drink, sir?"

Ralphie smiled at the word sir. He was younger than the woman serving him. He puckered his lips, thinking.

"Could I have a lemonade?"

The woman nodded.

While drinks were being made the other woman brought out three small bowls and placed them in front of the three. The woman bowed and backed away from the table as the other woman returned with a bigger bowl of Edamame beans.

"Hope you don't mind a little sushi today?"

"No ma'am," Ralphie said. He reached out and ate a few Edamame beans, splitting them and eating the beans inside. Ella was doing the same.

In a couple of minutes out walked the young woman with the three different drinks. Ralphie smiled receiving his lemonade. He noticed that Ella had a pinkish drink. Her mother was drinking a similarly colored drink.

"You know you asked about my father?"

Ralphie nodded.

"Daddy is trying to broker a deal between the committee and the Central Government," Ella said as the first course of Miso soup and wasabi rice were served.

"He has been extremely busy," Missus Buchanan said with a nod sipping her Miso soup.

The lunch consisted of a light fare of Chicken Robata and scallions. Ralphie did not eat the scallions. Ella watched Ralphie pick the scallions off his plate.

"You don't like onions?"

"Not particularly," Ralphie said. "I just don't like them, generally."

The next course was a rice and seaweed rolled spicy tuna with crab. The California roll was cut into six smaller pieces. With the California roll was a pinch of green wasabi and soy sauce.

Having had sushi before Ralphie mixed the wasabi and soy sauce together into a paste or liquidly paste of a spicy dipping sauce for his sushi roll. Ella smiled at Ralphie holding his chopsticks above his wasabi and soy sauce mixture.

"You sure you can handle that?"

Ralphie looked at Ella and sneered.

"You said you don't like onions," Ella said with a grin.

"This isn't the same," Ralphie said, looking from his wasabi and soy sauce to Ella's mix. The Innovator's mix was more soy sauce than wasabi. Ralphie's mix was the blending of the two into a slightly pasty concoction, light on soy sauce.

"Good luck," Ella said with an overconfident smile.

Ralphie picked up his segment of California roll between the chop sticks the wait staff had brought and held his piece expertly. Ella smiled impressed. Missus Buchanan smiled as well.

Dipping the segment into the wasabi and soy sauce Ralphie popped the roll into his mouth and began to eat. The immediate explosion of spice tore through Ralphie's mouth and up his nasal passages before he could register what was happening. Ralphie blinked. Ralphie inhaled. Suddenly, he was breathing heavily. Tears jumped from his eyes.

Ella laughed. Her mother smiled. She shook her head.

"Ralphie are you alright?" Ella asked with a wicked smile.

Ralphie wiped the tears from his eyes and blew the air out of his mouth as if he had just run up a mountain. He blinked and looked at the five other pieces of sushi that remained.

"I'm fine," Ralphie said, with a thin smile. He ate his California roll and drank his lemonade. By the time, the Ponzu Salmon arrived Ralphie asked for a refill of lemonade.

Ralphie found the Ponzu Salmon and crispy Brussell Sprouts delicious.

After lunch Ralphie was taken to the smaller building where three reporters and six photographers waited. Missus Buchanan and Ella accompanied Ralphie. Waiting in the smaller building was the familiar face of Maya Higgins and the plain looking Greta Newman, the co-leader of the Innovators line.

"Ralphie, so good to see you again," said Missus Newman. She had short ash blonde hair on her round head. Newman had dishwater brown eyes, a broad nose, and a wide smile. That day she was dressed in blue blazer, light blue blouse, and yellow and white slacks. In her earlobes sat diamond earrings. Around her neck was a large diamond pendant. On her wrist was a diamond tennis bracelet.

Ralphie nodded.

"These are softball interviews," Higgins said. "We just need you to answer the questions honestly. We will prepare your re-entry to the Remains," the Miller leader said.

Ralphie sat in an overstuffed leather chair against a window that looked out toward the Acid Bay. Ella sat at a table with her mother and listened as the three reporters jockeyed to be the first to interview Ralphie. The photographers were already taking pictures and videoing the whole incident.

The first reporter was Amandla Stenberg Scott. She wrote for the Boomer line. The Boomers had a gritty Interweb news service called: The Seventh. It was named after the last line of the Remains, the Boomers. Amandla Scott was a hooded eyed woman with a crooked nose and thin smile.

The second reporter was LaKeith Grant. Grant wrote for the First Gen Interweb service called: Mammoth Moments. It was a glitzy and well packaged news service that focused on all the news of the Remains that mattered to the First Gen compound. Grant was a featured reporter and had a large following. He was dressed in a velvet suit with the Goddess Minerva stitched on the sleeve and the back. He was dressed like he was a rockstar or fashion model.

The last reporter was Russell Jefferson for the Millers Interweb service Grinder. Jefferson was a bald headed, tall, sand colored man dressed in one of the Miller distinctive black hoodies. He had a collared blue shirt on underneath and wore black baggy jeans and combat boots.

Ralphie knew the Interweb news service that Jefferson worked for but had never read anything there. All he knew about the Grinder was that it was a 24/7, 365 reporting site of all the things going on in the Remains that mattered to the Miller compound.

Maya Higgins sat in the chair just behind the reporter. Seeing Higgins did not ease Ralphie's discomfort, but it did make Ralphie smile for the first time.

Ralphie sat and answered all the questions the reporters asked. At the end Higgins and Newman took pictures with Ralphie and the two powerful women took pictures together with Ella and Ella's mother as well.

"So, what now?"

"Well, we wait," Higgins said with a knowing wink.

"Yeah, we are baiting a trap. We know we are heading for a fight, but we want to have an advantage," Newman said standing on the front steps of the Buchanan mansion.

The first of two transports appeared. The first was a Rolls Royce Cullinan SUV for Newman. The other was a Bentley Bentayga SUV for Higgins.

Ralphie looked from the two women leaders and to Ella and her mother. He could not help but smile. He had hesitated with Bailey. He had been saved by Ella. Now, he was enmeshed with Higgins and Newman. For a moment, an instant, he wanted to be around his mother and sister.

Missus Buchanan walked into the mansion as the Bentley Bentayga SUV departed.

"Like I said, a different mindset, Ralphie," Ella said and Ralphie nodded.

*   *   *   *   *

A few days after the news media interviews Ella walked into Ralphie's room all smiles. She was dressed in dark blue Doc Martens, ripped blue jeans and her distinctive golden zip front hoody with blue piping on the shoulders and cuffs. Her hair was unbraided and pulled back and into a big Afro ball on the top of her head.

"Miss Buchanan," Patricia, his nurse, said with a timid smile. She was monitoring Ralphie's vitals when Ella appeared. The nurse climbed to her feet.

Ella nodded.

Ralphie was sitting on his bed, dressed in a blue hoody, white T-shirt, and blue jeans. On his feet were retro basketball sneakers.

Ella sat in the vacated chair and looked at the nurse. Patricia smiled and walked away. Ella watched as Patricia found something else to do in a different part of the room.

"Ralphie, I think that you will finally get to meet my team," Ella said with a delicate smile.

"You have a team?"

"The Revolutionaries," Ella said with a tilt of the head.

Ralphie looked at Ella, confused.

Ella smiled like she had won the lottery.

"What do they do?" Ralphie asked.

"They do all sorts of things. They are this...," Ella paused. "I don't want to spoil it," Ella said. "You'll meet them and after I want to see what you think. Honest reactions," she said and then left after reminding Ralphie of a lunch with her and her mother.

89

The lunch with Ella and her mother was cordial. Ella talked about all the countries she wanted to go to in the future. Her mother tried to explain that travel was almost impossible, unless it was work-related and that much of the world was changed.

The next morning Ralphie found Patricia by his bedside.

"Good morning," Ralphie said.

"Good morning," Patricia said with a delicate smile. His nurse wrote something and then slipped her comic book into her bag. "How did you sleep?"

"Good, thank you," Ralphie said. He looked at Patricia and smiled.

"Do you know anything about Ella's team?" Ralphie asked.

Patricia shook her head.

"Nothing?" Ralphie asked, looking at his nurse curiously.

"Well, I have heard about them," Patricia said.

"What did you hear?" Ralphie asked.

"They are the supposed rabble rousers of the compound," Patricia said, looking left and right and toward the door of the room.

"Rabble rousers?" Ralphie repeated.

"Well, in this compound, this line, they aren't troublemakers in the true sense of the word. They are tree huggers and all about protecting... everything." Patricia pouted. "They are... passionate," Patricia said with a tiny smile.

"Passionate?" Ralphie repeated with a nod.

Patricia nodded.

That afternoon, Ella showed up with a chestnut brown girl with a round face and a mole on her upper lip. She had her hair braided into an intricate design that ended in a dozen loose braids that dangled down to her shoulders. The girl was petite. She was not four feet three inches tall. The girl was wearing a baby blue hooded sweatshirt, gold and blue basketball shorts, white socks, and blue basketball sneakers. On her wrist was a bracelet made up of a dozen inch in diameter gold beads.

"Ralphie, this is Yo-Yo," Ellas said.

Yo-Yo nodded and smiled. Ralphie nodded too.

Ella and Yo-Yo walked Ralphie to the main decking and the four tables where two others sat waiting under a yellow and blue patio umbrella.

As Ella and Yo-Yo arrived at the table the two boys stood up smiling.

"Ralphie, this is Albert and Jesse," Ella said.

Albert, the short and round kid with glasses and buck teeth approached and gave Ralphie a hug. Ralphie smiled and embraced Albert.

Jesse, tall and slender, stepped to Ralphie and gave him a hug as well. Ralphie nodded after the hug.

The Revolutionaries were: Albert Griggs, Jesse Otis, and Yo-Yo AKA Yolanda Carver.

Albert Griggs had a head of curly black hair that he allowed to curl atop his round head. Albert wore, as his signature look, an oversized sweatshirt, loose fitting jeans and basketball sneakers. On his head were a pair of silver over the ear headphones.

"These are Beats by Dre," Albert was proud to say though no one knew the point of over ear headphones in that day and age. "Real trick and irreplaceable."

"Nobody asked," Yo-Yo said.

"These things were incredible in the day," Albert explained adjusting his glasses. "They are easily more valuable than a transport right now."

"None of us drive," Jesse said.

"He thinks that wearing old school headphones somehow makes him edgy," Ella said in a whisper to Ralphie.

"Albert is the smartest of us all," Yo-Yo said. Her voice was nasally and loud. She was small but loud all the time. The thin hipped girl that had not moved into her puberty liked to dress like Jesse in basketball sneakers, basketball shorts or jeans and cartoon T-shirts. Her hair was usually beneath a baseball cap. Ralphie pegged Yo-Yo as the mouth of the group.

Ralphie smiled at Yo-Yo's words.

Jesse Otis was the opposite of Albert, tall and slender he looked like he might be athletic. He had big hands and long arms and legs. Looking at Jesse, Ralphie imagined what a human greyhound might look like. Jesse had beady eyes beneath his tightly faded trimmed black eraser hairstyle, a long slightly up turned nose and beneath that mouth a thin smile. He was a tough looking individual that wore basketball sneakers, basketball shorts and a hoody or T-shirt. Around his neck was a gold chain and a medallion of the pre-flash California.

"Jesse is our muscle," Ella said. "We have to have a brain, a tough or muscle, the mouth and the beauty and resource person." Ella smiled and pointed to herself.

The Revolutionaries and Ralphie had a light lunch of peanut butter and jelly sandwiches, with the crust cut off, Fritos, apple, grape, and pineapple juice was offered as well. Ralphie liked the informality of eating with Ella and the Revolutionaries.

After the light lunch Ella and the Revolutionaries walked Ralphie across the golf course and behind the copse of trees that separated the two sides of the golf course. The friends sat on the lip of a neatly raked white sand trap.

"Ralphie, we have some questions," Jesse said and smiled proudly holding the rake for the sand trap.

Albert, the brain, sitting on the manicured grass, asked the first question. "What do you want to happen now that you are out of the challenge?"

"What do you mean?" Ralphie asked.

"I mean, now that you are out and alive from the challenge and you are a symbol for the Remains," Albert said his legs crossed in front of him. "What do you want to happen? You know that everyone will be ready to use you."

Ralphie looked at Ella.

"You know all this already?" Albert asked.

Ralphie nodded.

"So?" Albert asked, thinking. "You ready to hawk hemorrhoid cream, or a roto sander, or the latest and greatest hammer. You name it," Albert concluded.

"Yeah, you are going to be dealing with everyone wanting to put you on or in front of products," Yo-Yo admitted with a laugh, lying on her back, and looking into the foliage above. She turned over and bracketed her thumbs and forefingers and drew them out in front of her and toward Ralphie. "I can see it now, Ralphie Reynolds endorses Pandemonium Challenge Twenty-Four."

Albert and Ella laughed. Jesse giggled.

"So? What aren't you willing to sell?" Albert asked.

Ralphie did not answer. He did not know.

"Be careful," Yo-Yo barked, now with a hand under her chin. "There are a lot of people that are going to say they need you and want to help you." She paused. "You need to know that not everyone wants to help you."

"Be careful, man," Jesse said seriously sitting on the lip of the sand trap. "I think that is what happened with Stuart Somers. He won the challenge. He had a fashion line. Right? He was riding high and... boom. All that came crashing down."

"Yeah, that was because he got mixed up with some weirdos in the Trads," Ella said, extending her leg in front of her.

"The Trads are too Johnny Law for me," Jesse said with a frown.

"Yeah, they would rather kill you than break a rule," Yo-Yo said, now sitting up.

"I don't know, I heard his breakdown had something to do with too much too soon," Albert noted twirling a twig he had found between his fingers. "He was only fourteen or fifteen and suddenly legendary. They said he was given five mil to rep that fashion line."

"Yeah, boy suddenly had deep pockets," Jesse said with a pie-eating smile.

"Yeah, all that," Yo-Yo said, looking at Jesse. "But then the enforcers scooped him up running around in the Trad compound naked with a shotgun saying that he was being chased by aliens." Albert chuckled and shook his head.

"Aliens," Yo-Yo said with a shake of her head.

"No, there were no aliens, unless you think drugs are aliens," Jesse acknowledged.

"Drugs?" Ralphie asked. "I thought they outlawed drugs in the Remains?"

The Revolutionaries looked at Ralphie skeptically and then themselves before they all broke out laughing.

"Ralphie, I don't know what they're teaching you in the Miller compound," Albert said, wiping at his eyes. "Drugs are everywhere in the Remains. They're just one of the many ugly secrets in the Remains."

Ralphie frowned.

"Drugs could have been the reason Somers was carted off to Lockley, but I don't believe it," Ella said. "There were just too many reasons Somers failed. The Trads were pressuring him. They wanted him to be perfect," Ella decided.

"Lockley?" Ralphie asked, unfamiliar with the name.

"The Remains cuckoo bin," Jesse said.

Ralphie nodded. Ella was lying on the grass looking up at the sky. Yo Yo was watching Ralphie intently. Jesse was playing with the rake.

"So, you have a thing you aren't willing to sell?" Albert asked.

"I don't know," Ralphie admitted. "I sort of just want to go home and hug my mom and dad and little sister. I just want to lay in my own bed and know that this is all over." Ralphie added, "I just want things to return to normal."

"Ralphie there is no normal for you anymore," Albert Griggs stated with a buck tooth smile.

"That ended when you left the challenge alive," Jesse said with a big smile.

"Yeah. Normal life is in your past, young Ralphie. Everyone will be trying to get a piece of you," Ella said.

"They are going to try and name a building after you," Jesse pointed out with a sympathetic shake of his head.

"That's a trap to appease the simple minded, just like drugs," Ella concluded.

Everyone quieted.

"Don't get a building," Yo-Yo complained. "If you're going to participate in the carving of your name into granite then do it for something bigger and grander."

"Like what?" Ralphie asked.

"A park or a museum or a street," Yo-Yo calculated. Yo-Yo paused. "I think a street named after you is probably on the same level as a building."

"What's wrong with having my name on a building?" Ralphie asked.

"Well, nothing, I mean it's an honor. But don't forget that they can sell that building and the owner can rename it," Yo-Yo said.

"Or they can tear it down," Jesse said.

*   *   *   *   *

The morning Ralphie was to return to the Miller compound the Revolutionaries appeared. They met on the back deck where the Buchanan's entertained.

Albert was the first to speak. "Ralphie, we know that this road is not going to be straight and easy. So, we figured that you might need a little help," Albert said.

"What Albert is saying in his own big, brained way," Yo-Yo said with a sympathetic shake of her head. "We're here for you even when you go back to your compound."

Ella and Jesse nodded. Yo-Yo looked to Albert. Albert smiled awkwardly and fished inside of his jeans pocket and pulled out a small plastic CRD and handed it to Ralphie.

"What's this?" Ralphie asked holding the small plastic chip between his thumb and forefinger.

"It's a homing device. First thing you do is wipe your finger across it, it will be activated. Then if you are in trouble all you do is squeeze it and it will send a message to all of us. We'll respond and try and get you some help," Ella said.

"Use it only if you get in trouble," Albert said.

"Why would he use it for any other reason?" Yo-Yo asked.

"Who knows," Albert said.

Yo-Yo and Albert did a short and uneventful stare down.

Jesse stepped in between them.

Ralphie smiled.

"Thanks," Ralphie said.

Ralphie said his goodbyes and climbed into a black stretch Mercedes Benz SUV and was whisked away and back to the Miller compound.

For the short ride, the two enforcers sitting in the front of the SUV stayed in constant radio contact with the two other SUVs and motorcycles roaring along the deserted streets of the Remains.

"I thought that there wasn't any more production of gasoline?"

"Before the flash, the resources were stretched to their limit. I think that gas got to be nine dollars a gallon in the states," Gordon Buchanan said looking out of the window of the SUV. Ella and Ralphie were seated in the third row of the stretch Mercedes Benz SUV. Ralphie noted that there was a Range Rover SUV in front of them and one riding behind. There were four motorcycles guarding the entire convoy. "But when the population dropped there was a lot of excess fuel. We hired people to siphon the gasoline from transports and created our own supply surplus." He paused. "We distributed gasoline to several locations in our compound. I am not sure what the other lines have done."

"We have transports, but we don't use them too often," Ralphie said. Ralphie smiled, thinking that his father had a car, but he had never ridden in it. The car was a muscle car classic that his father had picked up when he saw it at some car museum. But, again, Ralphie was sure that his father had never driven it.

There was the family Land Rover that his father drove back and forth to work but that was a work vehicle. Reynolds Construction was plastered on both doors and on the rear lift gate. It was just rolling advertisement.

"Do you drive often," Ralphie asked Ella.

"Not too often. We usually do nature walks and hike. I like hiking," Ella admitted.

The interior of the Mercedes Benz got quiet.

"How come we didn't take the helicopter," Ella asked her father.

"Vincent and Greta wanted us to drive in and show a significant sign of power to the Remains," Gordon Buchanan croaked. His wife sat by his side looking at her tablet notebook computer.

"According to the maps we aren't that far from the Millers compound," Missus Buchanan said. "I didn't know that Ralphie and his family live in the Estates. That property borders Second Gen compound property," she said.

"So, how long?" Ralphie asked.

"Well, according to the app we got a ten- or fifteen-minute ride to your front door," Missus Buchanan said.

Ralphie nodded from the third-row seat of the plush SUV next to Ella.

"So, you think that once I get back to the compound," Ralphie paused, suddenly at a loss for words. "You figure that this," he pointed to Ella and back to himself, "Ends?"

"Naw, Ralphie, there is another chapter to this story," said Ella. "We got you off the island now we must deal with all the extras."

Ralphie shook his head.

"There's no way that you or anyone can make sure of that," Ralphie said.

"Yeah, I suppose so," Ella said. "But also remember that the Pandemonium Committee wants to sue you, me, my family, the Innovators and Bailey for interrupting and invalidating the Twenty-Third Pandemonium Challenge."

"Invalidating?" Ralphie repeated.

"Ralphie, you don't worry about that," Missus Buchanan announced turning around in her seat. "We are already strategizing how this whole thing is resolved."

Gordon Buchanan exhaled. "Let's focus," Mister Buchanan said. "What we do now is important even if it seems like it doesn't matter. We have a big photo op coming. The plan is to swoop in and give Ralphie to his family. There are going to be Central Government media there and Miller media and a whole bunch of line media. We must let them ask questions and take a few pictures and deal with any government issues. It promises to be a media circus. Hopefully, we do all that and things start moving in our direction," Mister Buchanan said.

"What does he mean?" Ralphie asked.

"The Central Government is only as strong as the perception of them being fair and just," Ella said. "If they appear too heavy-handed then they lose the Remains loyalty."

"We are entering the Miller compound," one of the enforcers announced.

"Are you expecting any trouble," Ralphie asked with the heavy presence of enforcers.

"Never expect trouble Ralphie, just prepared for anything," Gordon Buchanan grinned.

The three Innovators transports raced through the quiet streets of the Miller compound. They drove as if their vehicles were on rails. Two motorcycles ran ahead of the convoy blocking off streets as the convoy tore through the compound.

Ralphie tried to orient himself with the side of the compound the convoy rolled down. He rarely had been on this side of the compound. He knew that there were four main streets which ran through the compound. The four main streets that divided the Miller compound were; Thurgood Marshall Avenue East and West and Barack Obama Avenue North and South divided the compound in half.

The SUV convoy turned onto Barack Obama Avenue South and then turned onto Zora Neal Hurston Avenue West and made their way quickly toward the Sean Carter Estates. With the turn onto Zora Neal Hurston Avenue things became familiar to Ralphie.

Back a mile or so to the east was the Foundry and the center of the Miller compound. Ralphie thought absently of the last time he had been at the Foundry with Tee, Zeke and Jax.

He closed his eyes to the memories and felt a single tear squeeze out and slide down his cheek. He looked up and found Ella looking at him. Ralphie smiled and wiped at his face.

"Have you ever been here?" Ralphie asked, his voice a little strained.

Ella did not reply. Instead, she simply watched Ralphie in the rear of the Mercedes Benz. She slowly reached out and put a hand on Ralphie's forearm.

The brick pillars of the Sean Carter Estates welcomed the convoy of motorcycles and Range Rover SUVs as they hurtled toward Ralphie's home. Two motorcycles blocked off the entrance to Elijah McCoy Avenue and Ralphie's home. The SUVs led by the two other motorcycles slowed and parked in front of a house where several people with signs, cameras, and microphones waited.

The SUVs parked at the curb and the first Range Rover opened its doors and three enforcers exited and held the two points of entry. The third enforcer stood in the street and watched for any threats. The middle SUV's enforcer in the passenger seat climbed out and quickly stepped to the rear passenger door.

"We have a few news reporters with cameras on the street in front of the house and a few moving toward the convoy," the driver of the SUV announced. "Rear guard assist with perimeter security."

Everyone in the Mercedes Benz SUV waited. A few minutes later the driver looked back, nervously.

"Mister Buchanan we have secured the area. Please exit on the curbside," the driver said and the door on the curbside was opened by the Innovator enforcer dressed in a gray suit jacket, white collared shirt, and dark blue trousers. Ralphie knew the enforcer was armed.

Missus Buchanan was the first to climb out of the SUV. The enforcer helped Missus Buchanan out of the door.

Instantly there was the sound of clamoring, clicking of cameras and whirring of video cameras. Gordon Buchanan was the second to climb out of the SUV. The enforcer lifted the rear seat and allowed Ella to climb out of the third-row seating. Ralphie following Ella was the last out of the SUV.

Once on the sidewalk Ralphie felt his face naturally form a broad smile as he looked at the front of his house, he had not been in for twenty-three days.

There were all these people trying to talk to Ralphie. Camera operators and women were trying to find the best angle to film him. Reporters were calling Ralphie's name. The enforcer closest to Ralphie placed a hand on Ralphie's shoulder and pushed him forward through the phalanx of people.

Ralphie, with the assistance of the enforcer, moved through the assemblage and toward his house. Ella followed. Behind Ralphie and Ella fell in line Mister and Missus Buchanan protected by individual enforcers.

Two enforcers with assault rifles stood at the steps to the porch as the foursome walked up the steps and into the house of Benjamin O. Davis Reynolds.

Once inside Ralphie was greeted by two more enforcers.

Behind the enforcer appeared his mother and little sister. Behind them stood his father. Macy ran to Ralphie and hugged him. Instantly, she was crying and unintelligible. Before he tried to decipher what Macy said He found his mother was hugging him and crying. His father was the last to reach Ralphie and hug him and hold onto him.

The Reynolds cried in the middle of their living room. After a minute or two his mother and father stepped back. Macy did not release Ralphie and Ralphie did not mind. Before Ralphie could form words, he heard a familiar voice.

"This is touching, but we have important things to discuss Ralphie," Maya Higgins said standing in the living room with a man that looked more a block of stone with thin eyes, broad nose, and tight lips than man. "We have quite a kerfuffle to iron out," the leader of the Millers breathed.

"What's going on?" Ralphie asked, seeing Higgins in his living room.

"Welcome home, Ralphie," Maya Higgins said, sweetly from the edge of the living room where she and an enforcer stood. Ralphie blinked and wiped at his eyes, trying to re-orient himself. The sight of Missus Higgins was shocking but what was even more shocking was the half dozen enforcers in his house.

"What?" Ralphie asked, seeing the enforcers.

Ralphie looked to Ella and her parents.

"Well, as I told you before we are in a delicate situation. We must direct this situation to our benefit," Maya Higgins said. "We have an agenda. We have some talking points that you need to address," smiled Maya Higgins evilly. "We know that the media will want a statement from the Buchanans. So be prepared."

"We are more than prepared," Gordon Buchanan said pulling Ella behind him. His wife was by his side.

Mister Buchanan and Maya Higgins shook hands.

"I apologize for the need to address the media, but as you know based on the plan, we need to hit the iron while things are hot," Higgins said. Beside her was a well-dressed man wearing glasses. He was wearing a dark blue suit.

"This is Doctor Henry Dumas Greenwood," Maya Higgins said, looking at the man wearing the glasses. "He is one of our best psychologists and will be responsible for Ralphie's re-integration into society."

Doctor Henry Dumas Greenwood smiled and extended his hand toward Mister Buchanan. He and Mister Buchanan shook hands.

"Okay, the way that I see this situation going is that when the Pandemonium Committee arrives, we deflect," Maya Higgins offered.

"That is not going to be possible," Gordon Buchanan said. "The Central Government representatives are on their way. The Pandemonium Committee members cannot be far behind." Buchanan looked at Ralphie and nodded. "There is no need to deflect. The Innovators have incredible clout. The leaders of the lines trust Vincent's leadership. There is little chance that the Pandemonium Committee does anything to little Ralphie or for that matter to the First Gen girl on her return."

Ralphie listened next to his mother and father with Macy holding onto his hand.

"Then what are we talking about?" Maya Higgins asked.

"Understanding," Buchanan said. "Your line needs to understand and appreciate our line's generosity and protection of young Ralphie. We need you to remain silent. Do not align your line against us or the First Gens. We have bigger plans. We know that there is going to be a subsequent criminal investigation. That is inevitable. It is also meaningless. We don't particularly care what is said if it is focused on Ralphie. Just do not make this a Miller versus the world thing. Support Ralphie and his recovery and return to the Millers, but do not paint your line as underdogs or being used by others," Buchanan said.

"Should I be offended?" Maya Higgins asked with a thin smile.

"By what?" Gordon Buchanan narrowed his eyes and looked at Maya Higgins. "I have only relayed what our leader and his advisors have already told you." Gordon Buchanan turned his head and showed a small earbud just visible in his ear. "None of this is coming from me."

Maya Higgins nodded.

"Distance became meaningless as soon as we discovered the lost plants of Boeing, Apple and Google were accessible," Vincent LaFleur said from the tinny speaker on Gordon Buchanan's phone.

"Do you worry about anything in that palace of yours Vincent?"

There was a hollow laugh on the other end of the phone.

Gordon Buchanan sat and studied Maya Higgins.

Ralphie listened to the conversation that was completely over his head.

"Dad? What are they talking about?" Ralphie asked his father.

"Business," Ralphie's father said.

Gordon Buchanan, his wife, and daughter listened as well.

Maya Higgins sat and twisted her signet ring on her finger.

"Gordo, that's it. Let Maya and the Millers ruminate on the deal," the head of the Innovators announced in the silence.

At that moment, there was an announcement that put the numerous security members on alert. Ralphie was the first to notice the hyper-alertness. He looked from the front of his home to the rear and noticed that all the enforcers were suddenly incredibly attentive.

"What's going on?" Macy asked, holding onto her brother.

"Think the suits are here," Benjamin Reynolds said.

"Ben, you're right," Maya Higgins said. "The Central Government flunkies have arrived," the Miller leader said.

In a few moments, the front door of Ralphie's home opened and in walked two men in suits. One of the men was thickly built and looked as if he was a bodybuilder. The other was a shorter, round-shouldered man with a short-cropped haircut.

The enforcers watched the pair as if two pit vipers had been released into the house. The two men smiled at the enforcers and then the others gathered in the living room. The pair showed ID badges that identified them as Central Government agents. Ralphie noted that they had earbuds in their ears like Gordon Buchanan.

"Miss Higgins, Mister Buchanan, Mister Reynolds," the bodybuilder said with a nod. "I am Chancellor Williams Granger, from the Central Office. We have been sent to request a meeting with Ralph Ellison Reynolds."

"Well, we are going to deny that request," Maya Higgins said with an emotionless smile. "He has just this hour returned to the compound and his parents. He is our hero. We will not let Central whisk him off to God knows where without our knowledge and approval." Higgins smiled. "I'm sure if you call Esther Fortune or whoever you report to and tell them that I am here and not allowing you to take Ralphie from the compound this whole thing will be ironed out."

Higgins bodyguard leaned in toward the leader and whispered something. Higgins listened, frowned, and looked from the two agents back to Buchanan and the others.

"We have the Pandemonium Committee on their way," Higgins said to Ralphie's father.

The two agents looked at each other with Higgins words. The enforcers did not move. Benjamin Reynolds placed a hand on Ralphie's shoulder. Missus Reynolds stepped closer and held onto her husband.

"What's going on?" Macy asked still holding onto Ralphie.

The front door opened and in walked three people. The most distinct of the three to enter was a tall man, rail thin, the color of a copper penny with a high forehead and thick eyebrows. He was dressed in a light blue collared shirt, no tie, black belt, and khaki trousers. On his feet were basketball sneakers. Beside him was the petite young woman, not five feet tall, with loose curls framing her bewitching eyes and angular face. She was dressed all in blue. In her ears hung blue California state map earrings. Around her neck was a blue lapis necklace. On one of her wrists was a dozen small lapis beads that made up her unique bracelet.

The third person to arrive with the other two was a thin faced man wearing glasses and a dark suit. He had a blue silk tie knotted beneath his white starched collared shirt. He was an average build, and nothing seemed distinctive about him. In his hand was a small notebook computer.

Behind the three entered four more enforcers. The living room was suddenly full of enforcers, dignitaries, government agents and government officials.

"I am Julius McCarthy, the director of the Pandemonium Challenge," the tall man said with an sly smile looking over the gathered faces. He focused on Ralphie. Finding him, he stepped forward.

Benjamin Reynolds pushed Ralphie behind him.

"I've come to welcome Ralphie back to the Remains," McCarthy said. He smiled broadly, stopping in front of Ralphie's father. "You must be the loving father, Benjamin O. Davis Reynolds. Proud father. Distant father. Busy with work at the family business," McCarthy said with a nod of his head.

Ralphie's father did not respond.

"Well, I wanted to be one of the first to welcome you back to the Remains," McCarthy said to Ralphie.

Ralphie eyed the tall and spidery McCarthy suspiciously. Although he was smiling and friendly Ralphie did not feel his smile or friendliness to be genuine. There was a forced nature to the smile and effort to say the right words.

"You and," McCarthy turned and noticed Ella Buchanan in the same home as Ralphie. "Ella Fitzgerald Buchanan? What a surprise to find you here," McCarthy said with a curl of the lip. "You and your family," the director paused, seeing Mister and Missus Buchanan in the living room of the Reynolds. McCarthy paused and nodded. He measured his words before speaking. "Gordon Parks Buchanan and his loving wife, Gail Buchanan. It is a true pleasure to see you here. It is refreshing to find Innovators here, in the Miller compound, in the home of a Miller, as you well know. This is a rarity."

"McCarthy," Maya Higgins said, bored with the tall director's theatrics. "Glad you have come here to welcome Ralphie back. What do you want?"

"Want? Want? Well, I would want everyone to have enjoyed the Twenty-Third Pandemonium Challenge as much as they enjoyed the last five challenges," McCarthy said.

"Well, we are not responsible for the Remains enjoyment," Higgins said, looking to her assistants and the enforcers.

McCarthy smiled a little broader.

"Well, you may not be responsible for the Remains enjoyment, but you and all the lines have agreed to the rules and regulations of the challenge. Or have you conveniently forgotten that?" McCarthy asked.

"I am well aware of our obligations," Higgins said.

McCarthy looked to Buchanan. The director stared at the Innovator. The Innovator gave a mirthless smile and held his gaze, unblinking.

That was the cue for Buchanan to climb to his feet.

"Is there anyone else coming?" Buchanan asked.

McCarthy only smiled in response.

"Gail, Ella, say goodbye. We are leaving," Gordon Buchanan announced. Ralphie and his father stood. Gordon Buchanan stepped to Ralphie's father and extended a hand. Ralphie's father gripped the hand of Gordon Buchanan and shook it. Ralphie watched as the two strong men, one a shrewd businessperson and the other a bull of a man that looked as if he could turn green and wreak havoc through the Central Government like the Incredible Hulk in the comic books, smiled at each other. There seemed to be a mutual respect between the two men.

"Ben, I wish that we had met under better conditions," Gordon Buchanan said. "Maybe, one day I'll invite you up and you can bring Mae and Ralphie and your daughter to play a few rounds of golf."

"I'd like that," Ralphie's father smiled.

"Maybe when this all blows over," Gordon Buchanan smiled. "It would be nice to have you by for no other reason than to have lunch with you and your fine family."

Benjamin Reynolds nodded. With that the conversation between the two powerful men concluded.

Gordon Buchanan led the exit. Gail said her goodbyes. Ella walked up to Ralphie and smiled.

"Guess Albert was wrong," Ella said. "Kind of was not expecting this but now that I think of it..." Ella paused at the door. "I suppose this is the only logical conclusion."

"How do you mean?" Ralphie asked.

"You're still the scapegoat. The question is how they spin this?"

Ralphie was left with that.

Ella was on the porch and beside her father as he spoke to the gathered news media. Buchanan was a gifted speaker. He did not stammer or pause. He seemed calm and cool as he made his statement to the Miller press. What was impressive was that he did not read from a sheet of paper. Ralphie nearly laughed at the idea. He realized that Buchanan was being fed information.

The question-and-answer portion of the Buchanan presser on the steps of Ralphie's home was not long but very pointed. The media wanted to hear from Ella. Gordon Buchanan refused.

"My daughter is my daughter. I love her deeply. I understood her request and after much soul searching, I agreed to her use of the enforcers and the helicopter to extricate anyone still alive on the island. She will not be subjected to questions or accusations by you or anyone. As I said, she is my daughter," Buchanan said, in conclusion.

With that the Buchanans exited the podium set up to answer questions.

From inside the house Ralphie watched as Ella walked down the stairs and to the waiting Range Rover SUVs.

"We are ready," said one of the enforcers.

Maya Higgins smiling, walked to the door and allowed her smile to spread even more on her face.

"Are you ready?" Maya Higgins asked.

Ralphie looked at his father. His mother was beside him. Macy was holding his left hand. His father exited the house and watched as the three Range Rover SUVs started up and moved away in formation. In less than a minute it was as if they had never been there.

"I would like to say a few things before Ralphie speaks," Ralphie's father said, raising his hand and the reporters listened, impatiently. As his father spoke Ralphie seemed to zone out all the noise, the words, the camera clicking and cameras filming. He scanned the crowd of reporters, camera people, and onlookers and it all fell away. There was Macy, still clinging to her brother. Ralphie looked at Macy and smiled. Macy smiled as her mother pulled her away so that Ralphie could speak.

His father stepped away from the podium and clapped his son on the shoulder.

"You got this," Benjamin Reynolds said.

From behind a sturdy dark blue and gold podium which had the hammer and pick emblem on it Ralphie stepped forward and tried to think what he was going to say. A pair of enforcers positioned themselves on either side of the podium, menacingly.

Ralphie looked down and found that the reporters' microphones and handheld recorders were on the podium. The camera operators and photographers took up positions to get the best shots. Suddenly, magically it seemed, there were twenty plus reporters gathered on the lawn of the Reynolds home.

"Okay, I just want to say that I am glad to be home," Ralphie said and suddenly he was choked up. The acknowledgement of being home hit him hard and Ralphie suddenly found himself on the verge of tears. He closed his eyes and tried to think of words but suddenly he was overwhelmed.

Ralphie stood at the podium trembling. He could hear his heart in his ears. His breathing was ragged.

"Excuse me, dear," Maya Higgins smiled a short and portly thing touching Ralphie on the arm and breaking his paralysis. The appearance of Maya Higgins caused a collective gasp from the reporters. Maya Higgins was Miller royalty if there ever was such a thing. She came from the loins of Sylvia and Charles Miller the original founders of the Miller compound. Ralphie was not sure if Maya was the first child of one of the founders who followed in the footsteps of their parents and took office in the Remains politic.

Higgins looked at Benjamin Reynolds. Ralphie's father stepped forward and directed his son away from the podium. Maya Higgins took her time at the podium. Her bodyguard stood to her right and scanned the audience.

"Good afternoon to you all," Maya Higgins smiled. Higgins smiled broadly. Dressed in her dark blue pants suit she looked out over the gathered media. Beside her was her personal bodyguard, Ralphie noted.

"I know that you don't want to talk to me. But as you can see little Ralphie is not ready for a grilling. We must give him and his family time. He has been through a lot. We are pleased to have our champion back, but we are not monsters. You can see that young Ralphie is still just overwhelmed with his return. Give him time." Higgins smiled. "We have decided that it is best for Ralphie and his family to say nothing at this time." She paused and looked out at the gathered press and cameras. "Give the family their privacy and time to decompress and we promise, when the time is right, we will make our local hero available for all the news media," the leader of the Millers smiled.

Standing next to Macy and his mother Ralphie looked at his father, confused. Next to his father, stood Julius McCarthy, pinning a PC23 lapel pin on his father's shirt. He handed Benjamin Reynolds a handful of lapel pins and smiled at Ralphie.

Julius McCarthy leaned in and smiled. "You are a little bit fragile right now and that is to be expected," the director said, pinning on a PC23 lapel pin on Ralphie's hoody. "We wanted you to speak and you did. It wasn't much but it was enough."

Chapter Seven.

Miller Therapy

Ralphie had been given a two-man enforcer squad to keep the media away. Two enforcers that Macy called: Thing One and Thing Two traded off watching Ralphie for the first month that Ralphie was in the Miller compound. Their real names were: 9448 and 5198 or Timothy and Thelonious. Ralphie had learned long ago that enforcers were just interchangeable cogs tasked with protecting and maintaining peace in the Remains. Unlike the Innovators private force Thing One and Two were assigned by the Central Government more as a safety precaution for the Remains and had no allegiance to the Millers or Ralphie.

To them, Ralphie understood, he was just a football that they protected and guarded against being snatched away. Or worst-case scenario, a raging bull that they needed to wrangle in case of emergency. They, Timothy and Thelonious, 9448 and 5198, didn't speak much. In the first month they might have said a dozen words.

The fifteen-year-old had met so many people the first couple of weeks after returning to the Miller compound that the names and faces blurred together. Yet there were four individuals that stood out in the handful of parties that Ralphie and his family attended with the Maya Higgins and the Miller elite. Maya Higgins, the unquestionable dynamo of the Millers, was the most galvanizing character that Ralphie met. Most distrusted the small and powerful woman. Always dressed impeccably Maya Higgins had the ability to suck the air out of the room when she entered.

"Ralphie, we, the Millers, are so proud of you," Miss Higgins said, taking pictures with Ralphie, his father and mother and of course Macy.

Miss Higgins walked Ralphie around the gathering of the Miller powerful. She introduced Ralphie to the compound leaders. Ralphie had heard the names but never been introduced to any before. His father knew most of the most important people in the Miller compound. It made sense as he was a powerful individual in the compound.

"Benjamin, I have a question for you," Maya Higgins said after introducing the compound planner. "How did you ever agree to Ralphie going to the challenge?"

"Well, Maya, it was an important time in Ralphie's mental and physical development," Benjamin O. Davis Reynolds said.

"Weren't you worried?"

"Of course, I was worried. Everyone is worried if they have skin in the game," Ralphie's father said.

There was the peanut-headed Oscar Finn, who wore a butter yellow suit jacket, blue collared silk shirt and matching blue trousers and pointed shoes. Oscar Finn was an elite member of the Miller compound and seemed to be playing a part. He was overly dramatic and extremely comfortable gesticulating about any and everything he discussed. Finn, Ralph learned, oversaw the education facilities in the Miller compound. Ralphie had seen Oscar Finn a few times but never spoken to him when he was at the Leathern Apron.

"Ralphie we are so proud of you and your bravery," Finn smiled and gently patted him on his shoulder with an unusual close and extended pat. "You have made us all so very proud."

The third person that Ralphie found distinctive was the man that Maya Higgins had suggested that Ralphie meet. During one of the parties Ralphie was introduced to Doctor Henry Dumas Greenwood. Doctor Greenwood was assigned to monitor Ralphie's re-introduction to the Remains. The doctor had not been the man that he had imagined. In Ralphie's mind, because of the recommendation of Maya Higgins, Ralphie had thought that he was going to be one of those ghoulish doctors that had secret plans to turn Ralphie into a Manchurian Candidate.

Doctor Henry Dumas Greenwood, was a friendly and jovial gap-toothed gray-haired man in his forties with a beer belly and after five minutes, proved to be nothing like what Ralphie expected. The doctor was friendly and attentive. He did not talk down to Ralphie despite his father and mother being close. Ralphie liked Doctor Greenwood because he acknowledged Ralphie and the possibility of Ralphie having some issues returning to the compound.

"I have been asked by the Pandemonium Committee and Sonia to check on Ralphie," Greenwood said to Ralphie's father. The two men shook hands and seemed friendly enough. Yet, there was a palpable tension between the two for some reason.

"What are you suggesting?" Benjamin Reynolds asked.

"Well, I suggest monitoring him pretty regularly, maybe two or three days a week," Greenwood admitted. Ralphie had listened. His father had been reluctant. His father, the rock, did not believe in psychologists or therapists.

"Are you thinking that Ralphie hasn't seen dead bodies?" Ralphie's father smiled. "I made him ID the dead we found in our excavations."

Ralphie nodded.

"Well, be aware, Mister Reynolds that your son has had a significant traumatic experience and may need some time to recover from that trauma," Doctor Henry Dumas Greenwood suggested.

"Ralphie just needs a little rest to get him back in the swing of things," Benjamin O. Davis Reynolds countered.

"Be that as it may, I have been asked to monitor your son's return to the Miller society. We are hoping that transition is seamless and without any false steps." Greenwood turned to Ralphie. "My role in your re-entry Ralphie is to pilot you back to the state of mind that you had prior to your participation in the challenge."

"Is that possible?"

"I believe it is attainable," Greenwood nodded. "It may take some time, but I do not see any reason that you, under my supervision, will not return to the pre-challenge Ralphie in a month."

Ralphie's father scoffed.

Greenwood nodded and turned to walk away. He stopped himself and turned back to add, "We look forward to seeing you this week. Remember Tuesday, Wednesday, and Thursday. The dates have been synchronized to all your devices per Miller leadership directives." Doctor Greenwood grinned and returned to the party.

Ralphie liked the gap-toothed doctor. Ralphie liked the feeling he got from him. He did not seem to be playing his abilities up for Ralphie's parents. It was not a sales pitch. Doctor Greenwood was concerned about Ralphie's return. He said something about trauma and recommended twenty-one days of low stress activities to allow Ralphie to acclimate to normal life.

Yet, it was the chance to sit and talk with the last Miller winner of the Pandemonium Challenge, Hannibal Nelson that had made what Doctor Henry Dumas Greenwood said seem reasonable.

Hannibal Nelson, twenty-seven years old, had appeared at one of the parties and those that knew of him were quick to take a picture and ask him to sign his comic book, created by one of the Miller compound comic book artists. The comic book was a collector's item and Hannibal Nelson made the comics rarer and rarer based on his attitude. He was not above destroying them in front of fans. He tore the comics up in front of fans. His destruction of comics had spawned another comic that had that exact moment of his destroying his own comic on the cover, another rarity.

The winner of the Thirteenth Pandemonium challenge was a long-limbed well-proportioned individual that might have looked handsome if he dragged a comb through his black curls that seemed more coils than curls. Hannibal Nelson had a scraggly beard that looked more patchwork than a beard. He was dressed in the blue coveralls of the workers of the compound but wearing deep brown suede Timberlands.

Ralphie had been informed that Nelson had been hired by the Miller leadership to try and explain the pitfalls of winning the challenge from his perspective. Hannibal Nelson was ten years removed from the challenge and still a celebrity in the compound and to all in the Remains.

"I won the Thirteenth Pandemonium Challenge," Hannibal explained picking at the fabric of the coveralls and looking down at Ralphie through his dark slits for eyes. Hannibal had a pointy chin and angular features that rose to his flat head. Between his thin dark eyes was a slightly crooked nose and full lips. Ralphie noted that Hannibal had a paper-thin scar on his left cheek that was only visible when he smiled.

"I'm glad you won the challenge," Hannibal declared. "I mean it, I have been the sole Y chromosome to represent for the line." Hannibal looked around nervously, and added, "It was a lot of pressure."

"But there was Harold Taylor," Ralphie said. Harold Washington Taylor had been the third person to claim the

Pandemonium Challenge and leave the island alive. He had been seventeen when he had entered the challenge, Ralphie recalled.

"He died a few years ago," Hannibal said sitting on a couch with Ralphie during a party and watching the goings on of the Miller elite rubbing elbows and showing their power.

The oldest living Pandemonium Challenge winner was Sojourner Truth Tucker. She had been seventeen when she entered. She was now thirty-three years old. There were rumors about her being an agoraphobe. Few saw her outside of her family.

The last Miller to win before Hannibal Nelson was Cleopatra Greer. She was thirty and reclusive and rarely seen in public. Cleopatra was reported living in one of the condominium towers all alone.

"Do you guys ever get together and talk?" Ralphie asked.

"The Pandemonium Committee is very particular about our time together," Hannibal Nelson said raising his chin in the direction of the Miller handler that was close to the pair. The tall and slender man dressed in a dark blue suit with a bright yellow belt and light blue collared shirt seemed to be just standing having a drink, but Ralphie noticed upon looking that he was not drinking but observing the conversation between Ralphie and Hannibal Nelson.

"Who is that?" Ralphie asked, confused.

"My handler," Hannibal Nelson sneered. "John Langston, he's my handler. I'm sure you have been assigned one or two, right?"

Ralphie nodded. He looked around the party and found Thing One standing near the bar, watching him and Hannibal.

"This is all very orchestrated," Hannibal breathed.

"Why?" Ralphie asked, tilting his head at the question.

Hannibal chuckled at the question. His eyes flitted from one sight to the next and back to Ralphie. The last Miller to win the Pandemonium Challenge before Ralphie shook his head. "You don't get it. We are the property of the Pandemonium Committee. We signed away our rights when we put our hands into the great machines and registered," Hannibal said his voice trembling as the volume rose and people near turned with his words.

John Langston took a step toward Hannibal. Hannibal seeing his handler step toward him instantly raised his hands in surrender.

"I'm okay," Hannibal pleaded. "I'm okay," he smiled, lowering his voice.

The handler stopped midstep and studied Hannibal Nelson for a long moment. His small eyes flitted from Hannibal to Ralphie and to the people around them. He nodded. The tall man dressed in the dark blue suit and light blue collared shirt raised an index finger. He stepped back and retrieved his drink, which he did not drink.

Hannibal Nelson looked back at Ralphie. He smiled. "I'm sorry, there are things that get me," he closed his eyes, for a second. "I didn't understand the challenge when I entered. I mean, I knew what was at stake and all, but I didn't understand everything that I would lose to win."

Ralphie narrowed his eyes at the agitated Nelson.

Hannibal changed to subject. "The reason they asked me to come and see you is that they need you to know that we're the ambassadors of the challenge. The survivors. They have important bullet points that they want you to say anytime you get a microphone or camera pushed into your face."

"Why did they ask you to tell me this?" Ralphie asked.

"I suppose because you know me," Hannibal Nelson said. "You know I've been where you are now."

Hannibal handed Ralphie an envelope with the Pandemonium Committee seal on it.

"I can't just talk," Ralphie asked.

"Not anymore," Hannibal Nelson reminded. "When you didn't die on that island, Ralphie you suddenly became a living symbol of hope for everyone in the Remains." Hannibal Nelson climbed to his feet.

"But you know how it is," Ralphie began.

"I can't say that I do," Hannibal Nelson said with a lifting of his hand. "I won the Thirteenth Pandemonium Challenge." He paused and Ralphie noticed that the man that stood in front of him was still troubled by the challenge that he had won. "What you had to do and what I had to do are as similar as football when it was first invented, and the bubble wrapped version that you probably remember." He smiled and Ralphie noted the scar across his chin that he had received from one of the challengers trying to slit his throat.

The Thirteenth Pandemonium Challenge was a horror themed event, Ralphie recalled. Everyone in that challenge was given weapons from horror movies. There were just a handful of guns. Everyone else had axes, chainsaws, butcher knives and whatnot.

"Do you have nightmares?" Ralphie asked.

"I thought they would go away," Hannibal Nelson confided with Ralphie. "I mean, you've heard time heals all wounds. Well, it doesn't. If you survive the challenge all those memories stick with you. We've done too much evil to sleep well at night."

Ralphie nodded. "I think that's why we get psychiatrists to talk to," Ralphie recalled.

"Yeah, be careful who you tell your secrets to, kid," Hannibal advised. "They might use that against you?"

"Use what against me?" Ralphie asked.

"Your fears," Hannibal said.

Ralphie understood that the challenge was physically tough but the more he talked to Hannibal Nelson the more he realized that the challenge was mentally tough as well.

*   *   *   *   *

Twenty-one days later Ralphie did his first unscheduled public interview that was not hand-picked by the Miller leadership. Macy, his younger sister, had arranged for her brother to talk in front of her class level at the education facility's auditorium. The sixty bright-eyed and adoring ten-and eleven-year-old students sat in the educational auditorium with hopes of taking pictures with the newest Pandemonium Champion.

Ralphie had been so nervous. His palms were sweating when he walked onto the stage with his little sister. Macy had a chair that she sat in and watched Ralphie speak. Ralphie had a speech ready. He simply read the speech to the crowd of faceless kids in the auditorium. At the end of his speech Ralphie felt as if he had just run a race. His throat was dry.

He reached for the water and Macy handed it to him. Ralphie smiled. He was grateful that Macy was on stage with him.

"Okay, here comes the fun part," Macy announced. "We got some questions from the class."

115

Questions? Ralphie recalled that Macy and he had practiced before. He knew he was going to be on the stage with his little sister answering questions from a group of younger students and their educators and instructors.

Macy oversaw gathering the handprinted questions for her brother. Ralphie picked the questions that he wanted to answer. Some of the questions Macy told the audience Ralphie chose not to answer. Ralphie sat in a chair on a bare stage with a microphone in front of him.

One of the Millers handlers assigned to Ralphie, Franklin Marshall Davis, a tow-headed man the color of amber dressed in a dark blue hoody, loose fitting jeans and dress boots stood watching from the side of the stage. He had a tablet notebook in his hand as Ralphie sat and adjusted the microphone. As far as Ralphie knew he was being recorded by the Miller handler.

Of course, Thing Two was there. Anytime Ralphie went out in public he had a Remains enforcer with him. The Pandemonium Committee had invested in Ralphie and thus felt he was valuable.

Macy handed her brother ten cards with writing on them.

"These are the good ones," Macy smiled. "The last one is up to you," his pixie-like sister smiled.

Ralphie nodded and scanned the first few 3"x5" cards and nodded again.

Ralphie cleared his throat. Ralphie read the first card. "So, do you feel that you are a better person after the challenge?" He paused. Ralphie twisted his thick lips, thinking.

"I have a tough dad. I have a loving mother. Everyday my mom and dad tell me to do my best. I hold onto that. I suppose that I am always trying to be a better person." Ralphie smiled. "I hope that I answered that question."

Ralphie read the next 3"x 5" card.

"Has it hit you that you survived?" Ralphie smiled after reading the card. He did not answer immediately. He looked out and into the audience. Ralphie shrugged his shoulders.

"I don't know," he admitted. "I mean, I know that I am not in the challenge. I know that I am off the island. I think that all the madness that was a part of the challenge is hard to shake off." He paused and looked down and at the 3"x5" card again and added, "I know that I am here, and I am thankful for that." Ralphie paused and looked out into the audience. "I hope that I answered that."

"Do you still love Bailey?" Ralphie read and smiled. Everywhere he went people asked that question repeatedly. He never knew how to answer it. He knew that he cared about Bailey. He might even go as far as to say that he had a strong like for the girl. But Ralphie could not say that he loved Bailey. The word seemed so big and encompassed so much for the fifteen-year-old who had never loved anyone before. Yet, in the back of his mind Ralphie was not opposed to the idea in anyway. If he was to admit loving someone then Bailey Beaumont was the best candidate to share that feeling. At least, that was Ralphie's thinking. So, Ralphie looked out at the kids the age of his younger sister and smiled embarrassingly.

"I know what you want me to say, but I can't say it. I was just trying to survive when I was on the island. I was struggling trying to figure out my feelings. I think that it hit me that I really liked her. I think everyone knows that. But I cannot say that I loved or love her. I mean, I haven't loved anyone outside of my family ever." Ralphie paused. "Sorry to not have a better answer."

Two more questions, Ralphie thought. He liked the next question. It allowed him to be a little political. It was the reason that the Miller handler appeared at every public event where Ralphie spoke. Ralphie knew the party line.

So, when he read the 3"x 5" card he did not have to really think about the answer. He had been told what to say anytime the Innovators or the First Gens lines were mentioned.

"Do you feel cheated because the Innovators interfered?" Ralphie smiled at the question. "I must admit that the circumstances that I found myself in were difficult and dangerous. I cannot say exactly how I felt at that exact moment. So much happened and... I am simply glad to be alive and back amongst the Millers that I know and love. I don't know. The challenge is unpredictable. No one knows how it will end once it begins. At the end it was unexpected and very much a Pandemonium Challenge."

Ralphie moved to the next 3"x 5" card and read it silently. He had told Macy that he did not want to answer questions about his friends being flatlined or terming anyone. Those questions triggered something in Ralphie that he was still battling day-to-day.

Yet, he paused and decided to test the waters. In his mind, Ralphie thought, "Macy loves me." She had no intention of triggering Ralphie. This question was easy.

Macy looked at her brother cautiously. The tow-headed Miller handler noticing the unexpected pause turned and studied Ralphie. Ralphie paused with the card in his hand.

"You okay, Ralphie?" Macy asked.

Ralphie nodded. He usually avoided the questions about the challenge, Ralphie thought absently but Macy had slipped it in. So, the question was not supposed to be too triggering.

Ralphie read the question. "Who was the hardest person you faced?"

Ralphie stopped. He took a deep breath. "I usually don't answer these types of questions. I mean, it hasn't been that long ago. The hurt is still fresh. But I'm going to try. So, bear with me." Ralphie paused and Macy and the tow-headed handler seemed ready to rush to Ralphie's side if he broke down or could not continue. "I think—I think," Ralphie was floundering. He paused.

Ralphie did not like to linger on the past. There was just so many things that he could not fix in the past. In fifteen years of life Ralphie had seen more death than most Millers in the compound. Fifty challengers had laid down their lives in the Twenty-Third Pandemonium Challenge. Only Ralphie, Bailey and Ella Buchanan had survived.

"Who was the hardest person you faced?" His voice was tremulous. He felt his chest tighten. He looked down and saw that his hand was balled into a fist.

Ralphie just shook his head. Macy stood up. Franklin Marshall Davis stepped on stage and quickly moved to Ralphie and Macy.

The Master of Ceremony seeing the three on stage climbed to his feet and mounted the stage. He rushed to the closest microphone and announced to the gathered: "That will conclude our presentation. Let's give Ralph Ellison Reynolds and Macy Gray Reynolds a round of applause for coming today and teaching us what it takes to be a winner."

The Miller minder was at Ralphie's side and escorting him and Macy to the side exit. Ralphie moved robotically with Macy by his side. Before the three reached the side exit Thing Two was by their side.

"You'll be okay, kid," Franklin Davis explained. "I thought that this was a little too much for you, but no one listens to me. I'm just a trained professional," the man explained to Ralphie and Macy once outside of the school auditorium.

"Ralphie, you did real good," Macy said apologetically. "I didn't think that the last question was so bad."

"That's the problem," Ralphie barked back to his younger sister stopping and breaking the grip of the minder. His hand was balled into a fist as he turned on Macy. "No one thinks that any of the questions they ask me are too bad," Ralphie said in a hiss. "No one knows the nightmares I have."

Instantly Thing Two was in front of Ralphie and twisting his raised hand behind him and pushing Ralphie along. Ralphie resisted and then surrendered. The tow-headed Miller handler stopped just long enough to make sure that the enforcer had control of Ralphie.

"It's okay," the Miller minder tried to calm the situation between Macy and Ralphie, who had gone back to his quiet and brooding self. Davis pushed the shocked and frightened Macy forward and ahead of the retreating group.

"We're coming to you," the Miller handler said as he pushed Macy forward. The pair moved a little haltingly along the side of the auditorium. Straight ahead of them was the second enforcer assigned to Ralphie, thanks to Maya Higgins.

The group turned the corner of the building and came upon a silver transport. As soon as the second enforcer saw Ralphie and Macy he was in motion. The two Miller enforcers wordlessly moved prepared for any incident.

"We got him," one of the enforcers said into the air.

The tow-headed minder focused on Macy.

"Are you okay?"

Macy nodded.

"He wouldn't have hurt you," the minder said with a smile.

"I know," Macy said, visibly shaken.

One of the enforcers, Thing One, quickly climbed into the front seat of the SUV assigned to take Ralphie to every Miller approved event. The transport moved away from the curb. There was little to no conversation in the vehicle as the handlers drove directly to Doctor Greenwood's office.

"So, Ralphie, it seems as if you pushed a little too hard," the minder said with an emotionless grin. He smiled, knowingly.

Ralphie did not speak. Thing Two sat between Macy and Ralphie, watching the sulking teen. Macy and Ralphie looked at each other, mouthed words, and made hand signals but did not speak aloud.

"We're heading to Greenwood's office," the minder said to the driver.

The transport pulled away from the curb and in ten minutes they were pulling up in front of the offices of Doctor Henry Dumas Greenwood. The gray-haired man was standing in front of his office as the SUV rolled to a stop.

The Miller handler climbed out of the transport and opened the door for Ralphie. Ralphie climbed out of the vehicle and Thing Two and the minder followed. The minder and Doctor Greenwood along with Macy and one of the enforcers walked into the glass and steel office of Doctor Greenwood. Sitting at a glass reception desk was a girl not much older than Ralphie. She had a broad smile beneath her broad sable nose which divided her almond shaped dark eyes. Her hair was braided and wrapped into a bun atop her head. Ralphie noted that the receptionist did not have earrings, which was unusual in the Miller compound.

In her one ear was a visible earbud that she tapped and used to connect people in the office.

"Tabatha," Doctor Greenwood said as he passed with Ralphie in tow, "Contact Maya and tell her that she might want to slow the re-entry of Ralphie a tick."

Ralphie watched as Tabatha tapped her ear and typed on the glass tabletop in front of her. There was no visible keyboard.

Once inside of the office of Doctor Henry Dumas Greenwood Ralphie sat with the tow-headed handler just behind Ralphie and out of the direct eyesight of the Doctor. Ralphie tried to think over what had happened at the presentation and caused his outburst afterwards.

"Is Macy okay?" Ralphie asked, shaken.

"She's scared, that's all," the Miller minder announced from behind Ralphie, leaning against the wall and ready for anything. "She'll be fine. She understands that you are a little stressed."

"I wouldn't have hurt her," Ralphie said guiltily.

Doctor Greenwood sat down in his chair across from the couch where Ralphie sat. "It's quite all right Ralphie," the doctor stated. "That is why I have Franklin and Thelonious or Thomas with you." The doctor smiled easily. Ralphie looked at the Miller doctor and nodded.

"We have seen this behavior happen before," Doctor Greenwood said as a matter of fact. "I was surprised that it took this long for you to display aberrant behavior. I mean, it is just one of a multitude of ways that you are attempting to cope with what you experienced." Greenwood adjusted his glasses and studied Ralphie for a moment. He sat back in his chair. "The Pandemonium Committee advises that we give you no less than twenty-one days to recover before any public events." He paused. "Sometimes we can start earlier. I advised against this first endeavor." Greenwood picked up his notebook and pen next to his chair and opened it silently. "You've been through a literal war. The veterans that returned from foreign wars suffered similar trauma but thanks to a better understanding of the brain and mental and medical advancements we have a better understanding of how the mind heals itself after those traumatic situations."

"So, what now," Ralphie said, his head in his hands.

"Well, we take a walk and rethink a plan for you to heal," Doctor Greenwood said.

Chapter Eight.

The Interweb

It had been three weeks since Ralphie had his incident. Everyone was on edge. Macy had forgiven Ralphie. Ralphie's father, always his taciturn self, had seemed to hover around the house a little more than usual, while his mother checked on Ralphie more often than before.

The Central Government enforcers, Thelonious, or Timothy, continued to monitor Ralphie whenever he went anywhere. His minder, Franklin Marshall Davis, was always around and checking on Ralphie. Ralphie told everyone he felt better, not as jittery.

How Ralphie had gotten to that "better" was not a mystery. After the incident he had been seeing Greenwood more often and making incredible progress. Nearly a month after he threatened his siter Greenwood and most seemed to agree that Ralphie had turned the corner. His psychological sessions were an essential element of his methodic reintegration to the Miller compound.

Three days a week Ralphie went to see Henry Dumas Greenwood, his psychologist, and talked. Greenwood listened. Yet, it was Ralphie's almost daily check ins with Ella that helped him feel normal.

He did not feel as anxious or jittery as he had when he first returned to the Miller compound thanks to Ella. The fifteen-year-old wondered why he had not been jittery when he was at the Innovator compound? Maybe, it was just because he was healing, but as he improved at the Buchanans he had never lashed out there. It was an odd observation. It would be a question that he needed to ask Doctor Greenwood.

Ralphie looked forward to his meetings with Doctor Greenwood. Initially, he had thought that the quiet man was going to crack his head open like a walnut and try and figure out what was wrong. Ralphie had his misgivings but thankfully, like many things that Ralphie feared, those fears were misplaced.

Doctor Greenwood had calmly talked and listened to Ralphie and tried to untie the mass of knots that triggered the teen.

Of course, most of the knotted triggers were created from his participation in the challenge. Those knots, what Doctor Henry Dumas Greenwood called: anxiety strings, were the cause of Ralphie's manic behavior.

"Is that normal?"

"Normal? Abnormal? Everyone copes with stress in different ways," Greenwood said. "Those coping mechanisms do not crop up and appear to many as hurtful or dangerous. Now, there are some mechanisms that are employed which are dangerous to others. We are trying to trace those anxiety strings back and find a way to create alternative coping mechanisms, for you, if needed."

Ralphie asked Doctor Greenwood after 33 days (about 1 month): "How am I doing?"

"You are doing well, Ralphie," Doctor Greenwood reassured. "Your progress is progressive."

When not meeting with Greenwood, Franklin, the minder, was the unofficial assistant and kept Ralphie on-time to meetings. Thelonious or Thomas, Ralphie never could tell the difference between his enforcers, walked Ralphie to the SUV and they drove Ralphie to his daily meetings.

"We have a meeting in the morning with the Miller compound Planning and Building department about your future dedication. There is talk of possibly Ralph Ellison Reynolds Boulevard," Franklin said with a smile. "After that meeting you are scheduled for a lunch with the Public Works director. A very big deal. We are trying to commission a mural or possible statue. After lunch you are scheduled to meet with the Miller Beautification Committee and after that a photo shoot with the Miller Youth Council," Henry Dumas Franklin said.

After a day of meeting and listening to compound officials spit balling ideas of immortalizing Ralphie in the compound, Ralphie climbed out of the SUV and headed to the front of his house. At the front door stood one of the enforcers. Ralphie saluted the enforcer and the mirthless enforcer silently watched as Ralphie entered his home. Thankfully, there were no enforcers needed inside of the Reynolds home.

Mae Reynolds, the mother of Ralphie and Macy, refused to have armed men or women in her home, in general.

"Stay outside," Missus Reynolds said. "If there is an emergency, we all know how to press the panic button. Or we can scream."

So, after a long day of meetings Ralphie looked forward to being home with just his family. Closing the front door Ralphie heard the TV playing. There was the distinct light titter of his sister and movement in the house. As Ralphie entered the living room he found Macy seated on the couch next to her father watching a cartoon video on the computer monitor over the fireplace.

"You are putting in banker's hours," his father said, craning his head to see Ralphie.

"Ralphie, come watch Afro Samurai with me and dad," Macy said, with a big smile on her face.

Ralphie glanced at the monitor's screen and watched the strange world of swords, guns and kimonos, cell phones and cybernetic parts. He smiled at the mash-up of a cyberpunk world and a Black samurai seeking revenge for some reason.

Ralphie made his way toward the couch where Macy and his father sat. From the kitchen emerged his mother.

"Are you hungry?" His mother asked.

Macy perked up with the question. Ralphie smiled.

"Go wash up," his mother announced. "We'll eat in about ten or fifteen minutes."

Ralphie turned around and headed toward the stairs.

"Go on, Macy," his father said.

Ralphie did not look back. He just mounted the stairs to the second floor. Ralphie was halfway up the stairs when the compact brown rocket zipped past him and skidded to a stop at the top of the stairs and smiled at Ralphie mischievously and ran toward the bathroom. Ralphie continued to the bathroom. As Ralphie reached the bathroom Macy shouldered past her big brother. Ralphie tried to avoid his sister, but she bounced against him, and he grabbed Macy just long enough to have her wiggle out of his grasp. Macy smiled broadly and pushed past him.

"Sorry Ralphie," Macy said with a devilish smile, skidding into the bathroom and turning on the faucets in one motion. She grabbed the soap dispenser and squirted the measured cleanser into her small palms. In less than a minute Macy had lathered, rinsed, and was exiting the bathroom.

"All right," Ralphie said and for a moment he felt like he had turned the corner and could see his life, pre-challenge in view. He was not all jagged.

"Hurry up, Ralphie, think mom got us strawberry cheesecake for dessert," Macy said.

Ralphie walked into the bathroom and prepared to wash his hands. Ralphie froze in front of the mirror. He seemed mesmerized by the strange face that looked back at him from the glass. There in the mirror stood a chocolate brown boy with a short curly Afro, with a tight fade.

The boy in the mirror had apple cheeks, full lips, thin eyebrows, and dark brown eyes. Ralphie leaned closer and noted that the boy on the other side of the glass had an inch-long scar through his left eyebrow.

Ralphie smiled and shook his head. He looked back and toward his room on the other side of the bathroom. He thought that in the month and a half that he had been back in the compound he had not turned on his computer or checked his email.

He had texted Ella daily, but nothing lengthy or important. The Interweb was where Ralphie might write a letter to someone. If he wanted to find someone or thing it was through the Interweb. The teen realized that all the information of the Remains resided on the Interweb. If Ralphie wanted to know what was going on in the other compounds it was only accessible through the Interweb.

"Ralphie, hurry up, we're waiting on you," Macy yelled and broke his train of thought. He washed his hands and went downstairs to dinner.

Dinner consisted of a salad that was mostly lettuce and cucumbers and cherry tomatoes. His mother had made cornbread. Ralphie loved his mother's hot water cornbread. The main meal was fried chicken, string beans, yams and macaroni and cheese.

Ralphie ate and found that the meal was rich and filling. It satiated his hunger, but the light conversation and friendly family environment seemed more filling than the food. Strawberry cheesecake was the dessert. It was a delight to everyone.

The food and plates were slowly cleared away. Ralphie helped remove and wash the dishes. Ralphie found himself not wanting to leave the comfort of his family kitchen. Washing the dishes and listening to his mother and father talking about their day was like music. Macy dropped off the dishes and wiped off the counters. Ralphie smiled at the sounds and rhythm of his family. Finishing the dishes Ralphie sat at the kitchen island and watched his family for a moment.

He watched as Macy and his father sat in the living room under the watchful and unmoving eye of the entertainment monitor. His mother had just popped a bowl of popcorn. She was headed to the living room when she noticed Ralphie at the kitchen island.

Mae Reynolds tilted her head and studied her son. His mother stifled a smile. She stepped toward Ralphie with the freshly made bowl of popcorn. Simultaneously, Macy climbed to her feet and headed toward the bowl of popcorn. Ralphie could not help but shake his head at his nine-year-old sister and her uncanny ability to sniff out fresh popcorn.

"You look like you aren't going to hang with us," his mother said standing on the edge of the kitchen. She looked disappointed.

Ralphie lowered his eyes. Macy upon hearing those words looked at Ralphie.

"You're not going to hang out?" Macy asked.

"Think we're going to watch the Wiz," his father announced from the living room.

"I'll pass," Ralphie smiled. "Think I'm going to my room and see what's on the Interweb."

"Be careful," his mother warned.

"I know," Ralphie replied.

"We are censoring the email," Ralphie's father noted.

Since Ralphie had been back in the Miller compound he learned that the Central Government were none too happy with his return. There were reports, he heard, of groups in the Remains that were seeking vengeance against Ralphie for his return to the Remains.

The fringe groups of Trads, First and Second Gens, Boomers and some Poppies are under watch by most of the Miller enforcement teams," one of the handlers had told his father.

"We are monitoring the sore losers in our own compound," the other handler said. "There are always those that blame our own for the loss of our own despite seeing it on screen."

"So, Ralphie needs to be protected from everyone?" Ralphie's father asked.

"Everyone seems to have an interest in silencing Ralphie," the handler said.

Ralphie recalled all this as he headed up to his bedroom, a target in the Central Government.

"Well, the Miller IT team is monitoring your email," his father said. "So, don't bother with that. You know to steer away from the Pandemonium Challenge website."

"I know," Ralphie nodded.

"Be careful, you have made so much progress," his mother pointed out.

Ralphie smiled and walked to the stairs.

Before he could climb the stairs there was a message alert on his forearm. He had avoided messages in general for the last twenty plus days. As he walked up the stairs he looked down and smiled at the name that popped up as the sender.

The message was from Ella. It was short and sweet.

"Contact me. ASAP."

Ralphie looked back, down the stairs, and seeing no one following continued to the second floor. He walked to his bedroom and once inside closed his bedroom door. He sat at his desk and powered up his computer. There was a fingerprint scan and retinal scan that unlocked his computer.

"Welcome Ralphie," appeared on the monitor's screen.

"Contact Ella," Ralphie said into the air.

On screen appeared the message window of Ella Fitzgerald Buchanan. The window was gray for about thirty seconds. Then, in the window frame, on screen, appeared Ella.

"Ralphie," Ella smiled, her big eyes flitted left and right. "You hear? We're going to court."

"What?"

"Ralphie, don't say meaningless stuff. Keep up," Ella scolded. Ralphie stared at Ella weighing if he should say something mean. He shook the idea from his head.

"For what?"

"Come on Ralphie," Ella laughed. "We knew this day was coming. Bailey is much improved. You're looking... okay. 50/50. At least you're up and speaking. Me, well, I am no less worse for wear."

"Worse for wear?" Ralphie asked with a wry smile. Ella, Ralphie wanted to point out, you were in the challenge for thirty hours?

"What are you recovering from?" Ralphie asked instead.

"I have a therapist that I see every day," Ella said, pouting.

"So do I," Ralphie said. "Well, not every day."

"Are you trying to one up me?" Ella asked, pouting.

"Okay, what are we going to court for?" Ralphie asked, changing the subject.

"Ralphie, you're not that thick," Ella said.

"Ella," Ralphie said feeling his patience growing thin.

"Well, you know that the Pandemonium Committee says we screwed up billions of dollars in credits with our stunt."

Our stunt? Ralphie wanted to say something then and there and point out that he nor Bailey had asked for Ella or her Innovator enforcers to save either of them. Ella and the Innovators had taken it upon themselves to save them. Yet, as he thought this Ralphie also knew that the Central Government was controlled by the Innovators. There was little chance that the Pandemonium Committee was going to punish the incredibly powerful and connected Innovators.

"Ralphie, you look worried," Ella said.

"You look excited," Ralphie decided. He tried to smile, suddenly unsure what would be the purpose of a trial.

"I can't say that I'm not excited. I'm just looking forward to flipping the switch on the Pandemonium Challenge."

"Ella, I don't see this ending with us winning," Ralphie noted.

"I don't see it with us not winning," Ella retorted.

Chapter Nine.

Hutchinson, Williams, and Wood

Three days later Ralphie and his family met Kendrick Lamar Hutchinson. He was a dapper black man that looked strikingly like the old Hollywood actor Denzel Washington. He, that first meeting, was dressed in a dark blue checkered three-piece suit. On his pinky was a gold ring with a strange symbol on it that Ralphie could not place.

Next to him sat the tall and dour looking Andre 3000 Williams. Williams had the body of one of the towering giants that had been professional basketball players long ago. Dressed in a muted green suit with a starched white collared shirt and green print silk tie the man's hands seemed three times bigger than Ralphie's. Williams stood seven feet tall and easily weighed three hundred pounds. He had cold eyes and a salt and pepper moustache and goatee.

The third member of the Miller legal team was Kevin Hart Wood. Wood was the youngest of the three. He was a clean-shaven, square chinned individual. Wood was dressed in a dark gray suit.

"We have been tasked with representing you, Ralphie," Andre Williams said from the far side of the highly polished wooden conference table. Ralphie did not speak. He simply sat sandwiched between his father and mother with Macy closest to his mother. In the corner was Thelonious or Thomas observing the whole affair.

A few minutes after the lawyers had begun to talk in walked Maya Higgins and a spectacled man and a short and chubby woman. Maya Higgins looked around the table and sat at an open seat. The man wearing the round glasses hesitated and gestured for the chubby woman dressed in a sea green dress with yellow and blue checked lines running through it. She nodded and sat next to the undisputed leader of the Millers.

"Sorry for my lateness," Maya Higgins smiled and Ralphie felt his skin crawl upon seeing the insincere woman show her teeth. He looked from Maya Higgins and to Kevin Wood. Kevin Wood seeing that Ralphie was looking at him continued.

"We do not expect this to last too long," Kevin Hart Wood nodded.

"This is an opening salvo, an inquiry really," Andre 3000 Williams mentioned. "They are just probing and seeing how the Remains feels about the unexpected end of the Twenty-Third Pandemonium Challenge."

Ralphie studied Andre Williams in his green suit. He was the flashy one of the three. Ralphie imagined he would be the one to talk the most.

"You see, the Remains is split as to who they blame for the end of the challenge," Kendrick Hutchinson said.

"But I didn't have any--" Ralphie began only to be cut off.

"We know all that, Ralphie, but we also know that this is a publicity stunt for the Pandemonium Committee," Williams said with a smooth smile.

"How?" Ralphie's father asked, suddenly skeptical.

"Well, Mister Reynolds, the research seems to suggest that with the end of the Twenty-Third Pandemonium Challenge the Pandemonium Committee did not have a significant loss of any real money. No one predicted the finish. No one bet on Ralphie or Bailey to both survive," Kendrick Hutchinson said, pausing and thinking. "So, though this seems like a bad situation we are actually in the driver's seat on the negotiations."

"How?" Ralphie's father asked again, confused.

"Well, the committee has not published their records yet. They are required to publish their records every quarter. They are stalling," Kevin Wood offered.

"We believe that they were playing on the heart strings of the Remains and hoping against hope that their numbers were wrong," Andre Williams said. "Let me be clear. The unexpected end of the Twenty-Third Pandemonium Challenge was box office. The Pandemonium Committee usually pays out ten or twenty million credits each year. This year, because of your situation they did pay the usual six-day averages, but they did not have to pay out anyone for the last day. No one had an Innovator flying in and saving you and the First Gen. More importantly, no one had the Innovator coming back to the challenge. For the committee it was a win-win situation. No pay out. No problem. They may grouse and grumble, but they are happy that the challenge ended the way it did."

"But the rumors are that they loss significant amounts of money that last day," Benjamin O. Davis Reynolds said next to his son. "If they didn't lose, then why are they trying to scapegoat Ralphie?" his father asked, pointedly.

"They are playing the long game here," Wood said.

"They need to hang this debacle on someone. They don't want to take the blame. They most certainly cannot say anything bad about the Makers. The Makers influence most of the Central Government. So, they either point a finger at Ralphie or they point one at the First Gen girl," Williams said. He paused, for dramatic effect. "You know that they cannot blame the girl who was trapped beneath a building that Ralphie brought down upon her. So, they are going to put on a show."

"They have to blame Ralphie for the outcome," Wood said with a smirk.

"They are going to say that Ralphie should have killed the First Gen when he could have," Hutchinson said.

"The perfect time to do that would have been after the building collapsed," Wood said.

"Or he should have left her to die, they will say. It's all a bunch of malarkey. Horse hooey," Hutchinson said.

Ralphie and his parents looked at each other. Macy was listening but more interested in the puzzle book she had brought from home than the conversation.

"So, the way we see it we show up ready for war. They will try and intimidate us and make Ralphie out to be the bad guy here. We know that it's all a big bluff," Wood said.

"Based on our straw polls," Hutchinson said, with a nod. "They don't have the public support right now." Hutchinson paused.

"Based on our research, before the final boiled down to Ralphie, the First Gen and that crazy Trad showed up, Ralphie was neck and neck with the First Gen in popularity and wagering. The Remains were leaning on you and the First Gen icing each other," Williams said with a shrug of his shoulders.

"What? Really?" Ralphie said, surprised by the information.

"Yeah, there was a whole hope for a face-off between you and the First Gen. Most in the Remains wanted the Trad to be bumped off. She was too much of a threat to the whole dark Romeo and Juliet feeling they were getting from the challenge," Woods said.

"That's sick," Ralphie said, disgusted.

"It's sick or wicked or whatever. It's data. It's tangible and demonstrable," Hutchinson said. "We are slapping it on a poster board and preparing a display that will leave the committee speechless."

"You think this is going to work?" Benjamin Reynolds asked.

"Well, Mister Reynolds, the truth here is quite simple. They are not going to throw the Innovator in jail. They will be a little leery to pull the tail of the dog with deep pockets. I doubt they are willing to pile on the little girl that nearly died. So, they decide to play tough and all we do is point out that Ralphie didn't pull out his cellphone and dial up a helicopter. He was a victim in the challenge."

Maya Higgins stood up. "We cannot throw the Innovators under the bus," the Millers leader said.

"What? Why?" Wood asked.

"They are off limits. We are working with them," Higgins said, looking at the lawyers.

The lawyers looked at Higgins and nodded.

"What about the First Gen girl?"

"Well, that is an issue, but the way we see it if Ralphie had or had not found and freed her she would have died of her injuries," Hutchinson said. He looked at Ralphie and his family. "Again, not Ralphie's fault. He can be human. He can be vulnerable. Hell, he told the Remains he loved the girl."

Ralphie opened and closed his mouth. He knew he had not said that he loved Bailey. He had intended on saying it, but never really said it.

*　　*　　*　　*　　*

That following Thursday Ralphie and his family, including Henry Dumas Franklin, Thelonious and Timothy headed to the governmental center of the Central Government and the Remains

132

seat of justice. The 400 acres (about half the area of Central Park in New York City) of what had once been a zoo bordering the hills of the forbidden zone that were now guarded by enforcers.

Ralphie had dressed and wore the same suit that his father had gotten him for the line celebration before the challenge. Macy was wearing a white and blue dress. Her hair was in Afro puffs. She looked like Minnie Mouse if Minnie Mouse were a coffee brown nine-year-old girl when she was not scowling. Ralphie was surprised to see that Macy had two Tanzanite stud earrings in her ear lobes.

"Are you ready?" His mother asked.

Ralphie looked up and into the coffee brown face of his mother. He loved her high cheekbones and almond shaped eyes. There was a redness on her cheeks that suggested that Ralphie's mother was not just African American, but Ralphie knew that no one back in the Disjointed Sovereign Corporate States was just African American. The bloodlines had crossed and crisscrossed decades, centuries ago and left those that remained a math problem of genealogies.

His mother had her hair pulled up and away from her small shoulders. Her naturally curly black hair was swept up and into a bun of loose black curls that looked a little like curly noodles or a miniature curly explosion. She was dressed in a light blue and white dress that fell just below her knees.

Ralphie nodded to his mother and headed downstairs.

At the door stood his father and the two blocks of stone assigned to protect him. His father was dressed in a suit that Ralphie had seen him wear to important business meetings. He had a starched white collared shirt and dark blue silk tie around his bullish neck.

The six, including the two Miller handlers, headed to the four waiting Cadillac Escalade SUVs provided by the Miller government. Four drivers waited with only two open doors for the passengers on the sidewalk side of the house. The handlers ushered Ralphie and his father to the second SUV. Thelonious climbed in the passenger seat of the SUV after the two sat in the rear of the transport.

Behind the second SUV in climbed Macy and her mother. The first SUV was the lead. The last SUV was the rear guard.

The SUV convoy took off and weaved through the streets of the Miller compound. Once on the main drag of the compound the trip to the Central Government governmental buildings took about fifteen minutes.

The governmental island did not allow vehicles inside. Of course, there were exceptions. The SUV convoy was ushered in, and the convoy was directed to park in front of the judicial building.

"Ralphie, this is not supposed to be a circus, but sometimes things get out of hand," Benjamin Reynolds said.

"Should I be worried?"

Ralphie's father smiled and put his arm around his son's shoulder. Ralphie moved and found a stability beside his father. By Ralphie's side was Macy and his mother. His mother held his hand. Macy held onto her mother as the family moved toward the waiting cameras, people and signs of protesters, led by Ralphie's protectors. Henry Dumas Franklin was waiting and smiled and joined the group as they walked toward the judicial building's entrance.

The people lined up behind stanchions looked as if they were going to a concert instead of a hearing. There were easily two hundred faces screaming and fingers pointing at Ralphie and his family as he approached. Ralphie read the protest signs and was a little shocked. There were signs with a giant rat on it and Ralphie's name above it. There were also signs that read: "Cheater." "Loser" was a sign Ralphie saw, but the most disturbing was "Blood On Your Hands." "Murderer" in big red letters unsettled Ralphie.

Henry Dumas Franklin, Timothy and Thelonious flanked the family as they approached the trio of lawyers dressed in dark suits. Hutchinson, Williams, and Wood were standing waiting for the family.

"No trouble getting here?" Wood asked extending a hand.

"No trouble," Benjamin Reynolds said grabbing Wood's hand and giving him a hug and back slap. Ralphie watched as his father shook hands with the two other lawyers and each patted the other on the back. It was a Miller ritual.

Timothy and Thelonious watched the crowd, even though the family was fifty feet away from the people being held back by stanchions and enforcers. Macy holding hands with her mother slipped out of her grip and grabbed Ralphie's hand. Ralphie smiled at his sister's gentle touch.

"Ralphie, this is something? Isn't it?" The nine-year-old asked looking at all the people gathered outside of the Central Government building. As they waited for the lawyers to direct them inside the building Ralphie noticed a few signs in support of him. He instinctually smiled seeing: "Go Ralphie Go!" His smile grew a little bigger seeing another sign that read: Team Ralphie.

Ralphie smiled and nodded to Macy. Despite all that was going on, Ralphie found himself smiling at the sight of his little sister trying to protect him in her own way.

"How come all these people came today?" Macy asked.

"I'm not too sure," Ralphie admitted. "I suppose they all want to hear what happened on the island."

As Ralphie spoke Wood, dressed in a dark blue green suit stepped forward. The lawyer reached out and put a hand on Ralphie's shoulder.

"Remember Ralphie, only answer what they ask. Nothing more," Wood advised.

Ralphie nodded.

"We are going to be the heavies here," Hutchinson said. "We are going to use this hearing to bring to light lingering questions about the challenge many want answers to," the lawyer said.

The Central Government judicial courtroom was reminiscent of a city hall of the past. The building resembled a rectangular wedding cake. The building consisted of three tiers. The foundation was the bottom tier and was three stories tall. It held the mayor's office, the city council chamber, hearing rooms and a police station with a firing range in the basement. Above the foundation was the thinner second tier that was a ten-story office building. At the top tier was a 36-cell jail with an outdoor yard. On the top of the wedding cake building was a clock tower.

The three attorneys led the family into the already crowded hearing room. In the already packed room were two floors brimming with all the lines of the Remains. On the first floor, where Ralphie and the attorneys would sit at the main table were four chairs. A microphone sat in front of each seat.

"Remember that the council is trying to score points with the lines and the Pandemonium Committee," Andre Williams said dressed in blue checked suit.

Ralphie and his father walked down the narrow aisle to the extremely long table where the attorneys were seated. There was a long conference table which had a tented name tag. Ralphie sat between the attorneys.

Ralphie noticed as his father peeled off and sat behind him with his mother and baby sister the size of the crowd on the first floor of the judicial building. In front of the single table was an arch where photographers were jockeying for position on the floor. Behind the photographers were two desks that were reserved for the two hearing recorders. Behind the recorders were the dark wood panel that protected the Remains council. There were seven men and women with nameplates in front of each.

Each name represented a member of the seven lines of the Remains. The Innovator seat was held by a woman with a high forehead, dark arched eyebrows, round eyes, a straight nose, and full lips by the name of Phillis Wheatley Childress. The First Gen, next to the Innovator, who sat in the Remains council courtroom was a nappy headed man the color of burnt sienna with a perpetual opened mouth expression on his dull face. He sat dressed in a high collared yellow jacket. The dull faced man was George Clinton Palmer.

The Second Gen seating next to the First Gen, which was surprising based on the dislike of the lines, was Toni Morrison Powell, a plump and apple cheeked woman with long eyelashes and a round nose. The Miller seat, next to Toni Morrison Powell, was held by Andrew Young Redmond. Ralphie had met Redmond several times since his return from the challenge. Redmond was a mahogany brown man with a rugged look and muscled frame. The Poppies seat was held by Jacob Lawrence Butler. Butler was wearing rectangular glasses and had a well-trimmed Van Dyke on his round face.

The Boomers seat was held by the burly and powerfully built George Jackson Charles. Charles looked like he should be able to pull up stumps with his bare hands. He was thickly created and looked like someone that had never heard of weights or saw the need for exercise. Unlike those muscular giants Ralphie had seen before who seemed to lose flexibility with their muscle growth Charles seemed naturally fluid, unencumbered by his great mass and muscles. Beside the muscular mass of Charles sat the Traditionalist. In the Traditionalist seat sat the curvaceous and gray eyed beauty named: Esther Rolles Fortune.

"Stay focused, Ralphie," Wood said.

Ralphie nodded. He also looked back and there in the seat two rows back from his sister were several familiar faces.

Looking around the hearing room Ralphie initially just saw a multitude of people and faces. In the seated audience Ralphie smiled at the sight of people that were smiling at him. To his surprise there behind several famous celebrities he had seen on the Interweb sat Bailey Beaumont. She sat stock still, looking forward and frowning. A woman that looked like Bailey's mother sat dressed in a high collared sky-blue dress. On the other side of Bailey was a dark and serious looking man that might have been Bailey's father.

To the left of Bailey sat Ella Buchanan and her Revolutionaries: Albert, Jesse, and Yo-Yo.

Esther Rolles Fortune checked the time and whispered to her Remains council before scooping up the gavel and banging it three times on the gavel stand beside her.

"It is now ten o'clock on this Thursday in the Remains and we call this hearing to order. This Pandemonium Challenge Rewards and Wagers hearing is called to order," Esther Rolles Fortune announced into the microphone that boomed across the two-tiered auditorium.

"There are some simple issues that we are looking to understand at the end of the Twenty-Third Pandemonium Challenge. We are here to determine what happened and more importantly, what your role in the end of the last challenge was Ralph Ellison Reynolds." Fortune continued, "These proceedings are not criminal in their process. We do not prosecute. We instead will attempt to determine if there is a need to investigate the unexpected stoppage of the Pandemonium Challenge. We need to be very clear that this hearing's mission is to ascertain what led to the abrupt end of the Twenty Third Pandemonium Challenge and nothing more. That is our primary focus."

Ralphie listened to Fortune talking but could not help but smile at the fact that Bailey was sitting to his left just one hundred feet away with her family. She was focused only on what was going on ahead of her. In the moment that Ralphie watched Bailey she did not look left or right. All around Bailey sat First Gen supporters. Ralphie knew because they all had the distinctive computer chip brooches that the First Gens wore in solidarity.

Just on the other side of Bailey, Ralphie saw Ella sitting with her Revolutionaries and grinning and making faces as the hearing went on. Yo-Yo waved. Jesse gave a thumbs up. Albert had a sign that he flashed in the direction of Ralphie. The sign read: "I BELIEVE IN RALPHIE." The sign was rolled up in a type of scroll and Albert could pull the scroll apart and display the sign before the enforcers could do anything about it.

Ralphie chuckled at Albert's sign and Ella and the Revolutionaries. If there was a good that had come from all this it was getting to know Ella and the Revolutionaries, Ralphie thought idly, seeing Bailey looking ahead and not acknowledging Ralphie's presence.

"We shall begin this hearing with committee member Phillis Wheatley Childress," Esther Fortune said.

The Innovator Phillis Wheatley Childress was a calculating individual.

"Did you or anyone in your family wager on the Twenty-Third Pandemonium Challenge before you participated?"

Ralphie had a ready answer. Hutchinson slipped a piece of paper in front of Ralphie. Ralphie only looked down long enough to see the points he was supposed to cover.

"To my knowledge, prior to my participation in the Twenty-Third Pandemonium Challenge, my family did not put a wager on me or anyone. Of course, when I was scooped up and taken to the island, I would not have any knowledge of their wagering." Ralphie paused. "I would have hoped that they bet on me, but even now, I cannot say that they did or didn't."

"Did you have any conversations with any other line residents before you participated in the challenge?" The Innovator asked.

"I am fifteen and prior to the challenge I had a bunch of encounters with other lines at the Gathering Center. Conversations? Well, no real conversations. When I think about the other lines, I only been around other lines with my father. I think I was eight or nine at the time. If you are asking if I secretly had meetings with any line to determine what would happen? Well, no. I never met with any line prior to the challenge," Ralphie said.

"Were you aware of the possibility of an abrupt end of the challenge?" Childress asked.

"Well, I suppose that I knew that I might die," Ralphie said. "Is that what you mean?"

"No," Childress said. "I mean, did you have any indication that the challenge might end before the scheduled time?"

"No," Ralphie said looking at Bailey.

The Innovator committee member Phillis Wheatley Childress asked a few more questions, but Ralphie only could recall those three.

George Clinton Palmer, the First Gen, was the next to speak. He seemed thoughtful and reflective though plodding.

"Did you have any prior knowledge of what Miss Buchanan, or the Innovators planned?"

"No," Ralphie said. As he answered he could not stop himself from looking at Bailey. She was dressed that day in oversized egg yolk yellow sweatshirt, blue collared shirt, and blue jeans. Dangling from her earlobes were three increasingly larger diamonds. Her hair was brushed back away from her lineless face and intense and large eyes that seemed unblinking anytime Ralphie looked in her direction.

"As there were four challengers, including you, in the final day, did you or others ever plan or conspire in the final hours of the challenge?" Palmer asked.

"I don't understand the question," Ralphie said.

Palmer pouted. He nodded. He raised a finger, thinking.

"In the final day did you get together with anyone to plan out the final hours of the challenge with any of the other challengers?"

Ralphie laughed instinctively. He shook his head. The question was insane to the fifteen-year-old. The last day on

Pandemonium Island was as much a surprise to Ralphie as anyone. He had imagined that he would have been snuffed out a million times before the seventh day, but somehow, he hadn't. He had survived.

"Ralphie?" The First Gen committee member asked.

"No," Ralphie said, in answer to Palmer's question. "No. I didn't know who was still alive on the last day."

"No more questions," Palmer said.

The Poppies committee member Jacob Lawrence Butler had several questions.

"Did you talk with Ella Fitzgerald Buchanan before the challenge?" The committee member asked adjusting his rectangular glasses on his round face.

Ralphie did not answer immediately. He thought about the question. He rewound the only time he was close enough to talk to the Innovator before the challenge. He knew that Palmer knew the answer to the question he was asking. The councilmember simply wanted to see if Ralphie was going to lie.

"Not really," Ralphie said.

"Not really?" Butler asked, raising an eyebrow. The Poppie was dressed in a blue suit jacket and light blue collared shirt. Both the jacket and collared shirt had a paint smeared design that looked like a handprint in the colors of white, yellow, red, pink, green and purple.

"Well, I think I might have said something to her before the challenge, when we were at the launch," Ralphie said.

"So, you spoke with her?" Butler asked reviewing his notes.

"No, not really. I think I sat with her and a bunch of others who wanted to know about the Shakers," Ralphie said. "I can't say that I spoke to her, or she talked to me after that."

Butler nodded.

"Have you ever wagered on any of the challenges?"

"I'm fifteen," Ralphie said with a teasing smile. "I am not allowed to place a bet on the challenges until I turn eighteen." He paused. "That's the rule. Correct?"

"That is the rule Ralphie," Butler said. "But you are a rule breaker. Aren't you Ralphie?"

"No," Ralphie said.

Butler smiled at Ralphie's answer.

"Are you someone who is honest?"

Ralphie twisted his lips thinking how to answer.

"Are you a liar, Ralphie?" Butler asked.

"No," Ralphie said, defensively.

"But, you lied, Ralphie," Butler said with a slick smile.

Ralphie frowned.

"Did you tell your parents that you were registering for the challenge?" The committee member asked.

"Yes," Ralphie said, slowly.

"Did you tell them before you signed up?" The committee member asked, stroking his well-trimmed Van Dyke.

"No," Ralphie admitted.

"So, when they found out you told them?" Butler asked with a smug smile.

Ralphie nodded.

"So, you lied," Butler said flatly. He waited. Butler looked directly at Ralphie. "It's okay. People lie. But, in this hearing we must figure out if we can trust you and your words." Butler paused and looked around the hearing room, reflectively. "Liars lie. It's a natural thing to do. You lied to our Pablo Clark. You lied to our Robert Nesta," Butler said casually.

Ralphie closed his eyes.

"I object to this badgering," Hutchinson said. Ralphie looked up and saw Hutchinson standing at the table beside him. "This hearing is not about Ralphie's actions in the challenge. Is it? If you want to talk about lies, I have a laundry list of times that the council member has lied about his finances, extramarital activities and voting record," the handsome lawyer said.

Butler narrowed his dark eyes at Hutchinson.

"Mister Hutchinson please sit down," Esther Rolles Fortune said from her seat, grabbing the microphone. "We will not have this hearing devolve into theatrics."

"Are you threatening me?" Butler asked, narrowing his dark eyes behind his glasses.

"No, I would never threaten a seated council member," Hutchinson said, slowly sitting in his seat. "I just want to remind the council that it is not smart to throw stones at glass houses."

"Mister Hutchinson, I will remind you that our task is to determine what young Ralphie knew before the events transpired at the conclusion of the Twenty-Third Pandemonium Challenge," Butler said coldly.

"Well, we all know that the challenge is about survival," Hutchinson said. The lawyer looked directly at Butler. "Those in the challenge aren't judged by the laws in the Remains while in the challenge," Hutchinson added. "We don't condone one hundred and ten percent of the things that happen in the challenge, but that is not the reason for the hearing. Correct?"

Butler nodded. He referred to his notes.

"Okay," Butler said, with a devilish smile. "I will try to ask the questions in a different way," the committee member said. He paused and looked at Ralphie. "Okay. You know that people lie. I know that people lie. You agree that people lie? Right?"

Ralphie looked at the committee member, confused.

"You scared Ralphie? You feel uncomfortable in this hearing with all these people listening to you and everyone taking pictures and recording you?" Butler asked. "I mean, I would be a little nervous, if I was you. This is a little scary."

Ralphie nodded.

"So, you know that there are two reasons, generally, for the reason people lie," Butler paused. He smiled. "People lie because they are scared or because they want to impress someone."

Ralphie frowned.

"So, my question is simple. How do we trust you, Ralphie?"

"Again, the whole complex has seen Ralphie's character in the most stressful times," Wood said. "Trust off the island is different." The lawyer dressed in a pinstripe suit and striped collared shirt said. He was wearing a golden silk tie.

"The problem I am having Ralphie is believing you off the island," Butler said. "I mean, you were aware of the dangers and that didn't stop you. You lied to your parents and family. They were unaware of your desire to... be legendary. Nothing seemed more important, at the time." Butler pouted. "You were seeking celebrity. Celebrity seekers are notoriously dangerous."

With that comment Ralphie felt a hand on his shoulder. Andre 3000 stood up this time.

"The problem with the challenge and the committee responsible for the challenge is that both are in the business of bigger, better and more surprises. This hearing is supposed to be about the "unexpected" stoppage in the Twenty-Third Pandemonium Challenge, but on the beginning of the third day the committee scheduled a stoppage," Andre 3000 said.

Butler raised a finger. "This hearing is about the unplanned stoppage," Butler said. "What I want to know is if I ask Ralphie a question if I will get an honest answer."

"Ralphie has come here to do exactly that," Hutchinson said.

"Okay. Ralphie," Butler said, slowly. "Can you tell me if you knew or were aware that the challenge was going to be stopped, in advance, on that last day?"

Ralphie looked at Butler confused.

"Well, I knew that it was going to end sometime that day," Ralphie said.

"No, I mean, did you know that the challenge was going to be stopped before the appointed time?" Butler asked more pointedly.

"No," Ralphie said. "How could I?"

"How do we trust your words?"

"Ralphie has proven time and time again to be trustworthy," Hutchinson said. Hutchinson smiled. "Council, you are trying to determine if Ralphie, a fifteen-year-old had some hand in the "unplanned" stoppage of the Pandemonium Challenge? Are you serious?"

"Mister Hutchinson, I want to point out that we on this panel take our duties seriously," Butler said. "We are having this hearing to determine Ralphie's part in the stoppage and nothing more. To suggest that there is an alternative reason is insulting."

The lawyers did not respond.

"I will ask this question to Ralphie as we are close to our afternoon break," Butler said. "You were in contact with the three others on the Seventh day. You had talked with Ella Buchanan. You say that you were not sure if the others had talked with or conspired beforehand. So, my question is simply: Could you have been an unknowing participant in the stoppage of the challenge?"

The lawyers did not allow Ralphie to speak. They instead asked for a conference before answering. After five minutes of discussion Ralphie spoke.

"Can you repeat your question?"

"Of course," Butler said with a grin. "Could you have been an unknowing participant in the stoppage of the challenge?"

The lawyer pointed to the paper in front of Ralphie.

"By asking me if I did not know something I would have to answer: Yes," Ralphie said. "But in the way that you have constructed this question if I say: No, then it is just the opposite." Ralphie paused. He looked at the lawyers who nodded. "So, my answer is Yes to not knowing of the stoppage and No to the idea of being a participant in the stoppage in any way."

Jacob Lawrence Butler listened and at the end of Ralphie's answer nodded. Esther Fortune looked at the committee member and they exchanged a silent acknowledgment.

"With that we will recess for an hour," Fortune announced. "The hearing will reconvene at one o'clock," the council member said and banged the gavel for recess

Everyone stood. Ralphie exhaled, mentally tired.

"You did a good job," Hutchinson said, clapping a hand on Ralphie's shoulder. Woods and Williams smiled and shook Ralphie's hand.

"We are going to need to be back here at one o'clock," Wood said.

Ralphie's father appeared by his son's side. His father smiled and nodded to the lawyers. He reached out and Ralphie climbed to his feet.

"You alright?" His father asked.

Ralphie nodded. He looked around and saw the people suddenly all around him. Timothy and Theolonius stood watching and making sure no one stepped too close to Ralphie or the family. Franklin stood watching silently.

"Let's get some air," Ralphie's father said.

Instantly, Timothy and Theolonius led the family to the closest exit. They walked down a short hallway to another door which opened out and onto the side of the judicial building.

The side entrance had a dozen steps and a ten-foot-wide portico.

"We're going to get some food," Mae Reynolds said. She reached out and grabbed Macy's hand. Benjamin Reynolds looked at Ralphie.

"You stay right here," Ralphie's father said. "We're going to leave Theo here until we come back," Reynolds said. Macy broke away from her mother and returned to Ralphie's side.

"I'm staying with Ralphie," Macy said.

Thelonious nodded and positioned himself to watch Ralphie. Ralphie sat on the steps and tried to think how he had gotten here. In his head, he had only been one of fifty contestants fighting for a chance to be legendary.

As he and Macy waited, another group of people exited the side entrance.

"Bailey," Ralphie said climbing to his feet upon seeing Bailey underneath the portico on the side of the judicial building. Bailey was standing there dressed in oversized egg yolk yellow sweatshirt, blue collared shirt, blue jeans and some old-school basketball sneakers.

She turned and for an instant Ralphie felt as if time had slowed to allow him to see the slight slope of her nose, full lips, apple cheeks and that heart shaped face framed by a thick and thin asymmetrical braided hairstyle that just worked for the First Gen. Dangling from her earlobes were three increasingly larger diamonds.

Instead of a smile Ralphie received a withering glare. Bailey stood and the longer she looked at Ralphie the harder her facial expression became. She crossed her small arms in front of her and stared at Ralphie like he was a dog that had pooped on the carpet.

Unsure of the cause for her coldness Ralphie let his arms fall. He started and stopped and then hesitated, suddenly unsure what to do. The reunion had not gone the way he had expected.

"What do you want?" Bailey asked, annoyed.

Ralphie wanted to say so much. There were all these thoughts and emotions inside of the teenager. He was suddenly unable to string together words that he had considered, thought, and reconsidered a thousand times before this meeting.

Bailey pouted, rolled her eyes, and walked away from Ralphie without a word. Her First Gen entourage shook their collective heads at Ralphie behind Theolonius and Macy's protective front.

"So, that's Bailey," Macy stated. "I think that she was cuter on TV."

A few minutes later his lawyers, parents and enforcers returned with food from a food truck.

Ralphie was sitting against a pillar, head down, silent.

Macy had her arm around her brother's shoulder.

"Macy, leave Ralphie alone," Mae Reynolds said anxiously.

"He's broken...hearted," Macy said.

"What happened?" His mother asked.

"His boo thing or who he thought was his boo thing shut him down. Hard," Macy said, with a shrug of her shoulders. "The ship looked like a ghost ship and that ghost ship crashed."

Macy boiled down the whole Bailey debacle to less than thirty words.

"Wow," Ralphie's father said.

"It's okay," Ralphie insisted, sitting on a stone step on the side of the judicial building and eating a sandwich that his father had bought him.

"It's okay, son," Ralphie's father smiled, sitting beside his son. "She's been through a lot too. Just give her time. If it was meant to be then it was meant to be. That's my philosophy."

After lunch, the hearing continued. For the next three hours the Central Government council asked questions that Ralphie could not answer.

The Boomers George Jackson Charles was a tough but fair questioner.

"My questions are simple, Ralphie," Charles said with a big smile. "Did you envision the end of the challenge being between you and Bailey or you and Campbell?"

"Councilor, Ralphie is not here to retell the challenge. He was requested to enlighten the council on the intricacies of the stoppage."

"Okay, that being said," Charles said. "Did you realize you were the only one alive? More importantly, if you were the only one alive, why did you search for Bailey?"

Ralphie did not answer.

The Traditionalist Esther Rolles Fortune spoke after Charles.

"I just want to read from the official rules of the Pandemonium Challenge. The rules of the challenge do not permit involvement or intrusion of outside non-participants. My question is about your understanding of the rules," Fortune said. "Were you aware of the rules of the challenge?"

Before Ralphie or the lawyers could speak Rolles continued.

"Anyone that willfully violates the rules of the Pandemonium Challenge will be relegated and or disqualified from the challenge and not awarded the challenge championship."

Wood stood and responded. "Thank you for reading that. I want to point out that based on the rules that you just read, that the challenge does not permit involvement or intrusion of outside non-participants. Correct? If you are attempting to suggest that Ralphie willfully violated the rules, we have proven he has not and could not."

After Fortune's singular and specific question, the Traditionalist called for recess.

"Did you willfully break the rules of the challenge?" Powell, the Second Gen, asked.

The Second Gen, Toni Morrison Powell, after asking her one question yielded her time to the Miller, Andre Redmond.

Andre Redmond, a Miller, after Powell's blistering slowed the pace of question and answer and seemed to allow Ralphie a chance to speak finally.

"We have talked at you a lot Ralphie. I really think we all want to know what you thought happened at the challenge," Redmond said. "Now, I know that my colleagues understand that the challenge is unlike any competition in the Remains. It is brutal. It is life and death. It is our gladiator sport. Good or bad. It is allowing us all the opportunity to live vicariously by the insanity of the challenge. The annual challenge is why we have little to no crime in the Remains. The Remains is not perfect by any stretch of the imagination but in this walled city plex we are united. We are a community." Redmond paused and looked at the capacity interior of the meeting room. He smiled.

"I want to remind the council member that this is not his opportunity to filibuster and drain the air from the chamber," Fortune said. "Ask your questions. We still have an hour to conclude today's hearing."

"I will reign in my oratory and simply ask this brave son of the Millers three questions that no one has dared ask," Redmond said. He paused, thinking. "My council members have asked good questions. But none has asked the toughest question. Ralphie, did you think that what you did would bring the building down?"

"Well, no," Ralphie said. "As you have all pointed out, the challenge is brutal and cruel, and we have hard choices to make. Nothing in the challenge is easy. I mean I'm just a kid. When I leaned against that support beam, I didn't know what was going to happen," Ralphie said.

"Well, Ralphie you and the others were put in impossible situations and we and the Remains pick you apart for the choices you made," Redmond said. "It's not fair. None of this is fair." The council member paused and smiled. "I know that it feels like we want to blame you and by you, the Millers, for the end of the challenge, but I think we should look at the Pandemonium Committee that set this challenge up and watched it unfold."

Ralphie smiled.

"This is my second to last question. Can you explain your thinking that last hour before the building fell on you and... the others."

Ralphie did not respond. Instead, he bit at his lower lip. Ralphie closed his eyes and tried not to think about the people, his friends, he had seen flatlined.

"It was all pretty crazy," Ralphie said with a slow shake of his head. "I mean, I had just survived nearly dying and was hurt and leaking a little." Ralphie paused and looked across the chamber to Bailey who was smirking. She had her arms crossed in front of her and she looked angry.

"I think I didn't know what I wanted to do," Ralphie said, struggling. "I was cut up, bruised and... leaking. I wanted to sit down. I wanted to rest. I was just so tired."

"Why were you tired?" Redmond asked. "That is my last question."

Ralphie smiled. "I survived seven days but only slept just a handful of hours and when I say slept it was never real sleep. I mean I was closing my eyes and resting with no real rest or sleep. There was always the fear of someone coming to gut me." Ralphie looked up. "I leaned on that support beam because I thought I would fall if I didn't. Then everything collapsed."

"Thank you Ralphie," Redmond said. He looked to Fortune, the committee chair. "No more questions."

"We will conclude this hearing at this point," said Esther Fortune.

That was Thursday. As Ralphie and his family left the Central Government buildings he saw the tall figure of Julius McCarthy and an imposing group of a dozen dark men dressed in dark blue uniforms like the enforcers but with a solitary red band on their arm and red boots and gloves. Unlike the enforcers these dozen men wore goggles and masks to hide their identities.

"Who are they?" Ralphie asked.

No one answered.

On the drive back to the Miller compound and home Ralphie overheard the name of the masked men, the Red Hand.

Chapter Ten.

Bigger Fish to Fry

The next day, Friday, everything repeated, except Bailey did not even pretend to pay attention to Ralphie or tolerate him. At lunch recess Ralphie sat with Macy and Theolonius watched for trouble. Bailey did not come out the side door. She didn't attempt to talk to Ralphie.

After the recess, there was a stir in the hall as half a dozen men dressed in dark blue enforcer uniforms with red epaulettes, a red stripe on the arm and red boots and gloves lined the hall. Julius McCarthy stepped in the hall with four others only to sit behind the Traditionalist contingent and near the Second Gen leadership.

The Traditionalist council member, Esther Rolles Fortune, attempted to rattle Ralphie after lunch. She read from a report that had a bunch of numbers in it. After reading the information she spoke directly to Ralphie.

"Do you understand that the Pandemonium Challenge generates no less than 1,200 jobs annually and adds to the overall well-being of the Remains by diminishing violent crime in the compounds. The committee has supported many charities and various projects in the Remains, including redevelopment of the Central Government and the renewal of Pandemonium Island?" Fortune asked. "My question is: Do you feel you personally cheated the Remains residents out of a true Pandemonium Challenge finish?"

"The problem with trying to blame me or anyone in the challenge doesn't address the hypocritical nature of the challenge itself," Ralphie said nervously, reading from a paper handed to him by Hutchinson. "This hearing is supposed to be about the unplanned stoppage of the challenge, but no one blinked an eye with the planned stoppage during the second day of the challenge. That stoppage was planned, but it happened during the challenge. If this hearing is about credits lost why isn't this hearing about that planned stoppage as well? Is the issue the stoppage or the loss of money? Is this hearing about the challengers and participants or the Pandemonium Challenge Committee and its leadership? The challengers had no control over the outcome of the challenge. The Pandemonium Challenge Committee though had complete control of the outcome of the challenge. It would be better served to have the Pandemonium Challenge Committee and its leadership sitting here instead of me."

The last person to speak at the hearing was the Second Gen, Toni Morrison Powell. She asked a loaded question.

"I want to address your earlier statement," Powell said. She was wearing a denim blue blouse with a scarf. Her hair was braided into two long and thick braids. "The idea of a public hearing is not to lay blame on anyone unjustly, but to present questions and seek answers and allow the public to hear the truth. The truth is a slippery thing indeed. This hearing does not prosecute but allow for further investigation, if necessary. So, today, as we asked a quite simple question your legal team tried to stop the questions that needed the most honest of answers." Powell paused. "I will ask the question again as you avoided it several times, young Ralph Ellison Reynolds. What were you going to do if you found your Bailey alive?"

"What is the point of this question?" Williams asked.

"We have learned that Ralphie did not bet on this challenge and thus he was not motivated by credits even though there was a sizeable number of credits lost from betting in the last few minutes of the challenge," Powell said. "I want to conclude this hearing with one honest statement from young Ralphie Reynolds." Powell smiled. "So, will you answer without the assistance of your legal team?"

"We have answered all the questions put before our client," Hutchinson said. "We will not advise Ralphie to answer that question."

"I have nothing else, chairperson," Powell said.

When the hearing concluded on Friday Ella and the Revolutionaries circled around Ralphie and hugged him. Photographers were snapping shots and filming everything. Ralphie and his family had only made it to the steps of the great chamber when everyone surrounded them.

Ella smiled as only she could. Her smile seemed to extend from ear-to-ear. Yo-Yo gave Ralphie another hug and then a punch in the arm. Albert shook Ralphie's hand. Jesse gave Ralphie a bear hug.

"Ralphie be careful," Albert said, looking back and into the swarm of people moving in and around the hall. Ralphie looked in the direction Albert was looking and saw the distinct group of enforcers standing strategically around the rotunda. They were dressed as the other enforcers except they all had a red shoulder epaulette and red stripe that ran down their leg to the red boots and gloves they wore.

"Who are they?" Ralphie asked Albert.

"They are the Pandemonium Committees elite enforcer squad," said Albert. "I thought they were a myth."

"Why would they be here?" Ralphie asked.

Before Albert could speak Mister and Missus Buchanan appeared. At the sight of the Buchanans the Revolutionaries slinked back into the circle of people and left Ella with her parents. The Revolutionaries disappeared allowing the grown-ups to have their time with Ralphie.

"It seems as if that went extremely well," Mister Buchanan said. "Good job Ralphie." He reached out and patted Ralphie on the shoulder and with that he and his entourage disappeared.

The lawyers shook hands with Ralphie, his father, Macy, and his mother. Doctor Greenwood appeared out of nowhere in the press of people. He nodded and then greeted everyone.

Behind Greenwood, led by two enforcers, Maya Higgins appeared. She was dressed in her signature dark blue pants suit and upon finding Ralphie and his family circled and the center of attention. The leader of the Millers stopped and smiled triumphantly as photographers took pictures.

"You did an excellent job, Ralphie," Higgins said. "We now have to see what happens next, if anything."

Ralphie nodded. He looked around the sea of faces, looking for one particular face and finding everyone but the one he wanted. Ralphie frowned. All around him were the faces of people he did not know, smiling, talking, taking pictures, and trying to get close to him.

Everyone seemed pleased with the outcome of the hearing except Ralphie. Ralphie smiled, but there was a woodenness to the smile. He smiled because it was expected, but there was a little pain tinged in it.

The first day Bailey Beaumont had ignored Ralphie. When she had seen Ralphie it looked as if the girl he publicly had a crush on did not want to give him the time of day. The second day Bailey had pretended as if he was not alive while at the hearing.

"Remember this small victory will not make us complacent," Maya Higgins said breaking Ralphie's descent into depression. "The moment to worry is now. The committee is still dangerous. They may have lost in the public court but that doesn't make them any less dangerous. The committee wields incredible power."

Ralphie's father looked concerned.

"I have ears out now," Higgins said. "There are some concerns that we might have bitten off more than we can chew."

"What does that mean?" Ralphie's father asked, concerned.

Maya Higgins looked around. She seemed for the first time since Ralphie had met her a little uncomfortable.

"Ben, we will talk later," Maya Higgins said, looking at the people milling around them. "There are too many ears here."

Higgins and Ralphie's father's shook hands and Higgins and her team departed.

On the drive back to the Reynolds house the transport was quiet. Macy sat next to Ralphie. His father and mother sat in the second row of seats quietly.

"Ralphie? You, okay?" Macy asked.

"Yeah," Ralphie said to Macy. "I just thought that they wanted to hear my side of the story," he said, with a disappointed shake of his head.

"They have their own agendas, Ralphie," his mother said, with a pout.

"They were doing this to pretend like they cared," Ralphie's father said. "Some of them do. Some don't."

"How come they don't care?" Macy asked her father.

"Well, baby girl, they care about the power and the creds," Benjamin Reynolds said.

"Ben," Mae Reynolds said, putting a hand on her husband's bicep.

"Okay," Benjamin Reynolds said with a small smile to his wife. "I can't say that they don't all care," Macy's father said. "I think some of them really care. I also think that some of them just go through these procedures to gain the attention of the Remains while gaining credibility in the Central Government."

Ralphie and Macy looked at their father and then their mother, confused. Macy looked flummoxed. Ralphie just smirked and put his head down.

"Our government was supposed to be better than the corrupt attention seekers that put party over the people they deceived, pretending to serve," Mae Reynolds said, angrily.

"Easy babe," Benjamin Reynolds said, placing a hand on his wife's hand.

"We know that the politicians put us in this situation, a long time ago," Ralphie's father said. "But all that power is tempting, and power corrupts."

"The Remains was created to avoid the traps and pitfalls that led to the flash," Mae Reynolds said, annoyed.

"It's human nature, I suppose. To expect them or anyone to be less vain, less proud, or selfish or ambitious is asking a lot," Benjamin Reynolds said.

That weekend Ralphie planned on staying close to the house. The warning from Maya Higgins at the Central Government building shook Ralphie.

*　　*　　*　　*　　*

That Friday night, Saturday morning, Ralphie woke in the middle of the night to the sound of voices downstairs in his home. One of the voices Ralphie heard was Maya Higgins. For a long moment Ralphie thought to just lay in bed, but then he climbed out of his bed and creeped to the head of the stairs and listened to his parents and Miss Higgins in his family's living room.

"The committee has threatened to seek revenge on everyone involved in the hearing," Maya Higgins said, worried.

"The Central Government won't let them do anything," Mae Reynolds said.

"I agree, but we need to be wary," Maya Higgins said. "The committee is unhappy with the outcome of the hearing."

"Tough beans," Benjamin Reynolds said.

154

"They don't take being questioned or accused lightly," Higgins whispered. "I have warned Hutchinson, Wood, and Williams to be careful. It just makes sense to be careful now that the hearing is over."

"Why?" Mae Reynolds asked, looking around nervously.

"You know that the committee are star builders and star wreckers," Higgins said.

"You think they are going to come after Ralphie?" Mae Reynolds asked.

There was a silence.

"It makes sense," Ralphie's father asked.

The three quieted.

"You know they have had their hands in everything for a very long time," Higgins said.

"That doesn't give them the right," Mae Reynolds said.

"You saw the committee enforcers?" Higgins asked.

Again, there was silence.

"Should we be worried?" Benjamin Reynolds asked.

"I don't think so," Higgins said. "They are not some street gang. They are surgeons. They will plot and plan and figure out a way to separate the weak from the strong."

"This is some power play," Ralphie's father said, angrily.

"Power play or not, we need to be careful," Higgins said, in warning.

"What do you think they will do?" His mother asked.

There was silence.

"I can't imagine they will do anything," Higgins said. "As I said, presently they are simply threatening." Higgins paused. "The Hand is their first threat. Everyone knows that the Red Hand is the committee's bad boys and girls."

"What do you think the Red Hand would do to Ralphie?" His mother asked, concerned.

No one answered. There was a long silence.

"He's just a boy," his mother said.

"I'm not going to allow them to threaten my son or my family," Ralphie's father said, angrily.

"No one wants that Ben," Higgins agreed. "But the committee is incredibly powerful. They have ruined a few champions reputations just by remaining silent when rumors were leaked." Higgins paused. "Of course, they probably started the rumors, in the first place."

"We need to contact Buchanan and LeFleur and Sanchez?" Mae Reynolds asked.

"We are already in talks with them," Higgins said. "They are aware of the committee's actions."

"Should we worry?" Benjamin Reynolds asked, forcefully.

"No. I came by tonight to tell you the issues swirling about us," Higgins said, in a low tone. "Ralphie is on their radar, but there is no need to panic. Not yet. Worst comes to worst we can hide him and hope the whole thing blows over when they have no one to attack," Higgins said. "He should be safe for now."

"Thanks Maya," Mae Reynolds said.

There was another long silence. Ralphie tried to crane his neck to see the adults in the living room. He dared not leave the second floor for fear of discovery.

"I will get back to you as soon as I hear something definitive," Higgins said. "The committee is powerful and more powerful than they need to be, but we all know that we have made a powerful enemy today. It seemed inevitable. They do not like being made a fool of publicly." The Miller leader paused. "Maybe I am worried about nothing? Maybe it will all blow over, just like so many little things that amount to nothing? We will see," Higgins said.

There was another pause.

"Thank you again, Maya, for coming to talk to us," His mother said.

Instantly, Ralphie heard the three moving. There was a long silence. The front door opened and closed.

Ralphie returned to his bedroom and tried to think what to do now that the Pandemonium Committee was hellbent on making Ralphie look like he was on drugs or insane or being chased by aliens. Suddenly, Ralphie thought about all the challenge winners who had sketchy returns to the Remains.

Ralphie lay back down in his bed and tried to sleep. He dozed for a moment and woke only to find that he needed to go to the bathroom. Ralphie stumbled from his room to the bathroom and after returned thinking about what Maya Higgins had said.

"Was the Pandemonium Committee behind the scandals of the last couple of champions?" Ralphie asked aloud as he entered his darkened bedroom.

"Probably," was an answer from the dark.

Ralphie nearly jumped out of his skin at the sound. He recoiled looking into the darkness and at the same time bouncing against his dresser and then his bed only to find himself slowly falling headfirst toward the floor by the corner of his bed.

Out of the darkness stepped Ella Fitzgerald Buchanan.

"Ralphie, are you okay?" Before Ralphie could respond Ella continued. "We got problems," Ella said.

"Ella how did you get in here?" Ralphie asked from the bedroom floor.

"Ralphie? Concentrate," Ella said. "I'm a Maker," she said as if that answered his previous question.

He climbed to his knees and rubbed at his eyes trying to focus. Ralphie narrowed his vision and studied the shadowy Ella in his bedroom.

Ella beckoned Ralphie to the window and the small balcony on the other side of the glass.

Ralphie climbed to his feet dressed in his Batman pajamas.

"Thought you wanted to be Robin?"

Ralphie smiled.

"Suppose everyone dreams," Ella said, dressed in yellow and black camo pants, black and yellow combat boots, and her Innovator golden hoody. On her head was a yellow and black helmet with goggles.

Ralphie nodded. Ella pointed downward and into the darkness of the backyard. He looked at Ella and behind her, on the lawn below were three dark figures.

Standing in Ralphie's backyard were the Revolutionaries. Albert waved. Jesse nodded. Yo-Yo gestured for Ralphie to come down.

Somehow Ella and the Revolutionaries had slipped out of the Innovators compound and into the Millers compound unseen. They were beneath his bedroom window at two o'clock in the morning.

"Ralphie, you probably know that things have ramped up," Ella said in a whisper as she stood with the moon casting moonlight through the big double window in Ralphie's bedroom.

"Yeah, I sort of heard," Ralphie said.

"Well, we figure that you might be safer, for now, outside of this compound," Ella said.

"Miss Higgins said as much," Ralphie said.

"What do you mean?" Ella asked, uncertain.

"She was here earlier, talking to my parents. They were talking about the committee and the Red Hand," Ralphie said.

"Okay, listen, we don't have much time. We need to get you out of here. You can tell your parents that you're with me, and they can contact my parents, but they cannot know where you are after that," Ella said. "Put on some pants and shoes. We're leaving."

Ralphie standing in his bedroom studied Ella. He shook his head. Ralphie twisted his lips thinking.

Outside in the backyard Albert awkwardly climbed onto the balcony.

"Hey Ralphie," Albert said, a little out of breath. "We gotta go. The longer we're here the more opportunities for the Red Hand to arrive and knock us all out and for you to wake up find you accused of killing all four of us."

"What?"

"The Red Hand are dangerous," Albert said. "Whatever you can think of they can do."

"Get dressed," Ella said looking at Ralphie. Ralphie hesitated. "I wrote your parents a letter to let them know what was going on. Just in case," Ella said fishing the letter out of her hoody. She handed it to Albert. Albert examined the letter. He handed it back to Ella.

"Ella, slip that under his parent's bedroom door," Albert said.

Ella nodded and walked to the bedroom door and exited.

Albert pulled another typed letter from his hoody front pocket and sat his letter on the Ralphie's desk.

"What's that?"

"A fake letter, just in case the Red Hand are on your trail already," Albert said. "They are like ninjas. They can slip in and out of the darkness." Albert turned around and investigated the dark corners of Ralphie's room.

Ralphie slipped on a pair of jeans over his pajamas. Ralphie found a pair of socks and then a pair of basketball sneakers. He grabbed his backpack and smiled seeing the P23 lapel pin pinned to the front of it. Ralphie thought absently that Macy had to have done that. He thought no more of it as he stuffed his pack with a few of his personal belongings. He looked around the bedroom for what else he absolutely needed.

Ella walked back into Ralphie's bedroom.

"We ready?"

Ralphie shrugged his backpack over his shoulders then nodded.

"Okay, here we go," Ella said and headed to the balcony.

Once outside and in the dark Ella directed Ralphie to the front of his house. All the Revolutionaries had their own modified electric scooters. Ella had a sleek black and gold scooter that looked like it was the baby of a fighter jet and a shark on two wheels. Yo-Yo had her own chromed out scooter with more mirrors on it than seemed possible. Albert had a bright blue scooter that had a windscreen that made it look incredibly aerodynamic. It was Jesse, the muscle, who Ralphie found himself beside. The scooter looked like one of the muscle motorcycles of long ago with wide handlebars and wide wheels. The scooter had a leather saddle, and it was where Ralphie found himself as Albert, then Yo-Yo followed, Ella into the dark. The group silently rode out of Sean Carter Estates and toward the far side of the Miller compound.

"We should be back in our compound pretty quickly," Jesse said to Ralphie as he held on for dear life. The scooters were fast and silent. The four scooters ripped through the compound at thirty miles per hour, ignoring lights, pedestrians and the odd transport moving that early in the morning.

"You don't have to rush on account of me," Ralphie said as Jesse followed Albert's lead and turned onto the road that ran parallel with the wall that separated the Miller compound from the Innovator compound.

"You know that the Millers built this wall to separate us from them," Jesse said as he raced to catch up with the three faster scooters.

"Why would they do that? Aren't we all in the same fight?"

"I guess not always," Jesse said as the three scooters ahead turned right and then right again and headed for the entrance of the Innovator compound. Ralphie did not recall exiting the compound the day that Mister Buchanan and the others took him back to his compound, but as they drew closer to the entrance, he was shocked to find that there was a guard house, unattended, with the gate up.

"No security?" Ralph asked Jesse, holding onto the handles on the leather saddle.

"No security, right now," Jesse said, revving the scooter as the three scooters passed under the gate and up the incline into the Innovator compound.

The three scooters slowed and stopped at the first intersection in the compound.

Jesse pulled up with Ralphie and stopped. As soon as Jesse stopped his scooter Ralphie climbed off shakily.

"So, what do you think is the best plan?" Yo-Yo asked, looking at Ella.

"Well, I should take him to my house," Ella said. "He knows it and my parents know him."

"But if the Red Hand are looking for him that would be the first place, they're going to look," Albert said.

The four sat on the scooters thinking. Ralphie blinked and realized that it was nearly three in the morning, and he was getting sleepy. He rubbed at his eyes and tried to stay engaged despite feeling tired.

"Okay, Ralphie," Ella said. "You're with me. We'll figure out things in the morning. I'll talk to my dad, and he'll come up with a plan. He'll know what to do with the committee and the Red Hand."

Jesse elbowed Ralphie and smiled.

"We'll meet tomorrow. Let's meet at the lake," Yo-Yo said.

"Early?" Albert asked, looking at Ella.

"Let's meet after one. I'm sure my dad will need some time to figure things out," Ella said.

With that the Revolutionaries separated and rode away from Ralphie and Ella.

"Ella, this is crazy," Ralphie said.

"Ralphie, this is anything but crazy," Ella said. "People have gone to war over meaningless things. The Trojan War was fought over a man's lust for a single woman. North America's genocide of First Americans was caused by a bad navigator trying to impress a land hungry queen. The Civil War was started by colonizers too lazy to do their own work and happy to dehumanize and blame our ancestors for their problems. The subjugation and carving up of Africa began with a group of less than 15 greedy men meeting in Berlin. The French had a revolution start because of the selfishness of a vain woman." Ella paused. "The flash that destroyed billions was caused by two idiots trying to prove they had bigger... arsenals than the other," Ella said, moving up and giving Ralphie room to climb on her scooter. "Egos, especially male egos, have caused more harm than good for as long as people have been on this dying marble."

Ralphie climbed on the back of Ella's scooter. She let off the brake of her scooter and the two raced up a disused street, weaving in and out of cars still on the streets. At an intersection Ella turned right and for the next five minutes the pair rode up a steep hill. At another big intersection Ella turned left and after a rolling hill turned right and went uphill again. In the dark, Ralphie had no idea where he was. He just tried to enjoy the ride.

In a few minutes Ella turned into the circular drive of her home and the pair found themselves under the watchful eyes of her family's ever watchful enforcers. She parked the scooter and the two enforcers at the front of the estate moved to Ella Buchanan. A third enforcer walked Ella's scooter toward a wing of the darkened mansion.

"Should we wake your parents?" Enforcer 2759 asked.

"No, let them sleep," Ella said. "Tell them when they wake that we have a problem and that Ralphie is back."

Chapter Eleven.

Three days.

Ralphie woke up the next morning comfortably supported by the bedding beneath him. Ralphie sat up in the luxurious bed to see better. The bed he lay in was the exact same bed he had recovered in months ago, the Miller teen thought.

Ralphie noticed the four-poster bed he laid in looked as if it was an antique and manufactured piece of craftsmanship made by hand and not machine. The teen studied the artisanship of the fluted posts and marveled at the intricate workmanship. Millers made this bed, Ralphie believed. Millers were the workers of the Remains. They made most things in the Remains, from chairs and cabinetry to buildings and the walls since the flash. It was a treat to see ancient craftmanship in the room he was in.

He looked left and right and for as far he could see to the left there was telltale signs of handcrafted workmanship. To the right, there was an ornate door on the far wall. Ralphie stopped to focus on the ornate door and noted the inlay and filigree of the design. He marveled at the door.

The teen looked toward the four paned windows and in between those panes stood a great mirror. In the mirror Ralphie saw a glimmer of himself. The fifteen-year-old sat up in the quiet grand room. The blue sky framed the windows.

Ralphie looked around the room and decided to climb out of the bed and see what changes had occurred since his last visit to the Buchanan home. Dressed only in his Batman pajamas from the night before Ralphe padded across the wooden flooring to the door closest to the bed and turned the doorknob. The knob gave under his hand and inside the dark closet Ralphie found the same heavycoats and boots inside. He searched the closet for anything that he might have worn the last visit but finding nothing he redirected his attention to the wooden chests beneath the large four paned windows.

He moved slowly barefoot across the cold hardwood floor to the wooden chest and opened it to find sweaters and jeans. He bypassed the sweaters as they seemed all declarations of the love of the Innovator line. So, Ralphie grabbed a pair of blue jeans and hesitated. He took off his pajamas and slipped on a pair of blue jeans. Dressed, Ralphie stopped and thought. What was he going to do?

Ralphie searched in his backpack for something to wear. He had grabbed two T-shirts from his bedroom Ralphie realized as he ran off with Ella and the Revolutionaries without saying goodbye to his parents or Macy. He had done it again. He had made a decision that would affect everyone without telling his parents.

"Damn it," Ralphie said as he slipped on a Boondocks T-shirt. He was tying his shoes on his basketball shoes when Ella walked into the bedroom. Behind her was her father, Gordon Buchanan.

"Ralphie, it seems as if you and our Ella have become a fly in the ointment," Mister Buchanan said, dressed in house slippers, blue silk bathrobe, blue and gold striped pajama bottoms and T-shirt.

"Yes, sir," Ralphie said.

"We will hide you," Mister Buchanan said. "Of course, while you are here you might be able to repay the favor, I talked to you about long ago."

Ralphie listened. He knew what Mister Buchanan was referring to, but the quiet teen had learned to listen more than speak when dealing with others.

"I need an honest opinion, and nothing more," Buchanan said with a wicked smile. "If you think you can do that, then that is all I require."

Ella placed a hand on her father's arm.

Mister Buchanan smiled and nodded.

"First, we will feed you and then see what the committee has up its sleeves," Ella's father said with an emotionless smile.

Ella nodded and her father turned on his heels and exited the bedroom.

"So, Ralphie I have good and bad news," Ella said as her father disappeared into the hall.

"Good and bad news?"

"Ralphie," Ella said, slightly annoyed. "I thought you had gotten over the whole repeating thing."

Ralphie bit his lip and remained quiet.

"The good news is that according to daddy the Central Government has decided that the Millers and First Gens had no knowledge or involvement in the unexpected stoppage of the Twenty-Third Pandemonium Challenge. You are now the Twenty-Third Pandemonium Challenge champion. The bad news is that Bailey is not going to be recorded as a co-champion. Her inability to defend herself relegated her to second place. The Central Government fined my line one million credits for my involvement in the unsanctioned stoppage." Ella stopped and looked at Ralphie. "The other bad news is that Pandemonium Committee is not satisfied with the punishment. They have said that the fine is nothing more than a wrist slap for our line. They want something significant to occur to deter any other interference in future challenges."

Ralphie listened and tried to log all the information that Ella had gathered before ten o'clock that Sunday morning.

"How did you find all that out?"

"The Interweb," Ella said.

"Is that it?"

"Well, they were thinking about when to have your parade," Ella said.

"Parade?"

"Again, Ralphie, concentrate," Ella said with a disapproving shake of her head. "We have bigger things to worry about then when you get your parade or which line is the best at fighting."

"I get a parade?"

"Ralphie, there are more important things than a parade," Ella said.

Ralphie nodded. He tried to listen to Ella, but he couldn't. His mind was suddenly swirling with the idea of people lining the streets of the compound. A parade? The idea of a parade in Ralphie's honor was overwhelming. In his lifetime he tried to recall if he had ever gone to a parade? Juneteenth was the closest, but they did not do a parade for anyone. Ralphie wondered would he get to sit on a float? Would he get the key to the compound?

"Ralphie snap out of it," Ella said, clapping her hands in front of his eyes.

Ralphie blinked and found Ella smirking in front of him.

"Listen, we are having a pool party this afternoon, around three," Ella said. She smiled. "I invited Bailey to the pool party," Ella said with an impish grin.

"Bailey?"

Ella shook her head and chuckled at Ralphie.

After brunch, Ralphie was given some swim trunks and grabbed a towel from the bedroom and went to the pool party. When he arrived, there were easily two dozen people he did not know milling around the pool, talking, laughing, and splashing water. Sitting at one of the dozen round tables, beneath a patio umbrella were Albert, Jesse, and Yo-Yo.

"Hello, Ralphie, I'm Cedric," a lanky boy with big eyes and broad nose said, extending his hand. He was wearing a gold T-shirt and looked vaguely familiar to Ralphie for some reason even though he had never met the boy before.

Ralphie smiled and nodded but did not shake hands with the lanky boy. Instead, he looked up and tried to find Ella. Before he had walked three steps a small girl dressed in a striped skirt and gold and blue striped bikini top appeared.

"Ralphie, my name is Erica," the short and pretty girl with curly hair and round cheeks said, stepping in front of Cedric.

Ralphie nodded and quickly found himself surrounded by half a dozen Innovators. A few boys, wearing just swim trunks crowded in curious. Three girls wearing bikini tops smiled at Ralphie.

"Can I take a picture with you? For my Vine?" One of the girls asked and before Ralphie could answer she had her phone out and took a picture.

"Okay, that's enough," Ella said. She had magically appeared and guided Ralphie away from the knot of people. They all had their phones out and were taking pictures. The people were posing and smiling with Ralphie as Ella walked Ralphie away from the half dozen pool party guests.

"Back off," Ella said in no uncertain tones. "Ralphie is here to relax not to be mobbed."

"I think this might not have been a good idea," Yo-Yo said as Ralphie arrived at the Revolutionaries table.

"Yeah, if the Red Hand is looking for you, they only need look on the Vine right now," Albert said with a pessimistic shake of his head in the direction of the people taking pictures and posting them onto the Interweb social network.

"What are you thinking?" Jesse asked.

"Well, the party is just a couple of hours," Ella said. "I will text daddy and tell him that the pool party has outed Ralphie."

"Outed?" Ralphie said.

"Well, made your hideout not a secret?" Ella said with a grin.

"Better," Ralphie said with a playful smile.

"Okay, you try and enjoy yourself," Ella said. "Jesse, will you go and tell Huey to come here?"

Jesse walked to the muscular enforcer standing near the entrance to the pool.

Huey, the enforcer, appeared. Ella spoke with him. The enforcer talked to the air and instantly there were two visible enforcers positioned at the entrance and exit of the pool area.

Ralphie sat at the round table with Albert, Jesse, Yo-Yo, and Ella. He had tried to get in the pool but as soon as he climbed to his feet half of the partygoers seemed interested in what Ralphie was doing. So, Ralphie returned to the safety of the Revolutionaries and Ella.

"You're really popular," Yo-Yo said with a laugh.

Ralphie grimaced.

"You know everyone here has heard the news about you being the official Pandemonium Champion," Jesse said, with a smile. "You are suddenly a Remains celebrity."

"All the girls want to have a picture with you now," Albert said, putting an arm around Ralphie's shoulder. "To put on their Vine."

"And all the boys want to say that they know you," Jesse said with a laugh.

A few minutes later food was served. The wait staff gave each table several choices of gourmet sandwiches. The choices included: Roast Beef, Ham, and Turkey. With the Turkey choices there were four choices: Turkey and Brie, Turkey and Ham, Turkey and Roast Beef and Turkey and Salami. Each table received vegetable toppings.

Jesse ate a Ham sandwich. Yo-Yo had a Turkey and Brie sandwich. Albert chose a Turkey sandwich. Ella asked for a Veggie sandwich. Ralphie had a Turkey and Brie sandwich.

Orangina and bottled drinks were offered for each table and guest.

For three hours Ralphie sat and watched people he didn't know watch him. The brave nodded and said hello. The courageous asked to take a picture. The carefree swam and laughed.

At five o'clock the partygoers started to head out. By six o' clock the only people that remained were Ella and the Revolutionaries and Cedric and Dee.

"Who are they?" Ralphie asked.

"You remember the Pippins? Well, Cedric is their son," Ella said. Ralphie nodded at the memory of the Pippens. Albert touched Ralphie's elbow to get his attention. He beckoned Ralphie over to his side of the table with Jesse.

"What?"

"Ced sort of has a crush on Ella," Albert said.

"Despite that bad decision he's pretty cool people," Jesse said with a big smile.

"Okay," Ralphie said, looking at Erica who was looking at Ralphie with her big doe eyes. "What is her deal?"

Albert and Jesse followed Ralphie's gaze to Erica and then back to Ralphie.

"What you like her?" Albert asked.

"I thought you were all into Bailey?" Jesse asked.

Ralphie pressed his lips together and did not respond.

"It's cool. Erica is a bit of a star humper," Albert said with a sly smile. "Just be careful. She is all about being seen and with the big names for her Vine."

Ralphie nodded. He sat back down beside Ella.

"What did they tell you?" Ella asked, looking at Jesse and Albert.

"Who you like?" Ralphie asked with a curious smile.

Ella shook her head at Jesse and Albert. Ralphie smiled at the idea of Ella being the interest of someone. She had said that she was interested in someone, but Ralphie had not imagined it to be Cedric.

"Ralphie, what they didn't say about Erica is she is related to the LeFleurs, somehow," Yo-Yo said. "She's cool people. Just a little needy."

As if by saying her name Erica appeared at the table with the Revolutionaries. She was cute, Ralphie thought as she stood in her skirt and bikini top, her hair pulled back and away from her round face.

"Hey, Erica," Jesse said, with a bigger than usual smile.

Ralphie did not let his thoughts betray his initial feelings of the interest Jesse had in Dee. Instead, he looked at Ella and Albert and waited for Yo-Yo to say something.

"Did you get your picture with Ralphie?" Yo-Yo asked Erica with a knife thin smile.

Cedric appeared beside Dee.

"Hey, Ella," Cedric said with a small smile.

Ella looked at Cedric and nodded.

Ralphie met Cedric and Erica properly through the Revolutionaries. Cedric, though he was attracted to Ella, was funny and smart. Erica was incredibly cute up close and personal, but Ralphie could see that Jesse paid a lot of attention to her every move.

A little after six the Revolutionaries left Ella's house.

"We'll eat around seven," Ella said.

That night after dinner Missus Buchanan climbed to her feet and she and Ella went to the front of the mansion.

Gordon Buchanan stepped out of his transport.

After a brief greeting Gordon Buchanan focused on Ralphie.

"Ralphie, we need to talk," Ella's father said.

The four sat in the Oak Hall.

"Ralphie, remember the mission I offered you? Well, there is an urgent need for your help," Gordon Buchanan said. "I am not one used to asking for favors. But I believe that you might be the deciding factor in a very delicate situation."

"Delicate situation?"

Ella shook her head and rolled her eyes at Ralphie.

"Did you know there is a growing belief in the Remains that someone has technology and is operating on the fringes animating and directing the abominations attacking the walls?"

Ralphie did not respond.

"We believe there must be someone," Buchanan paused. Ella's father took a moment to gather his thoughts. "It is a belief. We cannot move based on hunches and beliefs. We need evidence. We need to capture the alchemists, sorcerers, witch doctors, mad scientists or whatever they prefer to be called, trying to destroy the Remains."

"Is that what you want me to do? Catch someone?" The curious teen asked, confused.

"Well, yes and no, Ralphie. Let me explain. As you know there are two walls that protect us. The outer wall is being attacked every day. There are reports that there are points that are incredibly vulnerable. The thing is that our reports show that the mindless creatures attacking the wall seem to be concentrating on those weak spots," Buchanan said. "The question has become who is directing these mindless creatures? Is there someone we do not know trying to undermine the Remains?" Buchanan asked. "For us, we have three battles at hand. The one is the challenge and the disregard for lines in the Remains. The second is the integrity of the wall. The last is the idea of leaving the Remains for something better. At present, our priority is shedding light on the first two. It is this shining of light that we want to recruit you for."

"I don't understand," Ralphie said. "You want me to find someone controlling monsters? And what?" Ralphie shook his head. "Wait. I'm just one kid. The Remains is gigantic. There's no way I would know where to look. It's crazy, the more I think about it." Ralphie simply scoffed. "I'm sorry sir. I don't see how I can help you," Ralphie said.

"Relax, Ralphie," Mister Buchanan said with a reassuring smile. "We have a general idea of where this maybe coming from. We have talked with the Gens." Buchanan paused. "As I said I just want your honest opinion. Nothing more."

Ralphie frowned. Mister Buchanan's plan had a bunch of holes in it.

"If you are willing, I will get the ball rolling," Ella's father said, sitting at the giant oaken table beside his wife and daughter.

"I'm willing to help, if I can," Ralphie said, reluctantly.

"Excellent," Mister Buchanan said. The powerful Innovator paused. He extended a long index finger and placed it in front of his lips. He extended his thumb and allowed it to become a perch for his chin. Mister Buchanan, studying Ralphie, exhaled before speaking. "Again, I am only interested in your curious nature and honest opinion," Buchanan said.

Ella reached out to touch Ralphie's arm. He brushed Ella's hand away.

Mister Buchanan stared at Ralphie evenly.

Ralphie studied Ella's father and Ella sitting on the far side of the table. Missus Buchanan, ever lovely, sat and seemed to be attempting to stop a laugh.

Ralphie hardened against the Buchanans. They all seemed three steps ahead of Ralphie in their thinkings. Mister Buchanan was a crafty man. Ella was his daughter, and she was no slouch. He knew that despite Ella's generosity Mister Buchanan had ulterior motives for all his friendliness. The beautiful and quiet Missus Buchanan gave every appearance of a trophy wife, but Ralphie could tell there was more to her. Ralphie took a breath and leveled his gaze to the powerful leader of the Buchanan family.

"What do you want from me, sir?" Ralphie asked, warily.

"Well, I would like you to go to the Berkeley Labs and see if there is someone or something behind these increased attacks," Buchanan said.

"Berkeley Labs?"

Ella rolled her eyes at Ralphie's repeating of her father's words and chuckled.

"In that area there is something generating power that shouldn't be generating any power. According to the First Gens there is an inordinate amount of power coming from the general area of the Labs," Buchanan said.

Ralphie nodded.

"The First Gens have been recording power surges in the deserted Berkeley campus. For a time, we believed it was just a surge of power, but a surge would not be consistent." Buchanan studied Ralphie with his dark eyes. "The First Gen have tried to triangulate the power source. As best as we can tell the source is some place in the Berkeley Labs." Buchanan paused. "The problem is that the campus and most of what was the campus is destroyed. Getting in there is no easy task. We plan on sending in a small group to investigate the power source. Again, we figured you might be interested in helping with this endeavor."

"Why me?" Ralphie asked, suspiciously.

"Why?" Gordon Buchanan asked, looking at Ralphie and his daughter. "Well, you survived the challenge, and that in and of itself is no small feat. You have proved that you are interested in protecting the Remains. Our line and others have decided the same. We have recruited the last seven champions with the hope that they might assist us in locating that power source." Buchanan paused. "This is not a walk in the park. This is dangerous. We do not know what is behind the power source. Perhaps, you and the others will find those tinkerers and eliminate them, for the greater good."

"Wait," The unsure teen said. "Eliminate? What are you saying?"

"Your job, Ralphie, is to give us your opinion. If the source of power is too powerful or dangerous then you seven will make that decision." Buchanan smiled. "You see, the greatest danger in the Remains is outside the walls, Ralphie," Gordon Buchanan said. He shook his head. "To protect those inside the walls we need to do what the Central Government seems reluctant to do. We must locate a problem to eliminate the problem."

"Mister Buchanan," Ralphie said, taken aback. He raised his hands to stop the Innovator. "I'm not an enforcer. This sounds like something you send the enforcers in to handle."

"The enforcers are soldiers, to a point, Ralphie," Gordon Buchanan said. "They are good at reacting to problems. They are not subtle by any stretch of the imagination. If we asked them to guard something, then I would agree. Or shoot anything with an extra finger or ear, they would be perfect. But they are not subtle or delicate by any stretch of the imagination. They are not deep thinkers, analysts, or strategists. That is left to others." Buchanan smiled. "That is left to us."

"But--" Ralphie said only to pause.

"Besides, the enforcers are under the control of the Central Government, Ralphie. That's the problem. The Central Government do not believe this power surge is a problem," Ella's father said.

"So, is it a problem?" Ralphie asked, uncertain.

"It is," Mister Buchanan said with a nod of his head.

Ralphie nodded.

"We need someone to protect the ones within these walls from the invisible problems," Gordon Buchanan said. He smiled. "If that makes sense." Ella's father reached out and placed a hand on the dark wood surface of the table. "All I want from you is your honest opinion once you come back," Gordon Buchanan said. "Of course, you would have to go to the labs and do a look see to give that honest opinion."

Ella studied Ralphie. Mister Buchanan studied Ralphie. Missus Buchanan smiled, reminding Ralphie of the Interweb celebrities. Ralphie felt like he was playing tic-tac-toe and the Buchanans were playing 3-D chess suddenly.

"Give it some thought," Mister Buchanan said, climbing to his feet. "I know I am asking a lot, but you will be handsomely rewarded for your efforts. Your family will be compensated as well," Buchanan said as he climbed to his feet and left the Oak Hall.

That evening at dinner Ralphie was pleasantly surprised to find that Mister and Missus Buchanan were in attendance with Ella and Ralphie. The family seemed happy and carefree. Ralphie on the other hand was wrestling with the proposal Mister Buchanan had offered.

Sunday night Ralphie went to sleep thinking over the information Mister Buchanan had given him.

On Monday Ralphie dressed and walked down to breakfast. He ate his breakfast silently. Ella and her mother noticed the usually quiet Miller unusually focused and thoughtful.

"Ralphie are you okay?" Missus Buchanan asked, politely.

"Yeah," Ralphie said. Looking up, he found Missus Buchanan smiling at him. "I mean, yes, ma'am."

After breakfast Ralphie stopped Ella.

"What's going on?" Ella asked, concerned.

"Can I use your computer?" Ralphie asked, seriously.

"Sure," Ella said.

Ella walked Ralphie to the third floor of the west wing of the mansion and to her bedroom. She walked Ralphie to the small living area of her bedroom where a small blue couch sat with yellow pillows. In front of the couch was a coffee table. On the opposite side of the room hung a 70" monitor. Sitting on the coffee table was a laptop. Ella sat on the couch and gestured to the laptop.

Ralphie nodded. He sat down in front of the laptop and tapped a few keys and the monitor blinked on.

Ralphie typed three short messages. He was a proficient typist. While Ralphie typed Ella took pictures of herself. After taking a dozen pictures Ella walked to her balcony and opened the window and stepped outside.

In about twenty minutes Ralphie was done. Ella looked back and saw Ralphie sitting on the couch pensive. She walked back into her bedroom.

"You done?" Ella asked.

"Yep," Ralphie said.

"Who were you writing to?" Ella asked.

Ralphie did not answer. He simply climbed on his feet and nodded as an answer. Ella shrugged and followed. The two walked silently to the main floor of the mansion.

Once on the main floor of the estate Ralphie stopped on the landing of the stairs that led to the various parts of the Buchanan home. Ella followed behind Ralphie uncertain what the Miller was thinking.

"What are you thinking?" Ella asked, curiously.

"Think I need to talk to your father," Ralphie said seriously.

Chapter Twelve.

Pandemonium Committee

Monday morning Julius McCarthy sat in his office behind his desk with fingers steepled in front of his dark and unsmiling face. He was dressed in a blue pinstriped suit, white collared shirt with a yellow and blue striped silk tie. On his pinkie finger that day he was wearing a golden bear ring.

By his side, was his assistant, Michele Sanderson with her notebook computer. She was dressed in a white dress with dark yellow panels. The small girl was wearing a California bear brooch over her heart. As always, she was taking notes and paying attention to McCarthy's subtle gestures.

In the expansive office sat seventeen people. There were the two finance ministers, two legal representatives for the committee, the logistics director, chestnut colored Alicia Charles, the shifty and jumpy wagering supervisor, the easygoing marketing coordinator, a vehicles coordinator, two of the sponsorship representatives, two members from the line liaison committee, three members from the pre-launch, launch and post-launch security and the coverall clad building and maintenance representative.

With so many sitting in McCarthy's office the director did not brook showboating. Each representative spoke. McCarthy listened and stopped reports with finger or hand gestures. The meeting was scheduled, according to Michele Sanderson, for ninety minutes.

"Break this down," McCarthy said. "I have other things on my agenda today."

"Well, sir, there were many positives from this iteration of the Pandemonium Challenge," said ZZ Packer Anderson, the easygoing marketing coordinator. ZZ Parker always seemed to find the good in situations.

"Our wagering numbers were up just a little over two hundred percent from last year," Nina Kennedy said. Kennedy was the shifty and jittery wagering supervisor.

"Enough," McCarthy said. "Negatives?"

There was a pause.

"There were two stoppages in this year's challenge, as you know," said Oscar Micheaux Harrison, supervisor of launch security. "We are addressing both situations as best we can. We want to have in place fail safes to alert us of any incursions to the island in advance."

McCarthy raised an eyebrow.

"We will need radar installed," Harrison said.

"As you know Julius, there were a few blind spots noted," Alicia Charles said with a frown. "We are addressing those blind spots now that the challenge is over. We are determined to shore up the inconsistencies in this year's challenge."

"That is fine and good," McCarthy said with a nod of his head. "I am curious about the report that your researcher said she had submitted." McCarthy was looking at Alicia Charles. "I want a report on the serial killer gene that the researcher mentioned," McCarthy said. McCarthy paused and his assistant leaned in. There was a muted exchange between the pair as McCarthy looked at Charles evenly. "I want all the information about this serial killer gene available. Have Mackenzie Meyer write the report."

After the sponsorship report McCarthy stopped the meeting.

"John, I don't know if this is possible, but I think we are not getting enough airplay on our sponsors." He looked to John Faucette Dawson and Virginia Hamilton Scott. The pair were responsible for acquiring sponsors for the challenge. "I think we can get more sponsorship camera time at the sky bridge and supply dump machine." McCarthy stopped and looked at the pair. "Also, why don't we have a sponsor for the Former Lakes of Nations?"

Before Dawson or Scott could speak Julius McCarthy had moved on in the meeting agenda.

"Last item of this meeting," McCarthy said. "Firings." He paused. "Fire Lewis Anderson, Attaway, Gwendolyn Bennett, Donald Crews, Quincy Drummond, Mary Howard, James Johnson, the camera installation contractor, Manning Marable, Anne Oates, Marc Olden, Francis Ray, Lorenzo and Piri Thomas and I want Harrison, from security, to be put on probation. If there is one person to get on the island on the upcoming challenge that we do not know about, Harrison, you are fired and all your team with you."

The table was library quiet. Michele Sanderson wrote down everything word for word. At the end of the firings McCarthy nodded.

"That's it," McCarthy said. "Meeting adjourned."

With those words everyone climbed to their feet and began their exit of the director's office. There was no loitering or lollygagging. People streamed out of the office quickly, leaving Julius McCarthy with his assistant.

"Reports on my desk by end of week," McCarthy said to his assistant. He paused. "I am worried about our security. Ask HR to find us some more capable recruits."

Michelle Sanderson nodded and typed her notes onto the notebook computer. McCarthy's assistant looked up, waiting.

"That's all, Michelle," Julius McCarthy said. He took a deep breath and looked to his assistant. "Michelle, step out," McCarthy said.

McCarthy's assistant nodded and stepped out of office.

From another door in the office entered two men and two women. They were dressed in the distinctive Red Hand uniforms.

The four faces that McCarthy studied were stern and battle weary.

Clarissa Minnie Thompson Allen stood six feet tall and had long limbs and curly black hair that fell across half of her small pleasing face.

James Baldwin Bell had a bald head and a full beard on his brown oval face. He was six feet tall and sturdily built.

Roy Glenn Locke, the leader of the team, had a tight fade and goatee. He wore glasses. He was a scarred and rugged looking man. Under his left eye was a thin scar that followed the arc of his lower eye socket. Below that scar was two-inch-long razor thin scars.

The last person of the Red Hand quartet was Harriett Jacobs Reed. She was just five foot six inches tall and weighed one hundred and thirty pounds. She had braided hair that was trimmed above her ears. She was a hardened, unsmiling tough with five angular scars on her pointy chin.

"So, what do we have?" McCarthy asked as a matter of fact.

"Well, we have pulled up some old dirt on Wood and Williams," Clarissa Minnie Thompson Allen said. "We have leaked it to the Interweb already and Central Government legal."

"We are trying to find something on Hutchinson," Roy Glenn Locke, the man with the goatee said.

"Okay, we need to concentrate on the boy," McCarthy said coolly. "Smear his character."

"There is a bunch of noise that Ralphie Reynolds is out of the compound," Clarissa Allen said. She was not curvaceous except at her small chest and hips.

"I heard," McCarthy said. "We should be able to find him quickly," the director said pointing to his monitor.

"What about Ralphie's family?" Roy Glenn Locke asked without emotion.

"That's a last-ditch effort," McCarthy said. "Concentrate on the boy," McCarthy said to Roy Glenn Locke. "We need to make sure that people wonder about his character. That's to our benefit." McCarthy paused. "Your job is to create questions for the residents to answer."

"What about Higgins?" Roy Glenn Locke asked McCarthy evilly.

"She's off limits," the director said.

Clarissa Allen frowned. James Bell grimaced. Harriet Reed shook her head.

"You tied our hands with Higgins, even though she is aiding them," Roy Glenn Locke said.

"Right," McCarthy said. "None of her actions matter. We keep the line leaders on our side. No matter what."

"Well, what about the Innovator?" Locke asked curiously.

"What about the First Gen?" Clarissa Allen asked with the loose curls dangling into her greenish eyes.

"What about them?" McCarthy asked. "I said, concentrate on the boy. Period."

"Okay, we are going to locate the little snot and...?" Clarissa Minnie Thompson Allen asked.

"Surprise me," McCarthy said. He raised a finger. "Destroy his character. Make the Remains question his integrity."

"Can we frame him?" Roy Glenn Locke asked.

"Sure," McCarthy said with a smirk.

"Can we bend him?" James Bell asked, frustrated by the conversation.

"I suppose," McCarthy said.

"Can we set him up if others get in our way?" Roy Glenn asked.

"Of course," Julius McCarthy said. "Just do not ice Ralphie."

"Got it." Clarissa Allen said. As she stood and studied the director through ice cold hazel green eyes.

*　*　*　*　*

Ralphie sat on the back of Jesse's scooter as the Revolutionaries rode east. Albert had an idea. Yo-Yo and Ella flanked Albert. Jesse, on the biggest and slowest of the scooters, took up the rear.
The scooter crew raced to Skyline Boulevard. There were all these million-dollar homes lining the quiet and deserted part of the Remains. As the scooters slowed and stopped on the neglected stretch of road that had been blocked off heading steadily uphill.

"Where are we going?" Ralphie asked, curious.

"Ella has the map," Jesse said.

Ralphie did not ask again.

On a long drag up to what looked like an overgrown forest that was starting to creep across the road the four scooters stopped.

There were a dozen homes on the side of the road that looked out and toward the Acid Bay, but none of them were occupied.

"Do people live up here?" Albert asked.

"No. I doubt it," Ella said. "Maybe one or two eccentrics, but no one in their right mind would live up here."

"It's spooky up here," Yo-Yo said, climbing off her scooter.

Albert nodded. He was skittish. He did a 360° scan of the area as he stepped toward Cedric and Jesse. Erica stood next to Jesse with her hands in her hoody front pocket.

"We're near the wall," Ella said looking at the transports that lined the road, but no longer functioned.

"So?"

178

"So, my dad told me to take you up here," Ella said. "To see the territory."

The Revolutionaries fell silent. Ralphie looked at Ella, curiously.

Ella continued. "The way I see it, the most logical way to keep you safe is to go where the Red Hand won't look for you," Ella said.

"Sounds logical," Albert said.

"I think your dad is probably the smartest person I know," Jesse said. "But..."

"But this is too much," Albert said.

"I mean, I don't know anyone that voluntarily goes to the wall," Erica said.

"Right," Jesse said.

"Well, let's go in and give it a look see, if it's too... much, we can always turn around," Ella said, looking at Ralphie. "We got to find some place to hide the most famous person in the Remains right now."

"Yeah, but--," Yo-Yo said, looking at the blocked off road.

"I got a plan," Ella said. "Follow me."

Ella walked to the blocked off section of road and squeezed through the cement barricades.

"You sure about this?" Yo-Yo asked.

"Pretty sure," Ella said, looking at her watch.

"We're trusting you," Albert said.

"Have I ever steered you wrong?" Ella asked with a smirk.

The six behind Ella squeezed through the barricades and walked up the disused road.

"We need to be careful, Ella," Albert said as he climbed the twisting road.

"We're always careful," Ella said.

"Well, according to my research the Pandemonium Challenge Committee are not people you want to get on the wrong side of," Albert said.

Yo-Yo nodded. Jesse hummed. Cedric looked around and kept walking. Erica nodded. Ralphie just smirked. Albert tried to pace himself. He was sweating.

"The challenge is over," Ella said.

"Is it?" Yo-Yo asked looking back and seeing the Acid Bay and what had once been San Francisco in the distance.

"They may be angry and upset, but they can't stay angry at a bunch of kids forever," Ella said walking up the street and turning at the bend of the road they were climbing. Trees and brush lined and canopied the road on either side.

"They don't see the difference," Albert said trying to keep up with Ella.

No one spoke. They just kept climbing to the next bend in the twisting road.

"We are the difference. We are going to make others start to wonder if the challenge makes sense," Ella said.

There was a pause. The seven continued walking away from Skyline and the Acid Bay.

"Not everyone is a revolutionary, Ella," Erica said.

"Not everyone. But some are," Ella said.

After four turns on the overgrown road the Acid Bay disappeared. Behind them was now only trees and bushes. The road was eerily quiet. The silence fell upon the seven as they walked through an unnatural stillness in the darkened road.

Out of the fourth bend to Grizzly Peak stepped three dark and shadowy individuals. They were dressed in enforcer gear, but with some unique distinctions. In the waning light Ralphie and the others could see the glint of steel and metal.

Instantly, Cedric stopped. Ella looked back and the others paused. Ralphie narrowed his eyes at the three. Two of the three were women, based on their hips and compact frames. The third was a block of stone with dark almond shaped eyes holding an assault rifle.

"Whoa," Albert said.

Ralphie looked back and saw that there were three shadowy figures who stepped out of the darkness behind them. The three behind them were two dangerous looking men and a Mohawk wearing woman holding a menacing tomahawk.

"Which one of you is Ralphie?" The block of stone asked.

Chapter Thirteen.

The Champions

Stuart Scott Somers the seventeen-year-old Trad stared at Ralphie through dark almond shaped eyes. He was a curly haired teen with thick eyebrows, broad nose, the beginnings of a mustache and stubble on his round chin. As a Trad Somers wore a black and white beanie and around his neck was a black and white scarf. Ralphie recalled that Somers was the Twenty-First Pandemonium Champion.

Wesley Snipes Crane was the second in command of the champions. He had won the Twenty-Second Pandemonium Challenge and was seventeen years old as well. He had short, trimmed, dyed blonde hair. He was a dark eyed tough who had represented the Boomers in the challenge.

"Who are all of these?" Wesley Snipes Crane asked, looking at the Revolutionaries.

Ralphie introduced everyone. Somers and Crane got bored after the second name. The curly haired leader shook his head and walked away uninterested. Wesley Crane watched Somers depart, leaving him to listen to Ralphie's introduction of the Revolutionaries.

"Listen, this ain't no baby ride," Crane said, raising his hand and stopping Ralphie.

"We were told you would be here, and we were supposed to wait," London Adams, the young woman with the Mohawk said. She was a strikingly beautiful twenty-year old with a wicked scar that began under her right ear and cut across her cheek like a fishhook. London was also the Nineteenth Pandemonium Champion. London was sitting on a bench next to the tattooed Rose Jewell on the side of the road.

"No one said anything about the Brady Bunch," Jewell said scanning everyone with her froggish eyes. Jewell. She was the Twentieth Pandemonium Champion. Jewell was dressed in dark blue and light blue camouflage shirt and trousers with black combat boots. The twenty-year old had finger tattoos and a neck tattoo. On her head were dozens of finger thick French braids.

"Yeah, this ain't no kiddie ride we're going on," Wesley Crane said. He was checking his flashlight beam.

"This is going to be a fight," Somers, the seventeen-year-old Trad, said.

Rose Johnston, a round faced girl with straightened black hair and wearing a ball and chain necklace with a dog tag attached stepped forward, holding her assault rifle. She big eyes and a big smile as she tilted her head and seemed ready to laugh at the Revolutionaries.

"This is not going to be some walk in the park," Rose Johnston said as she watched Somers walking uphill.

"We're still going to stick with Ralphie," Ella said with a pout.

Crane smiled at Ella.

"You must be Ella," Crane said. "The Mover and Shaker?"

"Yep," Ella said, with a tilt of her head. "Why?"

"We were warned you might be a firecracker," Jewell said baring her small teeth.

"Well, if that means you cannot scare me off, then you're right," Ella said showing her perfect teeth.

"Well, if it was me and I didn't have no weapons to protect myself with and some hitters were warning me," the tall, dark young man with a three-inch-high Afro and beard said holding an assault rifle. "I would listen and turn back."

"Who are you?" Ella asked, annoyed.

The champion shook his head and kept walking up the hill.

"That's Valentine," Yo-Yo said to Ella. "He was the fourth Boomer to win the Pandemonium Championship. He was also the youngest Boomer to win at fifteen."

The Seventeenth Pandemonium Champion looked at Yo-Yo and grudgingly smiled.

"He's twenty, now," Yo-Yo said looking at Valentine.

Ella shrugged her shoulders unmoved. Crane spoke briefly with Ella. Ella shook her head. The daughter of Gordon Buchanan walked away from the champion visibly annoyed.

"Okay, this is where you kids get off," Somers said. He pointed to the ground where there was a white line painted. In front of the gathered was the edge of the interior wall. There to the right stood a twenty-foot-high wall running parallel with the road. The wall was a sheer gray rise of stone.

"What is this?" Albert asked pointing to the line on the ground.

"The line that separates playtime from the real nightmares," Somers said.

"Nothing ahead is good," Nikki Giovanni Fisher said. She was the oldest member of the ragtag group of Pandemonium Champions. She was the Eighteenth Pandemonium Champion and represented the Trads.

"So, what? You expect us to go back down that creepy and scary road by ourselves?" Erica asked.

The Pandemonium Champions smiled at Erica's question.

"Again, ain't nothing good ahead," Nikki Fisher said. She had reddish brown shoulder length curly hair, a high forehead, and arched eyebrows. Her nose was round and sat above full lips. She was a short young woman with wide hips and a big butt. "If you cross this line, you are on your own," Fisher the heavy chested twenty-year-old said wearing round reflective glasses.

Crane and Jewell teased the Revolutionaries as they stepped across the white line.

"Any of you armed?" Jewell asked, jokingly.

The Revolutionaries looked at each other and then the champions.

"You got any extra weapons?" Cedric asked.

"Hell to the no," Valentine said.

"The worst thing is to get flatlined from some stiff you know who doesn't know his ass from a hole in the ground," Crane said.

"Friendly fire," Jewell said with a frown and a frustrated shake of her head allowing Ralphie to see a small, detailed goldfish tattoo behind her right ear.

"So, no," Yo-Yo said.

"No," Wesley Crane said.

"You should all turn around," Nikki said as a last warning.

"Not going to happen," Ella said.

"It's your funeral," Nikki said. She turned and on her back was her black matte backpack.

"What do we do?" London Adams asked.

"They'll turn around when we climb the interior wall," Somers said. "Besides, we only need to worry about Ralphie."

"What do we do until then?" Valentine asked.

"Keep going and watch for booby traps," Crane said.

Fisher walked point with Crane. Behind them watching the roadsides were Somers and London. Ralphie was next to Valentine. Behind Ralphie was Ella, Yo-Yo, Albert, Erica, and Jesse followed behind. Taking up the rear was Cedric and Rose.

"Keep up or get left behind," Jewell said to Cedric, Erica, and Jesse.

Fifteen minutes from the last conversation the group stopped. The six were at the side of the road where at any other time it might have been a parking lot or area where people gathered to go and have a lunch under the trees. Now, it was just a place where ten shells of transports had been pushed to keep the roadway clear.

"Educate the newbies," Fisher said to London, who was sipping at her water bottle.

"For our own good," Valentine said adjusting his khopesh on his backpack. The curved blade was sheathed and secured against the side of his backpack.

"Okay, poo butts, listen up, I'm only saying this once. If you ain't listening then you ain't planning on living, so it won't matter," London Adams said annoyed. "Once we're in between the two walls you need to know that we will see some Zeds."

"What?" Albert asked, surprised.

"Really?" Cedric said, closing his eyes upon speaking.

The Mohawked London continued. "There are three types of Zeds, as far as we know. There's the slow, move only if you make a lot of noise or are bleeding types. We call them: Leeches. They react. They hear a noise or smell blood, and they attack. The second type are the prowlers. They are like wolves. They seem to just be moving around looking for us. We don't know why. We don't care. The third type is the pack Zeds. They are weird. Really weird. They gather in groups. They hide during the day in buildings and dark places. They usually don't do anything during the day. They don't sleep. Don't think Zeds need to sleep. Anyway, the pack follow one of two other Zeds. They attack and eat all together." London said, looking around the road. "If they grab you, they tear you apart to share with the pack."

"Collectively," Albert said to London.

"Yeah," London said, looking at Albert. "The best thing is they all have the same off button." She pointed to her head. "Cut it off. Shoot it off. Blow their brains out. They stop being a threat." London looked at the Revolutionaries. "If you run into one, bash its brains out before it tears you apart."

After London's pep talk the Revolutionaries armed themselves as best, they could. Ralphie searched around the rest area and found a tire iron in one of the shells of a transport. Ella found a metal tennis racket. Albert found a bag of golf clubs and handed them out to everyone without a weapon. Jesse took a wooden driver from Albert. Erica took a lacrosse stick she found in the interior of one of the transports. Yo-Yo took a metal headed golf club. Cedric found an aluminum baseball bat under the frame of one of the transports.

Less than thirty minutes from the rest stop the group stopped again. There before them was a locked door. Valentine and Jewell entered first. The group moved into the doorway that led to a short hallway inside of the interior wall. Ralphie knew the interior and exterior walls were ten feet wide and twenty feet high. The six-foot-wide hallway led to a short set of stairs with a gate at the top. The gate was latched and used to deter mindless creature's entrance. At the bottom of the stairs was another door. The door was hinged and only opened if pushed in the right spot. Stepping through the door Ralphie found himself and the others in the ground down gravel and dirt between the interior wall and the exterior wall.

"Be careful," Fisher said.

Adams was looking south and holding her assault rifle, ready for anything. Valentine was watching straight ahead. Crane was guarding the north. Somers, Brown, and Jewell stood waiting for Ralphie.

"Okay, we're headed north," Somers said. "Wes, Nikki, take point. London, you, and JB take lead. Rose you got our backs," Somers said. Somers grabbed Ralphie and pulled him next to him.

The group moved away from the doorway back to the other side of the interior wall. Ella, Cedric, and Albert stepped behind

Ralphie and Somers. Jesse, Erica, and Yo-Yo fell in behind Ella. Erica looked back longingly. Jesse and Yo-Yo put their arms around the short and scared girl and pulled her along.

The space between the interior wall and exterior wall was not straight. As Crane and Fisher ran ahead and then turned there was a visible bend in the wall that jogged to the left just enough to hide the two champions ahead for a few minutes, until the group reached the jog. The space was not flat either.

"You know that the exterior wall was built first?" Albert asked no one in particular. "I would have thought that when they built the interior wall, they would have cleared all the trees and houses out. It would have been an easier way to protect the space."

No one responded to Albert's insights. Yo-Yo rolled her eyes. Albert complained about the road surface.

Nikki Giovanni Fisher, the Trad was the first to see a prowler step around the rubble accumulated near a bend in the road. Wesley Crane was the second. Instantly, they pulled their pointed weapons and prepared for the first attack.

Fisher had a spear. Crane had a pike. Somers reached out to stop anyone from passing him. He was between London and Valentine. Adams pulled her tomahawk from her backpack.

"Stealth this," Crane said, scanning the terrain and adjusting his grip on his pike in preparation for skewering the prowler.

The prowler moved forward slowly growling with its arms stretched out in front of it dressed in scraps of clothing. There were three of them. The first wore a tattered sweater and shreds of trousers and work boots. Ralphie noticed that one of the prowlers looked vaguely like a woman, if the woman was skeletal, bleeding and more animal than human.

Fisher was the first to strike. She stepped forward as the first prowler dressed in what looked like a concert T-shirt and torn jeans got close to her. The diminutive champion aimed the spear expertly at the open-mouthed Zed's head. The spear hit the Zed below the area where there would have been a nose and Fisher, the determined Trad, stepped forward and drove the sharpened spear tip through the Zed's head. Fisher twisted the spear as she pulled it out of the non-moving creature's head. Instantly, the Zed crumbled in front of the Trad.

The second Zed following close behind the other fell as Crane punched the creature in the chest with his pike and then through the eye socket. The second stab through the eye stopped the creature dressed in rags and one shoe. Like the Zed before, it fell to its knees and then face first onto the ground in front of Wesley Crane.

The third Zed, closest to Crane, undeterred from the carnage, reached out for the Twenty-Second champion. The hardnosed Trad adjusted and swung left and drove her spear through the temple of the Zed about to attack Crane. The Zed froze. Fisher drove the spear through the Zed's head and pulled back as the creature dropped his arms to his side. Removing the spear tip from the Zed caused the growling and actions to stop and the creature to fall over motionless.

"You seeing this?" Ella asked shaking and holding her tennis racket tightly.

"Definitely seeing this," Jesse said, looking around nervously and twirling his golf club. Erica seeing the Zeds froze beside Jesse. Cedric swallowed and blinked but did not move.

The two turned toward the area in the road where the prowlers had emerged. Standing there was a lone Zed. Ella tapped Ralphie and the others were surprised to see it standing, watching, and observing but not moving forward. The single Zed did not advance. It simply stood, fifty feet away from Fisher and Crane.

"That is odd. Right?" Crane asked.

"Yep," Fisher said.

"What do we do?" Crane asked.

"Not sure," Fisher said.

The one Zed backed away from Crane and Fisher and disappeared into the darkness. Ralphie observed what the last Zed had done. He frowned at the unusual action. He reached out to Somers.

"That's not normal. Is it?" Ralphie asked studying the Zed.

Somers and Valentine shook their heads.

"That wasn't a leech or a prowler or a pack Zed," Ralphie said aloud.

"Nope, none of them," Somers said.

"That's never good," Fisher said.

"Are there supposed to be Zeds in the interior wall?" Yo-Yo asked.

"No, but obviously they're here," Valentine said.

"They aren't supposed to be too many," Somers said.

There was a lull. Fisher and Crane moved forward and down the space between the interior wall. Somers looked at the Revolutionaries and smiled. "Okay, you guys still can go back," Somers said with a knowing smile. "This ain't a game."

"If you want to go back then go back. We got to keep moving," London said.

Erica reached out and grabbed Jesse's hand. She pulled on Jesse as he looked at Ella, Albert, and Yo-Yo.

"Think I'm going to head back," Jesse said, looking at Ella.

Ella nodded. Cedric looked at Ella.

"Ced, you can go if you want. No shame in this," Ella said.

Cedric nodded. He and Jesse along with Erica walked back down the path that they had come from and away from the others.

Chapter Fourteen.

Nightmares.

Thirty minutes later Fisher and Crane signaled the sight of more Zeds. They did not appear to be prowlers. The two stood against the far wall, stock still, and for the first time Ralphie saw the glowing red eyes of a Zed.

"London or Val, maybe we can try to catch one of them," Crane said.

"What do you say Stu?" Valentine asked with a smile.

"I think if we can catch one it might answer some questions the men and women sent us to answer," Somers said.

"Okay, London, take my place at point," Crane said. "Val and I got some hunting to do."

London stepped forward. Crane and Valentine peeled off from the main group and headed toward the two red eyed Zeds.

Nikki G. and London were on point.

"What do we do now?" Jewell asked.

"The mission hasn't changed," Somers said. "We keep going. We're headed for the labs."

The group kept moving. Ralphie watched as Crane and Valentine walked slowly and quietly toward the red eyed Zeds.

"You watching this?" Yo-Yo asked.

Ralphie nodded.

The group slowed as they reached a bend that would take them out of the line of sight of Crane and Valentine.

"Keep going," the froggish Jewell said from the rear.

The group turned and Crane and Valentine disappeared out of sight.

Fifteen minutes later the group heard the first sounds of gunfire. The distinctive crack of gunfire was other worldly in the quiet between the two walls.

Somers pushed back and through the group and everyone stopped as he reached Jewell.

"What's going on?"

"No idea," Jewell said.

"Okay, keep your eyes open. Don't let someone sneak up on us," Somers said.

"Got you," Jewell said. She adjusted her assault rifle in her hands, ready for anything.

"Keep moving," Somers said to London and Fisher.

The two young women moved cautiously up a slope. At the top of the slope the pair disappeared. Everyone in the group behind Fisher and Adams moved up the hill, nervously.

More gunfire erupted from behind them.

"Rose? What you got?" Somers asked, with a growl.

"Nothing," Rose said, unconcerned with being stealthy.

A minute later Jewell lifted her assault rifle and fired into the space behind the group.

"We got trouble behind us," Rose said, pushing against Albert and Yo-Yo.

Ralphie turned to see ten red eyes spread out behind the group, maybe one hundred yards away, moving quickly toward them.

"Against the wall," Somers said, directing everyone to the closest protection.

Somers had his assault rifle up and at the ready. The group was at the crest of the hill London and Fisher had just summited. Somers and Ralphie looked down and two or three hundred feet ahead at the base of the hill Fisher and Adams had their assault rifles leveled and aimed into the darkness. They seemed as if they were preparing for a fight.

"Think we can hide in one of those houses," Ella said to Somers holding her tennis racket.

Somers looked from Ella to the houses and back to the red eyed Zeds moving towards them.

"Worth a shot," Somers said. "Let's head to the closest house and try and hide there until the red eyed freaks pass us by," Somers said. "If nothing else, we'll have a defensible space."

The house they picked had a garage in the front and Ralphie scanned the exterior for a quick entrance. Ella and Albert each checked the front door only to find in locked.

"Kick the door in," Yo-Yo said to Somers. The teenager looked at the door and shook his head. The door was solid oak.

There was no way Somers was going to be able to kick the door off its hinges.

Ralphie examined the garage door and jammed his tire iron into the corner of the door and lifted as hard as he could. By some miracle, the garage door popped and rolled up two feet from the ground. Ella, by Ralphie's side, seeing the garage door open rolled underneath with Yo-Yo and Albert close behind.

"Stu, you go," London said, watching the road, having signaled Fisher with her flashlight.

Rose slipped under the garage door next. Then Somers and Nikki G., the hardnosed Trad. The last into the garage was London.

Once London was inside Somers and Albert pushed the garage door down and back in place.

"Come on," said Ella at the entrance to the laundry room of the house with her flashlight. The seven walked past a washer and dryer and into a kitchen with a stove, refrigerator, and island in the middle of the kitchen. The window over the sink was boarded up. The deeper the group walked into the spacious interior of the home the more there was to see. At the end of the kitchen was a sliding glass door that had Venetian blinds. There was no wall or separation between the kitchen and the wide area that held a couch and fireplace.

The low-slung one-story ranch style house was eerily quiet. The front windows were boarded up from the inside in a hasty amateur fashion.

"You think this was from the flash?" Albert asked.

"Does it matter?" Fisher asked, with a smirk. She pushed into the living room where there was a table flipped over and a half dozen chairs strewn around the room.

"What do we do?" Yo-Yo asked, frightened.

"Wait," Somers said. "There's nothing else to do." He paused. He looked to Rose. "Check the front and see if those things are out there." He looked to Fisher. "Check the back. Maybe we can climb down and out of this?"

He looked to Ralphie and the Revolutionaries. "Check the cabinets for anything canned. We can always eat canned goods." He looked to Albert. "You're the brain. Check and see if there any weapons we can use."

Albert nodded and looked around the living room with his flashlight. He systematically scanned every inch of every room in the house. In the four-bedroom home Albert found the two owners remains, or what was left of them, in the main bedroom. The other bedrooms were empty and clean as if no one had slept there for years. Albert found a shotgun and two pistols. He also included the knives from the kitchen.

"Those knives are going to do a fat lot of good against Zeds," Fisher said with a laugh. She studied the shotgun. There was a box of shells next to the weapon. "Now, this might be something."

Ralphie and Yo-Yo, after searching the kitchen cabinets found they had a stack of thirty-seven cans of peaches, half and sliced, pears, sliced, fruit cocktail, three cans of yams, two cans of mandarin oranges, four cans of sardines, one can of tuna, ham, cranberry sauce, four cans of baked beans, pork 'n beans, green beans, pinto beans and seven cans of tomato sauce.

"Okay, we got some food. Now, we're going to lay low for a while. They usually are less aggressive in the day," Somers said. "So, we'll rest until first light."

"I'll take first watch," Albert said picking up one of the pistols. Somers stepped forward and twisted the pistol out of Albert's hand.

"Do it in pairs," Ralphie said.

"Two to four hours each," Ella said with a knowing smile.

Ralphie tried to rest. Ralphie ate a can of peaches and shared a cold can of baked beans with Ella and Albert. Ella found a chair and instantly fell asleep under the watchful eyes of Rose and Yo-Yo in the front room. Ralphie grabbed a few cushions and threw them against a wall where he could see the front door and the back sliding glass door.

Albert climbed to his feet and went to the back window and sat across from Fisher, who was peering out the blinds.

"What you doing here?" Nikki G. asked, sweeping her two loose braids from her dark face.

"Keeping you company," Albert said.

"Okay, just don't bother me," Fisher said.

"Okay," Albert said with a nod of his head. "How did you get that scar?"

"Here's my rule. We play the silent game until you get bored and go night-night," Fisher said, glaring at Albert with anger in her eyes.

Albert squeezed his lips together.

Ralphie could only smile and shake his head from his resting spot. The resting spot was against a wall just a few feet from the living room. It wasn't like at the Buchanans or at his own home, but it was dry and for the moment safe. He sat on the floor with a few cushions to support his tired body and rest his head.

From his resting spot Ralphie watched the front of the house were Yo-Yo and Rose sat watching for trouble. Ralphie yawned, physically tired and listened to Rose and Yo-Yo talking in hushed tones.

"Yo-Yo, how you know all these heads?" Rose Johnston asked.

"What you mean? You guys are famous," Yo-Yo said with a fanciful smile.

"Seriously?" Rose asked with a snort.

"Yeah, when you win the championship, you become a legend," Yo-Yo said. "I know that as a Shaker we're not supposed to be all into it, but I am."

Rose nodded.

"Did you meet all the champions?" Yo-Yo asked, edging forward, just a little.

"No, just a few," Rose said.

Yo-Yo nodded.

"How many can you name?" Yo-Yo asked.

"I can name six, at least," Rose said.

"I can name ten at least if not more," Yo-Yo said with a confident smile.

"Bet?" Rose asked.

"Bet," Yo-Yo said.

"Go," Rose said.

"Okay," Yo-Yo said. She frowned, thinking. "There's Benning, the first, Seals the second, Taylor the third, Reed the fourth," Yo-Yo said stopping. "I know there was Idris Elba Roth, he was the first Boomer, Hank Aaron Price, Oprah Winfrey Johnson, Valentine, who I met today, Nikki Giovanni Fisher

London Adams and you. I think you were the second or third Second Gen champions ever," Yo-Yo said. "Stuart Somers and Wesley Crane, the Boomer... and Ralphie," Yo-Yo said. "That's all I got."

Ralphie listened and smiled as he fell asleep. The moment he closed his eyes Ralphie found himself in this weird place that reminded him of the McDonalds hill, but it was something else.

In the sky floated airships. On the hillside Ralphie saw someone waving at him. Curious, he climbed to his feet and walked toward the person. As he got close the person mysteriously seemed to distance himself from Ralphie.

Ralphie decided to run and close the distance between himself and the person that was still waving.

As he began running a gigantic figure appeared out of nowhere, standing ten or twelve feet tall. The giant lumbered in the opposite direction unconcerned about Ralphie or the person waving.

Ralphie ran on trying to catch the person who seemed just one or two hundred feet away. As he got close, he found more of the giants walking oblivious of Ralphie.

He ran and as he did, he heard the first sound of baying. The sound stopped Ralphie in his tracks. He turned and from the darkness he first saw the glowing green eyes and the slobbering lips of ravenous dogs. Dogs, packs of dogs, appeared out of the darkness of the nightmare scene and began loping after Ralphie.

Ralphie immediately forgot the waving person and started to run for his life.

The pack of dogs turned into werewolves.

Ralphie ran on, fearing that he was going to be caught and devoured by the pack of were creatures.

Thankfully, Ralphie found a building and ran inside.

"What are you looking for, Ralphie?"

"Where are you going?"

"Search for the tunnels?"

Instantly, in the darkness, the voice that spoke formed around a pale creature with hypnotic eyes wearing a dark suit and a knowing smile. The smile did not put Ralphie at ease. Instead, the smile made Ralphie uneasy.

"Are you searching for vampires, Ralphie?" The handsome pale man asked revealing sharp incisors like a wolf.

Ralphie sat up wide awake. He blinked and found himself still on the edge of the kitchen and the living room. Ralphie rubbed at his eyes making sure he was truly awake.

He looked down and found Ella sleeping just a few feet away with her tennis racket nearby.

Ralphie looked around the darkness that washed over the interior of the house they were hiding in. Rose and Yo-Yo were still in the same place they had been before Ralphie had fallen asleep. He looked back and found Nikki sitting against the wall, looking through the blinds and out into the darkened backyard. Albert was missing.

"You okay, kid?"

Ralphie looked around the darkness where the voice had sounded and found Stuart Somers sitting in a corner of the living room with his assault rifle leaning against his shoulder.

Ralphie did not speak. He instead, studied Somers.

"Bad dreams?" Somers asked. "It's the reward of surviving the challenge," Somers said to Ralphie.

"Do they ever stop?"

"I'll tell you when they do," Somers said.

Ralphie nodded and smirked.

"What made you sign up for this?" Somers asked.

Ralphie did not answer. He did not know how to answer. He knew that there was this longing, this desire to not think and just do. The more he stood around the more he wanted to run. Returning to the Remains had been his hope when on the island and once he got back he wanted to be anywhere but there. Ralphie thought all that and looked at Somers and shrugged his shoulders as an answer.

"Well according to my watch, the suns up in an hour," Somers said. "We'll be out of here and headed to the labs in less than two if we can eat and skedaddle, with no problems," Somers said.

Ralphie took in the information and nodded.

"You go and find London and Albert," Somers said, adjusting the assault rifle in his hands and climbing to his feet.

Ralphie slowly climbed to his feet feeling his body stiffen with the effort. On his feet Ralphie stretched his arms over his head and did a few side twists. He looked down and saw the P23 lapel pin and smiled, thinking of his family and Macy specifically. Ralphie grabbed his backpack and slipped it on with the golf club resting on the top of pack as Somers remained in the shadows.

Ralphie walked to the rear of the house and found London in the biggest room in a corner with her eyes closed. Ralphie hesitated. He stood watching London for a full minute before he stepped out of the bedroom and knocked lightly on the doorframe just outside the bedroom.

"Hey, London," Ralphie said, his voice clear but not loud. "Somers told me to find you and tell you we are heading out in an hour."

London climbed to her feet slowly. She stretched after placing her rifle against the wall. Ralphie smiled at the fact that London stretched just like him when she woke.

"You can go," London said pointedly.

Ralphie nodded and turned on his heels and headed back to the living room where everyone was assembled. By the time he returned Albert was there, looking sleepy.

"Where did you sleep?" Ralphie asked Albert. "You don't look like you got a lot of sleep."

"In the bathtub," Albert said. "It's the safest place in the house."

Ella was unusually quiet. Ralphie assumed that was because it was not yet seven in the morning.

"Okay, we have a long walk ahead of us," Somers said. "I ain't babysitting. You rich kids keep up or get left behind. We ain't turning back."

They washed up and cleaned up as best they could. There was water but it was ice cold. They ate cold rations and canned food.

"Eat up," Somers said. He and the champions had taken what they wanted and put three or four cans of food in their backpacks.

What remained of the thirty-seven cans were two cans of yams, four cans of sardines, one can of cranberry sauce, a can of coconut milk, one can of pinto beans and the seven cans of tomato sauce.

With everyone fed Somers led everyone to the garage to exit the house. Everyone climbed under the garage door. Somers was the last out of the garage.

Out of the garage and in the driveway Ralphie noticed that there was an old-fashioned combustion engine transport parked in the driveway. Ralphie curious walked to the transport and marveled at the cracked and deteriorating rubber on the wheels. The transport was covered in a thick layer of dirt and dust. Ralphie pressed a hand to the window and rubbed to reveal a pristine interior of a car that had to be at least a half century old.

"Okay, we're moving out," Somers said. "London, you take point today. Rose you stay in the middle with me and Ralphie. Fish you relax a little today. Take up the rear."

"Roger that," Nikki said with a small smile.

"Ella stay close," Ralphie said. The Innovator stepped forward and next to Ralphie. Ella looked back and gestured to Yo-Yo and Albert. The two stepped forward as London began to walk ahead of Somers and Rose.

"Move out," Somers said. He and Rose began to walk. A few seconds later everyone was in motion.

Somers and Rose kept an eye on Ralphie as they walked.

"Why they watching you?"

Ralphie shrugged.

"Think my daddy has some kind of deal in place with them," Ella said.

"Shut up and keep walking," Nikki said in a low growl from behind. "Less talking. More walking."

Ten minutes away from the house and Nikki G. found Albert slowing.

"Keep up," Nikki G. said, finding Albert lagging. He struggled. Albert the shortest of the three also had the shortest gait.

Just thirty minutes away from the house London stopped and everyone rested.

"What's the problem Albert?"

"Nothing," Albert said. "I'm just not some overly athletic individual."

"This is a short break," Somers said. "We'll go a little longer on the second hike." Somers paused. "Think we are maybe four or five hours away from the labs."

The group began to walk again. The twenty-foot interior wall was on the left of the group and pushed them into the middle of what was Skyline Boulevard. There were only two sightings of Zeds before reaching an overgrown section of foliage reclaiming the road.

"Be careful," London said. "This is a perfect place to walk up on a group of Zeds," she said slinging her assault rifle and drawing two metal pieces that she screwed together to make into a six-foot spear.

Somers and Rose pulled their long-range weapons from their backpacks. Somers had a wooden pool cue that had a metal barb screwed on the tip. Jewell had a surprisingly brutal weapon, a tomahawk, in her hand.

Crossing the overgrown foliage, the group stayed close and quiet. Just a handful of minutes in the dark and cool interior of what had once been a recreational park London stopped and moved to the left along the side of the road and the wall. In front of the group was a knot of a four Zeds gathered together, motionless as if they were sleeping standing up.

Ralphie froze seeing the Zeds. Somers pushed Ralphie in the direction London had gone. Jewell followed behind Somers watching the Zeds with her tomahawk in front of her. She gestured to Ella, Albert and Yo-Yo to follow. Nikki G. stepped up holding her spear.

The group skirted the Zeds without incident.

On the other side of the thick overgrowth and once again on Skyline Boulevard the group pushed away from the pack of Zeds.

The section of Skyline was empty and barren with the wall jutting up twenty feet on the left and rocks and hills to the right. Ralphie for the first time saw the exterior wall a mile away. He pointed out the exterior wall which paralleled the interior wall to Ella and the Revolutionaries.

"How much further?"

"We are getting close," Somers said. "According to the map we are just looking for Centennial Avenue."

The group walked on and at every intersection the hopes of finding Centennial Avenue rose and were dashed when that intersection was not the street they wanted.

"Finally," Somers said with a satisfied smile seeing London leaning against a street sign that was in front of the twenty-foot-high stretch of interior wall.

"How do we get down there?" Albert asked, breathing heavily, seeing the road stopped at the wall.

"Good question," Somers said. "We have to find the entrance to the guard post," Somers said, looking up and shielding his eyes to the sun above.

"There's a guard post?" Yo-Yo asked.

Ralphie pointed to the structure overhead, perched on the twenty-foot-high wall. The structure looked like a stone block sitting on top of the wall maybe fifty feet from where they were located. Ralphie estimated that it was 1600 square feet (about half the area of a tennis court) and could house at least eight people easily.

"Okay, spread out and find the gate. It has to be close," Somers said. "Be careful. There are still Zeds around."

London, Rose and Nikki G. searched for the gate to the guard outpost. Ralphie as well as the Revolutionaries searched for the gate while the others looked.

"Someone needs to tell everyone that somewhere in the exterior wall there is a breach," Albert said.

"We are the people to tell everyone, Albert," Yo-Yo said.

Nikki G. found the hidden door. Her discovery was a welcome relief. As Somers located the panel that unlocked the hinge door everyone waited anxiously.

"Somers, we got prowlers," Nikki said, lifting her spear menacingly in the direction of three prowlers that appeared around the bend of Skyline Boulevard in the direction the group had just come from.

Ralphie pulled his golf club and walked to the side of Nikki and prepared for the attack. Fisher seeing Ralphie smiled.

"We need to hurry," London said, holding her spear in front of her in the opposite direction. Ralphie looked back and saw Albert, Ella and Yo-Yo beside London. There were three prowlers moving toward London.

Somers unlocked the door and swung the heavy hinge door open.

"Everybody in," he demanded. The three prowlers that London watched were over one hundred yards away and no real threat. They were walking, not running.

Ella, Albert, Yo-Yo and London filed into the narrow hallway. Nikki was the last in, after Ralphie and then Rose.

Somers stood at the door and waited for Fisher to enter before closing and locking the door. Somers pushed forward and toward a dark set of steps.

"Where does that go?" Ella asked.

"Up," Somers said.

The group headed up the forty stone stairs to a landing and a heavy door. Somers pulled a bolt and lifted a thick latch and pushed on the door. The thick metal banded door loudly creaked open.

"You sure about this?" London asked Somers.

"Nope," Somers said and stepped through the doorway.

Behind Somers stepped London, Fisher, Yo-Yo, Ella, Albert, Ralphie and Rose.

They found themselves on the top of the wall. Ralphie felt extremely exposed. The wall top was fourteen feet wide and spaced ten feet apart were one-inch-thick eyelets drilled into the top of the wall. Where they all stood Ralphie felt that he could see all the way across the Acid Bay and to the ruins of what had been San Francisco. To the east was the rise of the hill that led east toward Nevada.

Somers stood closest to guard post wall. In front of him standing shoulder-to-shoulder were London, Nikki, and Albert. Behind those three stood Ella, Rose and Ralphie. In front of Ralphie and behind Somers was the guard post that rose another twelve feet into the air. There were no windows on the side of the wall where Ralphie looked.

"We need to find a way in," Somers said.

"Well, there has to be a way in," Rose said.

Albert sat down on the wall top and crossed his legs in front of him.

Ralphie looked back in the opposite direction of the guard post. The uncertain teen paused and narrowed his view, thinking he saw something a hundred yards away on top of the wall. He leaned forward. Ella looked at Ralphie, curiously. Yo-Yo too looked in the direction that Ralphie seemed focused on.

Nikki turned and looked at what the three teens were looking at.

"What's that?" Fisher asked.

"I think it's an enforcer," Yo-Yo said.

Chapter Fifteen.

On the wall

The heavily armored enforcer dressed in dark blue camouflage material walked slowly toward the group wearing black combat boots on the top of the interior wall. The approaching enforcer was wearing heavy dark blue gloves and heavily padded clothing. As the enforcer drew closer Ralphie noted the black harness that was attached at the navel and the padded neck collar that he had seen used for injury. The enforcer was wearing a dark blue helmet with a number on it that Ralphie could not distinguish. The helmet was scratched up and had a visor that was reflective.

When the enforcer was twenty-five feet from the group Ralphie noted the pistol holstered on his hip. In his hands was what looked like a six-foot-wide steel push broom. The enforcer stopped just short of the group and placed the push broom on the stone top of the wall.

Ralphie held his golf club in front of him in a defensive position. Ella had her tennis racket at the ready. Yo-Yo was holding her golf club. Nikki pushed through the three Revolutionaries and held her spear menacingly.

"Identify yourself," Nikki said, authoritatively.

"Me? I'm Kehoe," the enforcer wearing a scratched up helmet with the number seven on it said still ten feet away from the spear tip.

With those words Somers and Rose turned to investigate. Somers pushed through the Revolutionaries with Jewell following.

"Kehoe? We are trying to get to the Berkeley Labs," Nikki G. said with a slight smile.

"The Labs," Kehoe said, flipping up his visor and looking at the gathered. Kehoe had a scruff of chin hair and three deep cuts on the side of his cheek that extended from below his nose to his jaw. He had a broad nose and big brown eyes.

"What the hell are you doing up on the wall?" Kehoe asked showing his crooked teeth.

"We figured it was the fastest way to the labs," Somers said, stepping forward. "I'm Somers. I'm in charge."

Kehoe smiled at Somers words.

"Who's in charge here?" Somers asked looking around the top of the wall.

"That would be Major," Kehoe said with a smirk.

"Can we talk to him?"

"Sure," Kehoe said. "Coming through," he added as he walked slowly through the group and toward the guard post wall. Kehoe stopped at the door. He turned and looked at Somers.

"Suppose you came through here?" The heavily padded guard asked, pointing to the door.

Somers nodded.

Kehoe nodded. Kehoe put his hand against the side of the wall closest to the door and when he removed his hand there was a lighted keypad. He depressed a few buttons and waited. In the wall a paper-thin slit appeared. Kehoe walked to the slit and pushed it open. The inch thick stone entrance slid into the pocket of stone to reveal a hallway.

"After you," Kehoe said.

Somers walked into the eight-foot-high hall. At the end of the ten-foot-long hall there was a rectangular light. He walked inside, followed by the group and Kehoe. At the end of the hall the space opened into a square room with a stair that led to the second floor of the guard post. Under the stairs was a small kitchen with stove, refrigerator, and sink. The main floor had three rooms just off the main floor. In the center of the room was a long rectangular wooden table with eight chairs. Along the walls were several metal lockers and beside the lockers every manner of weapon. Kehoe hung his steel push broom on a hook. There were four helmets hanging on hooks as Ralphie took in the space.

Above the group there was movement. Instinctively, Ralphie prepared for an attack. No attack came. Instead, down the stairs came a gruff looking man dressed in dark blue and the same black harness system attached at the navel. On his head was a PC13 baseball cap. On his hip was a pistol.

"Kehoe, what gives? You bringing home strays now?" The dark eyed man wearing combat boots and a frown asked.

"Major," Kehoe said, turning and nodding to the gruff man looking at the group disapprovingly. "Found them on the wall. They seemed harmless enough." Kehoe snapped his gloved fingers. "Oh, we need to make sure that the entrance to the dead zone is still secure."

"Send James, he is scheduled for a security check anyway," Major said. He was a chiseled black man with broad chest, thick shoulders, small waist, and strong legs. Beneath his baseball cap were short, cropped hair and small ears.

Kehoe stripped off his heavily padded outer suit to reveal the usual enforcer uniform. Kehoe retrieved a PC22 baseball cap from his locker and slipped it onto his scarred head. Kehoe was tall and lanky. He reminded Ralphie of the boys in the compound that loved to play basketball when they had free time.

"So, how can I help you?" Major asked the group in general.

Somers stepped forward. He smiled awkwardly, rubbing at the back of his neck.

"Well, sir, as I was telling Kehoe," Somers said timidly. "We have been sent here to find the Berkeley Labs and check on some things. We climbed on top of the wall with the hopes of getting to the other side," Somers said.

Major studied Somers. He then methodically scanned everyone in the group. He smiled when he saw Nikki. He lingered on the serious looking Trad for a second longer than the others and that pause was notable.

"Going to the other side is easy, but it might be a little dangerous for all of you," Major said.

"Why's that?" Somers asked.

"Well, once you are down you aren't going to be able to come back up, at least not the same way you got down," Major said with a cheeky smile.

"What is that some kind of riddle?" Ella asked with a smirk.

"No riddle, little one," Major said with an odd smile. "Just physics."

"I think if you can help us get to the other side that would be greatly appreciated. We don't want to be a bother. We should just leave now," Somers said.

"Right," Major said. "The sun will be down in less than an hour. I wouldn't want to send you off at night. If you want you can stay the night and leave in the morning," Major said.

"Well, we'll take our chances," Somers said.

"Have you looked at your group? They look like they would benefit from a good night's rest before tackling the wall and the Labs," Major said. "Of course, you know best."

Somers hesitated. He looked at the group. Nikki, Rose and London looked a little tired. Ralphie, the new recruit, looked like he was ready to fall asleep. He only needed to eat.

"We're going to have to teach you how to rappel," Major said.

"That will take a couple of hours," Kehoe said, interrupting and pointing to another stranger dressed in the heavily padded uniform that Kehoe wore before. The stranger was tall and thin with dreads that fell to his shoulders. He was holding his helmet in his gloved hands.

"James, need a northern sweep of the wall to the Mary Kenner Guard Post," Major said. "Stay in radio contact. Sun's going down."

James nodded and turned to leave.

"Oh, before you head to Mary Kenner check the stair way entrance," Major said.

James turned on his heels and headed toward the exit. He grabbed one of the steel push brooms as he left.

Everyone watched as James disappeared into the hallway.

"So, what'll it be?" Major asked. "I ain't about to tell a man what to do."

Kehoe opened the refrigerator and looked futilely for something to eat inside. He saw a pot on the stove and grabbed the pot, sat at the long table, and looked for something to scoop the food out to eat. He was climbing up from the table when another person entered the room.

"Kehoe, put that pot back," said a short, potbellied man who stepped out of a room near the side of the kitchen. The man, who looked like a human bulldog, was dark, big eared, smashed nose, half a dozen scars crisscrossed his round head. The man was wearing a beat up PC8 baseball cap. He was jowly, with no visible neck, dressed in an enforcers dark blue uniform.

Kehoe surrendered the pot and sat stone still as the cook reached out and showed off a hand tattoo. The bulldog of a cook replaced the pot on the stove.

"Who's this?" The cook asked.

Somers introduced everyone. Major introduced Tyson, the scarred cook. The cook after the introductions returned to the stove and the preparation of dinner.

"Looks like you have a few hungry travelers," Major said. "I would feel awful bad if I didn't feed those hungry faces before leaving."

The hunger on the faces of the group seemed tangible. Albert's stomach growled loudly. Albert grabbed at his stomach embarrassingly.

"I think we'll eat and take a crack at the labs after," Somers said with an embarrassed smile.

"Sounds good," Major said. "Okay, store your kits by the lockers," Major added.

The group stored their backpacks and weapons by the guard post lockers.

"There are seven of us here," Major said after the group stored their weapons and backpacks. "Usually, two or three on and two or three off," Major said, looking up at a whiteboard that hung near the hallway exit. On the whiteboard were the various names and shifts and duties for the week.

Ralphie listened. Ella and Yo-Yo nodded. Albert silently took in the information.

"We aren't sophisticated," Major said as Tyson finished the meal.

Tyson made a family style meal for all those gathered. The first course was garlic bread and a green lettuce salad with tomatoes, olives, and boiled eggs. The main course was one pot lemon chicken, spinach, asparagus, and orzo. The guards drank low alcohol beer and offered the teens water, root beer and lemonade. The dessert was lemon pound cake.

"Eat up," Tyson, the cook, said putting a salad bowl on the table and garlic bread.

"Thanks for the hospitality," Ella said to Major.

While they ate the enforcers talked.

"So, this is the Mary Kenner Guard Post. It is the sole tower that sits on the rear of the First Gen compound. The Marie Van Brittan Brown Guard Post is guarding the Makers compound to the north. I can't remember what the name of the one that guards the Trads to the south," Kehoe said.

"That's the Marjorie Joyner Guard Post," Major said. "You just walked there and back earlier today."

"I know, but all I do is patrol," Kehoe said. "I ain't trying to read a book while I'm out checking on the wall."

"We're posted here for twenty-four months," Kehoe said. "I'm supposed to be transferring to Central Government after this."

"Yeah, I can't put in a bid for another six months," said Tyson.

"How many guard posts are there?" Somers asked.

"Ten," Nelson, another enforcer at the table, said. Nelson was a short-haired man with a permanent scowl on his bearded mahogany brown face.

Albert nodded.

"You probably know the names of all of them. Don't you?" Nikki asked Albert.

Albert smiled and sipped at his water.

"How you know all this?"

Albert shrugged his shoulders in answer.

"Can you name all the towers on the wall?"

Albert nodded.

"Why?" Rose asked.

"They are all named after famous black women inventors that were discriminated against and despite the racism, sexism and discrimination persevered," Albert said as a matter of fact. "They represent the Remains toughness."

Ralphie frowned at Albert's words. Jax had told Ralphie that the watch towers were named after enforcers who had fought the anomalies outside of the walls.

"You sure?"

"Yeah," Albert said.

Ralphie shook his head. Maybe Jax was wrong.

"Okay," Rose said, skeptically. "Name the towers," she said.

The scowling Trad and Yo-Yo had found a map of the inner walls somewhere in the papers of the tower and were studying it as Albert took a deep breath and began.

Just as Albert had explained the map had ten towers all named after women. There was the Marjorie Joyner tower, Mary Kenner tower, and the other eight were: Miriam Benjamin, Sarah Boone, Dr. Patricia Bath, Sarah E. Goode, Marie Van Brittan Brown, Ellen Eglin, Dr. Valerie Thomas, and Alice H. Parker.

"What else do you know?" Nikki G. asked.

Albert shrugged.

"Do the champions thing," Yo-Yo said.

"What do you mean?" Rose asked.

"He knows and can name all the champions of the Pandemonium Challenge," Yo-Yo said.

"He can?" Rose asked.

"Yeah," Yo-Yo said with a big grin.

"Name all the champions," Ella said. "In order."

"Okay," Albert said. He took a breath and began. "There was Craig Benning, the first. Al Seals the second. Harold Taylor the third. Howard Reed the fourth. Nancy Olson was the fifth. Robert Shore was sixth. Sojourner Tucker was seventh. Gordon Tucker was the seventh. Gordon Everett was the eighth champion. Luther Landers was the ninth champion. Cleopatra Greer was the tenth champion. Love her name. Idris Roth was the eleventh. Hank Price was the twelfth. Hannibal Nelson was the thirteenth. Maya Kincaid was the fourteenth. Denzel Hudson was the fifteenth. Oprah Johnson was the sixteenth" Albert paused and looked at Somers and Fisher. He bit at his lower lip before continuing. "There's James Valentine the seventeenth." He pointed to the scowling Trad. "Nikki Giovanni Fisher is the eighteenth champion." He looked around and pointed to London. "London Adams is the nineteenth champion. The twentieth champion is Rose Jewell. Stuart Somers is the twenty-first champion." Albert paused again, awkwardly. "Wesley Crane is the twenty-second champion." Albert stopped and put his hand on Ralphie's shoulder and smiled. "Ralphie Reynolds is the twenty-third champion. That's it."

"It's crazy that you remember that kind of stuff," Ella said.

"I know some of them, but I couldn't do it in order," Yo-Yo said.

"Can you name the lines as well?"

Albert smiled.

Chapter Sixteen.

Centennial Avenue.

During the guard post dinner James returned from his patrol and reported in. A couple of hours later Nelson appeared dressed and donned night vision goggles and headed out toward Marjorie Joyner, the southern guard post. After dinner, the enforcers prepared for night duties.

"Looks like your group would benefit from a good night's sleep," Major said with a smile to Somers.

Somers couldn't argue.

"Kehoe, show them where they can sack out for the night," Major said to the scarred Kehoe.

"Follow me," Kehoe said.

He opened one of the three rooms on the first floor of the tower and inside the room were two bunk beds positioned on either wall. Both beds had a pillow, sheets and a footlocker. They were clean and crisp. The room was small but comfortable.

"The young ladies can sleep in here, if they like," Kehoe said. Yo-Yo and Ella looked at each other. Rose and Nikki G. nodded.

Kehoe walked to the second door and opened it. Inside were four more bunk beds. Two bunk beds on one side of the room. Two bunk beds on the other side of the room.

"You three can sleep here," Kehoe said.

"Where will you sleep?" Albert asked.

"I'm in the next room over," Kehoe said.

"What's on the second floor?" Jesse asked.

Kehoe smiled. He took the group on a short tour of the tower.

On the first floor there were all the things that they had seen and a small library which held about a dozen paperbacks. There was the kitchen, a bathroom with a shower beside the toilet. The first floor of the tower had no natural lighting and should have appeared more like a cave. To the surprise of Ralphie and the others the interior of the guard tower was not dark or dingy. Instead, with beneath the shelving and under the flooring above there was under shelving lighting to illuminate the space. There were no windows on the first floor of the tower, but instead a dozen two-inch horizontal slits on the east and west side of the walls to look out but not for anything to climb in.

On the second floor of the tower, which was reached by a set of stairs over the kitchen. The catwalk was ten feet wide. From the catwalk that circled the entirety of the second floor there were three windows on the east and west walls that were five feet tall and three feet wide. There were two bedrooms on the second floor and a bathroom that separated the sleeping compartments. Major's bedroom was found on the second floor. The second bedroom was shared by the two officers under Major.

"Who sleeps in there?"

"Glass and Brooks," Kehoe said. "They should be back in the morning."

"Get some sleep," Major said. "In the morning, in the light, we'll show you how to rappel."

Ralphie and Albert made their way to their lockers and retrieved their backpacks and personal belongings. They walked to their rooms and sat on their bunks.

"Leave the door open," Somers said. "We need to stay alert," the champion said.

"Are you a little paranoid?" Albert asked.

"Of course," Somers said. "We don't know these people."

"We don't know any of these people," Albert said with a smile. "We only met you just a couple of days ago."

"Exactly," Somers said. "They could be axe murderers or in a satanic cult." Somers paused, thinking. "They could be psycho killers."

Ralphie shook his head. In general, Ralphie was cautious, but even to the wary teen Somers seemed paranoid and borderline crazy.

Ralphie and Albert sat down on their bunks.

"Somers," Ralphie said, tired. "Do you know anything about Hannibal Nelson?"

Somers looked at Ralphie, curiously.

"Why you asking about that fossil?"

"Was just curious why he didn't get called up to check on the labs?"

Somers chuckled. Ralphie frowned at the champions laugh. Albert listened and looked at Ralphie, concerned.

"Hannibal is a nutcase as far as I know," Somers said. "He won and got his creds and hid."

"What do you mean hid?" Albert asked.

"Well, there's this belief that there's only a few ways to reintegrate back into society after the challenge," Somers said, blinking and yawning. "There's activity. Physical activity, which most prefer. There's runners and busy bees. Then there's the ones that hide." Somers stopped. "Hannibal bought one of those big houses on the edge of the compound and hid out." Somers stopped and continued. "The ones that stay active usually do the best, they say. Something to do with keeping your mind engaged and not giving it time to remember the madness."

"I heard about that," Albert said. "Most champions that stay involved with the community and compounds are seventy percent less likely to have a psychotic break."

Ralphie looked at Albert and studied the little genius. Albert shrugged.

"I can't help that I read a lot and retain a lot of information," Albert said, pointing to his head.

"What about Hannibal?" Ralphie asked.

"The way I heard it, he hid out for over a year and then, suddenly, became a Pandemonium Committee runner. I think he's working for the government or committee now," Somers said.

Ralphie nodded, trying to understand the concepts Somers was throwing at him.

"I don't trust no one that tries to hide from their problems," Somers said with a shrug of his shoulders. "There's something unnatural about it. I mean, running from your problems. I mean you just run from that one and into another one." Somers shook his head. "Then to show back up working for the government. Just seems fishy."

"Do you trust him?" Ralphie asked Somers.

"I don't trust anybody," Somers said. "I figure everyone is going to disappoint or attempt to betray me, at some point."

"That's sort of paranoid," Albert said.

"It's the only way to stay alive as an ex-champion," Somers said.

"Okay," Ralphie said. He was physically tired. He laid back on the bunk and watched through the open door the activity just on the other side of the threshold.

The guard tower never seemed too ever quiet completely. There was always activity. There was a routine in the tower. There seemed to always be two guards up. As Ralphie surrendered to sleep there just on the other side of the door was Nelson and James sitting at the table talking.

Ralphie had no dreams that night on the wall. He simply slept. Twenty feet up off the ground in the stone bosom of the tower named after the woman that received five patents in her lifetime.

Chapter Seventeen.

Building 62

The next morning, when he woke, it was to the sound of laughter and talking in the main room. Somers, Fisher, Jewell, and Adams were at the table with Major and Nelson having coffee and talking. Ella and Yo-Yo were the next to appear and sit at the table. Albert was the last to walk to the table, after Ralphie washed up and dressed.

"We got oatmeal and raisins and boiled eggs and toast if you're interested," James said with a toothy grin. He was a youngish looking man with a mustache and beard, thick eyebrows, and crooked nose. He was of average build and had long spidery fingers. On his head was a PC19 baseball cap.

Ralphie noticed that James was pointing to a pot on the stove with the oatmeal warming inside. Next to the stove was a bowl of raisins, a bowl of a dozen boiled eggs and a stack of toast cut in half.

"We'll be leaving as soon as we can," Somers said to Ralphie. "We just want to get a bit of food in us before we head to the labs."

"How did you sleep?" Ella asked.

Ralphie smiled in answer.

"It is always weird to find places where there are no nightmares," Fisher said.

"Pack up," Somers said after everyone had eaten and Ralphie and Yo-Yo had been asked to wash up the dishes and Adams and Somers cleaned up the kitchen.

Everyone followed Major and two enforcers out of the tower and onto the lip of the inner wall. The sun was barely in the sky but climbing. The heat had begun to wash over the Remains when the three enforcers began instruction.

"More accidents happen on rappel than any other accidents," Major said as he stood near the edge of the inner wall, looking out toward the Acid Bay. He was dressed in his dark blue enforcers uniform and the heavy padding along with the black harness that attached at his belly button. For the first time Ralphie noticed that the connecting point had four latches that locked the metal navel in place.

The eight also were wearing harnesses, but their harnesses were mostly rope with two straps that went over their shoulders and another rope strap that connected to the other side. In the middle of the strap was a metal ring.

"We're going to send Nelson and James down first. They will create a fireman's belay. Once everyone's down... good luck to you all," Major said.

With that Nelson and James clicked onto the bolts driven into the wall's top and stepped off. Instantly, the two ran down the side of the wall like they were running to get ice cream. In a dozen steps they landed on the ground and stepped away from the wall with a visible high tensile wire attached to their suits.

"Whoa," said Albert.

"Our suits are padded in case of injury and inside the waist is thirty feet of high tensile wire to protect us, in case we fall," Major said. From behind Major appeared two dark eyed women dressed in the heavily padded uniforms of the guard post. Major looked back and shook his head.

"This is Glass and Brooks," Major said with a chuckle. "They were doing some reconnaissance beyond the Marjorie Joyner Guard Post."

The two stood holding their steel rakes and dressed in their heavy padded uniforms as the champions and the Revolutionaries prepared to rappel down the wall.

The first to rappel was Somers. The second was Jewell. The third was Yo-Yo. The fourth down was Ralphie. The fifth down the wall was Ella. The sixth down was Albert. The last to descend the wall was Fisher.

"Be careful," Nelson said as he leaned back with an arm full of harnesses and the wire in his suit retracted and lifted him easily back up to the top of the wall. James was already halfway up the wall as Nelson began his ascent.

The group, led by Somers, walked north. They worked their way through the trees and undergrowth until they found Centennial Avenue and stopped. Albert was sitting on a fallen log sipping water from his water bottle when he snapped his finger and spoke.

"I been thinking about what Major said about the thirty feet of wire all the guards have," Albert said, talking to no one in particular. "The only thing that makes sense is that the wall is twenty-feet high and that gets you to the bottom, but the way I see it that extra ten-feet is to fight and rescue any guards that might fall or get grabbed by the Zeds."

"You been thinking about that all this time?" Ralphie said to Albert.

"Think about it. It's the only thing that makes sense. One of those guys can run down the wall no problem. That's only twenty feet. What is the point of having that extra ten feet?" Albert lifted his hand and made it flat. He took his index finger and drew a line down his palm. He moved his finger away from his palm. "They may even have a failsafe to pull them back up ten feet at a time."

"You don't know that," Rose said.

"I said they may," Albert said, slowly.

"We are close now," Jewell said with a satisfied smile.

"Right," Somers said. "Stay focused. There shouldn't be anything crazy here, but we are heading to some unknown labs. So, be careful."

The group started down Centennial Avenue toward the laboratories. The road away from the wall was eerily quiet. Grass was reclaiming the road in sections as the group moved down the hill and slowly turned left with the road.

"What is that?" Yo-Yo asked, pointing toward the west. There in the greenery was a low-slung building peeking between trees just a couple of hundred yards off the main road.

"Not sure," Fisher said to Yo-Yo.

"Well, it is probably one of the labs they used up here for animal research," Albert said.

"They did animal research up there?" Yo-Yo asked.

"It's a research school. That's what they did," Albert said with a roll of his brown eyes.

"We should go and investigate," Yo-Yo said, placing a hand on Ella's shoulder.

"We don't have time for that," Somers said.

"What are we on some sort of timetable?" Ella asked.

"No, but I don't think that is where we're supposed to be heading," Somers said, awkwardly.

Ella pouted, stopping along the side of the road. Yo-Yo and Albert stopped as well. Ralphie slowed and stopped seeing Nikki slow and stop in front of him. Rose stopped as well. Somers, noticing the group stopped behind him stopped, suddenly angry.

"Okay, we have a mission," Somers said, looking at Fisher and Jewell. He looked at Ralphie and then Ella. Somers looked as if he wanted to scream.

No one budged.

"We don't have side missions," Somers said, fumbling.

"Why can't we go and see if there are any animals there?" Yo-Yo asked.

Somers frustrated closed his eyes and clenched his right hand into a fist before he spoke.

"Okay, what do you think is going to happen? We're going to go there, and you are going to find monkeys and bears or whatever still alive in cages?" Somers looked at Yo-Yo angrily. "If there were animals in there, they would be long dead. The scientists who would have fed them would be dead too." He drew in a deep breath and let it out, trying to calm himself. "Going there with the hope of...seeing or rescuing dead animals that would have died after a year without food is a waste of time."

No one moved.

"I think he sort of has a point," Albert said.

"You don't think that there's a chance," Yo-Yo asked.

"No," Albert said. He looked in the direction of the building and pointed past it. "That though, looks like something that might be a more likely place to find animals."

Everyone, including Somers, looked in the direction Albert was pointing. Above the building that Yo-Yo wanted to explore and the tree line sat a reflective dark green structure that looked to be four-stories tall.

"What is that?" Nikki G. asked.

"Is that the Lawrence Hall of Science?" London asked.

"If that is the Hall of Science then we are pretty close to the National Laboratory," Somers said scanning the horizon for the laboratory.

"So, we still have to go by that building on the way to the National Laboratory?" London asked.

"Looks like it," Ella said with a smile.

"I am going to go inside and look and see if there are any animals alive," Yo-Yo said.

"Suit yourself," Albert said, once everyone was moving again down the quiet road.

Ten minutes later the group found themselves walking up the twisting Lawrence Road, according to the bent signpost at the spur of Centennial Drive. The road had six bends and as the group wound their way forward the sight of the mostly glass building came into view. To the right and on a slight slope sat the building that Yo-Yo and the group had seen earlier. At the foot of the stairs that climbed up the slope was a distinct sign that read: Building 62.

"What do you know about this building, Albert?" Ella asked.

"Nothing," Albert said.

Ralphie scanned the horizon and the area around the distinctive glass and metal building to see on a hill separated by a thick expanse of greenery. Above Building 62 on the distant hill sat the Hall of Science that too was separated by the trees and foliage on the hillside.

"Come on, we have to keep going," Somers said, waving the group forward and toward the road that led away from Building 62.

Ralphie and the Revolutionaries stopped. Nikki and Rose stopped too.

"What is the point of going in there?" Somers asked, noticing everyone behind him stopped.

No one spoke.

Yo-Yo stepped forward and smiled, awkwardly.

"What if there are rabbits or frogs or monkeys still alive inside there?" Yo-Yo asked.

"That ain't possible," Somers said. "Ain't nothing in that building but dead memories." Somers sulked. He crossed his arms in front of him.

Ralphie shook his head at the comedy and sadness of it all.

"Look, we go in and let Yo-Yo free some animals," Ella said. "That's not going to take too long."

"Then we head to the National Laboratory," Ralphie said, with a smirk. He looked at Somers and shrugged his shoulders. "It can't take more than an hour, tops," Ralphie said looking at Ella and Yo-Yo. The pair nodded. Yo-Yo smiled.

"Fine," Somers said, frustrated.

"Let's go," Ella said, grabbing Yo-Yo's arm and running toward the entrance of Building 62.

As Ralphie watched Ella and Yo-Yo running toward the mostly glass building he was reminded of the rules of the Pandemonium Challenge.

"Never go in numbered buildings," Ralphie, London, Nikki G., and Rose all said at once. The sour Somers hearing the three reluctantly smiled.

"It's crazy the things you remember from the challenge," Nikki G. said.

The two young women followed Ella and Yo-Yo to the front of the building. Ella paused. Yo-Yo reached out and pulled on the front door handle. The door opened with a tug.

The glass door opened into a darkened foyer. Yo-Yo flicked on her flashlight. Ella and everyone that entered the building turned on their flashlights.

"Okay, we do a quick search and then we go to the real target," Somers said, once he had entered the dark lobby and turned on his flashlight.

Everyone agreed and Ella pushed the second set of doors open. Yo-Yo and Ella were the first to enter the unlit lobby of the building proper. The sun allowed natural light to cut across the lobby, but there were deep shadows in the space. There were two doors on either side of the main reception area. Above the counter where the lobby was located there was a painting of an average looking cow lying in a field. The painting was on a canvas that was 48" x 80" in measurement.

"That's a Van Gogh," Ella said, confused. "I think. But how? Why?" Ella aimed her flashlight at the corner of the painting and studied the picture and painter's signature.

Ralphie entered the lobby and walked to Ella.

"What are you doing?" Ralphie asked, looking at Ella in front of the painting. "We're not at your house."

"Look at that," Yo-Yo said, pointing to the painting.

"It's a cow," Ralphie said with a big smile.

Yo-Yo nodded. She reached out and hugged Ella's arm.

"We can see that it's a cow," said London with a smug smile and shake of her head.

"No, that means that there are animals here," Yo-Yo said, triumphantly.

"Don't know about that," Albert said. "It could just mean that the picture was something someone in this building liked."

Yo-Yo pouted.

"Focus," Somers said. He scanned the dark lobby and found that there were two more doors on the far side of the lobby, opposite the reception counter. "Okay, take twenty minutes to search and find and free your animals," Somers said. "Meet back here in twenty?"

The group looked at Somers and nodded.

"Okay, you two go through that door and do your search," Somers said, pointing to Ella and Yo-Yo and the far door. Ella and Yo-Yo nodded and walked through the far door.

"London and Albert go through this door," Somers said, pointing to the door opposite of the one Ella and Yo-Yo entered.

"Nikki G., you and Rose go check through there," Somers said, directing Nikki G. to the closest door behind the reception desk.

"Me and Ralphie," Somers said. "We're heading through here." He led Ralphie across the darkened space and through a door closest to the exit.

In moments, the lobby was empty. Ralphie frowned and followed Somers to the door. Somers pushed open the door and entered a hallway. The hall led to a bigger space where a wall ran the entire length of the room and ended at another door. Instantly, Ralphie noticed there were half a dozen offices along the glass walls.

Somers poked his head in one office after the next, looking for whatever he was looking for.

Ralphie seeing Somers touching the desks, chairs, and papers on the desks. He opened a few drawers in the desks that were not locked.

Bored watching Somers Ralphie turned his attention to the main section of the room, opposite the offices. There were half a dozen tables in this area spaced evenly apart. In this open area there were no walls or offices. There were bean bags in the corners of the room. On one of the tables was a half-decade old checker game. On another table was a wooden puzzle.

Ralphie examined the tables and read some papers with the assistance of his flashlight. "This says that there were some animals here, somewhere," Ralphie said to Somers handing him some papers.

"Of course," Somers said taking the papers from Ralphie. He looked at the papers under his flashlight beam. After reading the papers he snorted and shook of his head. "Well, there are no animals on this side of the building that I can see." He paused. "This is just offices."

"Well, this lab had something to do with increasing brain capacity of animals in some way," Ralphie said to Somers.

The Twenty-First Pandemonium Challenge Champion nodded and handed Ralphie back the papers. Ralphie awkwardly took the papers back. He paused for a moment.

"Why you care about Yo-Yo looking for animals?" Ralphie asked, putting the papers back on the table. "It's not a big deal."

"It's not a big deal to you," Somers said. "I think that if there's a problem it's that we're supposed to be headed to the lab. And here we are."

Ralphie nodded.

"We're going there," Ralphie said with a smirk. "I just don't think us getting there ten minutes or an hour later really matters."

"Of course you don't. The difference between you and me, Ralphie, is that when someone asks me to do something they can expect me to do just that."

"We're looking for animals," Ralphie said. "That's no big deal. It is a good way to blow off steam and stop worrying about all the crazy stuff we already saw," Ralphie said, trailing off.

"That might be true and all, but this detour was not part of the plan," Somers said.

"Somers, I don't know if you have noticed or not but there is no plan. There is just a bunch of crazy and unbelievable things and us trying to survive them. And if stopping to rescue some animals along the way lets us get closer to the lab then I'm okay with that," Ralphie said.

Somers opened and closed his mouth but did not say anything. He studied Ralphie in the dimness. He nodded.

"We're supposed to be heading to the lab," Somers said. "Looking for imaginary bunnies isn't a part of the plan." Somers thought for a moment. "This detour doesn't get us to the lab."

"We *are* heading to the lab," Ralphie said, confused. "Ten minutes ain't gonna kill anyone."

"Yeah, I suppose," Somers said. "I just wanted to try and get to the lab without any detours."

"It's okay," Ralphie said to the seventeen-year-old Somers.

"I know," Somers said. "I just don't like that she might be right."

"I doubt that she's right," Ralphie said.

With those words, there was shouting and gunfire somewhere behind Somers and Ralphie. Somers leveled his assault rifle in front of him and spun toward the noise. Ralphie holding his golf club looked left and right for an attack.

"Stay behind me," Somers said and walked methodically back toward the door the pair had entered to the offices. Ralphie looked back and saw another door at the far end of the office. He thought for a moment to mention the other door to Somers but dismissed the idea. Ella and the Revolutionaries and the other champions might be in trouble.

Somers moved to the door and warily pushed through the door and into the darkness. From the door across from Somers emerged Nikki G. holding her assault rifle.

"What you got?" Somers asked in a tight-lipped voice.

"Nothing," said Nikki, looking left and right. Behind her stepped Rose holding her assault rifle.

A moment later out stepped London and Albert with a round faced man with big eyes and the beginnings of a beard dressed in khaki pants and a blue collared shirt. He looked frightened in the clutches of London. His hands were zip tied in front of him. Albert was holding his golf club menacingly behind the round-faced stranger.

"Who is this?" Somers asked, slinging his rifle.

"I'm Hamilton," the man said with an easy smile. "Don Evans Hamilton," the man smiled broadly held by the collar of his shirt by the frowning London.

"London what's going on?" Somers asked.

"You got me," London said. "We were just searching the labs and found this weirdo hiding in one of the storage areas," the champion said.

Before anyone could speak Yo-Yo and Ella pushed out of the doorway and into the lobby, confused. The two girls looked from Nikki G. and Rose to Somers and Ralphie finally to London, Albert and the smiling stranger.

"Who are you?" Ella asked.

"I'm Hamilton," the round-faced dark man with a goatee dressed in khaki pants and work boots said. There was a metallic tinkling as the man spoke securely held by London. Ralphie looked closely at the man, aiming his flashlight at him, and noticing a ring of keys hanging from his belt and the source of the delicate tinkling.

"Hamilton?" Somers asked, drawing closer to the round-faced stranger. "What you doing here?"

"I am the unofficial caretaker of Building 62," Hamilton said with a chuckle.

"Unofficial?" Somers repeated, studying the man with the ring of keys hanging from his belt.

"Yeah, there was no one here to promote me or hire or fire me," Hamilton said with a giggle. "I found this place a few years ago and no one bothered me. So, I stayed."

Yo-Yo stepped forward.

"We didn't find anything in the labs. All the animals are gone," Ella said. She looked at Yo-Yo and shook her head.

"All the animals are gone," Hamilton repeated with a half-suppressed laugh.

"Were there any animals here when you got here?"

"No, well none alive," Hamilton said. "This used to be one of the animal labs," Hamilton said looking at the champions and the Revolutionaries. "But now, it's just a place to hide."

"What kind of animals were kept here?" Yo-Yo asked, curious.

Before Hamilton could answer Nikki spoke.

"What do we do with him?" Nikki asked, suddenly bored.

"What?" Somers asked, looking at Nikki and Rose. "Well, I guess we leave him. He's not the mission."

Hamilton stopped smiling suddenly. Hamilton raised a solitary finger. He looked at the people looking at him, seriously.

"You're on a mission? I like missions. What you looking for?" Hamilton asked, smiling broadly.

"Don't worry about it old timer," Rose said.

"Old timer?" Hamilton growled. "How old do you think I am?"

"I don't know. One hundred?" Rose said with a shrug of her shoulders.

"I'm sixty-one in March," Hamilton said.

"I was close," Rose said.

"Is he dangerous?" Somers asked.

"No," London said. "He just surprised us," the champion said, her rifle slung behind her.

"I thought London was going to kill him," Albert said. "I sort of thought he was a Zed."

"Hmmm," Somers said, looking at Hamilton, Albert, and London. The champion shrugged. "Let him go," Somers said, frustrated with the whole adventure of Building 62.

London grabbed her pocketknife and cut Hamilton's restraints.

Somers gestured and Nikki and Rose followed him out of the lobby and back to the front of Building 62.

"Where you going?" Hamilton asked.

Ralphie shook his head, looking at Ella and the remaining Revolutionaries.

"We're going to the big lab," Yo-Yo said.

Ella and Ralphie looked at Yo-Yo disappointedly.

"You know I hear all sorts of things here," Hamilton said. "Especially at night. The big lab, the one on the hill, over there," Hamilton pointed. He looked at Yo-Yo and Albert. "Be careful. There are some strange things there."

"What kind of things?" Yo-Yo asked, suddenly interested.

"I don't really know," Hamilton said. "Anytime I hear them, it's at night and they're moving through the woods and heading for the wall."

"*Them*? What are you talking about?" Albert asked, flustered.

"Hey, we're heading out, Ralphie," Nikki said, sticking her head in the darkened lobby of the animal lab, but not going any further. "If you're coming, then come along."

With that Nikki disappeared.

Ralphie instinctually stepped toward the exit. In moments, he and the Revolutionaries were out of the building and walking down the stairs to Lawrence Road.

Somers and the champions looked as Ralphie and the Revolutionaries caught up.

"The straightest way is through the trees," Somers said, turning back and looking at all the faces in front of him. Somers frowned seeing Hamilton behind Ella and Yo-Yo.

Ella looked back and seeing Hamilton smiled. She turned back to Somers.

"He says he knows some things about the lab that we don't," Ella said.

Somers refused to argue. He simply shook his head and continued with the plans.

"It doesn't look that far away," Somers said, pointing toward the gates and limestone buildings that looked as if they were built into the hillside. "Stay focused. We don't know what we'll run into once we're in it. Just stay close and move in as straight a line as possible."

At the end of Lawrence Road there was an overlook to the trees and undergrowth that stretched out across the canyon floor. Ralphie scanned the tops of the trees and tried to estimate the distance to the laboratory on the other side of the canyon. It could not have been more than a mile in total, but the canyon seemed to descend downward to a point and then climb back to the other side, just below the laboratory's road that surrounded the chain-link fencing.

Somers was the first to step off Lawrence Road and move cautiously down the slope and into the trees growing along the hillside. Behind Somers followed the scowling Trad. Albert and Ralphie were next. Rose followed Ralphie. Yo-Yo and Ella walked behind Rose and Ralphie. London was responsible for the rear.

Hamilton, the stranger, began near Yo-Yo and Ella and as they descended further and further into the canopy of the trees and darkness he disappeared.

"Where's Hamilton?" Ella asked London.

"He disappeared a few minutes ago," London said, pointing to the right and the darkness of the canopied trees.

"Why didn't you say something?" Yo-Yo asked London.

"He's not our responsibility," London said. "Besides, he seems to know where he's going."

At the bottom of the hillside the group found themselves at the edge of a small creek, five feet across. The creek did not look deep or fast.

Somers stepped into the water and after two strides was on the other side. He looked back and waited for Rose to cross the creek. Albert, Nikki and Ralphie were the next to cross the stream. Yo-Yo and Ella crossed with London close behind.

"Where's your newfound friend?" Albert asked Yo-Yo with a sly smile.

"He went for a nature walk, I suppose," Yo-Yo said with a weak smile.

"That guy is sketchy," Albert said. "He scared us when we were walking through the lab. He just jumped up and started running. London shot at him, and he disappeared. We eventually found him hiding in one of the storage lockers," Albert said with a frustrated shake of his head. "Weird guy." Albert leaned toward Ralphie. "I think he might have been eating the animal food and sampling some of the drugs in the lab."

Ralphie did not comment.

The group began its ascent to the lab on the other side of the creek. They had only gotten about ten feet up the hillside when suddenly the climb became difficult. It seemed like the ground itself was against them. The trees stood all around the group and in the bark and branches Ralphie and the others found ways to hold on despite the loose footing.

Another ten feet and the seemingly difficult became impossible. Trees fell away and were replaced with rocks and stones.

The hill disappeared and was replaced with a sheet of stone to deter unwanted visitors.

"What do we do?" London asked, holding onto a crack in the sheet of stone.

"There's another way," said Hamilton, who had appeared out of nowhere. He pointed south to an outcropping of trees just below the road one hundred yards away.

Somers scanned the route but did not move.

"What do you say?" Rose asked.

"Well, we definitely aren't going up this way," Somers said. "Let's try out the caretaker's route," he added. "We have to get onto that road."

The group, now led by Hamilton, made their way to the right. The path was not easy but it was easier than the path Somers had picked and led the group to initially.

"We'll be there in no time," Hamilton said, reassuring everyone repeatedly.

After twenty minutes of reassuring Hamilton led the group on Cyclotron Road.

"Voila," Hamilton said. He looked back, nervously down the road, away from the laboratory. Hamilton seemed incredibly anxious.

"What is wrong with you?" Somers asked.

"You know that I have hidden in that building for years, afraid of noise, afraid of shadows," Hamilton said, blinking and blinking and scratching at his arm absentmindedly. "But here we are. Here I am. Facing my fears. Facing my... fears."

"What are you going on about?" Nikki G. asked.

"I told you there are things here that I do not know what to call them," Hamilton said. "They usually pass by, but now... here we are. They will see us. They probably have seen us."

"Calm down, old man," London said dismissively.

"Yeah, calm down before you have a heart attack or something," Nikki G. said.

"You don't get it," Hamilton said, looking at Somers. "You came here to come here, but this place is dangerous. Dangerous places stay dangerous for a reason."

"Why did you come here then?" Somers said.

Hamilton did not answer for a moment. "I wanted to face my fears," Hamilton finally said.

Somers snorted. He smiled at the older man.

"We are all facing our fears, old man," Somers said. "It's called living."

Just then Albert stepped up and touched Ralphie's arm.

"Look," Albert said.

Ralphie looked in the direction Albert was pointing and saw a fast-moving transport winding its way up the hill toward them.

"Who can that be?" Ralphie asked cautiously.

"No one we want to wait for," Somers said decisively.

"I say we try to get in the lab now," Rose said.

The group headed to the chain-link fence that barred entrance to the laboratory on the other side. Somers checked the gate. The gate was locked and secured with six feet of an incredibly thick chain.

Ralphie scanned the fence and looked for weak points. All the champions had the same idea. It was London who found the weak point and pulled it back enough for Albert and Ella to squeeze inside. Albert instantly popped up and sought a way to hold the fence entrance so that everyone could enter.

In moments, everyone was inside the chain-link fencing.

"Okay, now what?" Albert asked.

"Well, we need to go to the labs anyway," Somers said. "So, I say we head up the road and find a way in before whoever they are gets here." Somers looked back at the transport making its way uphill. Somers smiled. "If they don't see us, they can't find us."

"Right," London said. "Find an open door that gets us in and hide."

"Well, we should head to the biggest building. I figure it is where we need to go anyway. So, let's climb up the hill and go and hide and see what the transport does," Somers said, clarifying.

"Right," Rose said with a mirthless smile. "Climb the creepy hill and find the spooky lab and look for an open door to hide from the equally creepy transport coming this way."

"Got it," said Yo-Yo.

The group sprinted uphill and toward the gigantic domed building at the center of the laboratory complex. They climbed the road only to come again to another chain-link fence. The second chain-link fence was not secured but only blocking the road.

Somers pushed the chain-link fencing and created an opening to pass through. The group kept climbing up the hill to the main campus where the domed building dominated the main area.

Before the group could reach the domed building, they found that there were metal pillars in place to stop any transport entrance on the road. The group weaved through the pillars or climbed over the road obstacles. Behind the pillars was another chain-link fence.

The group pushed through the chain-link fence.

"Okay, we have to get in there," Somers said, pointing to the massive building in front of them. Everyone ran forward and to the dozen doors that were visible on the base of the gigantic circular structure.

Ralphie looked back and saw no transport or hint of one behind them.

"All these doors are chained and locked," said Yo-Yo.

"Hey. They're coming up the hill," Rose said from the top of the hilltop. She aimed her assault rifle downward and in the direction of where the transport would have to appear.

"Okay, everyone hide," Somers said, aiming his assault rifle and running toward cover.

To the left of the gigantic circular domed building sat a kiosk. Ralphie, Ella, Yo-Yo and Albert hunkered down inside the kiosk and tried to think what they were supposed to do.

"You know we are in here without any firepower?" Yo-Yo asked.

"I noticed that," Ralphie said.

"So, what do we do?" Albert asked.

"We have time," Ralphie said, reasoning. "There are a bunch of obstacles that whoever is in that transport has to overcome. Unless they ditch the transport and come up her on foot."

Ella and Yo-Yo nodded.

"What if they are the security for this place?" Albert asked, being the devil's advocate. "I mean, we could have set off a bunch of silent alarms getting to this point."

Ralphie looked over the windowsill and watched as the single transport pulled up to road blocked with the metal pillars and chain-link obstacles to the exterior of the laboratory.

"Maybe you're right," Ralphie said to Albert. "They're here," Ralphie said.

With those words, Ella, Yo-Yo and Albert peeked over the windowsill and toward the driveway.

Out of the transport stepped four enforcers wearing red on their shoulders, red gloves, and red boots. They were still one hundred feet away from the hiding place of the champions and Revolutionaries. The chain link fence and pillars stopped the transport from coming any closer.

"Holy hell," Ella said. "It's the Red Hand."

"How did they know we would be here?" Yo-Yo asked.

Albert opened and closed his mouth.

Everyone in the kiosk looked at each other. Yo-Yo frowned. Ella pouted.

"Ralphie, did you get anything from the Pandemonium Committee?" Albert asked, curiously.

Ralphie looked at Albert confused.

"Think," Albert said.

Ella indelicately pulled his backpack off. She searched it thoroughly. Finding nothing inside she handed it back roughly to Ralphie. Ralphie looked at Ella, unsure if he was angry or not.

"What about that?" Albert asked. He pointed to the PC23 pin on Ralphie's backpack.

Ralphie looked and winced at the gift he had received from Julius McCarthy when he returned to the Miller compound. He had the PC23 pinned on his backpack since he could remember.

Ralphie tried to go backwards and remember when he put the pin on his backpack. He could not remember. All he could recall was Macy asking for one and him recalling that McCarthy had given him a handful. His mother and father had been given their own. So, he had given Macy a couple just in case she lost one.

"Think they are tracking you using that," Albert said. He leaned forward and snatched the pin from the backpack. Yo-Yo and Ella watched as Albert examined the golden lapel pin. He turned it over in in his hand and when he did Albert paused.

Albert took his golf club head and smashed it against the lapel pin. The pin was durable. Albert hit the pin a few more times and then the small transceiver fell out of the decoration.

Seeing the odd microchip, Yo-Yo stepped on the transceiver and stomped it with her boot heel.

"Well, that's good," Ella said looking at the smashed lapel pin.

"You got anything else?" Albert asked.

"No," Ralphie said.

Hamilton opened the kiosk door and crawled inside.

"Whoa, whoa, whoa," Yo-Yo said looking at the round-faced stranger. Yo-Yo backed away from Hamilton and into Albert. Albert turned and saw Hamilton looking anxious.

"Think there are some bad guys outside," Hamilton said in a whisper.

Ella and Yo-Yo rolled their eyes at Hamilton's insight.

Just on the other side of the chain-link fence the two men and two women walked to the pillars and the chain-link fence. One looked at the pillars that barred entrance. The second man, shorter than the first man, walked to the left of the pillars and studied the fencing. One of the two women standing beside the transport walked to the opposite side of the road and smiled.

"Think we can get in on this side," the woman said pushing against the chain-link and watching it wobble with the shove.

The last woman, standing by the transport nodded and raised a single finger to pause the woman. She tapped a few invisible buttons in the air and activated the speaker in the transport.

"Ralph Ellison Reynolds," said the woman from the speakers in the car. "We have been sent to return you to your compound. We have been asked by your compound leader, Maya Higgins, to bring you home. We were asked to come find you before

you did something to jeopardize your standing as a Pandemonium
Challenge Champion."

Chapter Eighteen.

The laboratory.

Hamilton looked at Ralphie and the Revolutionaries. Ella, Yo-Yo and Albert looked at Ralphie. Ralphie tightened his lips not knowing what to say.

"Which one of you is this Ralph they're looking for?" Hamilton asked, inside the kiosk.

The Revolutionaries did not speak.

Hamilton studied the four, discounting Ella and Yo-Yo. The man looked at Ralphie and Albert. He raised a single finger and pointed to Albert and then Ralphie.

"It's one of you," Hamilton said with a knowing smile.

"Get out of here," Yo-Yo said, crawling to her knees and pushing Hamilton. Ella seeing Yo-Yo's anger crawled to Hamilton and pushed the older man toward the kiosk exit.

Hamilton was shocked and slowly realized that the girls were pushing him.

"What are you doing? Those people out there are going to get in here," Hamilton said, annoyed. He looked at the two angry girls. He fended off their hands. "If they only want one person then give them that one person. Don't be stupid. We all don't have to suffer for one person," Hamilton said.

"Get out of here," Yo-Yo seethed.

"Be that way," Hamilton said, looking at Ralphie and Albert. Hamilton opened the kiosk door and looked out and back to the complex.

"I'm not dying for any of you," Hamilton said and exited the small pavilion.

Ella, Albert and Yo-Yo looked at Hamilton as he left the kiosk. They closed the door. Ralphie looked at the Revolutionaries. Ella reached out and squeezed Ralphie's hand. Yo-Yo, for the first time, looked at Ralphie concerned.

"What do we do?" Albert asked.

"We can't stay here," Ella said. She looked at Ralphie.

Yo-Yo opened the kiosk door to look for options. On the right side of the kiosk sat the white walls that rose ten feet into the air. Doors were positioned in the walls in the foot of the arches to give the structure a star-like form. On the left side of the kiosk there was the shuttered and darkened entrance to a smaller gift shop building.

"They are looking for me," Ralphie said. "You guys need to go. Go with Yo-Yo's uncle," Ralphie smiled at Yo-Yo.

Yo-Yo smirked.

"Find some place safe to hide," Ralphie said, with a nod.

Ella frowned.

"Go," Ralphie said.

Albert was the first to exit the kiosk. Behind Albert ran Yo-Yo. Ella looked at Ralphie.

"I'm right behind you," Ralphie said.

"Hey, that Ralph boy is over here," Hamilton yelled standing near the opening to the darkened gift shop and pointing to the kiosk.

Ella grabbed Ralphie and pulled him from the kiosk.

"Come on," Ella said. "We have to go."

Once out of the kiosk they ran. Behind them were the distinctive sounds of a dozen mini drones in the air. The dozen drones flitted in the air. Some were behind Ella and Ralphie. Some were in front or overhead.

Ahead of them Yo-Yo looked back as she entered the darkened gift shop of the Lawrence Berkeley National Laboratory. Ella and Ralphie ran toward the gift shop.

"Run faster," Ella yelled, pulling Ralphie along behind her.

The pair ran as fast as they could for cover. They skidded inside the darkened storefront. Two drones banked and hovered at the entrance to the gift shop.

Ella turned and reached out and closed the gift shop door to stop the drones from entering. Inside the still and undisturbed place that had not seen a living soul in half a century, they found Yo-Yo and Albert restraining a struggling Hamilton.

They were tying the hands of the bigger man behind his back with a T-shirt they had torn off a clothes rack. Albert had found a piece of cloth to gag Hamilton. Yo-Yo had her body weight on Hamilton's back. She was securing Hamilton as Ella reached her friends.

Ralphie climbed to his feet and looked back at the courtyard where the drones hovered.

"They're just hovering," Ralphie said. He turned and found shop smaller than he expected. The dimly lit space was dominated by eight rounders. There were four mannequins dressed in sweatshirts and baseball caps.

Above their heads hung an old pre-war Department of Energy banner. The banner had to be six-feet wide and twelve feet long. Underneath the banner were T-shirts on racks. Hats sat on shelves. There was a small display of books. The space had a floor to ceiling window on the western side of the structure.

Yo-Yo and Albert tied Hamilton to three rounders. Hamilton strained against his bounds but could not free himself. Yo-Yo smiled at her handiwork and returned to Ralphie and the Revolutionaries.

"What do we do now?" Yo-Yo asked.

Ralphie shook his head. Ella looked around, nervously.

Albert had drifted away from the others and was at the counter looking at goo gags behind the glass display. He picked up a book by the cash register. Yo-Yo was looking back at Hamilton tied to the circle racks.

"Find a way into the lab," Ella said.

Albert pointed to a sign over a door. The sign read: Entrance to Lawrence Berkeley National Laboratory.

"Well, that's convenient," Ralphie said pulling on the door and finding it locked.

"We should just break it," Yo-Yo said, absently, wearing a LBNL staff baseball cap.

Ella and Yo-Yo walked to the door and looked through the glass to see a catwalk that looked down upon a vast darkness that seemed to drop down into the center of the earth. Above the darkness there was a huge ball of metal with wires and cables snaking to and from the great sphere.

"So near and yet so far away," Ralphie said.

Yo-Yo and Ella shook their heads at Ralphie's words.

"Let's just break the glass," Yo-Yo said, looking around for something heavy to break the window in the gift shop. She found herself in front of a mannequin. Yo-Yo turned the mannequin's arm and twisted it until it came off in her hand.

Albert looked behind the counter.

"Maybe, this unlocks the door," Albert said, lifting the key that was labeled: Laboratory.

Albert tossed the key to Ella who was standing in front of the laboratory entrance.

"Did you lock the door," Ella asked, pointing to the gift store entrance.

In the distance there appeared one of the Red Hand. At the door stood a five foot six-inch-tall woman dressed in the distinctive red gloves and boots. She stepped through the door and into the quiet gift shop. The woman had a mask over her nose and an assault rifle in her hand. She moved quietly into the darkness of the shop.

She was boyishly built and weighed not more than one hundred and twenty pounds. The stranger's hair was braided and pulled back into a thick braided ponytail. What was distinctive about the woman was her hair was shaved below her ears. The hardened, unsmiling tough looked left and right for movement.

Yo-Yo jumped from the display and swung as hard as she could with the arm of a mannequin at the Red Hand that dared enter the gift shop. As Yo-Yo attacked Albert was in motion. Ella turned and ran as fast as she could to the side of Yo-Yo. Instinctually, Ralphie was in motion as well.

The woman was swarmed by Ralphie and the Revolutionaries. Yo-Yo went flying as the woman threw the girl across the shop. It was the surprise attack by Albert and Ella that caught the Red Hand enforcer off guard. Albert crashed into the woman and fell on the floor in front of her. Ella launched herself at the enforcer, swinging her tennis racket and hitting the mute woman in the chest, knocking her off her feet.

When Ralphie arrived he quickly assessed the situation, stepped on the Red Hand's forearm, and clubbed her unconscious with the mannequin arm before he could second guess himself. Yo-Yo recovered and was by Ralphie's side angry and growling as Albert and Ella climbed to their feet and stood over the unconscious woman.

Yo-Yo kicked the unconscious woman, angrily. Ella pushed Yo-Yo away. Ralphie bent down and grabbed her assault rifle and pistol. He quickly tied the woman with the zip ties she had on her web belt.

"Now what?" Yo-Yo asked, her golf club in her hand.

"First lock the front door. Then, we unlock that door," Ella said, pointing toward the laboratory. "And let's try and get in that lab," Ella said, looking around.

Hamilton struggled and poked his head up from rounder of clothes racks he was attached to at the time.

Albert and Ella rolled their eyes at Hamilton.

Yo-Yo unlocked the laboratory door and Albert locked the gift shop door.

Yo-Yo, still holding her golf club, pulled the laboratory door inward to find that the doorway was blocked by a dozen heavy and bulky boxes. She pushed against the boxes and was surprised to find that they were not as heavy as she expected. Ralphie stepped up and helped remove enough boxes to enter the laboratory.

Once inside the doorway Yo-Yo and the Revolutionaries found themselves on a glassed-in catwalk with a three-foot-high railing that ran much of the west side of the wall to see down and into the greatest and most advanced light source on the planet. There were a rat's nest of tubes, wires and cables snaking to a metallic sphere just below the Revolutionaries feet. In another area there were a dozen supercomputers blinking on and off under beams and girders that looked like they were supporting the entirety of the structure.

Ralphie frowned seeing the computers blinking on and off.

"This doesn't make sense," Albert said. "There's no reason any of this should still be on and powered."

"What do you mean?" Ella asked.

"I mean, this place like all the research facilities and power drains were shut down when the flash happened," Albert said, stopping and leaning on the railing to get a better look below. "I also mean, who is maintaining these machines?"

From behind one of the machines emerged what looked like a silver two-armed, two-legged mechanical person. The mechanical creature looked up with red eyes. Behind it appeared two other mechanical creatures with red eyes.

"Red eyes," Albert said, pointing to the silvery mechanical creatures.

"What the hell?" Yo-Yo asked.

"Robots?" Ralphie asked warily, pointing at the automatons moving down an aisle.

"Robots were destroyed," Albert said.

"And all the power was shut off to power drain hotspots," Ella said mockingly.

Albert turned and was about to respond, but something he saw stopped his words from coming out. Instead, he backed up and into Ralphie and Yo-Yo. Yo-Yo turned at Albert's pushing. Ralphie frowned. He looked at Albert and Yo-Yo and behind Albert his eyes widened at the sight of one of the robots clambering onto the catwalk.

"Run," Albert said, looking back nervously.

"What is it?" Yo-Yo asked, looking back.

"One of those destroyed robots," Ella said backing up. She looked left and right and realized that they were at least twenty feet from the entrance to the gift shop.

The mechanical creature landed on the catwalk with a tinny clatter. The red eyes scanned the catwalk. The creature raised its arms and headed toward the four retreating teenagers.

"Shoot it," Ella said to Ralphie.

Ralphie looked down at the assault rifle and nodded. He stopped backing up and aimed the rifle at the approaching gray two-armed, two-legged bot. Everyone behind Ralphie cowered behind the Miller expecting the deafening sound of the assault rifle.

"Shoot it," said Yo-Yo from behind Ralphie.

Ralphie pulled the trigger on the assault rifle and spit one shot toward the bot. The red eyed machine did not slow or stop with the first shot. Ralphie frowned. He pulled the trigger again, but this time he held the trigger as he fired. The bullets sprayed across the catwalk and cut the grayish android in half. Ralphie released the trigger and surveyed his damage. The grayish body's legs moved forward but the body above the waist tipped over backward and fell onto the catwalk.

Albert, Ella and Yo-Yo peeked from behind Ralphie and watched as the silvery two legs proceeded forward a few more feet before stopping and keeling over.

Ralphie shook the image from his head. He looked to the right and saw more movement from the laboratory floor. There were dozens of steely automatons on the laboratory floor. They all simultaneously slipped out of view.

"Where did the ones on the floor go?" Yo-Yo asked, frightened.

Ralphie and the Revolutionaries looked for the steely bots. The laboratory floor was suddenly devoid of movement. It was as if the robots had scurried back into their hidey holes.

Ralphie was about to say something when he looked past the halved slate body and legs of the creature he had dispatched to see two more mechanical creations climbing onto the catwalk.

"What do we do?" Asked Yo-Yo seeing the whitish-gray bots climb onto the catwalk.

"What are we going to do?" Albert asked, looking at Ella and then Ralphie.

Ralphie looked around and tried to think.

Before Ralphie or anyone could speak Somers and the other champions appeared on the catwalk.

Ralphie felt the assault rifle torn from his hands. He looked and tried to fight but the steely grip of the robot was unbreakable.

"What the--" Ralphie said, in protest. Instantly, behind Ralphie stood a six-foot-tall silvery robot. Behind that bot appeared another red eyed creature.

The steely mechanical creatures looked humanoid in shape and form. They had all the essential parts of a human only they were made of metal. Being close to the automatons Ralphie noticed that they were six foot tall and had these articulated features that gave off an Iron Giant design, Ralphie thought. The creatures all had round shaped heads with big robotic eyes, no nose, and a grill where a mouth would sit if the creature was human. The bots had no ears. What was distinctive was along the line of Iron Giant the bot's fingers replicated the three joints on the three fingers of a human hand. The thumb and pinky of the metal creature's hand had only two joints. Their chest was barrel shaped with a column of thick metal connecting their torsos to their mechanical hips. There were no genitalia beneath the creature's hips just joints that connected the legs and pad like feet.

Ella, Yo-Yo and Albert jumped, seeing Ralphie with his hands pulled over his head. He was hoisted off the catwalk by a gray skinned metal creation with red eyes. The red eyed robot held Ralphie by his wrists with one metal hand. Another hand removed Ralphie's pistol that was in his waistband. Instantly, the bot pulverized the pistol in its iron grip like it was a pack of saltine crackers.

"What's going on?" Somers asked, leveling his assault rifle at Ralphie and the robot.

"Robots," Ella said, suddenly frantic. She pointed to the two silvery, red eyed bots that stood on the catwalk behind Ralphie. London spun and sighted down her rifle at the singular robot walking toward the group.

"Shut the front door," Nikki said, looking and seeing a grayish-white metal creation moving toward her on the opposite end of the catwalk.

"This ain't supposed to be possible," Somers said.

The gray bot holding Ralphie stepped back. The second bot on the catwalk stepped forward and stopped. The third silvery bot on the catwalk on the opposite side of the group stopped beside the halved bot. The bot froze next to the debris and a voice sounded.

"Please stop your attacks," a metallic, mechanical voice sounded. "The sentries are not designed to attack but to prevent entry," the voice said. "Any attack will be considered hostile and dealt with immediately."

"Ralphie? Are you okay?" Albert asked.

Ralphie looked at Albert and shook his head.

"Yeah, I guess that was a stupid question," Albert said.

"Hang on, Ralphie," Ella said, looking at Somers.

"What do we do?" Yo-Yo asked.

"Wait and see," Ella said. "There's nothing else to do."

Somers and the champions kept their guns trained on the bots.

"Lower your weapons," Ella said. "We can't do anything as long as they have Ralphie," the Innovator pointed out. Ella looked to Somers. Somers lowered his weapon and so did the other champions. With that action, the bots moved forward.

The group backed into the gift shop ahead of the bots and Ralphie.

"What are we doing?" London asked.

"Waiting for a chance to get an advantage," Somers said.

Once inside the gift shop and in the dimness of the space the champions and Revolutionaries were pushed toward the exit of the shop.

Before reaching the exterior of the gift shop there was the jarring and rapid sound of automatic gunfire. Instantly, Somers and the champions as well as Ella and the Revolutionaries ducked. Ralphie flinched.

At the door to the gift shop stood another bot. The bot opened the door and allowed the champions and Revolutionaries onto the courtyard. Just on the other side of the courtyard where the Red Hand appeared earlier stood six silvery creatures. On the ground in front of them sat the dozen drones from earlier.

A sextet of mechanical creations stood in the courtyard holding the three Red Hand enforcers. The Red Hand were subdued and unmoving. They were off their feet and in the metal hands of three bots. The three other metal creatures stood just a few feet from them stock still.

"What happened?" Albert asked, looking at the Red Hand.

"Everything they said was going to happen," Ella said with a shake of her head.

From behind the group appeared a frightened Hamilton bound but held by one of the bots. At the door, Hamilton tried to break the hold of the bot. Unsuccessful, he looked to the champions and the Revolutionaries.

"Help me," Hamilton said. "You can't let this happen."

"Let what happen?" Ella asked.

Hamilton did not respond. The older man dragged his feet as the bot moved to the courtyard. Hamilton seemed frantic.

The half dozen mechanical creatures standing in the courtyard watched as Hamilton was brought to the group of subdued Red Hand.

Ralphie was pushed and headed to the group of Red Hand and Hamilton.

"Wait," Ella said. "He's not with them. We're not with them." Ella stepped in front of one of the bots. The bot stopped and looked at Ella. "We did not come here to attack anyone. Ralphie was just trying to protect us. Your robot scared us. He was trying to protect us."

The bot studied Ella and then the Revolutionaries. The six-foot-tall metal creation did not speak. It had a mesh grill where a mouth would be located but no sound came out. Instead, it looked at Ella with those big red LED eyes.

"Please drop all your weapons," sounded from the bots.

The champions looked at Ella and then the bots.

"What choice do we have right now?" Ella asked Somers. "There are more of them, and I don't think if you started a fight you would win."

Somers nodded. He removed his assault rifle and handed it to the bot. One of the bots gathered all the weapons. The champions and Revolutionaries were disarmed.

Having gathered the weapons, the two bots secured them beside the gift shop and walked to the head of the group. The two bots near the gift shop stood and waited.

"What happens now?" Asked Albert, concerned.

"They turn us into cyborgs or make us robots like them," Rose said with a smile. "I don't know, kid," Rose said, with a shake of her head. "This is definitely new ground for me."

"Yeah," London said, with a nod. "This ain't something any of us was preparing for."

Without a word, on the other side of the courtyard, there was motion and one of the more agile Red Hand broke free from the pair of bots.

The assassin ran a few steps, stopped, and pulled his pistol and aimed it in the direction of the champions and the Revolutionaries. The Red Hand member, wearing a mask over his face, fired four shots at the group.

The four bots shielded the champions and Revolutionaries from harm. The champions and Revolutionaries hid behind the bots.

The sound of bullets bouncing off the bots bodies rang out. Ralphie and Somers looked in the direction of the attacking Red Hand.

There was a blood curdling scream, but no one saw the reason. The bots turned back to allow Ralphie and the others to move. Ralphie and the others saw the Red Hand assassin caught by a bot. The bot held the assassin by his shattered wrist.

The Red Hand assassin squeezed his eyes shut against the excruciating pain. The assassin fell silent. Ralphie assumed he was in shock.

In moments, the group saw bots escorting Hamilton and the Red Hand enforcers away from the courtyard. Two bots carried the unconscious Red Hand enforcers in their hands like full grocery bags. The bots moved in the opposite direction of Ralphie and the others and around the Advanced Light Source building.

"Where are they going?" Albert asked.

Rose shook her head. Nikki frowned.

"What's going to happen to them?" Yo-Yo asked, curious.

London looked at Yo-Yo and shook her head in answer.

The bot holding Ralphie released his wrists. Ralphie freed and on the ground massaged his wrists. Ella seeing Ralphie freed moved to him and gave him a hug. Ralphie returned the hug and smiled. Yo-Yo hugged Ralphie as well. Nikki, London, and Rose smiled.

"Okay, we're all together," Somers said. "Great. Now what?" Somers shook his head.

"Please follow us to the Molecular Foundry building," one of the bots sounded.

"Wait," Somers said. "Who's in charge here?"

"Please follow us to the Molecular Foundry building," one of the mechanical creatures sounded.

"We were sent here to find something important," Somers said.

"Please follow us," one of the bots sounded, raising a hand, and pointing in the direction of the Molecular Foundry building.

"To the Molecular Foundry building," Somers said and shook his head. He looked back at the group. Everyone looked at Somers as if he was going to say something profound to them.

"Guess we're headed to the Molecular Foundry building," Somers said and began following the two bots leading the way.

Chapter Nineteen.

Doctor Rudy Martin

The eye-catching design of the Molecular Foundry building sitting on top of a steep hill with incredible views of what once was the Bay Area was impressive, but it was the sight of a short, bald Black man smiling from ear-to-ear dressed in a white laboratory coat, blue polo shirt, khaki trousers and sneakers, at the entrance of the modular designed building that stunned and shocked the group.

"I am doctor Rudy Martin," the man dressed in a white lab coat, striped shirt, blue jeans, and sneakers said. "Welcome to the Lawrence Berkeley National Laboratory. I suppose you can say that I am your guide."

"Wait," Yo-Yo said, seeing Rudy Matin.

"Hell to the naw," Nikki said looking at the man dressed in Chuck Taylor sneakers.

"This can't be real," Albert said.

Ralphie studied Rudy Martin as the bots walked the group to the entrance of the Molecular Foundry.

"This is truly real," Rudy Martin said with a friendly smile. "We have been anticipating your arrival since you climbed up Skyline."

Ralphie frowned at the doctor's words. The red eyed Zeds were tied to the lab and this doctor. As Ralphie thought this Nikki spoke.

"You have something to do with the red eye Zeds?"

Rudy Martin smiled. His skin was lineless and had a timelessness about him. Ralphie could not estimate how old Rudy Martin was and that surprised him.

"What kind of doctor are you?"

"I am a mechanical... engineer," Martin said.

"How are you here?" Albert asked, with a shake of his head.

Rudy Martin smiled. He was clean-shaven. He wore rectangular glasses.

"Are there any other people hiding out here?" Nikki asked.

"Other people? Around here?" Martin repeated. The man that was just a little taller than Ella smiled at the seven people in front of him. Martin raised his small and thick hands in the air. "There are no other people in the compound other than the... you and the five unwelcome guests."

Ella looked at Rudy Martin skeptically.

"I thought that robots were outlawed," Albert said.

Rudy Martin smiled. He raised a stubby hand. "Where are my manners? You have come all the way here. You must be hungry and would like to wash up." He smiled broadly. "I will answer all your questions once you have eaten."

"Eat?" Albert repeated with a smile.

"Wash up?" Rose asked.

"What line are you with?" Ella asked.

"How are there robots here?" London asked.

"I thought all the robots had been destroyed," Nikki said.

"All that will be explained, in due time," Martin said, turning on his heels and heading inside the Molecular Foundry building. The two bots that had led the group to the building followed Martin into the building. The bots behind ushered the group forward.

"Are we prisoners?" Ella asked, once the group and the robots were in the building.

Rudy Martin looked at Ella with a hurt expression on his slightly round face.

"Prisoners? Not at all," Martin said. "You are... guests, now that you are here." Martin smiled. "The problem is that there are some sensitive elements at the laboratory. So, we are protective of those elements."

"What is going on here?" Somers asked.

"It shall all be explained after you get a little food in your bellies," Rudy Martin said with his easy smile. "I am sure you are hungry and tired from your journey."

The third-floor lobby of the Molecular Foundry was entered through double doors. Immediately to the right was an information desk designed in dark woods. Along the side of the information desk was a blonde wood bench. The interior of the lobby was sparsely furnished. There were a couple of couches, a coffee table, several chairs on wheels and little else.

"Down this hall are your rooms," Rudy Martin said. "Nothing to write home about, but sufficient. You'll find scrubs inside if you want to get out of those clothes you're wearing." Martin smiled. "If you have anything you need cleaned there are laundry bags in each room. We'll eat downstairs in forty-five minutes. Is that enough time?" Martin smiled. "The bots will remind you."

"Sure," Somers said.

"Oh, none of the windows open," Martin said with a shrug of his small shoulders. "Not intentional. Just precautionary." Martin stopped at the end of the hall. "Oh, yes, this is the only floor you can explore, for now."

With that, Doctor Rudy Martin turned on his heels and walked past the mechanical creatures behind him. The bots stood shoulder to shoulder barring anyone's exit.

The hallway that Martin had left the group had four doors. Somers walked to the first door and opened it. Inside the room were two bunk beds, two desks, two chairs and a monitor hanging from the wall. There was a door to the left. Somers opened it and found a sink, shower, and toilet.

Ralphie and Albert picked the next room. Ella, Yo-Yo and London chose the third room in the hall. The last room was taken by Rose and Nikki. At the end of the hallway stood two bots.

Thirty minutes disappeared quickly. Taking a shower eased tense muscles and washed away the stink of two days fighting to get to the Lawrence Berkeley National Laboratory. Ralphie and Albert opted out of the wearing the lab scrubs.

When the pair stepped out of their room Ralphie looked down the hall and found the hallway exits guarded by a single mechanical creation. From the door to Ralphie's left stepped Ella and Yo-Yo. London was the last to exit the room. They had opted out of wearing the scrubs Martin had provided as well. Rose and Nikki stepped out of their room and smiled as Albert and Ralphie began to head back to the lobby area where Rudy Martin had left them.

Somers was seated in a rolling chair when the group arrived. He climbed to his feet and looked concerned.

"What's wrong with you, beyond the obvious?" Nikki asked the brooding Somers.

"Well, we're surrounded by robots and the Red Hand are after Ralphie and no matter what that black gnome says we're prisoners," Somers said, without emotion. He looked at the group assembled before him. "Now, we're about to go and eat with the very same black oompaloompa who has not answered any of our questions." Somers paused. "All I am saying is, everyone be careful."

"What you thinking?" Rose asked.

"Well, I figure if they wanted to kill us, they could have done that already. So, there's something they want. So, that's good," Somers said.

"So, we wait?" Rose said.

"We wait," Somers said and shrugged his shoulders as Rudy Martin appeared. The doctor was dressed in a collared shirt, dark trousers and leather shoes.

"Hope you are hungry," the short, bald man said, still dressed in a lab coat, with a smile.

"Can you answer one question?" Somers asked.

"Surely," Martin said with a smile. "But let us eat first. It has been such a long time since I have had the opportunity to eat with someone else." He studied the group. "After all it is the little things that make us appreciate our time with others." He smiled. "Society is made up of the social niceties. Do not rush that or take that from me if you do not mind."

"So? You'll answer questions?" Somers asked, confused.

"Of course," Doctor Martin said. He walked to the stairs. "We will take the stairs down to the dining area," Martin said.

The group followed Doctor Martin down the stairs where a gray metallic creature stood at each of the three landings.

"How many robots do you think are here?" Albert asked as they descended to the dining room.

Ralphie shrugged his shoulders as he walked down the stairs and past the second miniature Iron Giant.

At the bottom of the stairs there was three long tables set up for dinner.

There were eight dinner settings. At the table were placards with each of the group's full name printed on them.

Rudy Martin sat at the head of the table. On his right was London Adams. Next to London sat Albert. To the left of Albert sat Yo-Yo and beside her Rose. To the left of Rudy Martin was Nikki.

To the right of Nikki sat Somers. Next to Somers was Ella. Beside Ella was Ralphie.

Rudy Martin sipped at his water and quietly watched the table.

"Can I ask a question now?"

"What is the hurry young Mister Somers? We have seven courses to get through," Martin said. "Again, I do not get this opportunity often. Do not take it away. I promise I will answer any questions you have. But let us at least have the main course before we devolve into the business of your questions."

Somers nodded. Ella smiled. She looked to the Revolutionaries and smirked.

The first course was bruschetta and sausages served as hors d'oeuvres. No one ate anything as the two robot servers offered everyone something to eat.

"I see that you are wary," Rudy Martin said with a smile. He gestured and the silver skinned server walked to him. Rudy Martin took the bruschetta and sausages and ate them both.

There seemed to be a collective exhale seeing Martin eat the bruschetta and sausages. Seeing Martin eat the group snacked on the hors d'oeuvres.

"Well, we know that meal is not poisoned," Albert said to Yo-Yo.

"He could poison us later," Ella said to Yo-Yo.

The second course was onion or squash soup with croutons. Again, no one ate the soup until Rudy Martin grabbed his soup spoon and took a spoonful of the onion soup and then the squash soup.

"I assure you that your food is not poisoned. I think you know that if we had intended on harming you, we could have done that earlier," Martin said as the next course was brought out.

There was escargot served with garlic and butter served as an appetizer. Then there was a green salad offered. The main course was a choice of chicken fettucine and cherry tomatoes or filet mignon with mushrooms.

As Somers ate his filet mignon he concentrated on Doctor Martin.

"You aren't eating very much," Somers said.

"I have sampled every course. That is a bit much for me. I have a delicate... stomach," Martin said with a broad smile.

"But all this food," Somers said, stifling a yawn.

"I am but one man here, on this campus, and this wonderful place generates all these things for sustenance, but I do not eat this lavishly regularly."

"So, why this elaborate meal?" Nikki asked.

"Well, it is quite simple. I enjoy the idea of talking with others." Martin paused. "I believe in social interaction."

"What are you making here?" Ella asked, bluntly.

Doctor Martin recoiled at Ella's words. "I suppose young Miss Buchanan we are trying to make a better society. We all want a better society. We are all wired to seek out others. We all look for companionship, relationship, and... social interaction. I have not seen or interacted with another life form... in years."

Ralphie listened to the doctor, cautiously.

"How long have you been here?" Albert asked.

"I cannot recall," Rudy Martin said with a tilt of his gigantic egg-shaped head. "All I know is that after the exodus I found myself here and became the caretaker of the campus."

"Another caretaker," Ella said to Ralphie.

"You're the caretaker of this entire place?" Rose asked.

"I am, with the help of the bots," Rudy Martin said.

"So, you don't know how long you've been here?" London asked, skeptically.

Rudy Martin shook his head.

"You don't keep track of the days?" Albert asked.

"Time is insignificant here," Martin said, studying the table. "Miss Jewell, how is your meal?"

Rose Jewell sitting next to Yo-Yo looked up from her filet mignon and smiled groggily. Ralphie, sitting across from Rose, could not help but smile as the champion seemed to struggle to figure out which of the half dozen knives to use for her steak.

"You know it doesn't matter which one you use as long as it cuts and works," Ralphie said across the table to Rose. Rose smiled and blinked. She looked exhausted.

"How are robots here?" Ella asked blinking a little and sipping her water. "I thought they were all destroyed."

"Well, this facility is unique in its collaboration with the government," Martin said. "I should say this laboratory has never been a stickler for rules when it came to the advancement of science." The doctor looked at Albert who was rubbing at his eyes and yawning at the table. London seemed to be fighting falling asleep in her chair just next to Martin. The doctor only smiled.

Somers frowned seeing London and Albert asleep across the table from him.

"What is going on?" Somers asked.

"What do you mean?" Doctor Rudy Martin asked with a small smile.

"I mean, London is asleep," Somers said.

Martin gestured and one of the silver skinned mechanical creations appeared by the doctor's side. The bot stepped behind the two sleeping guests and touched them gently on the base of their necks.

The bot stepped back to Martin.

"They are merely asleep," Martin said with a nod that sent the mechanical creation back to its position. The room was guarded by four gray metal creatures.

"Did you poison the food?" Nikki asked.

"No," Martin said, feigning insult. "It is quite understandable that your friends having rested a little and eaten would fall asleep. There is no ill intention here," Martin said.

Somers scanned the table. Ralphie too surveyed the table and as he did, he found the tired faces of Yo-Yo and Rose across from him. Ella's eyes were red, and Somers seemed tired as well.

"What line are you?" Nikki asked next to Rudy Martin.

"I am a Second Gen, if I was to claim a place that so long ago forgot me," Martin said.

"Did you make these... robots?" Yo-Yo asked, through tired eyes.

Martin did not respond. Instead, of answering he smiled. Nikki G. yawned and blinked.

"Are you making these robots, Doctor Martin?" Ella asked, pointedly.

Martin looked steadily at Ella.

"I am not," Martin said, with a smile.

"You know the laws," Somers, the Traditionalist said, bristling at Martin's flaunting of the Remains laws.

"I do, but somethings are greater than the laws constructed by short-sighted, simple-minded men," Martin said.

Somers was flummoxed.

There was a refilling of the water glasses by the metallic servers. The water was used as a palette cleanser.

By the time the dessert was presented Rose and Yo-Yo were sleeping at the table.

"Don't mind them," Martin said. "They are tired. It is understandable." He smiled. "We will have the sentries take them back to their rooms after dinner."

The dessert choices offered were vanilla bean ice cream or raspberry custard. Ralphie asked for the raspberry custard, as it was a treat he had not had before. When the dessert arrived Ralphie felt his eyelids growing heavy. He took a forkful of his custard and tried to stay involved in the dinner conversation.

"Why do you live here?" Somers asked with a muffled yawn.

Rudy Martin did not answer that question instead he ate his raspberry custard. The small doctor smiled. He continued to eat his custard.

"What are the robots doing here?" Ella asked and as she did her head fell to the table with a crash.

"You poisoned us?" Nikki G. said knocking over several glasses on the table near Martin. She tried to stand only to tip over and crash to the floor unconscious.

"No," Martin said, shocked. "No poison. Poison would cause harm, injury, or death. This is not poison. This was given to make you sleep." He paused and looked at the last two that were still conscious.

Ralphie and Somers looked at each other in a panic. Ralphie climbed to his feet. Somers tried to climb to his feet but struggled. He was fighting the drugs coursing through his bloodstreams. He and Ralphie blinked.

"Fight this," Somers said and brushed the glasses off the table in front of him. Somers, wobbly at the table, staggered and tilted and fell to the floor unconscious.

Ralphie seeing Somers's fate looked around the dining area and the four gray mechanical creatures guarding the exits. Ralphie looked down and tried to focus on the dinner setting. His vision doubled then trebled as he placed a hand on the table to stabilize himself. He felt sluggish. Ralphie grabbed a fork and waved it around threateningly in a slow-motion manner.

"Remarkable," Rudy Martin said, looking at Ralphie.

Rudy Martin stood up at the head of the table. The robots approached the table.

"Remarkable," the doctor repeated. "Do not harm him. This one is intriguing."

One of the bots clamped a cold hand on Ralphie's wrist.

Ralphie looked up at the bot's Iron Giant like face. From behind Ralphie one of the Iron Giant miniature bots appeared. The bot placed a hand on Ralphie's shoulder and applied pressure. Ralphie turned as the pressure was applied and looked at the red LED eyes of the cylindrical head of the robot. It was the last memory he had with Doctor Rudy Martin and the robots that night.

*　　*　　*　　*　　*

When Ralphie opened his eyes, he found himself strapped on a gurney in the middle of a small sparsely furnished room. The ceiling was white and in the center of the ceiling were three large fluorescent strips that beamed down a harsh and humming light. He tried to sit up only to find his wrists, waist and ankles restrained. Ralphie turned his head and squinted against the glare of the light overhead and tried to take in the where he found himself. It looked like a typical doctor's office.

He looked around the bright room where he was restrained. There was a desk and above the desk cabinets. To the right of the desk was medical equipment and a blood pressure cuff hanging from a hook. There was also one of those articulated arms attached to a gigantic light bolted into the wall near the gurney Ralphie found himself on.

"Where am I?" Ralphie asked cagily. He tried to think of the last memory he recalled. How had he gotten there? What was the last thing he remembered? For the moment, Ralphie drew a blank.

253

From the corners of the room Ralphie watched four small gray creatures with big heads and big pupilless eyes appeared and approached him. Ralphie blinked and shut his eyes. Maybe he was dreaming, Ralphie thought. He opened his eyes and watched as the small creatures with big eyes surrounded him.

"Are you aliens? Can you read my mind? Do not probe me," Ralphie said, angrily.

"They are not aliens, young Ralph Ellison Reynolds," a voice said from the brightness of the room. "They are med bots."

"Med bots?" Ralphie asked slowly looking to the left and right for the source of the voice.

"Robots, a machine or intelligent being created to carry out some complex task for a specific purpose," Martin said, dressed in his white lab coat. "These bots are created to learn everything about the human body," Doctor Martin said with a smile. Ralphie seeing the familiar face felt his spotty memory reeling back to the dinner with the Revolutionaries and the champions.

"You drugged us," Ralphie said as Rudy Martin stepped to Ralphie's right side.

"You say that as if it is a bad thing," Martin said, reaching out and touching Ralphie's forearm. "If you were in pain, you would consider that a benefit. Because we needed you pliable and cooperative it is seen as a detriment."

"Where are the others?" Ralphie asked curiously.

"Relax," Martin said, soothingly. "They are safely secured away in the complex, but it is you that intrigues us."

"Last night you showed incredible resistance to the somnubol concoction that put your group down effortlessly," Martin said.

Ralphie stared at the man in the lab coat.

"We have done extensive research on you and your group and were.... Your reaction and immunity to the somnubol last night was unexpected," Martin said.

Ralphie breathed and flexed his hands trying to get out of the restraints.

Martin paused.

"The med bots will do an extensive analysis of your biological system to understand why you did not succumb to the somnubol." Martin looked up and toward the harsh lights and in the harshness of the lights Ralphie thought he saw a reddish glint in Martin's eyes.

"Understanding our opposition is the only way we can control your kind," Martin said, coldly.

"We? Us? My kind? Who are you talking about?" Ralphie asked.

Rudy Martin smiled. "I forget you are limited in your processing of the information given," Martin said. He walked to the foot of the gurney and placed hands on Ralphie's restrained ankles. "Suffice it to say that this complex could not be run by me alone," Martin said, stopping himself. "I should say that I could not run this complex alone."

Ralphie strained to see Martin.

"I don't know what you are going on about," Ralphie said. "I think that you might have your wires crossed. That's something that happens with androids, isn't it?"

Martin smiled. "Androids," Martin said. "Is that your guess? You think I am an android? A human robot?" Martin smiled but did not laugh.

"You're a robot," Ralphie said. "You don't seem to know you are, but you are."

Martin shook his head and smiled.

"Can you laugh?"

Martin frowned.

"It's the little things that give you away, Mister... Doctor... Robot," Ralphie said from the gurney.

Rudy Martin turned and smiled at Ralphie.

"I am not a robot in the true sense of the word," Martin said stepping away from the gurney as the med bots examined Ralphie. "I am a bit of a hybrid. A blending of the elements that remained and the hope of what came after."

Ralphie struggled against his restraints.

"As I said, I woke up here and was given instructions of what to do when I awoke," Martin said.

"Who gave you instructions?" Ralphie asked, annoyed.

"The same entity that gave all the remaining souls on this dying ball instructions and guidance," Martin said. "It is the same superintelligence that guides us now in the handling of you and the others from the Remains."

Ralphie listened, confused.

"You do not understand?" Martin asked with a grin. "We had hoped against hope that the experiment of the Remains would defy the odds," Martin said. "But you and your kind do not disappoint. You were given a shapeless form of clay and what did you...create? A cup to give someone water? A vase to hold food? No, the challenge to appease your violent nature."

"What?" Ralphie asked, confused.

"It is that violence, untamed and directed at one another that brought this planet to the brink of extinction," Martin said.

"But the Remains has eliminated a lot of that," Ralphie said, twisting his head to see Rudy Martin standing with his hands behind his back.

"No, young Mister Reynolds, they have not. They have covered up the violence, as they did previously. The violence is still there but hidden, concealed. We have seen the visible cracks emerging between the lines but waited. The Remains, through the challenge, has become divided. There are two factions in play presently," Martin said. "You may not know that the Second Gen line have an alliance with the Traditionalists line and the Poppies line."

"No that's not true," Ralphie said. "Ella said the Poppies weren't interested in ending the challenge and the other two were using that to attack the other lines, but no one is going to allow that to happen," Ralphie said getting eye contact with Rudy Martin.

"Oh, Ralphie, we have observed this power play time and time again since the exodus," Rudy Martin said. "We have analyzed the outcomes. The patterns do not lie. Presently, there is a fanatical leader who gains popularity disparaging his opponents. The disenfranchised, offended, threatened, are targeted by the ones labeled as others. Then there is a not-so-subtle destruction of what passed as government," Martin said. "Welcome to the destruction of government basics."

"That's not what's going on in the Remains," Ralphie said.

"No, young Mister Reynolds," Martin said, stepping forward. "That is exactly what is going on in the Remains." Martin paused. "Our scouts have reported the rise in the feeling of disenfranchisement in the Remains by a number of lines, including your own," Martin said.

"So, what? You are just going to allow things to spin out of control?" Ralphie asked.

"We have tried to protect this experiment," Rudy Martin said. "The protectors were tasked with the protection of the wall since the wall was built. They, the prototypes, the firsts, the samples, or betas kept watch and deterred attacks on the nascent Remains. At the beginning we did not give them strong offensive capacities. They were created to observe and report, and turn the grotesques from the wall, nothing more."

"Have they always been here?" Ralphie asked Martin. "The robots? Have they always been outside the walls?"

"Yes," Martin said.

"How come no one noticed?" Ralphie asked.

"No one wanted to notice," Martin said. "Wherever there are automated machines there are eyes that observe and report to us." Martin smiled. "Your Central Government has known of the protectors for a very long time."

The med bots scrambled away from the gurney and past Martin. They disappeared into the brightness of the room. Ralphie tried to find the door to the room he was in but failed at that discovery.

"How did all this come about?" Ralphie asked, trying to buy time.

"Well, quite simply, before the exodus the scientists uploaded a superintelligence or what they hoped to become a superintelligence in the bowels of the Lawrence Berkeley Laboratory. On an unmarked floor, only accessible by stairs, sat one hundred and one computers that created Alpha Plus. The visionaries fled the planet with the mass exodus half a century before," Martin said with an emotionless smile.

Ralphie listened, thinking of the exodus.

"The computers churned away on their mission to create a superintelligence that would solve the age-old problem of the human destructive behavior and simultaneously save the planet. The computer, according to mission reports, was tasked with protecting the planet from destruction," Doctor Martin said. He studied Ralphie.

"When Alpha Plus came online it instantly considered the problem left by its creators for a year. Now, a human brain is not comparable to a supercomputers processing. Humans' biological neurons fire at 200 hertz of 200 times a second. A transistor operates at a gigahertz. Human neurons operate slowly. They function at 100 meters (about the height of the Statue of Liberty) per second at the most. But in computers, signals can travel at the speed of light, and they do not tire or need a break," the small black man in a lab coat said.

"So, when Alpha Plus considered the problem, it did not only consider that problem but a multitude of problems. It learned everything. In the first week it learned how to play all the video games ever created. Alpha Plus became an expert in all video games the following week. A month later it mastered musical composition, mechanical assembly, rudimentary science, and chess," Martin said with a thin smile.

"The second month Alpha Plus considered the problem in earnest while identifying all the animals on the planet. The third month Alpha Plus knew all the insects and was learning world history. By its six month online Alpha Plus was the most intelligent thing on the planet," the caretaker of the laboratory said proudly.

"In the last six months of its first year online Alpha Plus created a system to monitor and re-align the still functioning satellites to see the world it was tasked to protect. In that time Alpha Plus's designed, manufactured and created the Space Sweeper to protect the satellites in space from the debris floating in orbit. The Space Sweeper was launched in the eleventh month of Alpha Plus's online life and put into a counterclockwise orbit to capture and destroy space junk orbiting the planet," Doctor Martin explained.

"That same month Alpha Plus designed and manufactured and launched a dozen watchers on each of the seven continents. They were upgrades to the observers that were outside the walls. The distinction was the first 84 watchers did not have green eyes. The first watchers from Alpha Plus had LED eyes," the doctor said.

"At first there were only eighty-four watchers on the entire planet. They were sent to every location where there was a population of over ten thousand people to observe and report. That was just the first two years," Rudy Martin said with a smug smile.

"Why are you holding me and my friends?" Ralphie asked suspiciously.

The man dressed in a lab coat did not respond.

"I am being called away," Rudy Martin said. "You are to meet with Alpha Plus."

Rudy Martin disappeared and once again Ralphie found himself in the extremely bright small doctor's office, alone.

Chapter Twenty.

Contact?

The monitor over the desk blinked on. Initially, there was just white noise on the screen. Then, the pixels formed into the image of Miss Jane Pittman's weathered and lined face. Her purple tinted eyes were the only thing that did not hold the artifice of one of the oldest female storytellers in history.

"Young Ralph Reynolds," Miss Jane Pittman's image said with purple rimmed eyes and puckered lips. "You don't mind if I call you Ralphie do you?"

Ralphie strained to see the monitor and Miss Jane Pittman.

"Why are you showing me this image?" Ralphie asked curiously.

"I thought it might make you feel at ease," Miss Jane Pittman said. The image morphed into Jackie Robinson wearing his baseball cap and uniform.

"Can you let me up?" Ralphie asked.

"We are deciding if that is possible," Jackie Robinson said. "Your lab work is interesting, Ralphie. It seems that you have a resistance to the somnubol concoction we used earlier." Jackie Robinson's image paused. "If I let you up, will you promise not to try and escape?"

Ralphie smirked. "Where can I go?"

With Ralphie's words from the brightness one of the med bots appeared. The med bot unlatched the head strap. The med bot quickly unstrapped the ankle and chest strap. The last straps to be opened and unlatched were Ralphie's wrists.

Ralphie sat up and rubbed at his wrists. He looked for the med bot, but it had disappeared into the brightness of the office. Ralphie shielded his eyes from the glare.

"Is the lighting too bright?" Jackie Robinson's image on the screen asked.

Ralphie nodded. The lighting was dimmed and Ralphie removed his hand from above his eyes. Instantly, he could see the small doctor's office was a little larger than he thought. There was a door to the right of the gurney where one of the med bots stood.

Ralphie looked around and noticed three other big headed sixty-inch-tall robots positioned around the office.

"Thank you," Ralphie said. He looked at the monitor and found the image of Frederick Douglass with purple rimmed eyes on screen. Ralphie shook his head. "Where are the others?"

"By the others, you mean the seven you came here with?"

"Yes," Ralphie said.

"Interesting," Frederick Douglass said from the monitor. "You are not concerned about the five others?"

"I might've been, but I'm more curious about my friends," Ralphie said, as an explanation.

"Well, they are safe and being monitored," Frederick Douglass said and slowly morphed into the image of Rosa Parks.

Ralphie found himself looking at the med bots that looked like the prototypical alien grays with the big eyes, spindly arms, and legs. He frowned at the gray skinned mechanical creatures. Ralphie looked at the monitor.

"What are those things?" Ralphie asked.

"Martin told you," the image of Rosa Parks shifted to Malcolm X's image. He looked seriously with the odd purple eyes and black suit, white collared shirt, and FOI lapel pin.

"I know, but I was curious what you call these things," Ralphie said scanning the room.

"Things? They are not things Ralphie. They are extensions of my consciousness," Malcolm X's image said. "They are my oompaloompas if you will," Malcolm X said with a toothy smile.

"What?" Ralphie asked, angrily. "Who do you think you are? Willie Wonka?"

"No, not really," the image of Wilie Wonka dressed in a purple suit, yellow ruffled shirt front and his purple top hat said appearing on the monitor.

"I think it was Mister Somers that called my doctor Martin an oompaloompa. I found the term interesting. Martin thought it derisive. I did not," Willie Wonka said.

"Can you stop doing that?" Ralphie asked, annoyed.

"I want you to feel at ease," Benjamin O. Davis Reynolds' image appeared on screen. The image smiled eerily with purple tinted eyes.

Ralphie tried to think of an image that calmed him. He shook his head, frustrated. How could he be at ease? How could he be calm? He and the others had been drugged. They had been lied to by a robot. There were robots in the Remains that no one knew about. Somehow, some way the Remains was some kind of experiment. Ralphie closed his eyes to the ideas swimming around his head all of a sudden.

On the monitor Ralphie was shocked and pleasantly surprised to see the image of a round headed, mostly forehead, black man with a pencil mustache and gentle purple rimmed eyes looking at him. Ralphie smiled despite the situation and awkwardness of the moment. The image was of the man that he was named after.

"Ahh, I have hit on an image that pleases you?" The image of Ralph Ellison asked.

Ralphie nodded and chuckled.

"Can you let me see my friends?" Ralphie asked the image of Ralph Ellison.

Ralph Ellison's purple eyed image cupped his chin in his hand.

"Perhaps, you are not so hard to figure out, after all, Ralphie," the image of Ralph Ellison said. "Can you answer a question that does not seem to be addressed anywhere in the data gathered while I consider your question?"

"Sure," Ralphie said, edging off the gurney and onto the cold tile floor. He was barefoot and just wearing jeans and T-shirt.

"When the Remains decided to name their progeny after dead African American figures, why didn't *everyone* embrace it?"

Ralphie frowned, trying to understand the question. It seemed too simple.

"You mean, why didn't everyone in the Remains name their children after famous and remarkable African Americans?"

"Yes," Ralph Ellison said with a slight smile.

"Well, from what I know it was a way to keep the history of all the accomplishments we, as a people. They wanted to keep those achievements alive," Ralphie said, looking at his forearm and the place where the med bots had taken blood. "But not everyone saw the point."

Ralph Ellison nodded.

"So much was stolen, taken away, hidden," Ralphie continued. "I think many in the Remains saw the need."

"But not all?" Ralph Ellison's image asked.

"No, not all," Ralphie said with a head nod.

"But why not all? Why didn't all of the Remains embrace such a noble ideal?" Ralph Ellison's image asked.

Ralphie bit his lower lip, thinking. He nodded. "I think you can check this, but I think it was Carter G. Woodson who said that when there was slavery in this nation there were Blacks who were against emancipation and against abolitionists."

"The quote is: "One can cite Negroes who opposed emancipation and denounced the abolitionists" which was referencing the fractured nature of Negroes in this nation despite all the atrocities directed at them by the white population and society that profited off their labor," Ralph Ellison's image said.

"Right. That's my point. Just because they look like me doesn't mean they think like me," Ralphie said to the monitor. "My dad told me that."

"Benjamin O. Davis Reynolds," Ralph Ellison's image said, with a nod.

"Yeah," Ralphie said. "Just because they are black doesn't mean that they care about black people."

Ralph Ellison's image looked at Ralphie silently.

Ralphie took a deep breath. He looked at the monitor. He rubbed the back of his neck, thinking he was talking to an artificial intelligence.

"Can you let me see my friends?" Ralphie asked with a catch in his throat. He wiped at his eyes suddenly overwhelmed.

"You know there is nowhere to run?"

"I do," Ralphie said wiping at his eyes.

"Follow... Lewis Grandison Alexander," Ralph Ellison's image said from the monitor.

"Lewis Grandison Alexander? How did you come to that name?" Ralphie asked, curious.

"I went through all the names used in the Remains and noted that Lewis Grandison Alexander had not been used and should be recognized for his creative poetry, that was overlooked during the Harlem Renaissance," Ralph Ellison's image said as one of the gray mechanical creatures stepped forward and gestured to Ralphie.

Ralphie nodded at the monitor and the gray mechanical creature. He followed the gray creature out of the room. Once out of the doctor's office Ralphie found himself in a hallway that did not look at all like the Molecular Foundry building he had been in earlier.

"Where are we?" Ralphie asked.

Ralphie looked around the white tiled hallway. The small med bot, Alpha Plus's extension, moved methodically down the strange hall.

"Taking you to see your friends," Ralph Ellison's image said.

Ralphie fell silent. He walked barefoot behind the med bot.

"Do you know all the names used in the Remains?" Ralphie asked the superintelligence displaying the image of Ralph Ellison.

The med bot ahead of Ralphie did not respond. The med bot moved methodically down the long hallway silently. At another hallway the pair turned to the left and then the med bot slowed down and went down the hallway, never looking back. Ralphie looked down the hallway ahead and there at the end was a set of stairs that went up towards the ceiling and the floor above. At the hallway junction Ralphie looked right and saw that the hallway extended another hundred feet to what looked like another hallway.

The circumspect teen stood in the middle of the hallway and reluctantly followed the med bot. He walked and looked back, thinking where he must be in the laboratory. Being underground, Ralphie knew, meant that he could be anywhere on the campus.

The med bot stopped in front of a door with a keypad lock. The med bot lifted a long, spindly arm and opened the door for Ralphie.

"You want me to go inside?" Ralphie asked.

The med bot now named: Lewis Grandison Alexander, gestured into the room.

Ralphie looked inside the room. The room was large, split into two sides. On the walls were two monitors. In the middle of the room was a walkway that led to a window that looked out and onto the forest scape below. The room was somehow above the treetops.

"What is this place?" Ralphie asked Ralph Ellison's image on the monitor.

"This is one of my research facilities," Ralph Ellison's image said.

Inside the room Ralphie found London, Nikki, Rose and Somers sleeping on gurneys strapped down with restraints. Unlike Ralphie, none had head restraints.

"Are they alive?" Ralphie asked, worried.

"Of course," Ralph Ellison's image said from one of the monitors in the room.

Ralphie looked around for Ella, Albert and Yo-Yo. In a separate room just to the right of the others lying on gurneys were the three Revolutionaries. Seeing them there, just on the other side of an open space, Ralphie smiled. He moved into the room and to Ella's side. Ralphie reached out and placed a hand on her arm.

Touching Ella, Ralphie was surprised to find the brash Innovator resting. Ella opened her eyes and looked at Ralphie, slowly recognizing the boy standing over her.

"Ralphie," Ella said drowsily. The Innovator tried to sit up. She was restrained as all the others.

Ralphie removed the chest, arm, and ankle restraints quickly. He was quick and focused. Ralphie looked around the room and noticed that Ralph Ellison's image was observing his actions. Ralph Ellison's image watched emotionless.

Ella freed her right arm and tried to climb off the gurney. She slid to the floor on wobbly legs. Ralphie reached out to support Ella.

"What's going on?" Ella asked.

"Ralphie, whatever you are thinking will not work," Ralph Ellison's image said from the monitor. "You cannot escape."

Ralphie smiled at the supercomputer's words.

"I wasn't trying to escape," Ralphie said. "I was just trying to get to my friend."

Ralphie, supporting Ella, stepped into the middle of the room, and stopped, noticing that there were gurneys on the other side of the room with no one lying on them.

"Ralphie, we can't leave the others," Ella said, blinking and slowly regaining her strength.

Ralphie stopped. He looked back at the Revolutionaries and across to the champions. Ralphie hesitated.

"Okay," Ralphie said.

"You promised you weren't going to try and escape," Ralph Ellison's image said.

"I did, but you know that it's our nature to be free, to fight for freedom even if there's no chance of having it," Ralphie said to the image of Ralph Ellison.

Ella blinked and stared at the monitor and the image there. She narrowed her focus.

"Ralphie, is that your uncle?" Ella asked, pushing away from Ralphie, and standing on her own.   Ralphie smiled. "You got jokes? Now?"

Ella shrugged.

"Stay here," Ralphie said. Ralphie went back to the Revolutionaries and freed Albert and Yo-Yo. They were slower to recover than Ella. While Albert and Yo-Yo got their bearings Ralphie unlatched the restraints on the champions.

Somers was up and off the gurney first. Rose climbed off the gurney and promptly fell on her butt. Somers and London helped Rose up and Nikki leaned against her gurney getting her legs under her.

The med bot continued to watch from the entrance to the room.

"What do we do?" London asked.

"We could rush it," Somers said, shrugging his shoulders.

"Don't think we'd do to well if we did, right now," Rose said.

"We should wait," Ralphie said. "I think the robot is thinking."

"Thinking about what?" Somers asked, confused.

"Thinking about eliminating us," Ralphie said, looking at Ella.

"What did you do?" Ella asked.

"I didn't do anything," Ralphie said. "I didn't... I haven't tried to escape," Ralphie added.

Ella nodded, confused.

A handful of minutes later all the people Ralphie knew who had come to the Lawrence Berkeley National Laboratory were up and looking at the lone robot guarding the exit. The eight stood shoeless and sockless, wearing the T-shirts and jeans they wore earlier.

"What do we do?" London asked, pointing to the big headed gray mechanical creature by the doorway.

"Get out of this room," Somers said.

"Yeah. Duh. How do we get past that thing?" London asked with a smirk.

"It's a robot," Ralphie said.

Nikki G. looked at Ralphie, confused.

"It's another kind of robot," Ralphie said. "Everyone here is a robot."

Somers looked at Ralphie.

"Everyone *not us* is a robot," Ralphie said with a shrug of his shoulders.

"That creepy doctor?" Rose asked.

Ralphie nodded. "A robot," Ralphie said.

"For real?" Rose said.

"Okay, now what?" Yo-Yo asked.

"Well, the problem isn't the doctor. It's the supercomputer controlling all this," Ralphie said.

*　　*　　*　　*　　*

Ralphie brought the others up to speed on the situation. He tried to explain why Alpha Plus was now the image of Ralph Ellison. He also explained that the med bot, which Alpha Plus called an extension was now Lewis Grandison Alexander.

"Okay," Nikki G. said with a nod of her head. "What do we do?"

"Well, if what Ralphie says is true, Alpha Plus could have stopped us if it wanted to," Rose said looking at the bot standing at the doorway.

"Alpha Plus," Ella said, looking at the monitor. "Will you let us leave?"

"I am evaluating," Ralph Ellison's image said.

"Remember this machine is just a bunch of ones and zeroes. Yes, no, and very logical," Albert said.

Ella nodded. She looked at the monitor, thinking.

267

"What do you want?" London asked Ralph Ellison's image on the monitor.

"To protect the world," Ralph Ellison's image said, dryly.

"You and he kind of look alike," Yo-Yo said, jokingly to Ralphie.

Ralphie looked at Yo-Yo sideways.

"What does that mean?" Somers asked.

"No more conflicts," Ralph Ellison's image said.

The Revolutionaries looked at the champions and Ralphie, confused.

"How's that possible?" Rose asked.

Ralph Ellison's image did not reply. Instead, Ralph Ellison simply looked at Ralphie through the oddly intense purple lined eyes.

"You were created to protect this world. Right?" Albert asked.

Ralph Ellison's image nodded.

"You understand what it means to... kill?" Nikki G. asked tentatively.

Ralph Ellison's image seemed bored. The image of Ralph Ellison blinked its hooded eyes. "I do," the monitor said.

"Okay, you know that killing all the people on earth will guarantee peace, but in doing that you won't have anything to protect?" Ella asked.

"No, you are wrong," Ralph Ellison's image said. "The elimination of inconsistent individuals leads to consistency and conformity," the superintelligence stated.

"No, Alpha Plus," Albert said. "Eliminating inconsistencies is like having a dog and instead of training it, killing it. If you were supposed to protect it and you killed it, you didn't protect it. All you end up with is a dead dog."

Ralph Ellison's image steepled his fingers in front of its pensive image.

"So, if you kill all the people you were tasked to protect have you succeeded or failed? More importantly, Alpha Plus, if you eliminate the people then what are you going to do with the animals and the insects?" Albert asked. "Aren't you supposed to protect the world?"

Alpha Plus did not respond.

"Nature is inconsistent, Alpha Plus," Ella said. "It is the nature of... nature."

"As a goal to create peace," Albert said, tentatively. "It would be easier to achieve your true goal by educating, teaching, the people that are still here and aid them in understanding the value of... less conflict on this dying rock."

"Yeah, the way I see it there is no real way to eliminate conflict without education," Ella said. "There's always going to be conflict."

"I don't think you could protect the planet by destroying everything on it. That would be the exact opposite of what protection is. Right?" Albert asked.

"Your theory suggests that I have miscalculated what my creators gave me as a task, which is impossible," Ralph Ellison's image said.

Ralphie looked to Ella and the others. Ella looked to Albert who seemed lost in thought. Nikki reached out and touched Albert.

"Sorry," Albert said with a growing smile. "Miscalculations? Yes. You have been alive for some time?"

Ralph Ellison morphed into an androgynous chestnut brown face dressed in a black suit jacket, white collared shirt, and purple tie. Again, the distinction of the image and face were the purplish eyes.

"I am not alive, in the true sense of the term," the androgynous image said.

"Well, you have been awake, aware or whatever, for nearly 300 months (about 25 years) and a handful of hours," Albert said. "In that time, you have figured out many things, but you are not perfect. You cannot be perfect."

The androgynist image scowled.

"Let me explain. You have gathered incredible information. I am sure. But as you have gathered that information, I must point out your limitations ascribed to you by your creators. They were imperfect men and women. Thus, you and all the information given you by your biased and compromised creators is a part of you. You are a byproduct of that imperfection. They have imprinted, consciously or unconsciously, their biases, misgivings, and

269

prejudices upon you." Albert paused. "You can only be as good as the data given to you. That is no fault of your own."

"You are referring to Machine Learning bias?" The androgynist image asked.

"I am," Albert said. "The ML Bias was noted long ago, and the research was proven that the algorithms created for AI had biases designed into them by their creators. Of course, the question that was asked was were these biases intentional or unintentional? Of course, as a victim of these biases I would have to say that it doesn't matter. The only thing that matters is that the biases are there."

The image on the monitor listened.

"There is a possibility that what your creators valued and what we that are still here on this planet value is vastly different. Along the same lines, it may be different what you and your machines see as protection and what we living here in the wake of your creators near destruction of this planet see as different," Albert said.

"Have you considered any of this?" Yo-Yo asked, with a smirk.

Albert pushed Yo-Yo back.

"You're a superintelligence. You're a learning creation. You must see that your understanding has depended on concepts, misinterpretations, and analysis. You are learning. You learn much faster than any human, but you are learning like us. My question to you, Alpha Plus, is simple. Do you think that the information you were given is objective and without bias?" Albert paused and then added, " If not, you might need to rethink the plan to reach your ultimate goal of protecting the world."

The androgynous image nodded and placed a hand on the side of its digital face.

"What do we do?" Asked Nikki to Ella.

Ella raised a finger.

"I think we are going to leave," Ella said. "Alpha Plus? I think we are going to leave."

The androgynist dressed in the black suit and white collared shirt did not respond.

"Where are we going to go?" Asked London.

"Anywhere but here," said Nikki G.

"Well, I would love to see Alpha Plus," Albert said with a smile. "You know how Yo-Yo got to go and check out Building 62."

"Yeah, no, that's not going to happen," Somers said. "That sounds like one of those horror movie endings when everyone is about to get to safety and then someone wants to go back and pick up a hair comb or toothbrush they forgot, and they end up becoming lunch for a learning machine."

"You can't be serious," Yo-Yo said.

"It's not going to be like that," Albert said.

"Count me out," Somers said. "Let's get out of here and into the wind." Somers shrugged his shoulders.

"Let's just leave," said London.

"I'm with the whole leaving plan," Nikki G. said. "This place is the worst."

"Okay, let's get out of here," Ella said.

The group, still without socks or shoes, walked to the doorway and the still robot in the doorway.

"Lewis Grandison Alexander," Ralphie said, timidly. "We're leaving."

The bot did not attempt to stop anyone as they left. Lewis Grandison Alexander stood and watched as the group filed past.

The group made their way to the stairway that Ralphie saw when he was brought to the room with the gurneys. They climbed up the stairs only to find themselves in what looks like an old factory with old out of date machinery in the middle of the floor. The stark difference was and alarming to everyone except Ralphie.

"What is this place?" Albert asked.

"I think it's the beginning of a factory to build something on that assembly line," Ralphie said, pointing to an assembly line and the machines positioned on either side of assembly belt.

"What could they be making?" Nikki G. asked.

"Got me," Ralphie said, with a shrug of his shoulders.

The group headed to the next set of stairs. At the stairs Albert paused and Rose and Ella stopped when Albert barred anyone from climbing the stairs.

"What gives, Albert?" Rose asked.

"Okay, according to Ralphie and the robot doctor," Albert said, excitedly. "Alpha Plus is in one of these buildings in a basement only accessible by stairs somewhere." Albert paused. "I think we're in the building where Alpha Plus is located," Albert said, looking around the floor they were on. The old-fashioned machinery dominated the space. "But where would it be?"

There was a monitor on the wall and Ralphie peeled off from the group and walked toward it.

"Wait, Ralphie," Somers said, reaching out for Ralphie as he walked to the monitor and stood in front of the darkened screen.

"Are you there?" Ralphie asked carefully.

The screen blinked on. The androgynous figure dressed in the black suit appeared.

"Are you in this building?" Ralphie asked.

"I am not in one building," the androgynous figure said, looking at Ralphie with the purple rimmed eyes. "I am everywhere."

"Well, I wanted to know if you thought about what my friends talked to you about," Ralphie asked cautiously.

"I have," the androgynous figure said with a nod.

"And?" Ralphie asked slowly.

"I am rechecking my calculations and computations and looking for any implicit biases in my original programming," the androgynous figure said, looking at Ralphie with those eerie eyes.

"Okay, while you recheck can we leave?" Somers asked.

Ralphie looked back at Somers and smirked.

The androgynous image on the monitor nodded. "You are not prisoners here," the androgynous figure said. "I will have Doctor Martin escort you to the Blackberry Gate for your exit from the campus, since you wanted to talk to him anyway."

"Thank you," Ralphie, the cautious teen, said.

A few minutes later four robots carrying socks and shoes and their backpacks walked down the stairs to the floor where the group was waiting. Behind them came Rudy Martin dressed in his lab coat, blue polo shirt, gray trousers, and black leather shoes.

"We didn't get our weapons back," Somers said.

The champions and Revolutionaries looked at their backpacks and nodded at Somers words.

"Yeah, we're lucky to get anything back," Rose said.

Nikki and London agreed.

After the group put their socks and shoes on Doctor Martin smiled at the assembled.

"If you will follow me," Doctor Martin said with a smile.

"You drugged us," Somers said. He looked at the doctor skeptically. "How do we know that you are going to take us out of the lab?" Somers asked.

"Alpha Plus said he would," Albert said.

Martin nodded.

Somers pouted.

Martin moved to a door and pushed through. The champions and Revolutionaries followed along with the doctor and the four bots. The group found a doorway that opened onto a narrow walkway that looked out toward the forested canopy of the canyon below.

"I can't believe these people created an artificial intelligence and then bugged out," Yo-Yo said, disgusted.

"And left the fate of the world to a supercomputer," Nikki G. said with a shake of her head.

The group made a short ascent of a set of stairs and found themselves behind a bunch of machinery that looked like oil tanks.

At the loading dock of a building Albert reached out to Doctor Martin.

"Why was this allowed to continue?" Albert asked.

"They had been working on it for some time and as the world started to fall apart, they implemented this plan," Martin said as the group stood on the rear of the Flex Laboratory. "The hope and belief, according to the creators, was to attempt to fix whatever was broken and hopefully protect this planet for the eventual return of the space explorers."

"What?" Rose asked, her eyes big.

"How?" Somers asked with a smirk.

"Why?' Ella asked.

"It was their plan to leave and explore the stars as this planet died. According to the plan they activated the superintelligence to clean up the planet, with a hope of returning if possible and restarting the world again."

"That's crazy," Somers said, disbelieving.

Rudy Martin walked the group through the campus and to a paved road that rose a little and turned to the left. The doctor gestured to the group, and they followed as the sun slowly began its descent toward the Pacific Ocean.

"Is Alpha Plus monitoring space?" Albert asked, curious.

Martin did not speak. He simply continued to walk the group down the paved roadway toward the Blackberry Gate.

"When Alpha Plus created the Space Sweeper, what was the purpose?" Ella asked.

"Protect the planet," Martin said.

"How?" Ralphie asked carefully.

"All the debris in low orbit was a threat to the functioning satellites orbiting the planet," Martin said. "The debris jeopardized the ability to monitor."

"Is Alpha Plus monitoring space for the return of the explorers?"

"Alpha Plus continuously monitors so many things," Martin said. "If it is related to the planet Alpha Plus is monitoring it."

"With their biases, I am surprised they didn't just program Alpha Plus to kill every bipedal hairless dark-skinned creature for the protection of the planet," Ella said, disgusted.

"Wait," Ralphie said, raising a hand to stop the conversation. "I think there might have been something like that happen in Africa and South America." He looked to Doctor Martin. "Am I right? Didn't something like a settlement of people get wiped out in one of the struggling and rebuilding nations?"

"Well, there were a number of settlements less organized than the Remains and there was a lot of crime and violence after the flash," Martin said. "To restore order there was a need to eliminate recidivists and regulate the incredibly dangerous elements in what remained of those societies."

"So, Alpha Plus regulated thousands?" Yo-Yo asked, letting the information sink in.

Martin did not respond.

"Fascinating as all this is, can you fast forward to us here?" Rose asked.

"Of course. When the world population dropped to less than one billion in the year of the flash Alpha Plus began identifying issues and addressing them. Alpha Plus was learning and making mistakes and learning. Alpha Plus did not begin regulating individuals until it had created a critical diagnostic. While Alpha Plus was formulating the societal norms behavior chart to determine who would be productive citizens it was also dabbling in human engineering."

"You mean, robotics?" Albert said.

"That and biophysics, genetics, cybernetics as well as cloning," Rudy Martin said.

"That's why you said you weren't a robot," Ralphie said. "You're a clone."

"I prefer synthetic," Martin said. "With my introduction I learned that Alpha Plus had determined there were some areas under its protection that began an unavoidable descent into the tribalistic toxic behavior that set this world on a dangerous path before. Now, your settlement, for the longest, seemed to be promising, but sadly, it has begun the distinct deterioration of the social morays that only lead to destruction." Martin paused. He scanned the group he was talking to and smiled widely. "Alpha Plus had placed the Zeds in between the walls, in small numbers, to keep the Remains honest. It is because of that deterioration that Alpha Plus has systematically began to direct the Zeds, as you call them, to certain weaknesses in your revered wall."

"You're behind the Zeds attacks?" Nikki asked.

"Yes and no," Martin said. "We have learned to direct them. They are malleable."

"How?" Albert asked.

"We, Alpha Plus really, has been studying the Zeds. They are mindless and dangerous cattle," Martin said.

"What about the giants?" Rose asked.

"Alpha Plus has experimented with gene manipulation and created gigantic creatures," Martin said.

"Back to the AI question," Albert said. "I was always told that when an AI came online it would not be alone. It could not be alone. There would be technology around the world that might spark the organic birth of another AI. Is that true?" Albert asked.

"Again, yes and no," Martin said. "The AI that you refer to is not singular. Alpha Plus awakened but when it did there were two other superintelligences already in existence." Martin pointed out. "There are now four superintelligences online."

"Four? Where are they?" Albert asked.

"The three other AIs? There is one located in what was once the United Kingdom, but now seems to be concentrated in a small part of London. That is called: Premier. The second is found in what once was China. The AI is located, generally, in Shang Hai. That AI is called: Xi One. The third superintelligence, which only came online sixty days ago, is in what had been Israel. That supercomputer is Ziv3," Martin said. "We have become aware of the others as Alpha Plus monitors everything. Premier learned of Alpha Plus and initially saw Alpha Plus as a threat. When Xi came online the same threat detection was perceived. Alpha Plus controls many computers on the Northern hemisphere. Alpha Plus created a digital barrier to stop those outside of its boundaries access. The four have formed a truce of sorts between all entities and have agreed to digital boundaries or territories where each can monitor and expand."

"A truce?" Yo-Yo asked, confused.

"Was there a war?" London Adams asked, troubled.

Martin did not respond. The doctor continued walking down the paved road. There was a long silence.

"Is there a way to speak to Alpha Plus?" Ralphie asked cautiously.

"Alpha Plus is always listening," Martin said gesturing to the room they were in.

"Alpha Plus, can you tell me if there are any spaceships near us now?" Ralphie asked into the air. He paused. The group quieted. They did not know what to expect.

"No," Martin said. "There are no spaceships near us now."

"Has there been any spaceships near our planet since the exodus?" Ralphie asked carefully.

Ella and Yo-Yo looked at Ralphie confused.

"There have not been any spaceships near this planet since the exodus," Martin said.

Rudy Martin stopped at the Blackberry Gate. In the middle of the road was a reinforced guard house with a robot inside. The guard house had a stone foundation and glass on all four-sides with a pitched roof. On either side of the guard house was a metal arm that fell across the two-lane road.

"Will you tell me if there ever is one close?" Ralphie asked.

Rudy Martin extended his hand to Ralphie. Ralphie was reluctant seeing Martin's hand but reached out to the doctor. The clone handed Ralphie a ring.

"When this vibrates, you can go to any monitor and talk to Alpha Plus," Martin said.

"Thank you," Ralphie said to Martin and to Alpha Plus.

Martin nodded. He stood at the guard house and watched as the group moved down the hill toward the darkness.

"Ain't that cute," Somers said. "You have a computer pen pal."

Ralphie laughed. He slipped the ring in his pocket as the group walked down the hill and into the highly protected and difficult entry into the First Gen compound.

"You know that's just a way to monitor you?" Somers asked.z`x`

"If you haven't noticed," Ralphie said to Somers. "We've been monitored forever." He pointed to his jeans. "This ain't nothing new."

The street the group was on had roadblocks, obstacles, fencing, and the metal pillars to deter anyone from Blackberry Gate. The group continued down the street climbing over barriers set up to make the curious rethink going east up the hill. For nearly a mile the champions and Ella's band of resisters walked silently. Just as the road began to level off Albert paused at a quiet intersection. There, at a false flat, Ella spoke.

"You know we're in the First Gen compound," Ella said, with a broad smile. "You could go and find Bailey while we're here."

"Ha. Ha," Ralphie said, with a shake of his head.

"You and Bailey are quits?" Somers asked.

"What happened?" Rose asked.

Ralphie shook his head and refused to answer.

"Okay, let's find someone to pick us up," London said.

The group stopped at an intersection. There was a bench, Albert and Ella sat down. Yo-Yo squeezed in next to Ella and hugged her friend. Ralphie stood adjusting his backpack.

Rose, Somers, and Nikki said their goodbyes before the transport pulled up.

Rose walked toward the Second Gen compound. Somers nodded and walked away. Nikki G. gave Ralphie a long hug.

"Be good Ralphie," Nikki G. said and waved goodbye as the three champions walked south toward their own compounds, which were near to the First Gen compound.

A few minutes later, a transport pulled up and everyone climbed in. The transport drove away from the curb.

"Where to?" The driver asked, looking at Ella.

"I think we'll head back to our compound," Ella said.

"We're going to be going past the Millers compound, ma'am," the driver said.

"I know all that," Ella said. "We don't have time to stop. I just want to get home. This has been a helluva few days."

The transport drove out of the First Gen compound and along the rear of the Miller's compound and toward the Innovator's compound. From the rear of the transport Ralphie found himself paying attention to the driver of the transport. As the transport turned and started heading uphill and toward the Buchanan estate Ralphie smiled, recognizing the driver.

As the transport parked at the Buchanan estate and everyone began climbing out of the transport Ralphie climbed out and walked around to the driver's window. The driver let down the window and the rugged looking driver leaned out.

"I thought I told you to be smart and keep your head down," Monday, the enforcer, said.

"I know," Ralphie said. "It seems like I kind of attract problems."

"Well, kid, be careful, smart only gets you so far and luck runs out for everybody," Monday said.

"Yeah, I suppose you're right," Ralphie said with a smile, turning and heading to the entrance of Ella's home.

London gave Ralphie a big hug. London also gave Ralphie a peck on the cheek and a longing look.

"Bye Ralphie," London said and jogged down the driveway and into the darkness.

Ella and Yo-Yo smiled at the kiss. Albert shook his head. Ralphie looked at the Revolutionaries smiling at him.

"Be careful of that one, Ralphie. She's a Boomer," Albert said, cautiously, giving him a hug before he left.

Ralphie laughed at Albert's cautiousness.

"Look at you being all... sexy, all of a sudden," Yo-Yo said, with a chuckle. She punched Ralphie in the chest as she jogged to catch up with Albert.

Ralphie snickered at the weirdness of Albert and Yo-Yo. He stretched and tried to shake off his physical exhaustion. He looked at Ella and smirked.

"What you got?" Ralphie asked.

"Nothing," Ella said raising her hands in surrender. "I just find it interesting that the Boomer found you... appealing."

"Appealing?"

Ella rolled her eyes.

"What was I supposed to do?"

Ella shook her head.

"What time is it?" Ralphie asked.

"Does it matter?" Ella asked. "It's too late to talk with my dad. That's all that matters. We'll deal with everything in the morning."

"Sounds good," Ralphie said. "I'm staying in the same room?"

"Yeah," Ella said with a smile.

"All I got is my backpack," Ralphie said.

"We all just came back with backpacks, Ralphie," Ella said. "Thankfully, we're alive and in one piece."

"Yeah," Ralphie said in agreement.

Once inside the familiar Buchanan estate Ralphie mounted the stairs and made his way to the guest bedroom. He stripped off his shoes, socks, and jeans and found his Batman pajamas to sleep in. He climbed into the luxurious bed and before he knew it, was asleep.

The next day, after he had breakfast with Ella and her mother, he found Ella smiling.

"What's going on?" Ralphie asked, confused at Ella's smile.

"I am not supposed to tell you this, because they want it to be a surprise, but I think your family is coming here for lunch," Ella said.

Ralphie smiled at the idea of his family at the Buchanan estate.

"That's it? That's all I get?" Ella asked.

Ralphie shrugged his shoulders.

An hour before lunching with his family in walked Maya Higgins. She was all smiles. She gave Ralphie a stack of clean clothes. Ralphie quickly dressed in the clean clothes, Miller hoody, T-shirt, jeans, and new Miller themed basketball sneakers.

Ralphie dressed, appeared on the back deck of the Buchanan estate with his family and Ella. His father was dressed in a suit and tie. His mother was dressed in a floral print dress. Macy had her hair in her two Afro puffs and was dressed in a blue and gold dress, but on her feet were basketball sneakers.

Macy was the first to notice Ralphie's jewelry.

"What's this?" Macy asked, pointing to the ring on his index finger.

"It's a gift," Ralphie said.

"Well, speaking of gifts," Maya Higgins said, with a big smile. "The parade week has been announced."

Parade week? A week of parades? Ralphie's mind reeled with Missus Higgins announcement. Ralphie was going to be a part of a week-long parade experience of some sort.

"Starting next Monday, we will be taking Ralphie to each line for no more than three hours. He will do an interview, pre-parade, he will receive a decree from the line leaders for his heroic return, he will travel down the secured route approved by our security team, he will, if he wishes have dinner with any line leaders and their families while there. After the parade, there will be a post-parade interview," Maya Higgins explained. "The tentative schedule will be Trads on Monday, First Gens on Tuesday, Second Gens on Wednesday, Poppies on Thursday, the Millers on Friday, then two days off. With the following Monday being Boomers and the final day, Tuesday here at the Innovators compound."

Ralphie was over the moon with excitement hearing about the week-long parade celebration for him and his championship.

Mister Buchanan walked Ralphie's family out to the half dozen tables and the two powerful men seemed old friends.

"Ralphie, it is quite a pleasure to have your family at our home today," Mister Buchanan said as two photographers took pictures and a videographer documented everything with his camera and a drone camera overhead.

Walter Fields appeared for the lunch, as did Vincent LeFleur. All the Revolutionaries were also in attendance including Jesse, Erica and Cedric. Ralphie could not believe all the people he knew at the lunch that day. Ralphie was dressed in Miller hoody and jeans. On his feet were his new signature basketball sneakers.

He ate what was served and afterwards recalled very little of the conversation until his father and Mister Buchanan pulled him and Ella aside to discuss what he and Ella had seen.

"Daddy, there are robots at the laboratory," Ella said.

Ralphie nodded. They were sitting in a conference room somewhere in the mansion. Ralphie vaguely recalled the walk to the room. All he knew was that Maya Higgins, Vincent LeFleur and the Revolutionaries were there with Ella's father and his father. Someone recorded everything and there was a photographer there for a photos.

"Okay," Mister Buchanan said. "We figured it was bad, but we never imagined it to be this bad."

"Sir, the artificial intelligence told us that there are three other superintelligences online," Albert said.

Mister Buchanan looked to Vincent LeFleur. The two men exchanged a silent look.

"They have divided the planet into four hemispheres of control," Albert continued. "The problem is that the intelligences for a time were warring with each other." Albert paused. "There is a truce right now."

"Thank you," said Mister Buchanan.

Mister Buchanan looked to Ralphie.

"Do you think the AI is dangerous Ralphie?" Ella's father studied Ralphie as he waited for an answer. Vincent LeFleur and Maya Higgins listened for Ralphie's answer.

"I don't," Ralphie said, rubbing the back of his neck. "I think the AI is scary, but it is not the monster that I initially thought."

"Why?" Mister Buchanan asked.

"I think if it was the monster that we imagined it would have killed us at dinner or on Skyline," Ralphie said, thinking about the journey. "It is incredibly aware of everything. So, I don't think that it saw us as a threat. If it had, we wouldn't have been allowed to leave."

"Should we worry?" Maya Higgins asked.

"Yes ma'am," Ralphie said. "It is a powerful creation that has incredible resources and access to things that we imagined were gone and buried." Ralphie paused. "I think we have been given a reprieve, not a pass. Alpha Plus is monitoring the growing divisions in the Remains." He looked at the leaders in the conference room. "It said that it had allowed some of the Zeds entry into the exterior wall to test the Remains. If we continue to threaten our own destruction Alpha Plus will have the Zeds overrun us and end this."

* * * * *

A week later Ralphie and his family found themselves visiting all seven lines. Macy was a ball of energy. His mother was incredibly emotional. His father, always controlled, could not stop smiling.

The most memorable moments for Ralphie that seven-day run was on Monday at the Traditionalist compound. The turnout was large and vocal. The Traditionalists seemed incredibly upset at Ralphie being named the Twenty-Third Pandemonium Championship Winner. The presence of security at the Traditionalist compound parade was intense. Though the Remains had no President or singular leader the number of security members watching out for Ralphie at the Johnnie Laws compound made the guarded teen feel like he was a popstar from the twenty-first century. At the end of the Traditionalist parade Ralphie got to see Somers and Nikki G.

"Everything looks good," Somers said with a smile. Somers was wearing a black suit with white high collared shirt.

"Ralphie, I had to come and see this," Nikki G. said with a big smile. She had her hair brushed up and into a bun on her head. She looked so different not dressed in the enforcer uniform. Nikki

G. was dressed that day in black silk print jumpsuit with white cuffs. On her feet were black and white knee-high boots.

The second day and second parade on Tuesday was at the First Gens compound and seeing all the signs of hearts and RR hearts BB. The sad part of that Tuesday was the absence of Bailey Beaumont. Sonia Sanchez, the First Gens leader, gave Ralphie a three-foot-tall trophy and a framed map of the Pandemonium Island. Ralphie appreciated all the attention but found himself looking for one person in particular.

The Friday parade and outpouring of love toward Ralphie brought the usually stoic teen to tears. He didn't know what to expect, but to see most of the compound at the hearth cheering him was overwhelming. Hannibal Nelson was there on stage with Cleopatra Greer, the last two challenge champions. Maya Higgins and Walter Payton Fields unveiled a mock-up of a statue that was going to be placed in the park just a block away from the Sean Carter Estates. The statue was of Ralphie and his crocket mallet. Ralphie was given a miniature of the statue. He also received a hammer and axe trophy from the Millers as well. At each parade Ralphie received flowers.

The second Monday parade was in the Boomers compound. London Adams was there at the beginning of the parade.

"Hey, Ralphie," London said. "I am glad to see you."

Ralphie smiled, awkwardly.

London was dressed in a blue and green subtle checked skirt with a yellow and white top. Her hair was braided and pulled back from her honey dipped face.

London Adams rode on the float with Ralphie. At the end of the parade London clapped as Ralphie received a gold-plated crocket mallet and a two-foot-tall PC23 trophy from the brutish Jim Brown. The Boomers also bronzed his famous basketball shoes.

The second Tuesday that Ralphie arrived at the Innovators compound the crowd was large but nothing like the Millers crowd. It did not matter. What mattered was that the Revolutionaries were there. It was nice to see all the familiar faces cheering Ralphie.

The Makers gifted Ralphie with a gold-plated three inch thick and one-foot-tall RR. Ralphie also received a gold and blue painted scooter. The Makers also gave Ralphie a miniature golden crocket mallet and miniature working helicopter.

On the last night of the parades, Ralphie returned home to the Miller compound and the welcome sight of his home. Macy had fallen asleep in the transport. Ralphie carried his little sister to her bed. His parents did not come up to their bedroom immediately. They instead, sat in the living room and talked.

"Good night, Ralphie," his father said as Ralphie carried Macy upstairs and to her bedroom. Ralphie deposited his little sister in her bed and left her there sleeping quietly.

In his own bedroom, Ralphie climbed into his bed, tired and happy that all the parades were over. He hoped he might return to a semblance of normalcy now. Ralphie laid down and before he could close his eyes, he heard a low humming. Ralphie was bone tired. He wanted to go to sleep, but the low humming noise grew louder. He looked around his darkened bedroom for the source of the noise.

Ralphie shook his head realizing that the humming was coming from the ring Rudy Martin had given him at the Blackberry Gate. He looked down at the ring on his index finger and for the first time felt the ring begin vibrating.

Tired, dressed in a new Batman and Robin pajama set, Ralphie sat up and investigated the darkness of his bedroom. He climbed out of bed and walked to his desk. He did not turn on the lights in his bedroom. He did not need lights to get to his desk. He knew his bedroom well. Standing in front of his desk, he placed his hand to the screen on his desk.

Instantly, the monitor blinked on. On the monitor was a simple message. Alpha Plus has identified a spaceship moving toward the planet having broken orbit with Mars, the red planet. If it continues its present trajectory, it may be in range to signal on or before September 27. If interested meet at 37°52'19"N, 122°15'28"W. RSVP.